**SHE FORGOT EVERYTHING
EXCEPT THE FEEL OF HIS HANDS
UPON HER BODY.**

*She let him undress her and then helped him. His
lips traced a fiery path along the sleek curve of her
neck, and he paused briefly to run his tongue over
the throbbing pulse in her throat before he moved
slowly down her creamy shoulder to find her breast.*

*Eagerly, she responded to his caresses as his hands
blazed a torrid trail along her flat abdomen to the
silken flesh of her thighs. His velvet touch increased
the tender ache in her belly, and her thighs opened
of their own volition as his questing fingers
wandered.*

*A moan of pleasure escaped Jamelyn's passion-
swollen lips. "I love you," she murmured as, finally,
their bodies moved in unison, singing together the
age-old song of love until the slow cantabile changed
in rhythm and the madrigal filled their souls and
their voices could be heard as they cried out in
rapture...*

Fawcett Gold Medal Titles
by Cordia Byers:

CALLISTA

NICOLE LA BELLE

SILK
AND
STEEL

Cordia Byers

FAWCETT GOLD MEDAL • NEW YORK

A Fawcett Gold Medal Book
Published by Ballantine Books
Copyright © 1985 by Cordia Byers

Library of Congress Catalog Card Number: 85-90630

ISBN: 0-449-12746-X

Manufactured in the United States of America

First Edition: July 1985

*To James, my knight in shining armor,
my husband, my lover, my friend, my life.*

Chapter 1

Disturbed from their resting place in the trees, the ravens,
Scotland's ancient symbols of death, soared upward. The
flapping of their blue-black wings and their caws of protest
sounded in the still morning air of August 1333 as they
came to rest upon the granite towers of the keep named in
their honor. In the distance the hoofbeats of war-horses and
the clang of armor could be heard nearing the castle of
Raven's Keep. The reflection of the morning sun on polished
steel flashed through the trees, alerting the inhabitants within
the domain of Lord Cregan that soon the English troops
would lay siege to their small fief near the Moorfoot Hills.

No sound issued from the battle-hardened warriors of
Raven's Keep. They waited patiently for their enemy to
appear before the granite walls. Their war-tensed nerves
longed to see the Englishmen come close enough for the
arrows from their longbows to find easy targets.

A cow lowed from the entry bailey of the castle, and the
cry of a child could be heard through the stillness of hushed
expectancy within the great walls. Wise to the ways of war,

1

the villagers had taken refuge against the approaching troops within the keep. The serfs gave to their Lord of their toil and in return were protected against all enemies.

The Scots warriors did not take their gaze from the approaching forces. The rattle of harness and the clang of steel rode upon the morning air as the English army neared. Burning wood crackled beneath the heavy iron caldrons filled with animal fat. The heat would melt it into deadly liquid to be used against their enemies if they tried to scale the walls. Death was in the air, and all present knew their lives depended upon the leadership of the lone figure standing on the observation tower.

The mail-clad figure, with the stature and size of a youth, was the heir to all Raven's Keep. Lord Cregan had been slain along with most of his troops at Halidon Hill. Now King Edward's soldiers approached to take what was rightfully his heir's.

The sun reflected upon the fine steel mail, making the heir's slender form appear as a silver statue adorning the black granite walls of Raven's Keep. With the hilt of a sword securely gripped in one hand, the Scots leader moved not a muscle as the English forces halted at the edge of the forest. One lone rider approached bearing the white flag of parley.

Keen emerald-green eyes watched as the soldier halted before the closed gates and shouted, "Open to the soldiers of King Edward of England. By right of victory, he claims this fief as his own."

With bated breath the Scots listened to the strong, confident voice of their leader. "King Edward of England has no claim upon this fief. I am heir to Cregan, and none will claim what is mine."

The brisk breeze stirred the red plume adorning the messenger's helm. "Then are you prepared to go against the king's forces? We are here to take Raven's Keep whether it is your wish or nay."

With one quick motion a slender arm raised the broad sword high over the shining hood of mail. "It shall be nay,

English dogs. You'll not take Raven's Keep nor put any more good Scottish men under your blade."

Realizing the dangerous position he was in, the messenger quickly turned his horse back toward the main English force. Had he glanced back, he would have seen the sword lowered as a signal to the archers and might have had a chance to save his life. The arrow pierced the mail beneath his arm, and he crumpled to the damp earth.

A snarl of rage issued from the black-visored helm of the English knight who had led King Edward's troops to this foreign land to lay claim to the fief of Raven's Keep. He kicked his huge destrier sharply in the side, urging him forward. His war cry echoed eerily across the glade as he signaled his troops to attack. Rushing forward, they stormed the walls of Raven's Keep. The battle raged and took a heavy toll on English life, but the troops did not retreat until night made it impossible for them to see the enemy.

Ordering his men back into the safety of the forest, Lord Justin St. Claire reined in his lathered mount and swung down from the saddle.

"Damn," he swore as he pushed the visor back from his sweating face and looked once more at the dark outline of the keep. His squire, Gibbon, ran forward to offer him assistance in removing his heavy armor but was pushed roughly aside by the black knight's gauntleted hand. Lord Justin St. Claire was furious. He had been sent to this godforsaken land by his king and had been assured there would be no resistance. Through narrowing indigo-blue eyes, he surveyed the slaughter that had been reaped upon his men that day. He had come unprepared for a siege. He had no war machines to batter down the stone walls, nor did he have enough men to continue fighting such a battle as the one that had taken place that day.

Angrily his eagle-like gaze swept over the keep, seeking out a weakness in the battlements. He had to find a way to enter the castle without detection. The gates had to be opened.

Justin's shapely lips firmed into a tight line as he looked at the seemingly impenetrable fortress and vowed beneath his breath to see the young hellion who led the Scottish bastards pay with his life for this black day.

Removing his gauntlets, Justin threw them to the ground and flexed his tired hands before removing his helm. Running his long, tapering fingers through his dark, sweat-matted curls, Justin let his gaze sweep over the assembly of his men. With the knuckles of his broad hand, he wiped away the beads of moisture from his brow as he ordered, "Make camp and see to the wounded. Godfrey, come with me."

A tall blond man, whose handsome, boyish good looks had made many a lady's heart flutter within her breast, rose from his position near the fire and came forward. His youthful face was smudged with the grime of battle and a frown marred his forehead as he asked, "What are your plans, Justin?"

Lord St. Claire absently ran his hand over his dark, stubbled chin and along the firm line of his jaw as his gaze went once more to the Scottish keep. "We must find a way in or we'll not survive another day such as today. King Edward did not expect any resistance, but I see now that it will not be easy to claim what is mine."

A devilish grin quirked Sir Anthony Godfrey's lips. Slapping his friend on the back he said, "Such things are like women, Justin. If they're too easy to get then they're not as pleasurable."

Anthony's humor was lost on Lord St. Claire. Justin's scowl deepened, the smooth planes of his brow furrowing as his lips twisted into an angry grimace. "Those bastards will rue this day," he vowed. "They will pay with their lives for the foul deeds they have done. I've lost some of my best men to their arrows. No Scottish swine is going to survive if I have my way."

Well understanding his friend's black mood, as he had also lost several friends upon the battlefield, Anthony stared at the stone walls. "What are your plans?"

Justin drew his gaze away from the Scottish stronghold and scanned the group of men who sat nearby until he saw his sergeant at arms, Jacob Reeves, leaning against an oak, his lean, deeply-lined features alert to any command. Justin studied the wiry, older man who had served him faithfully through many battles in the past before turning once more to Anthony Godfrey. He looked at his friend speculatively while he assessed the feasibility of his plan. At last, he said, "Do you think you and Jacob can find a way in tonight?"

Anthony shrugged his wide shoulders. "If anyone can, it will be me. Have you forgotten it was I who slipped into Lord Bingham's keep and stole his daughter away without anyone ever suspecting a thing?" Anthony crinkled his lips mischievously at the memory of that night and the pleasure he had enjoyed from it.

"Aye, I had forgotten that escapade, but this is not some frolicsome jaunt, Anthony. I would have you keep your life, though there are some fathers of deflowered virgins who wish it otherwise."

At the memory of the many escapades he and Anthony had enjoyed during their youth, Justin's mood lightened a small degree. Each of them had been full of devilment and schemes to prove his manhood. His white teeth reflected the firelight as he slapped his friend on the shoulder. "I'm depending on you, Godfrey. I do not want you to enter the keep to find the prettiest maid. All I want is the gate lowered at dawn."

Anthony's chest swelled with feigned indignation. He tried to force his features into an expression to show he was hurt that Justin would suspect him of other things. Failing in the effort, Anthony threw back his blond head, his roar of laughter floating across the still night air. "I will do my best to keep my baser needs in control until at least daybreak, but I cannot guarantee it much longer."

The tension of the day broke. The two lifelong friends laughed until tears shimmered in their eyes. In normal circumstances Anthony's small jest would have drawn only a few chuckles, but after a day of death, their laughter was also a means of celebrating that they still lived.

When at last they sobered and wiped the dampness from their eyes, Anthony and Justin settled by the fire. The bond that existed between the two men made them as close as brothers, though their striking good looks contrasted like night and day. Where Justin was dark, with blue-black hair and deep blue eyes, Anthony was fair, his hair a golden blond, his eyes pale blue as an early spring morning sky. In personalities, they differed also: Justin was the more serious, while Anthony was always ready to make a jest. The diversity between them seemed to bind them closer together.

Both men's handsome faces were serious as Anthony listened to Justin's instructions while they gulped down the hastily prepared meal of roast venison. The meal concluded, Justin leaned against the rough bark of a large oak and looked at his friend.

"It will be dangerous to try to scale the wall, but with Jacob's help, I think it will be feasible," he said.

Anthony wiped the meat juices from his hands on his chausses and replaced his razor-sharp dagger in its sheath. "Aye, it will be rough, but what are a few Scots against good Englishmen? They are all heathens, and I doubt they have as much sense as an average man."

Deep lines etched a path about Justin's sensuous mouth as he looked into the flickering flames of the campfire. "Godfrey, those senseless Scots nearly won the day this afternoon. I would suggest you do not take them too lightly. It is imperative that the gates be opened to us or all is lost. It must be tomorrow. We came ill-prepared for this task. Our forces cannot be reduced any more if we plan to secure the fief as our own."

Anthony unlaced the leather strips that held his hauberk in place and removed it, leaving on only his dark wool tunic and chausses. Standing, he flexed his sword arm, massaging the tired muscles before bending to retrieve a long length of hemp rope. At its end dangled an iron hook with three barbed points that would catch in the crevices of the stone wall and help Anthony's climb. Securing the hook in his belt, Anthony wrapped the rope about his lean waist. Turning to Justin, he extended his hand in farewell. Justin stood and clasped it firmly before pulling the younger man into his arms. They hugged liked brothers, their eyes meeting for one brief moment before Anthony motioned to Jacob and the two blended into the dark night.

Justin watched until he could no longer discern his friend. His deep scowl revealed his concern for Anthony's welfare as he turned back to the duties at hand. "We need ladders constructed to scale the walls. There is much to be done before we can rest." His orders were firm, and the men hurried to obey.

Anthony and Jacob crept stealthily among the trees and kept to the deepest shadows as they made their way to the stone wall of Raven's Keep. Occasionally they heard the voices of the guards on the turrets above their heads as they pressed their backs securely against the granite stones. From years of experience the older, graying man, whose smaller frame possessed as much agility and strength as his tall companion, led the way without making a sound. They inched their way along the walls to the rear of the keep in the hope of finding a weak point in the defenses.

Only two towers at the front corners of the castle provided observation for the guards. At the rear wall, Anthony smiled to himself. It would be much easier to climb the rough stone and make their entrance from this vantage point. Justin had been right to assume there was a way into the Scottish lair.

Anthony's lips curled in disgust at the foolishness of the Scotsman who claimed the fief. Had he been an Englishman he would have placed extra guards at this weak spot in the castle's defense. Anthony motioned to Jacob, and the two men settled down to wait until the sky began to lighten. At that time they would make their move. Justin would draw the Scots' attention to the front wall as he ordered his troops to try to scale it. In the meantime, Anthony and Jacob would infiltrate from the rear. From there they would cross the bailey and hopefully lower the gates to the English troops.

The Scots warriors were battle-weary and tried to find a small measure of rest at their posts. There were no extra men to relieve them from their duties. Their numbers had

been severely reduced at the battle of Halidon Hill, and now
it took all to keep the walls secure against the English.

In the distance they could see the flickering light from
the enemy campfires and knew that when the sun rose the
battle would once more rage. The sound of axes against
the tall timbers also told them that when the morning came
the English would try to scale the walls of Raven's Keep.
In that event their arrows would be useless and all that would
be left to them was the animal fat that had been kept boiling
all day. Its stench permeated the cool night breeze, but the
soldiers paid little heed. Their own sweaty bodies matched
the foul odor that rose from the bailey.

One tall, barrel-chested warrior with bright red hair left
the small cluster about the fire and climbed the narrow stone
steps to the gate tower. "Jami," he called softly, "ye'd better
get some rest. By dawn the bastards will be at it again and
we'll have much to contend with if the sound of those axes
proves true."

Eyes the color of a stormy sea turned to gaze up at the
burly Scotsman. "Aye, you are right about that, Shawn.
They came expecting us to meekly give over and found they
were ill-prepared to face us. They can try and scale our
walls but the oil will put a stop to such ideas when it burns
the hides from those dogs."

Placing one massive hand on the slender, mail-covered
shoulder, Shawn McDougal said, "Then get yer rest. I'll
keep an eye on them tonight."

Wearily the heir of Raven's Keep nodded. "I think I will
take your advice, old friend." Without another word the
leader of the Scots turned and left Shawn to his vigil.

A light mist rose over the damp earth of the Scottish
lowlands as the first gray fingers of dawn crept across the
black velvet sky. The rattle of harness and armor echoed
across the green vale as the Englishmen prepared for battle.
All the inhabitants of Raven's Keep were also at their battle
stations ready to meet the enemy. Lord Cregan's heir had
returned to the observation post an hour before the first
sounds of war issued across the once peaceful meadow.

As the sky turned to mauve and then to lavender, giving the English enough light to see the Scots at their posts, Justin slid his black helm over his head and held up his hand to command his forces to attack. Arrows whistled through the still morning air about the Englismen's heads as they rode out to face the enemy again. Justin could hear the cries of his men who were not fortunate enough to avoid the piercing death that flew so swiftly from the castle walls.

The foot soldiers hurried along with their newly constructed burdens. They used the tall ladders slung over their shoulders to try to fend off the arrows as they rushed toward the walls. Luck was with quite a few of them; many were able to place their ladders against the black granite battlements. They obeyed Justin's shouted command to climb without hesitation, not suspecting the terrible death that awaited them from above.

Desperate for survival, the Scots used their last weapon. They lifted the boiling oil and poured it over the walls onto the unwary soldiers. The Englishmen grabbed futilely at their heads, the sizzle of their own flesh reaching their ears as they tried to prevent themselves from being cooked alive. Their screams of pain echoed across the battlefield, making all other deaths seem insignificant compared to the agony that had been inflicted upon them. They jumped from their high perches and writhed upon the ground, tearing the remaining tatters of their clothes from their burned bodies before death finally and mercifully claimed them.

Hearing the first battle cry, Anthony and Jacob threw the hook over the rear wall and began their ascent up the creviced surface. With ease they reached the top of the turret and quickly dispatched two guards. Stealthily they crept down the narrow steps to the bailey and maneuvered across it without drawing notice until they reached the stables. They exited near the main keep, warily keeping to the shadows.

Hoping to draw attention away from the gate, Anthony lit a torch and tossed it into the nearest stall filled with dry hay. It blazed instantly, but before the neighs of the frightened horses reached the Scotsmen, the horrible cries of the dying Englishmen pierced the air. A shiver ran up Anthony's spine at the sound of their agony, and he looked up to see the great vats being lifted to rain down scalding torture.

Without thought for his own safety, Anthony ran toward the main gate and released the lever that held it in place. It groaned but did not move. Grabbing his dagger from its sheath, Anthony began to saw through the massive rope. He worked feverishly, knowing he had only a few moments to accomplish his aims before being discovered. As the rope began to unravel and the gate slowly inched its way open, Anthony turned to see a broadsword coming down. The bright flash of its shiny surface reflecting the morning sun was all the warning the young Englishman needed. He jumped to the side. However, his movements were not swift enough to keep the blade from tearing through his soft wool tunic and opening his right side.

The dagger slipped from Anthony's fingers as he grabbed his injured side and stared at his assailant. He recognized the lone figure from the gate tower before he collapsed to the hardpacked earth.

Jami turned to face Jacob as he rushed forward to avenge his friend. From instinct that had been drilled into the young heir over the years of Lord Cregan's rule, the broadsword was once again raised against the enemy as the English troops surged through the open portal. Their horses trampled all in their path as their steel blades slashed out to annihilate the Scots.

Their last defense penetrated, the men of Raven's Keep fought with a fury born out of desperation. All that was left to them was this final attempt to save their lives. With brave determination bred down through the centuries, they fought the enemy hand to hand, slipping in the mud caused by the gore of the dead. The combat was fierce. Steel clashed against steel, battle axes rang loudly against shields, and cries of men and horses filled the bailey as the Cregan heir led the last futile fight against King Edward's troops.

Greatly outnumbered, the Scots were soon overcome by

the English soldiers. Most lay dead or dying, but their leader refused to acknowledge defeat. Surrounded by Justin's men, the heir kept them at bay with the sharp, bloodied blade of the broadsword. Backed up against the stone wall for protection, Jami parried each thrust of the Englishmen's blades with a swiftness surprising in one so small.

Justin's eyes narrowed dangerously as he watched the blood-spattered figure fight with fiendish cunning. His expression grew hard, the light in his eyes deadly. This was the lone figure who had ordered his messenger slain. Urging his huge war-horse forward, he ordered his men away and climbed from the saddle. His gauntleted hand gripped the hilt of his blood-encrusted sword as he strode forward to avenge the death of his men. He would fulfill his vow and make the Scots bastard rue the day he ever raised a sword against Justin St. Claire.

A breathless, tension-filled silence hovered around the remaining Scots and their captors. Their eyes never left the two leaders who faced each other for this final battle.

Justin's lips curved into a grim semblance of a smile as he surveyed his opponent. He knew his size and experience would see him the victor of this combat. However, he was determined to make the bastard suffer as his men had before he forfeited life at the point of his sword.

A snarl of rage escaped the smaller figure as Jami lifted the broadsword to destroy the enemy that had invaded the walls of the castle. Justin easily parried the first thrust of his opponent's blade and threw back his head, laughing. "Scots dog, your death will be slow," he vowed. The violent tone of his voice sent shivers down the spines of the stout-hearted soldiers who heard it.

Emerald eyes flashed with rancor from the soot- and blood-smudged face of the Cregan heir. "'Tis you who will slip into hell with the rest of your English troops, and it will be my sword that will open the door to let you in, vermin."

The flash of Jami's blade halted other words as the battle began in earnest. Sparks shimmered in the air as metal met metal. Justin toyed with his adversary. He could hear the

Scot's heavy breathing and knew that at any time he could easily overpower the smaller man and put an end to it. But that was not Justin's plan. He was enjoying himself at the Scot's expense. Assured of his success, Justin became careless, a mistake his opponent quickly took advantage of. Jami's sword slashed through the sleeve of Justin's mail and opened his arm from shoulder to elbow. Clenching his teeth tightly as the searing pain burned up his arm and into his shoulder, Justin's self-control vanished and his anger exploded. With the expertise born from years of experience in war, Justin's blade cut through the air for the final thrust. The young Scot adroitly avoided the main part of the blow that would have brought the combat to an end. The quick movement kept the sword from piercing the vulnerable area of the heir's chest, but failed to prevent the razor edge from opening the flesh from the shoulder down to the waist.

Justin drew back his sword as he saw his opponent's left arm go limp and hang loosely at his side. The end had come. Preparing to send the Scot's soul to eternal damnation, Justin watched as the Cregan heir swayed before him and then fell facedown at his feet.

The Englishman's anger still boiled within his blood. He raised his sword high to give enough force to sever the head from the slender body, but before the blade could descend it was halted in midair as a burly, redheaded Scotsman broke away from his guards and ran forward. Throwing his own body over his leader, Shawn McDougal covered Jami protectively as he begged, "Slay me, my lord, not the heir. 'Tis all that is left of the Cregan clan."

Startled by this new turn of events, Justin paused as he looked down at the huge man trying to shield his leader. He felt a grudging admiration for the man's courage and loyalty; however, he could not let the slaughter of his troops go unavenged. "Get away, Scotsman. Your time will come soon enough."

The man's bushy red head shook violently from side to side. "Nay, my Lord. The Cregan blood is as noble as your own. It should not be let as if this were a pig at slaughter.

The heir fought bravely to protect what belonged to the Cregan line."

Justin considered the Scotsman's words and let his sword arm fall to his side. "Aye, you are right. See to him and then I will decide how the heir of Cregan will meet his fate," he said.

Grateful for the momentary reprieve, Shawn did not question Justin's plans for the future. He gathered Jami's unconscious form into his powerful arms and strode up the steps of the keep. At the huge double doors two of Justin's men fell into step with Shawn McDougal and escorted him down the narrow stone steps to the dungeon. His concern for his leader etched deep lines across Shawn's craggy features as he gravely descended into the dark bowels of the castle. With each step he prayed he could save the life of the heir of Cregan.

Tiny lines of pain fanned Justin's deep blue eyes as he watched the Scotsman disappear with his burden. His wound burned from his own salty sweat running into it. Clasping his arm together with his other hand to stanch the blood, he turned to survey the damage done by the battle within the small confines of the bailey. His eyes widened slightly to find Jacob at his side and then narrowed again as he searched for his friend.

"Where is Sir Godfrey?"

The look on Jacob's face as he waved in the direction of the gate made Justin forget his own pain. Justin strode quickly across the body-littered yard to where Anthony lay propped against a stack of hay near the entry wall. Kneeling, Justin quickly surveyed the wound inflicted by the Scotsman.

"Anthony, can you hear me?" he asked.

Anthony's blond lashes fluttered open and his face screwed up with pain as he squinted up at Justin. "Aye, but my side hurts like bloody hell. Did you kill the bastard?"

"Who?" Justin asked absently as his fingers eased back the torn wool of his friend's tunic to examine the long gash in Anthony's side.

"The damned leader. He was the one who pierced me nearly through."

Justin shook his head as he helped Jacob lift Anthony and carry him toward the castle. "Nay, but his time will come. I have said I would decide his fate later."

Anthony's words were nearly a moan as he mumbled, "Let it be soon. I would like to know the bastard is in hell before I decide to join him."

Though Anthony's words were riddled with pain, a sense of relief swept through Justin. He knew his friend would recover if he could still jest. Carrying Anthony between them, Justin and Jacob strode up the steps and into the castle. The moans of the injured and dying filled the great hall where they had been brought to have their wounds tended by their comrades. Justin's men had secured the Scots in the dungeon and now turned their attention to the welfare of their friends.

Seeing the disorder that reigned within the castle, Justin released Anthony into Jacob's care and turned to take control. He ordered chambers prepared for the injured and servants found to help care for them so that his men-at-arms could return to the duties for which they had been trained.

As all scurried to do his bidding, Justin let his own weariness overtake him. He released a long, tired breath as he reached to remove his helm. In that moment a streak of hot pain ran up his arm, reminding him none too gently of his own wound. Clenching his jaw, he bellowed for his squire. "Gibbon, where in hell are you?"

The angry tone of his master's voice made Gibbon choke on a sip of cool ale. He coughed and spluttered as he lowered the tankard to the rough surface of the wooden table and hurried forward.

"Bring bandages and water to see to my arm," Justin ordered as he turned and made his way up the stairs that led to the main floor of the castle. His silver spurs clanged loudly in the stillness as he crossed the common room to the master suite. Justin glanced absently at the whitewashed walls that bore the relics of armor from times past. Heraldic tapestries and clan tartans adorned the cold stones, and for a moment Justin sensed the pride that had been handed down through the years in the Cregan clan. Those tarnished shields and rusty lances told him the reason behind the young Scot's feverish attempt to keep his heritage. Justin knew he would have reacted similarly; however, that did not change his feelings nor help the searing pain that shot up his arm with each movement.

Justin paused briefly upon the threshold of the master suite, his keen eyes surveying the austere chamber that had been Lord Cregan's domain until his death. The only luxury the room afforded was a heavily padded and sadly worn leather chair before the fireplace. Without further thought to his surroundings, Justin chose the chair and settled himself in it as Gibbon rushed into the room, his young face flushed and his breathing rapid in his hurry to do his master's bidding. The young squire helped Justin remove his armor and mail before cutting the soft wool tunic away from the wound. The fabric had dried to Justin's arm and Gibbon swallowed nervously as he pulled it loose, trying his best not to hurt his master further. Justin flinched slightly as the material came away but gave no other sign of pain as his squire washed the deep gash and then bound it tightly with white linen.

Gibbon grinned at his master as he finished his ministrations, a look of secret triumph playing over his still boyish features. "I've found the wine cellar, my lord, and have brought you a bottle of the old Lord's finest burgundy."

Tentatively Justin tested his injured arm and then settled back in the chair. He ached from head to toe. Wearily he ran his hand through his raven curls and a semblance of a smile touched his lips as he looked up into the pleased face of his squire.

"Gibbon, that's exactly what I need. Bring the bottle and then go and find a tub, if one exists in this pile of stones, so I might bathe. This afternoon will end the last of the Cregan Clan and I must look presentable."

As the heavy oak door closed behind the squire, Justin rose from the chair and flexed his aching muscles. The tall four-poster bed looked inviting and Justin could not resist the temptation. Stretching out across the soft down mattress, he rubbed his hand over his face. Soon he would sit in judgment on the heir of Raven's Keep and then it would belong to him.

Staring up at the soot-blackened beams of the ceiling, Justin asked himself if such a small fief as Raven's Keep was worth all the lives that had been lost.

Chapter 2

The sun was at its zenith as the Scots were led out from the dark dungeon and assembled under guard in the bailey. They squinted against the brightness and stared in dejected silence at the tall knight upon the granite steps of the castle.

Justin watched the procession with his bandaged arm held close to his body while his other hand rested upon the intricately worked hilt of his sword. He calmly surveyed the ragged bunch of warriors as they lined up to watch the punishment meted out to their leader. Justin's face mirrored none of his thoughts, nor did it reflect any sign of the pain that had made it impossible for him to find any rest during the previous hours. Once more clothed in black, he stood motionless before the assembly as an expectant hush fell over them. To many of the Scots his taut, unyielding body and his shrewd gaze reminded them of the ancient symbol of death, the raven. The sight made a chill creep up from the soles of their boots to tingle uneasily along their backs and raise the hair at the nape of their necks.

A small sound drew Justin's attention to the massive

double doors of the castle. His lips firmed into a hard line
as Shawn McDougal emerged from the dim interior supporting his leader. Justin's flinty gaze held no warmth for
the Scotsmen as he raised his arm and pointed at Jacob.
"Take McDougal and place him with the rest," he ordered.

Jacob grabbed Shawn's arm to lead him away but the
burly Scot tried to resist the smaller man's efforts. At the
slight shake of the heir's hooded head, however, he stopped.
Shawn's thick red brows lowered over his green eyes as his
scowl deepened and he reluctantly obeyed the silent command. His craggy, weather-roughened features were lined
with anxiety as he released his hold upon the narrow waist
of his leader and saw the heir sway. Shawn could nearly
feel the effort Jami had to put forth to remain standing. The
burly Scotsman balled his beefy fist in frustration as he let
Jacob lead him to the rest of the well-guarded prisoners.

Two guards remained behind the Cregan heir as Justin
stepped forward. His tall frame dwarfed the smaller figure.
Looking down, he saw the beads of sweat that dotted the
young Scot's brow and knew the willpower his adversary
exerted in order to remain erect. From the pain in his own
arm, Justin had to respect the youngster's courage. Justin
knew the wound from his sword had been much more severe
than the one he had received, and the Scot suffered greatly
from it.

Taking his gaze away from the Cregan heir, Justin looked
at the group before him. His voice was firm, his tone conveying a warning to anyone who dared dismiss his words.
"Know as of this moment, that I, Justin St. Claire, a knight
in King Edward Third's service, do call this fief of Raven's
Keep my own. I was sent here by King Edward, the sovereign of both England and Scotland, to claim it. All who
have opposed the king's wishes will not go unpunished. It
was an act of treason to defy His Majesty's troops and your
leader will be the first to suffer the consequences, to let all
know that King Edward's word is law and will be obeyed."
With a slight motion of his large, shapely hand, two soldiers
came forward and dragged the Scots chieftain into the center
of the bailey.

An angry rumble issued from the cluster of Scots as they watched the Cregan heir placed against the whipping post. Deep lines etched Justin's set lips as he looked from the Scots to their leader tied with hands overhead to the rough wooden pole.

"As Lord of this fief, I am showing clemency to your leader," he declared. "If he survives the fifty lashes, he will be sent back to England as prisoner of the crown instead of forfeiting his life for the foul deeds he has committed on this day."

Another outraged rumble passed through the assembly of Scots, but they were quickly subdued by the sharp tips of the pikes used by their guards.

Justin gave one regal nod of his raven head in Jacob's direction to indicate the punishment should begin. The wiry little man swaggered across the bailey, enjoying the moment he would see Anthony's attacker receive his punishment. With one swift movement he ripped the hooded tunic away from the slender back. A moan escaped the Cregan heir as shocked gasps issued from the nearest Englishmen. Their eyes grew wide with surprise at the sight of the body exposed to them.

From his position, Justin could not see what had aroused such a reaction from his men. All he could see was short, hacked-off hair and a bare back. A furrow creased his brow as he strode forward to investigate his men's curious behavior. Following the direction of their eyes, Justin's own widened in amazement at the sight of the well-shaped breasts exposed to his view.

"Damn!" Justin swore under his breath as his hard, icy gaze swept over the Scots, searching out Shawn McDougal. He clenched his square jaw tightly and his eyes narrowed to mere slits as he stared at the Scotsman. "Cut her down. Bring McDougal to the common room immediately!" Justin turned on his heel and strode angrily back into the castle.

Jamelyn tasted her own blood as it trickled down the inside of her lip. She had bitten it in her effort to remain quiet when her hands had been tied over her head. She had also tried to suppress the moan that escaped her as her tunic was torn away but had failed. The searing agony that burned along her injured side had been too much. Her defenses were still weak. Jamelyn could feel the warm sticky wetness of her own blood as her wound reopened and it took every ounce of strength she possessed not to cry out in anguish when her hands were roughly unbound. She concentrated her thoughts totally on remaining silent. Her stubborn Scottish pride would not let her yield. She would not let the Englishmen see her suffering though her wound ran from the tip of her left shoulder along the curve of her breast to her slender waist.

In the face of this foreign enemy, Jamelyn would show all the courage she possessed. She was the last of the Cregan line and had been claimed as the clan's chieftain after her uncle had been slain in battle. She was determined to show all the valor of such a position. They had been defeated in battle but not in spirit.

Shadows danced before her pain-glazed eyes and blackness threatened to take her into its grasp, but Jamelyn fought to remain conscious. She was the leader of these brave Scots. If death was to be her fate, she would go into its waiting arms with the dignity instilled in her by generations of Scots who had fought and labored to keep their country free of the hated English.

Clenching her teeth, Jamelyn exerted all of her willpower to remain standing, but her knees did not obey her mind. They gave way, and she slumped against the rough wood before the English guard lifted her into his arms and carried her into the castle she had called home for the past ten years. Each step was torture. The steel mail that covered his arms bit into her tender back and lacerated side as he took her once more down the slime-coated steps to the black bowels of the dungeon.

Without consideration for her damaged body, the soldier dumped Jamelyn roughly upon the vermin-infested, rotting rushes that had been thrown into the cells years ago. Jamelyn's nails bit deeply into her palms. She felt the skin break from the pressure but did not cry out. The pain in her hands helped her control the shriek of agony that bubbled in her throat. Dazed by pain, she heard the heavy door clang to on its rusty hinges and knew she was finally alone. She gave way to the weakness that stole over her and let the blackness take her out of her misery.

Lord Justin St. Claire paced the common room of Raven's Keep. His arm throbbed with each step, adding to the fury that had been building in him since learning the leader of Clan Cregan was a woman. Gibbon watched his master warily, sensing the dangerous mood that possessed Lord St. Claire. He knew it best to leave his lord to his own thoughts when the man was deviled by such black fits of rage or Gibbon would chance the back of his hand. Thankfully, the young squire had been fortunate enough not to have witnessed Justin's rage often. Only once before had Gibbon seen him in such a fury as now possessed him. It was several years earlier, when he had first come to serve Lord St. Claire.

Gibbon remembered that time well. At the tender age of eight, it was his first experience with death. Lord St. Claire had given Gibbon permission to ride with him to his uncle's estate near the border of England and Scotland. They were to escort Lady St. Claire back from there to their home in Leicester. Gibbon had looked forward to the outing. He wanted to see Lord St. Claire's younger brother Richard, who had been sent for training with his uncle. Four years separated the two boys in age, but when Gibbon had come to Leicester they had become fast friends until Richard had been sent north for training under Lord Richfield's direction.

The memory of that day was branded upon the young squire's brain. When Lord St. Claire's party arrived at Ancroft it was to find Lord Richfield's household in a state of turmoil and mourning. Lady St. Claire's body had been found near the cliffs at the edge of the estate, and young Richard had disappeared. It was thought that his body had been thrown off the cliffs and had drifted out to sea. Several head of cattle had also vanished, and it was presumed by all that Scots raiders had crossed the border to murder and steal.

Even now a cold sweat would bead Gibbon's brow at

the memory of what followed. Lord St. Claire had been like
a wild man until he tracked down the men he thought responsible for the death of his wife and brother. He had put them
to death personally and defied any of his men to interfere.
None tried. They all had loved and respected their master's
wife and had been very fond of young Richard St. Claire.
Even had they not thought so highly of Lady St. Claire and
Richard, they would not have interceded because they did
not want Justin's wrath to fall upon them.

Gibbon released a silent sigh of relief as Jacob roughly
shoved the redheaded McDougal into the chamber. A flicker
of pity swept through the young squire for the man that now
had to face Lord St. Claire.

Shawn McDougal stood straight with his chest out and
back held rigid before the English knight. His square jaw
jutted out obstinately as he vowed to show as much courage
as his Jami had done. She had displayed more pluck than
many a man would have done in such a condition. And he,
Shawn McDougal, would not dishonor his leader by doing
otherwise. Grimly he faced the broad-shouldered Englishman and waited to learn his fate at the black knight's hands.

The intractable expression on the Scotsman's face and
his resolute stance added fuel to Justin's already seething
anger as his cold gaze swept over Shawn. His words were
scathing as he spat insultingly, "McDougal, are you Scots
too cowardly to face the enemy without letting a woman
lead you?"

A muscle in Shawn's jaw twitched angrily and his green
eyes narrowed at Justin's offensive remark. "Nay, we follow
only our chieftain. Jami is the Cregan heir, and in Scotland
a woman can hold the title."

Exasperated as to what his next move should be, Justin
ran his long, tapering fingers through his raven curls. He
ordered, "Take him below until I decide what to do with
the lot of them."

Turning to Jacob, Justin asked, "What did you do with
the chit?"

"The guard took her back to the dungeon to await further
orders, my lord."

"Damn it, has everyone here lost all reason? The girl was injured. Have her brought to one of the rooms and see to her wounds."

Justin strode past the group of men and climbed the stone stairway to the bedchambers to see his friend. He pushed the heavy door of Anthony's chamber open to find his friend leaning back upon the pillows. Anthony casually sipped a tankard of ale and looked as if he did not have a care in the world. His smooth-shaven cheeks crinkled in a smile at the sight of Justin.

"It's about time you came to tell me how you avenged my wound. Did the bastard suffer much?" Anthony demanded.

Justin's raven curls shimmered with blue highlights as he shook his head, then pulled a stool to the side of the bed and sat down. "Nay, my friend, the one who wounded you is now being brought to the chamber next door."

Anthony's blond brows arched in surprise, then his brow furrowed in confusion. "Something is not right here. Have you grown soft in your elderly years?"

Justin's eyes twinkled as he ran a shapely hand over his stubbled chin and suppressed the smile that threatened. "Nay, I thought I might let you mete out the punishment once you have fully recovered."

Anthony pushed himself up on the pillows, a frown of irritation and pain caused by the movement crossing his handsome face as he stared at Justin. "By God, I will happily take my own sword to the Scotsman who did this if I cannot depend upon my friends to avenge me."

At the look on Anthony's face, Justin could no longer hold back his laughter. "Scotswoman" was all he said.

Anthony gazed at his friend as if he had lost his wits, and his blue eyes narrowed slightly in puzzlement. Shaking his head as if he had not understood the word, he repeated, "Scotswoman?"

"Aye, it was a wench that nearly put you beneath the Scots sod."

Anthony swore, "Be bloody damned, I don't believe you. Did you receive a knock upon that thick pate of yours?"

Throwing back his head, Justin guffawed, the sound of his mirth echoing down the long corridor beyond. "Nay, my friend. It seems at last the fairer sex has had its revenge upon you after all these years. I would suggest you give that sword arm more practice with a weapon and less raising it to toast the beauty of a fair maid so often. Next time it might prove fatal."

Anthony still could not believe Justin; he put his finger to his ear and shook it as if to clear his hearing. "Justin, the jest is up. Now tell me what you did to the chieftain of the clan."

Justin's laughter faded as he sobered and looked at his friend. "I do not jest, Anthony. The chieftain is a woman by the name of Jami. I have ordered her to be taken to the chamber next door and cared for. Then perhaps I will be able to decide what to do with her once she has recovered."

Again Anthony shook his head in disbelief. "Has the whole bloody world turned upside down?"

Darkness was creeping across the horizon and the first stars had come out to flicker like tiny candle flames against the black sky as Jacob knocked on Justin's chamber door. He entered when he heard Lord St. Claire's rough command and crossed the bare wooden floor to stand before his leader.

"My lord, the girl is awake."

Letting out a long, tired breath, Justin set the tankard of ale on the table at his side. He was weary to the bone. It had been a long, exhausting day and it had not yet ended. He must see the girl who had reaped such havoc upon his men. He had to make a decision about her fate and that of her men. Rubbing the aching muscles in his neck, Justin nodded as he stood and followed Jacob down the dark stone corridor to the chamber where Jamelyn lay.

Justin motioned his vassal to remain outside and then strode into the room. He paused at the side of the tall four-post bed and looked down at the slender figure within. The rush lamp illuminated her small form to Justin's keen scrutiny. A sense of amazement swept over him as he gazed at the Scots leader and realized he had faced her in combat and had come close to being defeated.

She now lay with her eyes closed and it gave Justin time to take into account the feminine features he had not noted previously. Her face was now free of the blood and soot that had coated it during the battle and Justin could see that her complexion was smooth; no scars marked its creamy surface. Her forehead was high over a thin aquiline nose and her eyebrows were finely arched, making her look slightly haughty even in repose. Her cheekbones were delicately sculpted and feathery thick lashes cast gentle shadows upon her pale skin.

Justin wondered briefly how he had misconstrued her gender. His gaze was drawn upward to her shaggy mop of hair. It had been carelessly cut to look like a man's, and he realized at that moment that her actions had also been those of a man. She had fought with a skill not known to most women and it was that that had obscured her femininity in the heat of battle.

Sensing Justin's presence, Jamelyn fluttered her thick lashes open. Confusion flickered briefly over her ashen features until her memory of the day returned. Even in her weakened state, Jamelyn's rancor glimmered within the shining depths of her green eyes. Her hands clenched the sheet until her knuckles grew white as she stared up at her enemy.

Seeing her hatred, Justin's own anger resurfaced and emerged harshly as he said, "They say you will live."

Jamelyn pressed her pale lips firmly together as she eyed Justin with open hostility. She refused to cower though she was now at this man's mercy.

Leaning against an intricately carved bedpost, Justin crossed his arms over his wide chest as he gazed down at the girl who refused to speak to him. "I would suggest you tell me who you are and why you have defied the king's orders."

Still Jamelyn refused to speak.

Rankled, Justin's indigo eyes narrowed slightly, giving evidence of his irritation. The girl's silence revealed her determination to resist, though her life now rested within his hands. Justin's anger bubbled through his veins as his own resolution to dominate the defiant creature flared into life. "Your silence will do you no good, wench," he told her.

Only her bright emerald eyes answered Justin. In them he read the message Jamelyn intended to convey.

"They tell me you are chieftain of Clan Cregan but from all I can see you are nothing more than a young girl playing the role of the leader of your Scots. If you were more you would care for the lives I have the power to dispatch to eternity."

The welfare of her men broke Jamelyn's resolve to remain silent. "English dog, do what you will to me but do not sacrifice good men's lives because they obeyed my orders."

Justin smiled but the smile held no warmth. His eyes were deadly cold as he said, "So you admit you ordered my messenger killed?"

Jamelyn nodded her shaggy head. "Aye, and I would do it again. Raven's Keep is my domain and King Edward has no right to order it taken."

One black brow arched sardonically as an angry scowl etched its way across Justin's craggy features. "King Edward is the sovereign of this land. It was ceded by David the First to him two years ago, and it is your duty to obey."

"Never!" Jamelyn ground out between clenched teeth before turning her face away. Her side ached unbearably. She knew she had to hold back what strength remained within her to face what this man would do to her when she recovered enough to stand punishment.

Jamelyn's small action of defiance further inflamed Justin's anger. She had dismissed him as if he were one of her vassals. "Then I have no choice left to me," he said. "The executions will begin at dawn."

Justin's words had the desired effect of gaining Jamelyn's attention once more. Her head snapped about, her eyes sparkling with ire as she faced him. She tried to push herself upright but only succeeded in raising herself to her elbows because of the excruciating pain that seared her side. Taking a deep breath to try to quell the agony racing through her body, Jamelyn spat, "Is that your good King Edward's justice? To slay men who only obeyed the orders of their leader? It is I who should be the first to die."

Justin noted the moisture that beaded Jamelyn's upper lip and forehead from the effort it took her to speak. Though she had caused much destruction, he could not stop himself from admiring her courage and willpower. "Then do you offer your life in exchange for those of your men?" he asked.

Clenching her teeth tightly against the pain, Jamelyn nodded. Her rancor-filled eyes never wavered from Justin's as she stared unflinchingly into the face of her enemy.

"Then so be it. You will be the one to pay for the crimes committed against the crown," Justin said calmly as he watched Jamelyn's complexion turn a deathly white. "I will leave you now to await your fate," he added and then strode from the chamber without a backward glance as Jamelyn slumped back against the pillows.

The door seemed to cause the thick stone walls to vibrate as Justin slammed it. Striding briskly across his chamber, he threw his mantle over the softly padded chair. He was still seething over the young woman's defiant attitude. Justin had expected her to plead for her life, but to his surprise she had agreed to meet death willingly to save the lives of her men.

His fingers clenched around the neck of the wine decanter briefly before he poured a large measure into a silver cup. Absently he studied the ruby liquid as he swirled it about the gleaming interior of the vessel, his thoughts never leaving the young girl down the corridor. He had told her she would be executed and now he had to keep his word. Justin's lips turned down into a grim, forbidding line at the thought. He had no liking for it no matter how stubborn or stupid the girl might be. It went entirely against all the vows he had taken when he had become a knight. He had sworn to protect women, not put them to death. Had the heir been a man as he had first surmised, Justin knew he would have no compunction about sending him quickly to his maker. Damnably, that was not the case.

Justin paced his chamber, trying to find an option that would keep him from breaking his chivalric vows while meting out a punishment to justly fit the crimes committed. A glimmer of an idea began to form in the back of his mind as he halted before the writing desk. He stared briefly at the parchment lying upon the smooth surface before seating himself and picking up the quill. He sharpened it with the razor edge of his dagger and spread the parchment out before him. Dipping the quill into the inkwell, Justin began to write. He would send a missive to King Edward informing him of the events that had transpired at Raven's Keep and let his sovereign decide the fate of the young hothead who lay recovering from the wound he had inflicted.

Justin reread the missive to his king before sanding and sealing it. As he pressed his signet ring upon the hot wax, he felt satisfied for the first time since learning the heir of Cregan was a woman. It was now out of his hands. All he had to do was wait for the king's decision. Whatever Edward decided, Justin would obey, no matter what fate his king chose for the young woman.

"Gibbon," he shouted and heard his squire scrambling about in the adjoining room. The young man had taken the small chamber next to Justin's so he would be close at hand if needed. Gibbon hurried into the room still hitching up his chausses and crossed to his lord. Justin handed him the letter and said, "Take this to London and see that you return quickly with an answer from the king."

Gibbon bowed to Justin and then hurried to obey. Though no question was voiced, Justin saw the perplexed look on the young man's face as he left the room and smiled as he settled himself in front of the fire, stretching out his long legs. Gibbon was only eighteen years of age but Justin knew he would have to look long and hard to find a more loyal man.

Crossing his hands over his hard, flat middle, Justin's blue gaze reflected the dancing flames as he watched them leap in the grate. Tonight he would rest; tomorrow he would begin to secure Raven's Keep as his domain. The fief was small but Justin knew he must make all who lived within its boundaries know that he was now the master. If he was to insure the peace of the area there could be none who kept their loyalty to the Cregan heir.

Justin was not the only person within the walls of Raven's Keep whose mind wandered over the events of the future and the past. Jamelyn lay in the large four-poster and stared unseeingly up at the black-beamed ceiling. She had tried to find some measure of rest, but her throbbing wound combined with her tumultuous thoughts would give her no peace.

She reflected over the events that had led up to this day and her defeat at the hands of the English. It had been ten years since her arrival at Raven's Keep. At the tender age of eight she had watched her family succumb to the plague. It had swept across Scotland, annihilating families and whole communities in only days. Jamelyn had lost both parents and two brothers to the dreaded disease in the short span of two weeks. Strangely, she had not been touched as it ravaged all the inhabitants of her father's fief. She had been orphaned with no one to see to her welfare except her great-uncle, the Lord of Raven's Keep. King Bruce had been the sovereign of Scotland at that time and had ordered Lord Cregan to accept her as his ward.

Jamelyn's lips crinkled up at the corners at the thought of that dear old man. At first she had been frightened by the old warrior with his harsh voice and rough manners. She had been a timid little thing upon her arrival, and Lord Cregan had done little to soothe her feelings. He had never married and the only women he allowed within his castle were the cooks. Jamelyn well remembered his loud, harsh pronouncement of his feelings toward the fairer sex. He had proclaimed with unbridled emotion that he didn't have any use for females, from the bitches in his kennel to the ones who prepared his food. His white beard had stood out dramatically against his ruddy complexion as he gruffly stated that his king had ordered him to care for her and it was his duty to obey, but he wanted her to know from the outset that he had no liking for the task. He was a man of war, not a mother hen. And if Jamelyn had any thoughts to the contrary, she had best rid herself of them or life would be hard on her within his household. Without ceremony he stated that he didn't believe in foolish fripperies that females desired and he would not condone a bunch of chattering servants underfoot when he wanted to rest. Bluntly he told Jamelyn not to expect anything from him except room and board.

Fortunately, Jamelyn had found one among Lord Cregan's vassals who would take her under his wing—Shawn McDougal. He had comforted her in her loneliness and had eased her fright of her great-uncle by explaining to her that Lord Cregan was a good man at heart and one whom his vassals would follow to the end. That, Jamelyn reflected, had been what they had done. The reason she had lost Raven's Keep was that most of her uncle's vassals had died with him at Halidon Hill, leaving only a small force behind to protect the fief.

Jamelyn's thoughts lingered on her faithful friend, Shawn. At his side she had learned much about warfare. He taught her to ride, to handle weapons, and to win Lord Cregan's love. It had not been an easy matter to accomplish, but as the years passed and Lord Cregan watched Jamelyn grow as efficient and knowledgeable as any of his vassals, he began to realize she was not like the females he had known and despised. From a distance, Lord Cregan could easily forget her gender as she mastered the arts of warfare.

The old lord noted the courage she displayed when facing an adversary and the quick mind she possessed. He glowed with pride at the respect his vassals bestowed upon her. They treated Jamelyn as if she were Lord Cregan's son. The relationship that developed between the old man and his young niece was wary at first until it grew into a close bond of love and respect. In his effort to demonstrate his feelings to her, Lord Cregan had made Jamelyn his heir and had gifted her with the badge of honor, the tartan of Clan Cregan. It was a sign to all that Jamelyn was his choice as chieftain if he should fall in battle.

In the dim light provided by the rush lamp, Jamelyn remembered the day her uncle had given her the red and black tartan. She had worn it with pride and a stubborn determination to make Lord Cregan proud. She had vowed to protect with her life Raven's Keep and all who resided upon the fief. Jamelyn's delicate lips turned down at the corners as tiny lines etched across her smooth forehead. That vow she would keep, for the English knight had already told her the fate that awaited her and she accepted it. All that was left to her was to see that her men did not receive the same. St. Claire had vowed to spare them, but she knew better than to trust an Englishman's word.

Gingerly, Jamelyn moved her arm to test it. She was relieved to find she had not lost the use of it completely. She had regained some movement in her hand and her fingers tingled from lack of use as she flexed them. Clamping her jaw tightly shut, Jamelyn threw back the covers and pushed herself upright. She gasped at the excruciating pain and beads of sweat broke out across her furrowed brow. Visibly pale and panting, Jamelyn forced her mind back to the matters at hand. Now would be her only chance to help her men and she must not fail them. Their lives depended on her and she was determined to see her loyal followers free before the English dogs could prevent it.

Cocking her head to one side, Jamelyn listened intently. The castle was silent. The English soldiers had ended their victory celebration some hours before. From the sounds that had emanated from the great hall earlier, Jamelyn knew they had enjoyed the contents of her uncle's wine cellar to the fullest extent. The Englishmen had drunk deeply, thinking their enemies safely locked away in the dungeon.

Fortunately for Jamelyn and her Scots, the foolish English curs had unwisely surmised she would be unable to offer any problems because of her wounds. An acrid smile crept to Jamelyn's pale lips. The stupid English did not know their enemy well or they would not have misjudged the Scots so easily. The tall knight would have placed a guard at her door.

With her right hand, Jamelyn retrieved the tattered remains

of her tunic. She awkwardly pulled it over her head and felt faint as she raised her left arm into the soft wool sleeve of the garment. Her body trembled from the effort. Bracing herself on her balled fist, Jamelyn took a deep breath as she slid her long, slender legs over the edge of the bed. She eased her feet to the cold, rough wood floor and tentatively tested her strength.

In her weakened condition, Jamelyn knew she could not manage to put on her chausses and gave no thought to her immodest attire of only the tunic, which covered her to midthigh. She thought little of leaving her feminine attributes exposed when more important matters lay heavily upon her mind. It was seldom that Jamelyn even acknowledged her gender. Only at that cursed time of the month did she consider herself a female. Each month she suffered horrible belly cramps from it. She had striven so hard over the years to overcome the liability placed on her by her sex, yet each month she had the physical reminder. Jamelyn was ashamed of that weakness and cursed nature for making her a woman.

The chamber spun dizzily before Jamelyn's eyes as she took a few wobbly steps. She grasped a bedpost for support and leaned her head against the cool wooden surface. Nausea churned her insides, for the pain had intensified with each movement. With a trembling hand, Jamelyn wiped the beads of sweat from her brow and moistened her dry lips as she gained courage to take a few more steps. She was grateful to find the room now steady as she released her tight hold upon the post and slowly made her way across the chamber. Though her side still felt as if it were filled with red-hot coals and her knees shook with each step, Jamelyn managed to reach the table, where a decanter of wine and a goblet rested.

Vexed at her own weakness, Jamelyn filled the goblet. Her hand shook as she placed the decanter on the table. With both hands firmly clasped about the goblet to steady it, Jamelyn gulped down the contents and prayed the ruby liquid would fortify her. As the wine reached her stomach, she could feel its warmth spreading through her, easing her agony to a small degree. Her wound still ached unbearably, but the wine helped Jamelyn feel much more like the person she had been instead of some inadequate female. Jamelyn poured another goblet of wine and drained it also. She had not eaten since before dawn and the effects of the alcohol made her slightly giddy as she wiped a few stray drops of the Burgundy from her lips. It renewed her courage and her small chin jutted out defiantly as she crossed the chamber and eased the stout wooden door open. Warily, Jamelyn peered into the darkened corridor. It was deserted as she had suspected.

Jamelyn's lips curled into a sneer of disgust as she eased the door open further and crept into the hall. Holding her wounded side, Jamelyn stealthily made her way along the cold stone corridor to the unused servants' stairway. At the top of the winding stone steps, Jamelyn leaned against the rough stones and took several deep breaths to steady her quaking knees. For one frantic moment, she thought her legs would no longer support her. The muscles trembled violently, threatening to give way beneath her. Pressing her thin body against the wall, Jamelyn drew from the last of her reserves. With effort she pushed herself once more upright. Brushing the cobwebs from her path, Jamelyn descended the dark stairs to the door that led to the dungeon.

Jamelyn's heart pounded in her chest as she peered down into the dark passage. Her head felt light, and it took a moment for her to bring her eyes into focus and see the glimmer of light at the bottom where a guard had been posted near the entrance to the cells. Her strength was quickly fading. Sensing that she did not have much left, Jamelyn eased down the steps, her eyes scanning the area for a weapon to use against the guard. Her gaze fell on a cudgel that had been carelessly thrown into the corner by one of the soldiers in his haste to refresh himself from Raven's Keep's larder.

Hugging the deep shadows, Jamelyn crept to the cudgel. Slowly she lifted the heavy object with her right hand, weighing it in her trembling grasp. She would have to take the guard unawares. She did not have the strength to face him outright. The lives of her men rested upon her ability to move swiftly and strike hard. There would be only one chance for her to succeed.

With her breath held, Jamelyn peered around the corner to see the soldier sitting under the torchlight with a tankard of ale propped on his belly. His eyes were closed and the tip of his dark, stubbly chin rested against his chest. From the sound of his even breathing, Jamelyn suspected he had also imbibed freely of her uncle's ale and dozed from the effects.

Jamelyn's grip tightened about her weapon as she silently crossed the short space on bare feet. Bracing herself, she hefted the cudgel upward and ordered her weak body to respond to the commands of her mind. Some infinitesimal sound aroused the guard. An expression of surprise flickered briefly over his face before the weapon descended upon his shaggy head. A shallow cry escaped as he fell forward, unconscious at Jamelyn's feet.

The cudgel slipped from Jamelyn's fingers. She braced her hand against the wall as she listened for any noise from above responding to the guard's cry. She released a long, trembling breath of relief when she heard nothing to indicate that her actions had been discovered.

Jamelyn bit her lip to hold back her own cry of pain as she bent to retrieve the ring of keys from the guard's supine body. She tasted the salty tang of her blood as she once more managed to stand erect. She swallowed back the nausea that rose in her throat and breathed deeply to try to stem the erratic pace of her heart. Her legs felt as if they were turning to jelly as she forced them to move toward the first cell. The key scraped in the rusty lock as Jamelyn twisted it and then pulled the ring on the solid wooden door to free the cell's occupants. Her vision had begun to grow fuzzy and it took a moment to recognize Shawn McDougal's ruddy face. Giving way at last, Jamelyn stumbled forward into his burly arms.

"Shawn, you must unlock the other cells so all the men may flee. Tell them to use the tunnel beneath the wine cellar."

The dim light from the torch illuminated the deathly pallor of Jamelyn's features as Shawn gazed down at the young woman within his arms. Deep lines of worry furrowed the brow above the green eyes that reflected Shawn's concern for Jamelyn. However, he obeyed her commands before turning his attention to her welfare. With great tenderness, Shawn eased Jamelyn to the damp floor and quickly set about opening the locked doors.

The Scots blinked their eyes against the light as they moved quietly from the cells to where their leader lay. Shawn lifted Jamelyn into his arms, but she protested. With a strenuous effort and Shawn's support she once more stood on her feet. An affectionate smile briefly played about her ashen lips as she looked at the beloved faces of her men. "Go to the highlands. You will be safe there. Use the tunnel," she whispered, her voice growing weaker by the moment.

A hushed mumble of protest escaped the battle-hardened Scots, but it was halted by Jamelyn as she shook her head. "They plan to begin executions at dawn. Now is your only chance to save your lives. Go now. I am your chieftain and I command you to obey."

Jamelyn watched the expressions play over the faces of her men. They disliked slipping away in the night like a pack of vermin. However, they were true Scots and knew they would have to escape to survive so they could return to fight another day. Silently each stopped before Jamelyn and placed his balled fist across his chest as a sign that they would always be men of Cregan, then crept up the stairs and slipped quietly into the wine cellar. From there they would make their way into the maze of tunnels carved out through the centuries by the deep silent river that flowed underneath Raven's Keep to the sea. It would not be long before they were out into the cold Scottish night, breathing the air of freedom. The fog would obscure their exits from the tunnel and from then on they would blend into the rugged countryside.

When only Shawn and Jamelyn were left, she looked up at her friend. "Go with them. I cannot travel in this state and I would see you free, Shawn."

Adamantly, Shawn shook his red head. "Nay, Jami. Ye'll come with me or I shan't go."

Dark shadows were once more fluttering before her eyes and Jamelyn could feel the warm trickle of blood as it seeped down her side through the bandages. Her pain-glazed eyes pleaded with Shawn as she slowly shook her shaggy head. Her last word was spoken in desperation as she tried to make Shawn obey. "Go," was all that passed her lips as she slumped limply against Shawn McDougal and felt the velvet darkness accept her into its black arms.

A severe scowl marked Shawn's craggy features as he lifted the light burden into his arms and glanced up the dark stairway. Jami's only chance of survival was for him to get her away from Raven's Keep and see to her injuries before she bled to death. He could not leave her behind even if it cost his own life. If it were found out that she had helped her men escape, the English devils would unleash all the furies upon her young head.

Intent upon their escape, Shawn crept silently up the stairs. In his anxiety over Jamelyn's injuries, he failed to note the tall figure in the shadows as he made his way toward the door leading to the cellars. He stumbled slightly as the sharp point of a sword pierced through his leather tunic, but he did not drop his burden. Staggering, Shawn braced himself against the rough stone and faced the black knight called Justin St. Claire.

Justin's eyes glittered dangerously as he held the tip of his sword against Shawn's throat. "Your folly abounds, McDougal. Did you think to escape so easily?"

Silently Shawn returned Justin's stare as he held Jamelyn protectively against his broad chest. He could feel the warmth of her blood as it seeped through her tunic as well as his own as it ran down the crevice of his spine.

The pressure increased on the tip of Justin's sword. It bored into Shawn's flesh as the knight's eyes narrowed with malice. "Answer me, man, or shall I have done with it now?"

Mentally, Shawn said his Hail Marys as he awaited his death. His gaze never wavered from Justin's face. He saw the flicker of surprise as the black knight's eyes adjusted to the dim light and he recognized the burden Shawn carried. The pressure eased against the corded muscles of the Scot's neck as Justin said, "Do you care so little for your chieftain that you would see her dead?"

Clearing his throat, Shawn spoke in a voice hoarse from the tautness his impending demise had created. "Nay, I would see her live."

Harboring unconcealed contempt for the Scot's reasoning, Justin stepped back and pointed with his sword in the direction of the stairs. "Take her back to her chamber."

Shawn did not move to obey but faced the black knight stalwartly. "'Tis better she die within my arms than suffer your punishment."

Justin's eyes flashed with icy-blue lights as he stared at the Scot. "You try my patience. If you care for your life and that of your leader, you will obey me."

By some second sense, Shawn perceived Justin's reticence in putting a woman to death. A spark of hope flared within him as he looked up into the handsome face of the English knight. Perhaps Jami's fate was not to die by this man's hand. Shawn glanced down at the ashen figure within his arms and prayed he was making the right decision as he turned and made his way back up the stone steps to Jamelyn's chamber. If he was not, Shawn vowed to die in his effort to save Jamelyn.

Justin kept his sword to Shawn's back as they climbed the steep steps, and the knight watched in silence as the Scots' warrior tenderly lay the girl upon the bed. He tended her gently as if she were a babe as he removed the bloody tunic and unwound the stained bandages to see how much damage Jamelyn's courageous efforts had inflicted upon her. Justin wondered about the relationship between the strong man and the skinny, boyish girl as his eyes came to rest upon her softly rounded breast.

Noting the direction of Justin's gaze, Shawn quickly covered Jamelyn's thin body before turning to the black knight. "She needs new bandages. Her wound has reopened."

With arms crossed over his hard chest and one boot

resting negligently upon its toe, Justin leaned against the solid door. His gaze rested speculatively on the Scot and justly surmised from the man's worried expression that he could now get the answers he desired. His voice was calm but seemed to hold an unspoken threat as he said, "First, there are a few questions I would have you answer before she is tended."

An angry glint flickered in Shawn's eyes as he squared his shoulders and looked at the Englishman. The contempt he felt for his captor was reflected in his stance. However, Shawn also recognized the determination on Justin's face and knew if he refused, Jami would suffer. It chafed against the grain to give way to the man's demands, but his love for Jami overshadowed all else. Accepting his defeat, Shawn glanced down at the pale young woman and said, "What would you know?"

Justin's keen gaze swept scornfully over the Scotsman. McDougal would be easily manipulated. His love for the girl would be the lever Justin would use against him. "First, I would know how you escaped your cell and crept up here to try to help the girl escape."

Shawn tensed. His battle-roughened fingers fidgeted nervously with the coarse material of the counterpane as his gaze flickered uneasily from Jamelyn to the black knight, who scrutinized his every move. Shawn's determination to protect Jami at all costs glowed within the green depths of his eyes as he raised his chin and said, "I unlocked the cell."

A muscle twitched in Justin's cheek as his anger simmered against the Scotsman. "Damn you, Scotsman, I will hear no lies." With one long bronzed finger, Justin pointed at Jamelyn. "Her life depends upon your truth. Now answer me," he said.

The muscles across Shawn's barreled chest contracted and beads of sweat broke out across his brow as he looked at Justin's angry countenance. He knew Jami's life would be forfeit if he told the truth. Staunchly he defended his lie as he wiped the moisture from his forehead with one broad blunt-fingered hand. "I do not lie. Check the dungeons and you will find that I released the others as well. You have only the two of us to execute at dawn."

For one unguarded moment, Justin's face mirrored his surprise at this new bit of information. He had only caught McDougal by accident when he had gone to the kitchens in search of another bottle to help him sleep and had surmised that the Scotsman alone was attempting to escape. Justin realized he had indulged more deeply in the wine than he had thought. His normally acute senses had been dulled by its effect, and he had failed to check the dungeons to see if anyone else was as clever as Shawn McDougal in effecting a means to flee Raven's Keep.

Abruptly Justin strode from the chamber, bellowing orders to his men in an effort to rectify his own foolish mistake. Shawn listened to the castle erupt in a clatter of arms and complaints as the English soldiers were roused from their sleep. His shoulders sagged, his wound throbbed, and his words lay heavily upon his mind. He had possibly condemned both his friends and Jami to death. He had been a fool to tell the black knight of the Scots' escape. He should have stalled for time to assure that Jami's men were in no danger of being apprehended. However, his concern for Jami and his own loss of blood had made him reckless.

Wearily, Shawn turned his attention to the matters at hand. He had to try to stem the flow of blood from Jamelyn's wound. With care he pressed the bandage against the jagged cut before wrapping the length of white cloth about Jamelyn's waist. When that was done he sank weakly to the side of the bed. Gently he brushed the stubby, soiled hair away from Jamelyn's forehead as he murmured, "Forgive me, lass." Shawn's lips thinned into a grim line as he gazed down at the ashen features of the girl who was more like a daughter to him than his leader. Taking her small hand within his own brawny grasp, he said, "Lord Cregan would be proud of ye, lass, if he knew of yer bravery. Ye have seen to the welfare of yer men and now must fight for yer life as you have never done."

Jamelyn stirred. A slight moan escaped as her thick lashes fluttered briefly before she opened her eyes to look up at her friend. A moment of confusion flickered in their emerald depths before she hoarsely whispered, "Shawn, you must go."

Shawn's shaggy red head shook slowly from side to side as he squeezed Jamelyn's hand comfortingly. "Nay, lass, 'tis too late."

Jamelyn squinted up at Shawn. Her hand trembled as it came up to rub her forehead as if to clear her mind of the fog that still lingered there and hindered her thinking. She moved her head on the pillow, her gaze sweeping over her chamber. She recognized her surroundings and her voice was filled with defeat as she said, "You should have obeyed me."

Before Shawn could reply, the door crashed open, its hinges squealing in protest as it slammed back against the wall. Justin crossed the short space in two brisk strides. His rage was apparent by the deep hue of his complexion. He reminded Shawn of a man the Scotsman had seen once who claimed to have come from Egypt.

A muscle in Justin's jaw twitched and his eyes burned with fury as he stormed, "By all that is holy, McDougal, you will pay for this. But first I would know how you managed to get the keys. Do I have a traitor in my midst?"

Shawn's fingers tightened about Jamelyn's hand, silently conveying his plea that she remain quiet. "I overpowered the guard when he brought our food and then I unlocked the cells," he said.

Justin's face suffused a deeper shade as he looked at the Scotsman. Something did not ring true in the man's explanation. The Scots had been served their meal earlier in the afternoon before Justin's men had started their victory celebration. Justin had found the guard unconscious, his tunic still damp from the ale that had spilled upon it when he was struck down. The man still lived but he could not confirm McDougal's words until he regained consciousness.

A statement McDougal had made earlier flickered into Justin's suspicious mind: "There will be only the two of us to execute at dawn." It gave him an inkling of the true culprit behind the escape. His scorching gaze swept past the Scotsman to come to rest upon the pale figure on the bed. The girl was the only person he had told what he planned to do at dawn. Emerald eyes met and clashed with indigo-blue as Justin said, "By your own words you have sentenced yourself to the gibbet. At sunrise you will meet your fate, McDougal." Justin's eyes never left Jamelyn's pale features as he spoke. He wanted to see her reaction to his words, and then he would finally know the truth.

Jamelyn's voice was weak and seemed to come from a far distance as she tried to raise herself upon her elbow. "Nay, Shawn did nothing. It was I who freed my men."

A look of triumph flashed in Justin's eyes as he gazed down at Jamelyn. He had been right to surmise that McDougal was lying to protect her. Looking at the sharp planes of her face and the way her bones threatened to protrude through her skin, it was hard for Justin to believe she could have the strength required to knock his guard unconscious and to release her men, but there was no other explanation. He had misjudged the girl but he would not make the same mistake twice. His eyes narrowing, Justin's expression held no compassion as he said, "Aye, you were the one to set them free. I suspected as much and your punishment will be to watch McDougal dance at the end of a rope."

Jamelyn clutched the sheet to her heaving breast as she forced herself up in the bed. She swayed with the exertion it took to move. Her head felt as if it were packed with lint as she pleaded for Shawn's life. "Spare him. He is innocent of any crime beyond his loyalty to me."

For a brief moment, Justin found himself contemplating the white globes outlined by the sheet. His eyes seemed glued to the sight and he had to drag his gaze back to the girl's face. Taking a deep breath, Justin tried to still the response of his body to her form. His reaction to the skinny chit puzzled him. She was not pretty and prettiness was one thing Justin had always required in his women.

The Cregan heir was too thin, no more than skin and bones. Her short hair did little to enhance her appearance and looked as if it had never been touched with soap and water as it lay matted against her head. Justin's sensitive nostrils contracted at the offensive odor that wafted through the air. He was a man of war and used to the smells of battle, but afterward Justin insisted upon bodily cleanliness. By the scent he surmised the barbaric Scots did not believe as he did.

Forcing his mind away from such inane matters, Justin said harshly "You ask for mercy when you have shown none to my men?"

Jamelyn collapsed back against the pillows, her face the same color as the white linen. Though her will was strong, her body was weak and she could no longer command it to do her bidding. Justin had to strain to hear her whispered plea, "Spare him and do what you will to me."

Justin's face gave no indication of his thoughts as he crossed his arms over his wide chest and leaned against a bedpost. His keen scrutiny swept over Jamelyn and Shawn as his shrewd mind took stock of the situation.

As he had done only a short while before with Shawn McDougal, Justin would use the girl's feelings for the Scotsman as a lever to assure a peaceful transition at Raven's Keep. "Wench," he declared, "your Scot will not die on the morn if you give your word you will cause no more trouble until I decide what to do with you."

Jamelyn's gaze traveled from the hard-set face of the black knight to that of her beloved friend and then back to Justin. Solemnly she said, "I give you my word as chieftain of the Clan Cregan."

"Agreed," Justin said, satisfied with her answer. Had she been any other female, he would have held some reservations about taking her word, but her actions had earned a grudging measure of respect from him. She had shown courage and loyalty usually found only in men and because of that Justin would accept her word of honor.

Striding to the chamber door, Justin pulled it open and bellowed for Jacob. The wiry little man appeared instantly and quickly obeyed his lord's command to have Shawn incarcerated in the dungeon and Jamelyn's wounds tended.

Chapter 3

Jamelyn spent the days following her men's escape in a hazy fog of delirium. Her wound festered and her fever soared. Strangely enough, it was Jacob who ministered to Jamelyn during her struggle for life. At first he resented the chore of caring for the girl who had nearly taken his friend Anthony's life. He cared little if the Scottish wench lived or died. However, as the days passed he began to understand the young woman and his sympathy for her grew. He learned small bits about her background as she tossed and turned while muttering disjointed phrases about her life at Raven's Keep and the trials she had faced. Though Jacob would never have admitted it, the small waif's valiant fight for life touched the heart he had thought long dead.

Jacob sat by her bed for hours watching her feverish thrashing. Alone with the sick girl, he was reminded of the lovely wife he had lost after their child was born. There was little physical resemblance between the two women. Where the Scottish lass was thin, his Mattie had been plump and well-rounded. He had often told Mattie, the more of

43

her the better since there was more to love, and it would be a sad day in his life if she lost weight. The thought of how Mattie had laughed at his jest still brought a smile to Jacob's lips. However, when he glanced at Jamelyn's flushed face, Jacob relived those horrible days when he had sat helplessly by his wife's bed and watched her succumb to childbed fever.

As each day passed, Jacob's determination to see Jamelyn live grew stronger. He would not let her slip away from life as easily as Mattie had. Never again did he want to experience the frustration and vulnerability he had known while waiting for Mattie's last breath to be drawn. If the girl died it would not be because he had sat by and done nothing.

Jacob used all the resources at hand to help Jamelyn recover. He forced vile-smelling herbal elixirs down her parched throat to reduce the raging heat in her body and bathed her brow with cool compresses, changing each when it grew warm. His attention to the Cregan heir did not go unnoted by his comrades. His duties as nursemaid had become a great joke among the English soldiers. Staunchly, Jacob bore their chiding in good humor, knowing well that his friends respected his abilities as a warrior no matter how they teased him about the Scottish lass.

The crisis came on the fifth day. Jamelyn's fever soared higher and she drifted into a deep, coma-like sleep. Jacob sat silently by her bed and waited. There was nothing more he could do. It was now in the hands of God whether the girl lived or died.

A splash of brightness from the afternoon sun illuminated the great hall before Justin closed the heavy oak door behind him. He strode across the vaulted chamber, noting the subdued atmosphere that greeted him. It seemed to hang over his men like a heavy blanket. He glanced uncertainly about the quiet hall as he removed his mantle and threw it across the back of a nearby chair. The usual jovial mood was missing. The men spoke in hushed tones or sat drinking their ale in silence. Several played cards, but without the ribald comments that normally accompanied their games of chance. Without realizing it, Justin's gaze was drawn to the stone stairway that led to Jamelyn's chamber as he wondered what had come over his men.

Anthony's chair scraped against the flagged floor, drawing Justin's attention. He crossed to his friend by the huge fireplace, a quizzical look playing over his handsome features. Anthony propped one boot upon the sturdy wooden bench before him and leaned his uninjured arm on it as he also glanced toward the passageway and then back to Justin. "The time has come. She will either live or die."

Justin's smooth brow furrowed slightly as he looked at Anthony. "Is that the reason for the pall that lies over the men?" he asked.

Anthony nodded his blond head. "Aye, it has been a great jest about Jacob mothering the girl, but she has gained the men's respect because of the courage she has shown."

Justin removed his leather gauntlets and tucked them into the wide belt about his waist. The heavy gold buckle shimmered from the light of the fire at his movement. "She has courage, Anthony, but she is still our enemy."

Anthony considered Justin's words briefly and then nodded his agreement. "My side still aches like hell as proof of that, Justin."

The stern expression faded from Justin's face as he smiled down at his friend and slapped him gently on the back. "But you have mended well. I knew it would take more than one small girl to do you in."

Tentatively, Anthony touched his healing side, his lips crinkling into a boyish smile. "For a while I began to doubt it."

A pregnant silence filled the great hall at the sound of Jamelyn's chamber door opening and closing. Justin and Anthony moved in unison toward the stairway as Jacob descended. Jacob stopped and stared down at the two men, his haggard face revealing his exhaustion. The men released the breath they had been holding as a slow, tired smile spread Jacob's bearded cheeks.

"It is over; she'll live."

The hall behind the three men erupted into a din as the

men laughed and returned to their normal routines. The heavy atmosphere evaporated like the morning mist. Justin could not suppress his own smile at the men's reaction. They were relieved and now expressed it by downing their ale and laughing at the slightest jest. Placing his broad hand upon Jacob's shoulder, the pressure of his fingers indicating his own thanks for the care his vassal had shown Jamelyn, Justin said, "You need rest. I'll go up and sit with the girl for a while and then Anthony can play nursemaid. The role might suit him well." Jacob nodded and chuckled at the look of distress that crossed Anthony's face at Justin's words.

The encroaching twilight shed little light into the bed-chamber through the narrow window in the castle wall. Raven's Keep had been constructed for defense, not comfort. Justin squinted in the gloom as he lit the taper beside Jamelyn's bed. He moved quietly so as not to awaken Jacob's patient, but as he turned to the bed, he was surprised to find her gaze upon him. He could not read the expression in the shining depths of her eyes as he pulled a chair close to the bed and settled his large frame comfortably in it. "Your fever has broken" was all he could think to say.

Jamelyn gave a nearly imperceptible nod and then turned her face away. At that moment she was too weak to face her enemy and hoped her actions would make him leave. Pretending sleep, Jamelyn listened as Justin rose from his chair and lit the fire in the grate. She heard the splash of wine as he poured it into a goblet and then the squeak of the chair as he once more seated himself at her side. The sounds were strangely comforting and soon Jamelyn's pretense blended into the truth. She drifted into a restful, recuperative slumber.

When Jamelyn's eyes fluttered open once more the fire in the grate was only embers. The English knight had not left her chamber but still sat quietly watching her. He smiled as she turned to look at him and said softly, "Jami is a strange name for a girl."

Justin stretched his long legs out before him and rubbed the back of his neck, not expecting an answer.

Briefly Jamelyn puzzled over Justin's words and then realized he did not know her by any other name than what Shawn called her. "Jamelyn." The word was no more than a hoarse whisper.

Unsure that she had spoken and that he was not imagining things, Justin leaned forward as he said, "Jamelyn? Is that your name?"

She nodded.

Justin rolled the name over his tongue as if tasting a fine wine. "Aye, that sounds more like a female."

Irritated by his reference to her gender, Jamelyn's green eyes glittered up at Justin. "I like it not," she said.

Justin leaned back in the chair and crossed his arms casually over his chest. With his raven head to one side, he studied the girl in silence for a few moments before he said, "Jamelyn was the name you were christened and that shall be the name you are called henceforth. You are no longer Jami as McDougal calls you."

Too weak to argue the point, Jamelyn conceded for the present as she thought, You can call me whatever you please, English dog, but I will always be Jami. Nothing would make her accept the name given her at birth. It reminded her too much of her femininity. She had labored too hard to gain the nickname of Jami. It was a symbol of acceptance bestowed upon her by her uncle's vassals, and no one could change that.

In the following weeks Jamelyn regained her strength slowly. She did not see Justin again after the night her fever broke. However, she often heard him bellowing orders to his men in the great hall or in the bailey below her window.

During her convalescence Jamelyn learned that not all Englishmen were brutal animals. The one called Jacob showed her kindness and saw to her welfare as if she were his daughter instead of his enemy. This revelation surprised Jamelyn. She had always considered all Englishmen to be brutes and had often been told as a child that they loved to devour young children. Jacob's tender ministrations made her realize that there were good men in every nationality.

As Jamelyn's body healed, her mind turned more often to the future and the welfare of her people. Jacob noted her long silences as she sat staring pensively off into space. He suspected the reason behind her subdued moods and tried to relieve her worries by telling her of the events that occurred about Raven's Keep since the day of their arrival. He saw the relieved look that crossed Jamelyn's face when he told her that all of her men except Shawn McDougal had escaped without detection. The grateful smile she bestowed upon Jacob swelled his heart and made him glad that he had been able to ease some of her troubles, even though he himself would have liked to see some of those Scots warriors hanged.

Jacob's news lightened Jamelyn's burden. She was also glad to learn that Shawn had not suffered unduly because of his loyalty to her. The English knight had kept his word and no harm had befallen her friend. He was still kept in the dungeon under lock and key and as long as she kept her vow, Shawn would remain safe. But how long would he live when her fate had been decided? Jamelyn puzzled over the situation. She had expected to be executed as soon as she recovered enough to mount the steps to the gibbet. Yet she grew stronger with each passing day and still the black knight had not come to tell her of his decision. She was treated kindly, more like a guest than a prisoner, and it confused Jamelyn. She could not know her fate had been decided in London by King Edward. Even as she spoke with Jacob, Justin's squire approached the keep in haste. Had Jamelyn suspected what her fate was to be, she would have once more offered her life in exchange.

Justin sat behind the dark wood desk, hunched over the thick tomes of records. It amazed him to find such meticulous documents kept by the old lord. From the state of the keep with its lack of servants and rustic furnishings, Justin would have surmised that Lord Cregan cared little for anything beyond warfare. However, the old warrior had cataloged each birth on the fief and each barrel of grain he received from his tenants.

Wearily Justin rubbed his eyes. Dust motes flew in the

air as he closed the thick leather volumes and leaned back in his chair. His gaze lingered on the ledgers, their bindings smooth and shiny from much use. A tired smile briefly played over his lips as he stretched his cramped muscles. At first Justin had thought Edward to be niggardly with his gifts when he gave Justin the right to Raven's Keep. Rich in his own right, possessing several estates in England, Justin was annoyed at having to fight to claim such a meager holding. But after reading the well-kept records, he realized the small fief had grown rich under Lord Cregan's rule. Its wealth was not visible to the eye, but Edward had known and thought it an adequate payment for the services Justin had devoted to the crown. The thick volumes improved Justin's outlook toward his king and Raven's Keep. After reading through them, he did not feel that all the long, exhausting hours had been spent in vain.

During the past weeks Justin had worked from daylight till dark to secure his fief. He had ridden over every inch of it inspecting the hamlet and seeing that all progressed well during the harvest season. The serfs reaped the products of their labor and as new lord, Justin would receive the yearly tribute.

The serfs' calm acceptance of him as their lord surprised Justin. There had been little trouble over the transition. That in itself was the enigma that brought a puzzled frown to Justin's smooth forehead. He had expected more resistance from the loyal Scots. Justin did not realize that the reason the serfs did not rebel against him rested only a few paces away from his own chamber. The peasants of Raven's Keep feared for their chieftain's life if they showed any sign of revolt against the English lord.

A loud knock interrupted Justin's train of thought and he looked up to see Gibbon stride briskly into the chamber after he was given permission to enter. His squire looked as if he had not slept in several days. His armor and mail were mud-spattered and a patchy stubble of golden-brown beard dotted his chin and jaws. His curly brown hair was matted with sweat as he removed his helm and bowed to Justin. "My lord, I have brought your answer from the king." Handing Justin the leather pouch, Gibbon watched as his master opened it and withdrew the rolled parchment. It bore the seal of the crown and Justin slit the wax with his dirk before unrolling it and reading.

A shiver of apprehension crept up Gibbon's weary spine as he watched the expression on his master's face. A deep scowl formed across Justin's wide forehead and his lips pressed into a tight, thin line as his complexion mottled with rage. Nervously, Gibbon backed toward the door, hoping to escape the fury he sensed beneath his master's still exterior. His flight was halted by Justin's words. "You had this directly from King Edward, himself?"

Gibbon could feel his knees begin to tremble and his voice quavered. "Aye, my lord. I accepted it from his own hand and he bade me to make haste back to Raven's Keep."

Justin's eyes sparkled with fiery lights as he seethed with anger. "That will be all for now, Gibbon. Send Sir Godfrey to me at once."

Trying to hide his look of relief, Gibbon bowed to Justin and quickly fled in search of Anthony Godfrey. He found Justin's friend in his usual spot by the fireplace in the great hall. Anthony's brow creased as he removed his feet from the table where he had comfortably propped them and looked up at the frightened squire. Wiping the ale foam from his newly-grown mustache, he said, "You say he is angry? That can only mean the king has condemned the girl to execution." With that Anthony strode briskly from the hall and took the stairs two at a time in his rush to Justin's chamber. The door to the room was partially open, and Anthony pushed it wide without knocking.

Justin's back was to his friend as he stared out the narrow slit at the domain of Raven's Keep. He was only aware of Anthony's presence when the lanky blond man closed the door. The sound startled Justin away from his morbid thoughts, and he swung abruptly to face his friend. The tempest that raged within him was clearly visible on his face. He threw down the parchment that was still in his hand saying, "I have received my answer from our good King Edward."

Anthony watched as the missive curled once more into a roll and then looked at Justin. "By the look on your face, Justin, and the sound of your voice, I surmise that King Edward has ordered the worst. When will the execution take place?"

Justin's fiery gaze riveted Anthony to the rough wood planking as his lips curled into an angry sneer. "Our good king has ordered it within the week. But I am the one to suffer his punishment."

Puzzlement knit Anthony's blond brows over his straight nose, his eyes expressing confusion as he asked, "Justin, have you angered the king?"

Exasperated, Justin shook his head before running his long, tapering fingers through his unruly blue-black curls. "Nay, our king has decided to reward me further. Read that and you will understand all."

Baffled by Justin's words and his outraged expression, Anthony picked up the missive and perused the contents. He studied it briefly and then a twinkle of mirth grew within the depths of his eyes. He tried to stem the bubble of laughter in his throat but failed. Dropping the parchment once more upon the desk, Anthony clasped his sides and roared.

His friend's hilarity at his predicament did little to ease Justin's feelings. His scowl deepened as he said, "Damn you, Anthony. 'Tis no laughing matter."

Anthony forced his lips firmly together. His face reddened and his eyes seemed to bulge as he tried to control his mirth. Wiping the tears from his blond lashes, Anthony looked soberly at Justin before his lips trembled and he exploded with laughter again. "By St. George, you are to pay dearly for taking this fief as your own, my lord."

With one vicious kick from his black boot, Justin's chair went flying across the room. He began to pace the chamber like a caged lion. Anthony backed out of his path as Justin raged. "Had I known this was to happen I would have slain the wench." The corded muscles of his neck were taut and a vein in his forehead protruded, throbbing with the blood that boiled in fury as he slammed his fist against the dusty surface of the desk. "By all that is holy, this cannot be happening."

Anthony held his injured side to keep it from aching. "Justin, you have to obey your king."

For one brief moment Justin considered throttling his friend to wipe the smirk off his face. A muscle in his jaw quivered violently as he tried to control his wrath. "What have I ever done to be vilified by our sovereign in such a way, Anthony?"

Anthony's sun-streaked head moved back and forth as he tried to make Justin understand Edward's reasoning. "Nay, my friend, our king needs your service to help keep peace on this wild border of his kingdom. That is why he has ordered you to marry the Scottish lass. By binding her to you, she will have to obey Edward. He does not mean you harm."

Justin rubbed his wide hand irritably across his face as if the action would wipe away the message that lay before him. "Our good King Edward does not know the girl or he would not think so foolishly." With a resigned sigh, Justin uprighted the padded chair and sank into it. He slumped against its leather back as he looked once more at Anthony. "I like it not, but I can see his reasoning. Had he ordered her slain, all of the lowlands would have joined forces against us. As it stands now Edward has a good foothold in Scotland."

Justin's wide shoulders drooped as he accepted Edward's command. His rage evaporated at the same time. The turmoil of Justin's emotions was mirrored in the dark depths of his eyes as he gazed up at his friend. "It is unconscionable, Anthony. After all the Scots have taken from me, I am now to wed one." Justin closed his thick-lashed eyes as if in pain and pressed the tips of his fingers about the bridge of his nose. "How can I marry the skinny wench knowing my beautiful Jessica lies beneath the dark loam of England because of the Scots?"

Knowing well the agony these memories brought back to his friend, Anthony tried to draw Justin's thoughts away from his dead wife. If he did not succeed, Justin's mind would also go to his brother, Richard, who had disappeared on the day of Jessica's death. "Are you forgetting Anne of Chester?" Anthony put in. "She will not take this lightly after warming your bed for nearly ten years with her eye on your name."

Justin's hand fell to the arm of the chair as he slowly shook his head. "Nay, Anne is another reason, but you know that I can never love another as I loved Jessica."

Anthony's voice reflected his sympathy as he said, "Aye, I know how you feel, Justin, but all of that is in the past." Crossing the short space between them, Anthony put his arm comfortingly about Justin's shoulders. "'Tis hard to accept, and you cannot compare Anne's beauty to that girl's. I sympathize with your plight, but we must look at the brighter side. Once you are wed and have the fief under control, you may then go back to England and renew your affair with Anne. You can forget the skinny wench you left behind."

Justin's sensuous lips curled at the corners as a bright light seemed to shimmer beneath the black clouds of his mind. "Aye, you are right, Anthony. The Cregan wench will soon learn who is her master and then I will be free to return to court."

Anthony slapped Justin good-naturedly on the back and laughed. "By the look of the wench, she will not live long. She is too skinny and if she dies, you will be free to wed again. Then you will have everything; but if you go against Edward, you will lose all."

The smile faded from Justin's lips as his fist balled against the arm of the chair. "I did not want to marry again. I have made no promises to Anne nor did I intend to do so. I care for her as much as I can care for any woman, Anthony. But since I lost Jessica any pretty face and shapely body does as well as another to satisfy my needs. It chafes me sorely to know that my future bride is of the race I despise, not to mention that she acts more a man than a woman. It would help a bit if she had a small amount of meat upon her bony frame."

Anthony's blue eyes twinkled with devilment as he said,

"Shall I have the priest summoned today or do you need time to adjust to the thought of your new bride? If it were I, I would need much time to consider taking that one to wed." With that he rubbed his healing side.

Justin grinned ruefully up at his friend. He welcomed the knowledge that he was not the only one who would be reluctant to marry the girl King Edward had chosen for him. Shaking his head matter-of-factly, Justin said, "Summon him today, Anthony. If I dwell upon it, I might not think Edward's favor worth the price. Tell Jacob to bring the wench to the hall when the priest arrives."

Jamelyn slipped the tunic over her head and pulled on her chausses, relieved to find the soreness nearly gone. It felt good to dress again. She was tired of wearing the robe Jacob had found for her in her uncle's chamber. But the feel of her own clothing against her skin only added to Jamelyn's restlessness. As her strength returned she began to yearn for her freedom. With each day that passed, her chamber seemed to shrink in size, adding to her distress. She paced the room trying to expend some of the growing energy and frustration her captivity aroused.

Tying the laces of her tunic, Jamelyn prepared herself for another day of pacing across her room. But at least today she would wear her own clothing instead of the long robe that hampered her movements. Jamelyn's gaze turned to the sturdy oak door, and she wished for the hundredth time that she could go through it, if only for a few brief minutes of freedom. But she knew that was not to be until the black knight decided her fate.

A commotion from the bailey drew Jamelyn's attention. She crossed to the narrow window and peered down, watching with interest as the guards scurried about to carry out the orders of their leader.

Instinctively, Jamelyn knew something out of the ordinary was afoot. The short hair at the nape of her neck seemed to rise as a cold chill of apprehension swept up her spine. She sensed the unusual activity had something to do with her. Warily she watched the English troops file into the yard below and line up. Jamelyn's gaze was drawn to the gates of Raven's Keep as a short, rotund figure rode through the entrance on a small highland pony. Jamelyn made the sign of the cross and squared her shoulders as she recognized the village priest. Jacob had told her that Lord St. Claire awaited a message from King Edward decreeing her fate and at the sight of the holy man, Jamelyn knew what that would be. It did not surprise her; she had expected it all along. At least the black knight was kind enough to send for the priest so that she might receive the last rites.

Mustering her courage, Jamelyn raised her small, oval chin and brushed the stubby hair away from her forehead with nerveless fingers. She staunchly swallowed the tightness that constricted her throat and took a deep, steadying breath. Determination darkened her green eyes, making them the color of the stormy sea. She would face her death bravely as she had been taught by her uncle and Shawn McDougal. The English dogs would not see her cower or beg for her life.

The hinges of the great oak door squeaked behind her and Jamelyn turned slowly to face Jacob. With chin in the air and back stiff, she looked at the Englishman who had saved her life and now came to take her to lose it. She forced her features to remain expressionless, hiding behind that vacant mask of trepidation that was sweeping over her thin body. Only her eyes gave evidence to any emotion; they burned with emerald lights of hate.

Jacob noted the scorching look directed at him, its heat making him want to recoil from the young woman he had grown fond of, but he had to obey orders and said, "My lord has instructed me to escort you to the great hall, Lady Jamelyn." Taking Jamelyn's arm, Jacob led her into the corridor.

Jamelyn jerked her arm free of Jacob's hold and preceded him down the passageway with head held high. She swallowed nervously as she entered the vaulted room and found all of the English soldiers assembled to witness the carrying out of the judgment. Her steps faltered at the entrance, and she turned to Jacob. "I would have my tartan," she said.

At the strange request, Jacob glanced uncertainly at Justin and saw him nod his consent. Quickly, he sought out the badge of honor and brought it back to Jamelyn. The young heiress of Raven's Keep draped the red and black wool plaid over her thin shoulder, bestowing one last loving caress upon it before raising her chin haughtily and walking toward the tall English knight who would administer her fate.

A hush fell over the English troops. Their respect for the young girl grew with each moment as she walked bravely toward their leader. Her steps did not falter, nor was there any fear written across her face. Only dignified and courageous acceptance of what was to come was reflected in her pale features.

Jamelyn stopped before Justin, her wide green eyes assessing his sober features. She came only to his shoulder in height and had to lean her small, shaggy head back to see his handsome face. The breath caught in her throat as she noted for the first time his comely appearance. She momentarily forgot the reason she stood before him as she took in his fine features. Her eyes lingered briefly on the iridescent raven curls that recklessly caressed his high forehead, which now puckered slightly in a frown. Her gaze was drawn to his intense blue eyes, fringed with long, curling black lashes, and she almost envied them. Any woman would have been pleased to possess their richness.

Unabashed, Jamelyn continued her inspection of her handsome enemy. She met Justin's penetrating stare unflinchingly before continuing her perusal. Her eyes traveled down his aquiline nose to his sensuous lips. Jamelyn sensed by their harsh line that the English knight did not like the duty his king had commanded of him.

Slowly Jamelyn's sea-green gaze moved along his square jaw, down his corded neck to his wide, velvet-covered shoulders, and then across his broad chest where patterns of intricately woven threads of gold seemed to add to its great dimensions. From there she took in his lean hips with the wide, gold-studded belt and his long, muscular legs encased in soft woolen chausses that clung to each well-formed muscle. Ruefully Jamelyn admitted the Englishman was a handsome specimen.

Tired of her gawking, Justin's wide-palmed hand closed about Jamelyn's upper arm and brought her around to face his men. His voice was firm and contained no warmth as his words fell heavily upon the assembly. "I have received our sovereign's command on this day, and you are here to witness his judgment be carried out."

Jamelyn's muscles grew taut beneath Justin's hand, and he glanced briefly at her shaggy head but could not see the expression on the girl's face. Swallowing back the distaste his next words caused him, Justin continued, "King Edward has decreed that the Clan of Cregan and the house of St. Claire be united by marriage."

Jamelyn flinched as if she had been struck and looked up with wide, startled eyes at the man towering at her side. Shock mingled with contempt in her expression as the words escaped her suddenly fear-stricken throat. "Nay, I'll not bed down with an English dog."

Her refusal seemed to echo from the vaulted ceiling through the stillness that had invaded the great chamber. With one swift movement, Jamelyn jerked free of Justin's imprisoning grip and fled toward the entrance of the hall. Dumbfounded by the turn of events, Justin's men seemed welded to the floor and made no move to stop Jamelyn's flight.

Being as surprised as his men by Jamelyn's violent reaction, it took Justin a moment to collect himself and charge after his fleeing bride. He caught Jamelyn as she swung open the heavy door, his hand coming down like a vise upon the nape of her wool tunic. He was not gentle as he hauled Jamelyn, kicking and screaming vile oaths, back before the stunned priest.

Shoving her roughly into the arms of the smirking Sir Godfrey, Justin eyed Jamelyn distastefully. "Hold the wench until the service is over. She smells like a pigsty."

Anthony wrinkled his nose in repugnance at his task. Justin noted Anthony's grimace and smiled sardonically. "After the ceremony, I want the wench scrubbed. She may be a little heathen, but I will not abide those crawly infestations upon my wife. I will not suffer because of the Scots' barbaric ways."

Justin's insult hit its intended target like an arrow through a bull's-eye. Breathing heavily, Jamelyn looked up at him through the red haze of rancor. Her lips curled away from her even teeth as she snarled, "English dog, I spit upon you." With that she spat at Justin's feet.

Justin's eyes narrowed dangerously, and the smile that spread his lips chilled the bravest of his warriors. "That would be more water than has touched your skin in many a day, I would think. Now, Anthony, clamp your hand over her mouth to keep her quiet. We must obey King Edward's command."

Jamelyn groaned in fury as she squirmed in Anthony's arms and fought against the suffocating hand over her mouth. How she wanted to tear the insufferable smile from the bastard's face. Her eyes burned with hatred and her fingers curved into talons as she tried to bite the broad palm that pressed her lips against her teeth. She failed. Trembling with unmitigated fury, Jamelyn eyed Justin St. Claire, silently vowing to put a knife in his back at the first opportunity.

Ignoring Jamelyn, Justin calmly looked at the pale, wide-eyed priest. The man's shock was clearly reflected by his slightly quivering, fat jowls. "You may now proceed with the ceremony," Justin ordered. "Make it quick, for I have more important tasks at hand."

The priest's eyes seemed to bulge with discomfort as he looked from Jamelyn back to the tall English knight. His loyalty was to the Cregan heir but the cold, stony expression on the Englishman's face made his breath catch in his throat and a shiver of fear pass along his spine.

It was an unusual ceremony, to say the least, but it was not within the priest's rotund body to protest that no banns had been read nor was the bride willing to participate. From the look on the raven-haired knight's face, the cleric quickly determined it would be in his best interest and that of all concerned for him to proceed as if nothing were out of the ordinary.

Swallowing nervously and clearing his throat, the priest spoke unsteadily as he began to read the vows. His eyes darted from Jamelyn to Justin, waiting for them to repeat the pledge. Beads of sweat popped out on his balding pate as silence filled the chamber.

Justin paused briefly, his eyes mirroring his resentment as he began to speak the vows. As he finished he turned toward Anthony, his nod instructing his friend to remove his hand from Jamelyn's mouth. As Anthony did so, Jamelyn shook her head violently and halfway spat, "Nay," before Anthony clamped his hand once more over her lips to still her answer. With a shrug of his wide shoulders, Justin, unperturbed by her stifled squeal of protest, repeated the vows for Jamelyn.

Knowing it would be futile to ask, the priest decided to forego asking the couple to kneel to be draped by the white linen as a symbol of unity. He blessed the union and then handed the parchment for Justin's and Jamelyn's signatures to the tall knight. His pudgy fingers trembled as he dipped the quill into the pot of ink.

Justin signed his name and turned to Jamelyn. "Sign your name or make your mark," he commanded gruffly. A grim smile played over his shapely lips as Jamelyn shook her head in denial. With calm deliberation, Justin took Jamelyn's hand within his own, forcing the quill between her fingers. His grip tightened about her hand, and she was helpless to prevent him from moving it to sign her name.

Satisfied, Justin handed the document back to the frightened priest for his signature to confirm to King Edward that his orders had been followed. When the priest scribbled his name, Justin handed him a pouch that jingled with coins. "This is for your church, Father," he said. With that Justin turned abruptly and left the hall without a backward glance at his new bride or his friend, who stood helplessly holding the still-squirming form of Lady St. Claire.

Anthony watched with impotent vexation as the priest quickly scurried from the hall, followed by Justin's men. No one paid any heed to the predicament in which he had been left. He did not know how he was to carry out Justin's order, as the vixen had not ceased her struggles even briefly. Anthony let out a long, exasperated breath. Having no other recourse, he finally released Jamelyn and tried to capture her wrist. For his efforts he received a sharp elbow in his injured side and he howled with pain. Gasping for air, Anthony managed to get a tenacious hold upon Jamelyn's thin arm. Bellowing for Jacob, he dragged her toward the stairs. "Damn you, Jacob, come and help me with this wildcat before she tears me apart."

With lips quivering slightly at the young man's plight, Jacob rounded the corner to give Anthony aid. Roughly Anthony shoved Jamelyn at Jacob and pressed his hand to his aching side. "See that she is bathed," he ordered before hobbling off across the hall for a tankard of ale to ease his pain.

Settling himself in his favorite spot by the fireplace, Anthony watched as Jacob calmly led Jamelyn up the stairs. Though his side burned from her attack, Anthony could not suppress the impish smile that played about his lips. The thought of Justin trying to bed the little wildcat lightened his mood. Ruefully he shook his blond head before taking a long, slow sip of the cool drink. Anthony felt sorry for his friend in more ways than one.

Jamelyn did not resist Jacob's firm hold upon her arm as she let him escort her back to her chamber. He had been too kind to her during her illness for her to lash out at him physically as she had done to the young Englishman. However, her feelings changed drastically a short time later when Jacob returned to her chamber, dragging a large wooden tub into the room. Her wide emerald eyes were filled with apprehension as she watched him fill it with steaming water. She eyed the wiry little man as if he had grown two heads and wondered briefly if he was the same person who had given her such tender care.

Finishing his task, Jacob turned to Jamelyn and told her to bathe. Rapidly shaking her shaggy head from side to side, her small chin jutting out stubbornly, she said, "Nay, I'll not bathe."

Sensing the difficulty at hand, Jacob let out a long, resigned sigh as he looked at Jamelyn's set little face. "Lass, Lord St. Claire has ordered you to bathe, and I must see that you do as he bids. Now come and I'll wait outside till you are done."

Crossing her arms over her chest, Jamelyn perversely turned her face away. "Nay, a person does not bathe in the autumn. If your high-and-mighty lord wants to see me dead, then let him hang me. It will be much quicker."

Jacob could not suppress his grin at the girl's antiquated idea. He knew many people believed that bathing was ill for the health, thinking the hot water weakened the muscles. But he had learned, as had most of St. Claire's men, that cleanliness was one thing his lord required. "Come, lass, and into the tub—or do I have to put you there?"

As Jamelyn turned to face Jacob she realized the venom she had expended earlier on others was now directed against him. Her eyes glittered like hard jewels in the sunlight as she said in a dangerously low tone, "Come near me and I'll scratch your eyes out."

Knowing well the young girl's temper, Jacob did not enjoy the task assigned him. It would not be simple, but he had a duty to perform and would do it. Shrugging resignedly, he advanced on Jamelyn. His eyes widened in surprise as a brass candlestick missed his head by only a few inches. "Hold now, lass," he ordered, but his words went unheeded as Jamelyn rushed to the fireplace and grabbed the heavy iron poker. She backed against the wall and waved it threateningly.

"English dog, come near me and you will regret it."

As a battle-hardened soldier, Jacob had faced many enemies and knew well when to retreat. The girl had nearly slain his master and Sir Godfrey and Jacob knew she would do her best to do the same to him. It was time to call in reinforcements. He would let Lord St. Claire handle his tempest of a wife.

Jamelyn relaxed slightly as she watched Jacob's hurried retreat from her chamber, but only for a moment. She braced herself staunchly against the wall, her grip on the poker tightening as she heard Justin's outraged voice coming closer. With her chin still jutting out defiantly she awaited her husband's entrance.

The chamber door slammed back against the wall with such force it seemed to make the room tremble. Justin's eyes sizzled with blue fire as he strode angrily into the chamber and approached his wife. "Damn you, wench. You will bathe. I'll not have such a stench within my domain."

The black look on Justin's face made Jamelyn back warily along the wall as he came forward. He lunged at her and tried to grab her weapon but she was too fleet. Jamelyn flitted across the room, overturning a chair in front of her husband. In hot pursuit, Justin could not stop in time to avoid it. He stumbled and crashed to the floor. Rage exploded within him as he hit the hard wood. Clambering to his feet, Justin raced toward the door to block Jamelyn's path. For all his large size, the knight was swift on his feet, and he caught his wayward wife before she could make good her escape. He grabbed her roughly by her short, stubby hair and dragged her back toward the steaming tub.

With one large hand, he grasped both of Jamelyn's slender wrists up over her head and then with a vicious yank, he ripped her tunic from her. Next her jerked off her chausses, leaving her totally naked before him. Still overcome by rage, Justin shoved Jamelyn into the tub and with one hand ducked her beneath the hot liquid. He held her below the surface of the water until he saw bubbles rise and then pulled her up for air.

Jamelyn gasped for the life-giving substance, taking deep breaths into her burning lungs. When the pounding in her head subsided slightly, she began once more to try to free herself. Calmly, Justin's flat palm clamped onto the top of her small head and pushed her once more below the water. Again and again, he forced Jamelyn beneath it until she was turning blue in the face from lack of air. At last he felt her resistance give way and he raised her, allowing her to lean weakly against the side of the tub. She gulped in deep breaths to keep from fainting.

Casually, as if nothing were out of the ordinary, Justin

took the bar of soap and proceeded to scrub Jamelyn none too gently from head to toe. He lathered her short hair and was surprised to find it a rich auburn gilded with shining copper when he rinsed the soap away.

Jamelyn's thin limbs were rosy-hued when Justin finished and poured a bucket of water over her. She sputtered with outrage as the cold water hit her warm body and Justin chuckled with malicious glee. He dragged her from the tub and pushed her toward the bed. "Find something clean to put on that skinny body," he ordered. "I do not want to see you attired in men's clothing again. You are now Lady St. Claire and will dress accordingly. Do you understand?"

Stumbling from the force of Justin's hand, Jamelyn landed upon the bed. Wrapping a sheet about her wet body, she brushed the dripping strands of hair from her forehead. Her face was pale but her lips set in a defiant line as she raised her chin and spat contemptuously, "I have nothing more to wear, my great Lord the Dog."

Exasperated that he had not broken the girl's spirit, Justin clenched his fists tightly at his sides to keep from throttling Jamelyn. Sparks seemed to shoot from his eyes as he took deep breaths to try to control his urge to strangle the wench. "Then I suggest you do as other women and make yourself appropriate garments." With that he turned and stormed from the chamber, slamming the door loudly behind him. Justin knew he had reached his limit; his patience had completely deserted him. If he stayed a moment longer in Jamelyn's presence, he would treat the vixen as she deserved and slay her.

Sir Godfrey lounged negligently against the wall outside Jamelyn's chamber. As Justin turned to lock the still-vibrating portal, Anthony arched one brow inquisitively and said, "Are you, my lord, having your first lovers' quarrel?"

Justin's hand stopped in midair as he swung to face his friend who was tempting fate. "Anthony, I warn you, your glib tongue is sorely fraying what friendship we have known." With that Justin gave Anthony his back and strode angrily to his own chamber, slamming his door on the other's laughter.

Still seething, he crossed the room in a few short strides and filled the pewter tankard to the brim with the rich red wine. He gulped down the contents without blinking an eye. The warm liquid had the desired effect, soothing his taut nerves as well as his rage. Refilling the tankard, Justin slumped into the padded chair and stretched out his long, muscular legs before the fire. With his elbow bent against the chair arm and one cheek propped upon his balled fist, Justin wearily reflected on the events of the day. It had been like a terrible nightmare, and he prayed without hope to awake and find himself once more in England.

Justin's gaze rested upon the ruby liquid within the tankard. He would have need of much more than one tankard of wine if he was to finish what his king had ordered. He had not seen the last of the Scottish vixen. He had to return to her and consummate their vows to make the marriage legal. Rolling his dark eyes heavenward, Justin prayed for strength to perform the act. Resting his raven head against the back of the chair, Justin propped one foot upon the stool before him as he thought, After this day no one can ever question my loyalty to the sovereign of England. He had put all of his deepest emotions aside to please Edward III.

The image of Jessica floated into Justin's mind, sending a wrenching pain through his chest at the thought of his golden-haired, blue-eyed wife. "Ah, Jessica," Justin murmured to the still room and squeezed his eyes tightly shut to stem the moisture that threatened. Rubbing away the dampness with the tips of his fingers, Justin took a deep gulp of wine. Bitterness tugged Justin's shapely lips down at the corners as he stared unseeing into the leaping flames and remembered the love of his youth.

Jessica, with the sweet smile and gentle disposition. Justin had loved her from the first moment they had met. The goodness she possessed glowed in the depths of her pale blue eyes. Those eyes always reminded Justin of sunshine and soft spring days, for they were the same shade as the sky on a clear morning. Her delicate features reflected her innocence of the cruelties of life, and Justin had wanted to take her into his arms and protect her forever. Always a man of determination, Justin had set out to woo Jessica and make her love him in return. It had been the happiest day of his life when she agreed to marry him.

Their marriage had lasted less than a year; then the Scots bastards had murdered Jessica and Richard. Those few months of marriage lingered within Justin's mind like a sore, open wound. He had been unable to heal it, to close off that part of the past and look toward the future with another woman.

A burning log sent a shower of sparks up the chimney, but Justin did not see them as his mind turned to the woman who awaited his return to London, Anne of Chester. At one time he had thought he was in love with the beautiful Anne, but that was before he had met Jessica. Then after Jessica's death he had turned once more to Anne as he desperately tried to put his wife out of his mind and heart. It had been a useless effort. He was attracted to Anne. What man would not be drawn by such a sexually alluring woman? She also had charm and wit, but that did not make Justin love her. He could go to her bed and satisfy his needs, but that was the extent of his relationship with Anne of Chester. Even if he did come to love Anne it would be to no avail at the present time, for he was not free to ask for her hand. It was a damnable situation in which he now found himself.

Taking another long swallow of wine, Justin rubbed his temples with the tips of his long, bronzed fingers and closed his eyes. He had generally been a fortunate man in love and war, but after this day Justin felt his luck had deserted him. He was now at the mercy of the fates, and they had tossed him into a sea of turbulence. The rough waves would drag him beneath the angry surface until all hope of survival died.

Moodily, Justin let his chin drop to his chest, his expression mirroring his glum thoughts. Justin's gaze rested upon the dust motes floating gently through the rays of the late afternoon sun that streamed in through the narrow window. It would soon be time to go to his bride. For the first time in his thirty-two years, Justin St. Claire found no pleasure at the thought of spreading a woman's thighs.

"Damn," he cursed before draining the tankard and then refilling it once more.

Night lay over the Scottish countryside like a dark, jewel-studded mantle by the time Anthony knocked on Justin's door to escort the new groom to his connubial bed. Justin was in his cups and hiccuped loudly as he bellowed, "Come in, damn you!"

Anthony's lips curled in amusement as he thought of several witty remarks with which to bedevil Justin as he took him to his bride. However, all such thoughts fled as the door swung open and he recognized Justin's state of inebriation. Crossing to his friend, he picked up the empty tankard from the floor and set it on the nearby table. He wrinkled his nose in distaste as the odor of the room assailed his nostrils. The heavy scent of wine permeated the air.

Anthony's blue eyes glowed with sympathy. He knew the pain Justin had suffered that day. A doleful expression played over Anthony's face as he looked down at Justin's slumped figure and thought of the young girl who was now Lady St. Claire. He pitied her as well. With his friend in this state, she would be the one to pay for all past grievances. Jamelyn St. Claire had nearly felled Anthony and had added to the damage that afternoon, but he would not wish such a fate on anyone, especially this young woman, who had gained his grudging respect.

The girl had fought bravely to defend her people and had been defeated. She did not deserve the treatment she would receive from Justin in his drunken condition. The wine would let down all barriers on Justin's self-control, and he would let his hatred for the Scots direct his actions. "Justin, let me get you to bed," Anthony said. "Tomorrow will be time enough to start your marriage."

Justin's head wobbled. He blinked almost in slow motion as he tried to focus his eyes. "Damn you, Godfrey. I will finish what my good king has ordered and be done with it. I will not live another day with such punishment hanging over my head." Hiccuping, Justin held out his unsteady hand to Anthony. "Now help me to my dear bride's chamber and cease your prattle."

A deep scowl etched a crooked path across Anthony's smooth forehead as he placed his hand firmly on Justin's shoulder to try to keep him from rising. "Nay, Justin. You are not in fit condition to honor your vows this night."

Anthony's argument roused the anger lying just beneath the surface. Shaking off his friend's hand, Justin clasped the chair arms for support and forced his wobbly legs to hold him as he stood. He swayed as he glared at his friend. "Not fit to bed the Scottish bitch, you say? I'm as fit as I'll ever be because I know I cannot do it when I'm sober." Justin's words were slightly slurred as he weaved back and forth on his feet. "To think of my beautiful Jessica . . . it makes me want to retch, Anthony. The only way I can obey Edward is to seek courage from the wine. Don't you realize it was the bloody Scots who took my wife and brother from me?"

Anthony placed a supporting arm about Justin's waist. He had no argument to counter his friend's words. If he were in Justin's position he would probably have done the same. Without another word Anthony helped Justin down the chilly corridor to Jamelyn's door and unlocked it.

Bleary-eyed, Justin mustered as much dignity as his besotted senses could command. He straightened his clothing and squared his shoulders as he faced the open door. His actions reminded Anthony of the times they had gone into battle together.

Anthony stood quietly outside the chamber as Justin stepped through the portal and then closed the door after him. For a moment Anthony stared at the solid wood and then turned on his heel and made his way back to the great hall. He ordered a large tankard of ale and gulped the contents down as Justin had done earlier. Its taste was bitter, but no more so than the taste that was already present in his mouth. "Damn Edward's scheming," Anthony muttered under his breath before shouting for more ale.

* * *

Justin squinted into the nearly total darkness of the chamber. Only one taper burned to illuminate the huge four-poster with its small occupant. He forced his eyes to focus on the object of his attention and then strode unsteadily across the room. Coming in contact with the bed, his wobbly legs would no longer hold him and he slumped down beside the wide-eyed Jamelyn.

The sound of Justin's entrance had awakened her, and she now sat huddled against the intricately carved headboard, clutching the muslin sheet to her chest. She tried easing away from the lean, rock-hard body of her husband, but his wide hand stayed her movements as he clumsily grabbed her arm and jerked her toward him. Even in his state of inebriation, Justin's strength was tremendous. He easily drew Jamelyn to him.

A shiver of fear swept over Jamelyn's slender body. For the first time in her life she was experiencing true, undiluted fear. She had faced armed men in battle, but never before had she felt as vulnerable as she did now. Choking back the panic that was rising in her throat, threatening to cut off her breathing, Jamelyn looked up into the face of her husband. What she saw there only served to remind her of the weakness that belonged to all of her sex. They had to submit to a man's desire, for they did not have the physical strength to prevent it. It made her detest her female body even more. It had been a vile trick played upon her by nature. Had she been born a male, Jamelyn knew she would have been able to die with dignity instead of suffering the degradation that now was to be her fate. She would not have been used as a pawn in Justin's and King Edward's schemes to conquer Scotland. The thought infuriated Jamelyn; rage at her own sex and at the man who sat swaying before her bubbled white-hot through her veins and surfaced to end her moment of panic. Her lips curled back into a snarl as she hissed, "Keep your hands off me, vermin."

A lopsided grin, which Justin thought to be his most charming, spread his lips as he foggily gazed at his wife. "Is that any way to speak to your husband?"

Jamelyn felt Justin's fingers slacken their hold as he

spoke, and taking advantage of the moment, she jerked free. With one swift movement, she threw the covers at Justin's head and scrambled to the edge of the bed as she spat, "I'll not submit to you willingly, bastard dog."

Justin fought the covers away from his face and shook his head to clear it of the wine fumes. Seeing Jamelyn's flight, he made to grab her, but she easily avoided his awkward movements. "Come here, wench," he ordered, but Jamelyn was already sliding her small feet to the floor. "Nay, you'll not have me."

Justin lunged at Jamelyn before she could move out of the reach of his long arms and grasped her firmly with both hands about the waist. He jerked her effortlessly back onto the bed. "Wench, I have no more liking for this than you. Let us be done with it. This one time is necessary. After that I will bother you no more."

Jamelyn struggled against Justin's iron grip as he pulled her easily beneath him. Clumsily, he removed his clothing and threw it across the chamber. His heavy body imprisoned Jamelyn, pressing her into the soft down mattress as his mouth came down to claim hers.

Jamelyn froze, stunned briefly by the contact of his lips upon hers. It was the first time in her life another person had touched her in that manner. However, the shock was only momentary, and she renewed her fight for freedom. She pushed against the heavy body that crushed her small frame but could not budge Justin as his hands ran through her short hair, which had begun to curl after the dirt and oil was washed away.

"Um," Justin murmured against her ear. "You smell more like a human now."

"Get off me, you great beast!" Jamelyn screeched as she clawed at Justin's bare shoulders.

The pain roused Justin from his stupor. He grabbed Jamelyn's hands and held them above her head to protect his eyes. "Lie still and it will soon be over," he ordered, and hiccuped.

The scent of wine filled Jamelyn's nostrils as she squirmed to rid herself of Justin's presence. She did not realize her own actions were detrimental to her cause. The feel of her slender hips moving against his made Justin's loins tighten, and he quirked one curious brow as he looked down at Jamelyn. "Are you eager then, my little vixen?"

His words further inflamed Jamelyn's fury. "You bastard," she screamed, but his mouth silenced her curses. Jamelyn did not have time to close her lips against Justin's assault. His tongue invaded her mouth to explore its velvety softness.

Justin felt himself swelling with desire as his tongue tasted the virgin sweetness of Jamelyn's mouth. His own reaction surprised him. In his wine-fogged mind, Justin wondered briefly how his body could respond to such a skinny wench.

Justin's hand traveled quickly across the bony shoulders to Jamelyn's full breast and then down to her flat belly. He parted her thighs to receive him but paused to shake his head as the wine tried to take him beyond conscious thought. He knew he had to finish the chore before he passed out. Spreading Jamelyn's slender legs, Justin positioned himself between them; but before he could thrust forward the wine finally claimed him. He slumped heavily across Jamelyn, his dead weight crushing her further into the mattress.

Struggling, Jamelyn managed to free her hands from Justin's slack grip. Using all the strength she possessed, she pushed his heavy body off her. Feeling bruised and battered, she sat up and looked down at the man snoring softly at her side. Outraged by all that had transpired during the past minutes, Jamelyn clenched her fists tightly at her side, her eyes burning with the first tears to moisten them since her family had died ten years earlier.

Taking a shaky breath, Jamelyn slid her bare feet to the cold wood floor, her gaze searching the chamber for a weapon to carry out the vow she had made that afternoon. Spying Justin's dagger amid his pile of discarded clothing, Jamelyn scurried across the room and retrieved it. The shiny ivory handle fit perfectly within her hand as she crossed back to the bed and looked down at the prone figure of her husband. She would kill the bastard. Raising the dagger above her head, Jamelyn let the razor-sharp blade fall swiftly toward its target, only to find her arm freeze inches away from his smooth, tanned back. She could not kill Justin St. Claire. If it had been only her life at stake, Jamelyn would have happily plunged the keen point between his ribs. However, she had Shawn McDougal to consider. Her friend was still locked away in the dungeon, and if she took the life of the Lord of Raven's Keep, then Shawn's would also be forfeit.

Knowing she could not kill Justin, Jamelyn's mind quickly searched for a means to flee the threat the unconscious man presented. If she remained, he would only try to finish what his drunken body had refused to do tonight.

The dagger fell from her nerveless fingers, clattering loudly against the rough floor as Jamelyn looked at the naked, sinewy body lying upon her bed. Jamelyn took in the wide shoulders, her gaze traveling down the small dip of his spine that ran the length of his muscular back to his well-rounded buttocks and then to the hard thighs that had pressed her so easily into the mattress. She knew she would not again be as fortunate as she had been tonight. She had been raised by men and knew what transpired between men and women. She had often listened to her uncle's soldiers as they bragged about bedding a virgin and seeing the proof of their deed upon the linens the next morning. She had learned men prized that red sign of virtue above all else. Jamelyn had been revolted by their stories and knew she would never enjoy being hurt in that manner. A chill crept up her spine, and she shuddered at how close she had come to that very thing.

Exasperated, Jamelyn ran her hand through her tousled curls. She had to find a way to solve her dilemma. Her eyes scanned the chamber once more but to no avail. The door was locked, the window too narrow. There was no means of escape and no way to avoid what had been decreed. Suddenly, Jamelyn paused as an idea that might save her bloomed into existence in her clever mind. A mischievous twinkle brightened her emerald eyes and a cunning smile played over her lips as she retrieved the dagger. She ran one slender finger along its sharp edge as the thought took root.

Laying the dagger beside Justin, Jamelyn strained to push him to one side. Taking up the weapon, she pressed her finger against the needle-like point and bit her lower lip from the stinging prick. Jamelyn was relieved to see several large drops of blood form on the tip of her finger.

Without further thought, Jamelyn smeared the bright blood on the muslin sheet. A small, triumphant laugh bubbled in her throat at her own ingenuity. The English bastard would think he had succeeded when he awoke.

Taking the blanket from the bed, Jamelyn wrapped it about her as she settled herself in the chair by the fire. She yawned and stretched her arms over her head contentedly. The English knight thought he had conquered her. He would soon learn that it took more than physical power to subdue Lord Cregan's heir. Curling her feet beneath her, Jamelyn lay her head on her arms and drifted off into a satisfied slumber.

Chapter 4

Jamelyn's thick, black lashes fluttered open with a start as Justin's moan awoke her from her light slumber. Her muscles ached from her cramped sleeping position. She stretched slowly with feline grace as she pulled the blanket closer about her to stem the morning chill that invaded the chamber. Warily she peered over the edge of the wool blanket at Justin as he raised himself on one elbow, squinting his bloodshot eyes against the bright sunlight that filtered through the narrow window.

Another moan escaped Justin's lips, and he covered his eyes with his hand to shield them against the agonizing light. With his thumb and middle finger, he massaged his aching temples before gaining courage to uncover his eyes once more. As if in slow motion, his hand dropped to his bare middle and he blinked several times in Jamelyn's direction. His brow furrowed with the effort, and he shook his head to clear it of the haze that remained from the effects of the wine. The motion gave him an unbearable headache; he fell back upon the pillows and covered his eyes again with his arm. In a dry, hoarse voice he ordered, "Wench, bring me water."

Only silence greeted his command as Jamelyn made no move to obey. Rolling onto his stomach, Justin glared across the chamber at the small, quiet figure of his wife. "Damn you, have you no sympathy for a dying man?"

Justin's pale features reflected the agony he was suffering, and Jamelyn's lips trembled slightly before spreading into a smile of delight. She was enjoying the Englishman's discomfort, to Justin's extreme annoyance.

Seeing he would receive no help from the girl, his scowl deepened and tiny lines fanned his red-rimmed eyes. He bellowed, "Gibbon! Bring me water to wash the foul taste from my mouth." The sound of his own voice made Justin's head feel as if an army was marching across his brain and he clenched his teeth tightly as he glowered at Jamelyn.

Hearing his master's angry command, Gibbon unlocked the door and hurried into the chamber. He had been waiting in the corridor near Jamelyn's room for Justin's summons. Seeing his master's figure upon the bed, Gibbon glanced uneasily at Jamelyn. He noted the pleased expression on her young face and could not help but wonder what had transpired between Lord St. Claire and his wife. Intrigued, Gibbon's gaze traveled back to his master, and he was surprised to see the angry glare Justin cast in his wife's direction. Suddenly becoming aware of the tension in the room, Gibbon realized with a start that Lady St. Claire's smile was derived from Lord St. Claire's misery. Gibbon hurried to do his master's bidding. He did not want Justin's anger directed at him as well.

Justin took the tankard of water offered by his squire and drained the contents. Feeling somewhat better, he sat up, swinging his long, muscular legs over the side of the bed, and ordered Gibbon from the room. Without argument, the squire obeyed.

Hanging his head, Justin ran his tapering fingers through his tousled, iridescent curls. His wide shoulders slumped as the rumble of his stomach echoed in the room. Suddenly he straightened, a green shadow seeming to cross over his features as he rushed to the chamber pot. His stomach ridded itself of the water, jerking spasmodically when nothing more would come. Cold beads of sweat formed on Justin's pale brow, and he wiped them away as he weakly crossed back to the bed and fell across it.

Jamelyn bit her lower lip to keep from laughing with glee at his plight. Tiny dimples deepened her smooth cheeks at the corners of her mouth as she watched the steady rise and fall of Justin's tanned, muscular back. She knew from the deep breaths he took that he was still fighting to conquer the nausea that unsettled his insides. Her eyes sparkled with scorn as she thought, It serves you right, English dog; you deserve much worse. Curling her feet comfortably beneath her, Jamelyn relaxed back into the chair.

Slowly, Justin's queasy stomach settled, but his head still pounded as if a mallet drummed against his temples in unison with his heart. Propping himself up on one elbow, he looked at his silent companion. The foggy haze left by the effects of the wine was slowly abating and his mind turned to the events of the previous night. He could remember nearly all that had transpired between him and the young vixen. Only one void remained. Justin could not be certain if he had fulfilled his mission. One raven brow arched over his bloodshot eyes as he gazed quizzically at Jamelyn. Wetting his dry lips with the tip of his tongue, Justin said, "I presume you are now truly Lady St. Claire on this morn."

Jamelyn's voice dripped with venom as she responded, "Aye."

Not satisfied by either her quick answer or his memory, Justin said, "Then you will not mind if I confirm it this morning. I'm afraid I cannot remember all that transpired last eve."

The auburn curls bounced in a riotous disarray about Jamelyn's small head as she shook it violently from side to side. "Nay, you'll not have me again."

His mood, already grey from his hangover, turned black as he looked into Jamelyn's stubborn little face. In his present state of mind Justin was not inclined to be tolerant of

Jamelyn's obstinate nature and he growled, "Come here, wench. I have no proof our marriage was consummated."

Contemptuously, Jamelyn regarded Justin, her eyes flashing like hard emeralds. "Your proof is beneath you, as was I when you took my virginity by your drunken thrusts."

Tiny lines knit Justin's brow over his slender nose as he frowned. He remembered the feel of the girl and the sweet smell of her hair as he positioned himself to take her, but he failed to recall what had transpired beyond that. Bewildered by his lack of memory, Justin raised himself into a sitting position and looked for confirmation of Jamelyn's words. It was there on the sheet where he had lain, the dark stain that verified his wife's words.

A sense of relief swept through Justin's sinewy frame. He had accomplished his mission and was glad for his lapse in memory. He had no desire to recollect something he had found so distasteful. Sliding his long, brawny legs from the bed, Justin stood naked before Jamelyn and gave her an elegant bow. "Then I shall bid you adieu, Lady St. Claire." Retrieving his scattered clothing, he slipped it on and, without another word, strode from the chamber.

The sound of Jamelyn's soft laughter wafted through the still room as the door closed behind her husband's lean form. Her eyes sparkled with mirth as she rose from the chair and strolled across the chamber to the narrow window. Taking a deep breath of the fresh morning air, Jamelyn raised her chin triumphantly. "I have won this battle, my lord, and will win again," she said aloud.

Knowing well his master's requirements, Gibbon had a hot bath awaiting Justin when he returned to his chamber. A satisfied grin lifted the corners of Justin's full lips, as he eased his aching body into the steaming water. Lathering the bar of soap, he rubbed it through the silky dark mat on his chest as he lay back and savored his accomplishment.

Justin had fared far better than he had thought upon awaking. He might still suffer the headache of the damned, but the wine had served the purpose he had desired. His marriage had been consummated and he would not have to bed the skinny wench again. Oddly, Justin's thoughts turned to the moment when his body had responded to Jamelyn, and he experienced a moment of unexpected regret. Pushing such an unwanted feeling firmly from his mind, he laid his throbbing head back against the rim of the wooden tub and surmised it was the wine that had made him react in such a way. Closing the thick, curling lashes over his eyes, Justin forced his mind to the things he needed to do that day.

His thoughts wandered over several items on the agenda; the first thing he intended to do was to have the keep staffed properly with servants, the second, to see Jamelyn clothed as befitted her station as his wife.

After reading the king's command the day before, Justin had thought his luck had turned sour. His mood had been so black, he could not see that any good would come out of the situation. Now, as the warm water relaxed him, Justin realized all was not lost. He would gain high favor with his king, and perhaps in the future, Edward would grant him the right to petition the pope in Avignon for a separation.

The thought heartened Justin as he lathered his raven hair and ducked his head beneath the water to rinse the blue-black strands free of soap. Standing, his lean body shimmering in the morning light, Justin felt more like himself. He stepped from the tub, dripping water on the wooden floor. Rubbing his muscular body vigorously with the soft linen towel, he was imbued with the feeling that he had his life under control once more.

Justin dressed without Gibbon's assistance. The soft velvet surcoat emphasized the wide breadth of his shoulders while the dark wool chausses complimented his shapely legs. Clasping his wide sword belt about his lean waist, Justin walked jauntily from the chamber. His spirits high, he wondered only briefly at the reason for his sense of well-being. His beautifully molded lips curled wryly as he surmised that he'd just needed to bed a woman to relieve some of the tension of the past weeks. Justin's finely sculpted features broke into a satisfied smile as he descended the stone steps to the great hall, whistling a happy tune beneath his breath.

Anthony studied his friend with keen interest as he entered the hall and could see no sign of effects from the previous night's drinking bout. His blond brows arched in surprise at Justin's good humor as the knight jested with several of his men before joining Anthony at the long table. He greeted Anthony congenially as he settled his large frame in the lord's chair at the head of the table. Anthony returned Justin's smile and watched as he heaped his plate with roast venison and brown bread. Curiosity bloomed within Anthony at Justin's mood as he watched him devour his breakfast without so much as a word to what had transpired the night before. After filling their tankards from the pewter pitcher of ale, Anthony raised his to his silent friend and chuckled, "To the newlyweds."

To his surprise, Justin's lips curled into a wide, satisfied grin as he raised his tankard and clicked it against Anthony's in a toast.

Knowing his friend well, Justin could easily sense Anthony's burning curiosity. A twinkle of devilment sparkled in the depths of Justin's eyes as he prolonged his friend's misery while he casually finished his meal. Draining his tankard, Justin leaned back in his chair and looked at Sir Godfrey's expectant face. "We've much to do today. I want you to ride to the hamlet and retain enough servants to see that Raven's Keep is well staffed. From what I can surmise, Lord Cregan cared little for the comforts of life with the exception of the food that was served. This place doesn't look as if it has been cleaned in several generations."

Trying to sound uninterested, Anthony perused Justin's fine features and shrugged. "Then I take it the honeymoon is over?"

Justin's lips twitched as he suppressed a grin and his brow furrowed. "Honeymoon? If you are asking if I did my duty to the crown, Anthony, I would prefer that you just state what you mean."

Letting out a long, exasperated breath, Anthony gave way. "All right, Justin. Did you bed the girl?"

Rubbing his hand over his chin and mouth to hide the smile Anthony's curious expression brought forth, Justin nodded casually as if nothing unusual had occurred. Pushing his plate away, he slid back his chair. "I am a loyal subject of His Majesty. I do what I am ordered and I would suggest you do the same and not worry about my sleeping habits."

Justin watched as Anthony's gaze traveled in the direction of Jamelyn's chamber. He sensed his friend wanted to know how the girl fared, but Justin knew Anthony would not ask because he realized it was none of his concern to interfere in Justin's affairs.

Anthony stood and stepped over the wooden bench, picking up his tankard. He drained it and set it back down as he said, "I'll see to the servants."

As Anthony strode briskly from the great hall, Justin released the smile he had been holding back. Justin could read his friend like a book. Most considered Anthony Godfrey a womanizer, but Justin knew he was far from it. It was true he had many women, but it was his boyish charm that won the fair maidens' hearts. Anthony was loyal to his friends and possessed a kind and gentle heart beneath his suave exterior. To people who knew him less well than Justin, Anthony projected an attitude of a jester so that none would suspect his other qualities. And it was his tender heart that had aroused his curiosity about Jamelyn's welfare. Justin glanced in the direction of his wife's chambers and wondered briefly what it was about her that caused all of his men to act so foolishly. She was a stubborn little hellcat. To Justin's mind, Anthony's worry had been misplaced in this matter. Putting the thought of his wife and friend from his mind, Justin strode out into the bright sunlight of the autumn day.

Jamelyn stared unseeingly down at the food Jacob had brought her a short while earlier. It was now cold and untouched. She had little appetite as she sat wrapped in the woolen blanket. After the previous night she had nothing left to wear, and it was that problem that she now faced.

Grimly, her feathery lashes shadowing her green eyes, Jamelyn surveyed the crumpled heap of rags lying where they had been thrown. Justin had torn the last of her clothing

into shreds when he had bathed her and then had the audacity
to order her to dress as a woman. Little did he know that
Jamelyn knew nothing about the construction of such articles
of clothing. Even if she did know how to sew, she had
nothing with which to work. As far as she knew, there were
no materials suitable for what Justin wanted within the domain
of Raven's Keep.

She had been given an order by the Lord and Master of
Raven's Keep, but it baffled her to find a way to fulfill it.
Though she did not like the idea of obeying her husband's
command, Jamelyn knew she could not keep wearing the
blanket to cover her nakedness. Her lips twisted into a wry
grimace. Had Justin asked her to shoot an arrow at a target
several hundred feet away, Jamelyn would have known how
to go about it. She did not like the feelings that were aroused
by this problem.

Holding out one slender, delicately-boned hand, Jamelyn
looked at the calluses that marred the smooth surface of her
palm before turning it over to gaze at the short, broken
nails. Her hands could curry a horse, mend armor, and use
a broadsword, but they could not do women's work. Jamelyn's lips pursed as she laid her cheek against her balled
fist and propped her elbow on the arm of the chair. It was
the first time since being accepted by Lord Cregan and his
vassals that Jamelyn had felt inadequate, and it disgusted
her. After all the years of working to overcome her handicap
of being a woman, she was now found wanting in that same
area. It isn't right to be condemned to this shell that suits
me so ill, she mused crossly.

Jacob's entrance quelled Jamelyn's gloomy thoughts. He
nearly staggered from the weight of the cloth in his arms.
Stacked nearly to the top of his head were a variety of
materials from soft, pastel wools to bright, gleaming satins.
Breathing heavily, he dumped his burden on the foot of the
bed and turned to Jamelyn, a smile of pleasure playing over
his lined face. "Lord St. Claire thought you would need
these to make suitable clothing for yourself."

Securing the blanket more tightly about her, Jamelyn
crossed the chamber on silent, bare feet. Tentatively, she

let her hand play across the exquisite fabrics, an awed expression flickering briefly over her face as she asked, "Where did you find this?"

Well-pleased by the look on Jamelyn's face, Jacob said, "In one of the chests in Lord Cregan's chamber, my lady. Do they suit you?"

Jamelyn sighed as she felt the rich material beneath her hand. As if speaking to herself, she said, "I did not know my uncle possessed such riches."

Puzzled, Jacob's bushy brows knit over his large, sun-reddened nose. "The chest was marked with a different crest, my lady. I assumed it might belong to you."

She drew her gaze away from the fabrics and one delicately arched brow rose as she asked, "Was it a lion and a raven?"

Jacob grinned and nodded.

The knowledge that her possessions had been kept from her further confused Jamelyn. Had she the time to consider it, Jamelyn would have known the reason behind her uncle's actions. He had kept all reminders of Jamelyn's past from her because she had become the son he never had. He wanted nothing to remind her of her femininity because he feared he would lose her to the woman that she was. By hiding the materials away, he put temptation out of her reach.

Jamelyn's hand strayed back to the fabric, her mind no longer on the mystery of her uncle's action. The feel of the soft material brought back images of the first eight years of her life. Her thoughts surprised her. It had been so long since she had remembered the happy days before the plague had taken her family. Her melancholy tone mirrored the ache in her heart as she murmured, "I did not know."

Seeing the sad, distant look in Jamelyn's eyes, Jacob said, hoping to cheer her, "There be jewels also, my lady."

Jamelyn did not reply as her fingers absently stroked the soft nap of a burgundy velvet. Sensing Jamelyn's somber mood, Jacob let the subject drop. "Will you need anything else, my lady?"

Drawing her mind forcibly away from recollections of the past, Jamelyn shook her head and let the velvet slip from her fingers. "Nay" was all she said before turning her back on the treasures Jacob had brought and returning to the chair by the fire.

Scratching his head at the girl's strange behavior, Jacob quietly left the chamber. He had learned quite a bit about the young Lady St. Claire during her illness, but for all that she still remained a mystery to the Englishman. The material would have thrilled most young ladies into squeals of delight, Jacob mused as he went to search out Lord St. Claire.

Finding his master in the newly-built stables, Jacob said, "My lord, I have taken the fabrics to your wife as you instructed."

Justin had been inspecting his bridle and saddle to make sure all repairs had been made after the battle and the long days he had just spent in the saddle riding over the fief. Without taking his gaze from the strap in his hand, Justin answered absently, "Good. Maybe now she will dress as befits a lady." Seeing no frayed edges in the leather, Justin placed the bridle on a wooden peg and glanced at his vassal. "I cannot imagine any woman choosing men's clothing over the fine fabrics in the chest. She must possess more than one mad streak."

Jacob fingered the stubbly growth on his chin; he was growing his annual winter's beard. Remembering the look of awe on Jamelyn's face, he looked up at the younger man. "I do not believe she knew of their existence until a short while ago."

Justin's raven head cocked to one side as he regarded Jacob, disbelief written in his eyes. "You jest, Jacob. My lady was Lord Cregan's niece. Surely the man would not have kept her dressed in such a manner if she did not choose to do so."

Picking up a piece of straw, Jacob placed it between his teeth, twirling it around with his fingers as he said, "Aye, 'tis strange, but my lady seemed surprised when I told her they came from her own chests locked away in her uncle's chamber."

Justin strode to the stable door and folded his arms over his wide chest as he leaned against the thick wood. His gaze traveled up along the dark granite walls till it reached Jamelyn's window. Considering what he had just learned from Jacob, Justin mused, "True, the old lord was miserly in every way except where his men and arms were concerned. There he spared no expense. His record books proved that. But it would have cost him nothing to let his niece have the materials and jewels that already belonged to her. What were the man's reasons?"

Justin's puzzlement over old Lord Cregan's actions and miserly ways was interrupted as he watched Anthony ride through the gates. The blond knight reined his mount to a halt before Justin, crossing his arms over the pommel of the saddle. He looked down at his friend and a rueful smile touched his lips. "I'm afraid, my lord, it will not be a simple affair to get the villagers to come to work at the keep."

"Why so?" Justin asked as he unfolded his arms and patted Anthony's mount on its muscular neck. "They have not given us any problems before this."

Nimbly, Anthony dismounted, his spurs jingling as he hit the ground. "Aye, but after hearing of their chieftain's fate, they have closed their doors and barred them against us."

The peaceful expression faded from Justin's face. Lines etched his sensuous lips as he said, "Why should that make a difference? If anything, they should welcome us after the marriage."

Anthony looked past the gate toward the hamlet beyond. His lips curled slightly at the irony of the situation. "Aye, that is what I thought, but in this case it is not true. The serfs think you have killed my lady because they know she would never accept an Englishman to husband."

Justin's scowl deepened as he growled, "Damn, I should have known everything was going too smoothly. That is the reason for it; they feared for the girl's life. It seems that since I received Edward's message everything that could go wrong has done so." Justin's disgust at the situation was reflected in his every word. "We will have to prove to them that Jamelyn still lives. Have two horses saddled."

Justin's stride was brisk as he made his way into the

castle and up the stone stairway to Jamelyn's chamber. He pushed the door open without knocking, his steps never pausing until he stood before his wife. "Get dressed, wench," he ordered, and his face flushed with anger as she made no move to obey. "I said get dressed. Obey me or suffer for your stubbornness."

Pulling the blanket about her thin body, Jamelyn returned Justin's gaze without flinching and then calmly said, "I have nothing to wear. You ruined my only garments last night."

"Be damned," Justin swore, running his long fingers irritably through his raven curls. He puzzled over the problem that now faced him. "Have there never been any women in this keep?"

At the negative shake of Jamelyn's curly head, Justin's lips pursed with disgust momentarily before an idea blossomed in his mind. "I will get Gibbon to lend you a few of his garments until you make your own. It should not take you long to stitch up a few gowns to decently cover that skinny body."

Jamelyn's delicate lips firmed into a mutinous line, her eyes sparkling like newly-cut emeralds in her pale face. Intractable, she raised her small chin in the air. "I will not make the fripperies you desire, my lord. I have no liking for gowns and such."

Her obstinacy rankled, but Justin, determined to keep his temper under control, said, "Wench, you are now my wife and will dress accordingly. I will not have you attired as one of my men-at-arms. I have already stated the fact and have sent the materials for you to use. I intend to see that you do so, no matter what your objections may be." His tone was firm, indicating he would abide no refusals.

Perversely, Jamelyn folded her slender arms over her chest and insolently turned her face away as she haughtily said, "Nay, I'll not lift a hand to obey you."

Jamelyn's defiance ignited Justin's already simmering temper into angry flames. With one swift movement, he placed his imprisoning fingers about Jamelyn's set little chin and jerked her to face him. Placing both hands on either side of her on the chair arms, he leaned forward until Jamelyn could feel his hot breath upon her face. Her dark-fringed eyes widened as she looked up into his flashing gaze. Justin's voice was low and deadly as he said, "You are now my wife and you will obey. One way or the other. Have you forgotten your Scot still incarcerated in the dungeon?"

During the past minutes all of Jamelyn's thoughts had been centered on defying the fiendish devil who was her husband. In the heat of battle she had forgotten Shawn as she pitted her will against Justin's. Guilt curled in the bottom of her stomach at the thought of Shawn, her friend and mentor, locked away in the dark, damp prison so deep in the bowels of the castle. Her eyes filled with seething rancor as Jamelyn thought, That is the reason you still live, bastard dog. Had Shawn's safety not rested within my hand, you would be dead and in hell by now.

Jamelyn's heart beat rapidly against her breastbone as she looked directly into Justin's eyes. In their blue depths she could see reflected her own image and her subjugation. Shawn was the pawn in this game of life, and Justin used him skillfully to make Jamelyn obey his commands. Jamelyn's hands curled into tight balls in her lap. She fought to keep them from reaching out and taking Justin's dirk from its sheath and slitting his throat. It would be so easy to spill his blood, and she would not regret one small drop that spread across the floor as his evil life drained from him. Trying desperately to maintain control, Jamelyn clenched her teeth and spat, "Nay, I have not forgotten anything, nor will I ever." She trembled violently from unleashed anger.

Justin towered over Jamelyn, satisfied for the moment that he had vanquished the vixen and that she would obey. "Then I will see to your clothing. We will ride to the village when you are dressed." Without waiting for her reply, Justin strode from the room in search of his squire.

Jamelyn's eyes narrowed suspiciously and her pale lips tugged downward as she propped her chin on her balled fist and waited for Justin to return. A speculative gleam brightened her green eyes as she wondered what Justin was about. The English knight did nothing without a reason. What scheme lay brewing in his devious mind? Why did he want her to ride to the village with him?

For the moment it doesn't matter as long as I can get out of this prison for a little while, Jamelyn thought as she scanned the bedchamber. That Justin had something in mind that would be to his advantage, Jamelyn knew well; but if it would free her from the confines of her room, it would be a welcome relief. Since the English had invaded the keep, Jamelyn had been restricted to her quarters. With each day she grew more restless, and it chafed against her already taut nerves. Like a wolf her uncle had once captured, Jamelyn wanted to snarl and bite at her imprisonment. She knew if she did not receive some measure of freedom soon, her end would be the same as that fierce beast's; he had died from his caged existence.

The silver spurs on Justin's smooth leather boots jingled loudly as he entered the room with a bundle of clothing under one muscular arm. Tossing it to Jamelyn, he ordered, "Now get dressed. I have little time to waste reassuring the peasants of your well-being."

Justin's words confirmed Jamelyn's suspicions about his motive for taking her with him to the village. Cocking her curly head to one side, a small, triumphant smile played about her lips. Copper strands gilded her auburn hair and it shimmered gold as she looked up at her husband. His words had also answered another question that had been puzzling Jamelyn. She had wondered at her people's calm acceptance of the English rule, and in her deepest moments of despair she had felt betrayed. Without voicing it, Justin had just told her the reason behind the serfs' lack of action. They had feared for her welfare. Jamelyn's heart swelled within her at this sign of their loyalty. However, when her villagers had heard of yesterday's events, it must have frightened them. They knew their chieftain well and with that came the knowledge that she would never willingly marry an Englishman.

It pleased Jamelyn to find the powerful knight was not so strong that he did not need her. To maintain the tranquillity of the past weeks, Justin St. Claire must prove that she still lived.

Noting his wife's gratified expression, Justin could feel the dark hair at the nape of his neck rise like a dog's bristles when sensing a fight with another mongrel. Her look of victory rankled more than any words she could have spoken. With his lips narrowing into a thin, hard line, Justin eyed Jamelyn. Her small, piquant face with its black-fringed, startling green eyes, did not mirror the shadows of defeat. Though he had conquered Raven's Keep and all it possessed, including its firebrand heiress, Justin saw only triumph reflected in her fascinating eyes.

In that moment Justin's hands ached to reach out and encircle the slender ivory column of her neck, breaking the indomitable spirit he saw in her provocative face. She stood before him with her head high and back straight, her little oval chin jutting out, daring him to do his worst. There was no fear in her demeanor, and Justin could not suppress the grudging respect the boyish girl aroused within him. Oddly, it cooled his flaming wrath so that there were only warm embers of anger resting beneath his calm exterior. Feeling as if he had suddenly lost something but could not quite put a name to it, Justin brusquely ordered, "Get dressed." Then he turned on his heel and left Jamelyn to wonder at the strange expression that had lingered for only a moment upon his handsome features.

Dropping the blanket in a heap on the floor, Jamelyn quickly dressed in Gibbon's clothing. As she had expected, they were too large for her, but with a few minor adjustments, Jamelyn was ready. With no further thought to her appearance, she hurried down the corridor, pausing at the top of the stairs and taking several deep breaths as she savored her freedom. The feeling was quickly swept away and replaced with annoyance as she saw her husband waiting below. Squaring her shoulders as if ready for combat, Jamelyn descended the stairs. "I am ready" was all she said as Justin took her arm to lead her through the great hall.

Jamelyn did not move, pointedly looking down at the bronze fingers encasing her upper arm and then glaring up at Justin as she jerked free of his hand. "I will not attempt to flee, my lord. I have given my word."

His lips twitched at the corners of his shapely mouth. "My lady, I was only trying to escort you from the hall as would any good husband."

Green light danced in her eyes. "I do not need nor want your husbandly concern, my lord. To me you are still the enemy and only the welfare of my people has kept me from putting your own dagger into your cold heart."

Bitterly, Justin smiled down at Jamelyn, his own gaze flickering with flames though his words were spoken in jest. "My lady, are all Scottish women so bloodthirsty?"

"Aye, if they have reason," Jamelyn replied tartly as she strode ahead of her husband into the bright, sun-filled court-yard of the keep.

Piqued by his wife's brusque manner, Justin remained a few paces behind Jamelyn. Her behavior did not surprise him; it blended well with the impression she tried to present to the world. From the top of her curly, auburn head to the bottom of her small feet, Jamelyn would not allow any of her feminine traits to be discernible.

Justin regarded her straight, slender back as she walked boldly toward the entrance. With her shoulders back and chin high, she looked as if she were going out to command a troop of guards. From the rear it would be hard for anyone to detect her true gender. The overly large tunic hid her feminine attributes well. Had Justin not known of her firm breasts and softly flaring hips, he would have thought he was gazing at a young man. Her mannerisms were more suited to his squire and that was what vexed Justin. He had always been a man who loved the soft, gentle ways of ladies; it was his ill luck to be saddled with a Scottish wench who possessed none of those qualities.

Stepping from the dim interior of the castle, Justin found Jamelyn was already sitting astride a huge roan stallion that pawed the earth and snorted as if eager for a brisk canter. She controlled the large beast with the ease of one well acquainted with equestrian skills. For a moment Justin stood fixed and stared at his young wife. A look of pure delight played over her delicately-boned features, her emerald eyes sparkling with pleasure at once more being on Red Devil's back. In that short span of seconds when she thought no one was observing her, Jamelyn's lips spread into an enchanting smile. The sight made Justin realize the girl was not quite the ugly duckling he had thought.

Dragging his eyes from the sight of his wife, Justin glanced at Anthony Godfrey, standing to one side, a bemused expression on his face as he held the reins of a small, dapple-grey mare. Seeing Justin's gaze upon him, he shrugged. "The stallion belongs to my lady," said Anthony. "She would not have the mount I chose. It is too tame."

Justin nodded that he well understood Anthony's plight. The choice of Jamelyn's mount did not surprise him. There was nothing normal about the young girl he had married. Without any comment, he mounted his own black stallion and led a small squad of soldiers and his wife to the thatch-roofed hamlet a short distance from the keep.

One main thoroughfare passed through the village. Cottages lined the sides of the muddy lane. As they approached Justin noted the stillness. No one could be seen about: no children played within the tiny yards adjoining each cottage, and the doors and windows were closed and shuttered to all who entered the hamlet.

Justin reined his black steed to a halt in the center of the village, his eyes cold, his expression unreadable as he leaned forward, crossing his muscular arms over the pommel of his saddle. The tone of his voice let the villagers know he would abide no more foolishness as he said, "People of Raven's Keep, I have brought my lady to choose several of you to work in the castle."

Shutters squeaked here and there as they slowly opened and the inhabitants who hid behind them warily peered out from the dark interiors. Upon seeing Jamelyn sitting astride her great roan, the serfs gradually unbarred their doors and quietly, with heads bowed respectfully and eyes downcast, came forward.

All was silent as Justin watched the serfs form a small, protective group before the Englishmen. Covertly, they cast guarded looks at the Cregan heiress, their blank faces mirroring none of the confusion her presence in the company of the English soldiers aroused. Justin regarded the bedraggled group thoughtfully and then reached across the small space that separated him from Jamelyn. Taking her hand, he raised it between them as he said, "As of yesterday, Jamelyn of Cregan became my wife."

As if a heavy downpour had washed the blank expressions from the serfs' faces, they stared sullenly up at Lord St. Claire and his lady. An oppressive stillness seemed to hover over the assembly as if the villagers held their breaths waiting for Jamelyn's denial of the English knight's words.

Jamelyn felt Justin's grasp tighten about her hand as he watched the silent group before them. Some faces bore only resentment; others were openly hostile. Fear for her people contracted Jamelyn's heart within her breast as she looked down into the work-worn faces of Raven's Keep's serfs. The words rose in her throat to shout out the circumstances of her marriage to the Englishman but she bit the inside of her lip to hold them back. By telling them the truth, she would only be causing them more suffering. Their loyalty would make it necessary to avenge her and that would provoke a revolt that could only end with the blood of her people seeping into the dark earth they had worked for generations. No good would come if they refused to recognize Justin as her husband and their lord.

Feeling the pressure of his long, bronzed fingers, Jamelyn gazed at the strong hand upon her own. That hand held the power to reap destruction upon the people who had given her their loyalty. Glancing into the set face of her husband, Jamelyn realized that he was once more placing the lives and safety of her people in her hands. Mutely aware of that fact, Jamelyn turned to look once more at the peasants who had given of their sweat and labor to see Raven's Keep prosper. Swallowing back the bile that rose in her throat, Jamelyn nodded as she said, "It is true. I am now Lady St. Claire and have need of your services."

An angry murmur rumbled through the group as one tall, redheaded man stepped forward. Angus McDougal was a distant cousin to Shawn and also sheriff of the hamlet. Pulling his large hat from his shaggy, cropped head, he bowed stiffly to Justin. "There be few here who know of such things, me lord and lady."

Justin released Jamelyn's hand as he leaned forward and studied the Scotsman. His keen gaze assessed the man skeptically. In a tone that brooked no argument, Justin said, "I have need of at least two healthy females to wait on my wife and serve in the kitchens."

Angus stepped back nervously, his eyes going once more to Jamelyn. His lined, weather-beaten features mirrored the distrust he felt toward her since the rumors of her marriage had been confirmed. He, like the rest of the villagers, felt betrayed. By her own admission, she had bedded the enemy willingly and that alone had shaken their faith in the Cregan heiress. A muscle twitched in Angus's ruddy cheek as he tried to conceal the bitterness that her actions aroused within him. The asperity in his voice could not be hidden, however, as he said, "Young Nora and Maille McPherson are the only serfs of age in the hamlet."

Justin glanced at his pale-faced wife. "What say you?"

Longing to get away from the eyes that condemned her, Jamelyn nodded her consent. At that moment she would have agreed to accept the devil himself, to be away from the place. Her throat constricted with painful emotion and her heart lay like lead within her chest. But her stubborn Scottish pride held her in good stead as she determined not to give way and let them see how their condemnation affected her. She raised her small chin in the air and balled her fist against the contempt on their worn faces.

The people of Raven's Keep had judged her and found her guilty of something over which she had no control. They did not realize her reasons for riding so meekly beside the English knight, nor did they know that her love for them had brought her to this fate. Stiffening her back, Jamelyn looked away from her people to the rolling hills beyond and thought, I have done my best for you, and in doing so, I have only succeeded in losing your loyalty and trust.

The hostile looks cast in his wife's direction angered

Justin. You ungrateful swine, he thought, she has fought bravely to defend all of Raven's Keep and now you condemn her for surviving. His cold gaze sought each resentful face until they sheepishly lowered their eyes to the muddy earth in submission.

"Hear me well, people of Raven's Keep," he commanded. "I am now lord of this fief and it is I whom you will serve as well as my wife. This is my last visit to appease you. From this day forward, when I send an order by my men, it will be obeyed or you will suffer the consequences. Have the girls sent to the keep immediately as well as several other women with strong backs, for it needs a good cleaning." With that, Justin kicked his horse in the side and urged him back toward the castle.

Jamelyn cast one last glance at the people she had loved and then did likewise. She rode silently back to the keep and dismounted before anyone could come to her assistance. Her slender shoulders drooped, feeling weighed down by the events in the village. Had anyone told her that her own people would treat her in such a manner, Jamelyn would have been the first to accuse them of lying.

Anxious to be away from the man who had caused all of her troubles, Jamelyn strode into the castle without a backward glance and fled up the stairs to her chamber. She needed time to herself to sort out her feelings and try to understand all that had happened.

Justin caught his wife as she reached the heavy, iron-hinged door. His fingers gently grasped her elbow to halt her flight and he turned her to face him. "Jamelyn, I would have you dine in the great hall this evening."

Justin's touch seemed to burn through the sleeve of her tunic, igniting her own angry resentment. Jerking free of his hand, she glared up at him. "So that you may gloat over your victory? Are you not satisfied with turning my own people against me? Have done with your torture and put me out of my misery."

Justin was confused by her sudden furious outburst, and his smooth brow puckered with a frown. "I have only tried to see to the welfare of Raven's Keep by staffing it with servants to serve you, my lady. As for your people, they will adjust in time."

"Nay, you know nothing of we Scots. My people hate the English as I do and now they have turned that hatred to me for bedding you." Swinging away, Jamelyn opened the door and slammed it shut behind her before Justin could say anything more.

"Whew!" Justin whistled under his breath as he rubbed the back of his neck and stared at the closed portal. He had not planned the turn of events that day in the village; however, Justin was not one to let even a small advantage slip through his long fingers. Thoughtfully, he turned his back on Jamelyn's door and walked down the dim corridor. He paused at the top of the stairs, a pleased expression flickering over his handsome features as he realized the full extent of all that had transpired. The peasants' loyalty to Jamelyn had been firm and unshakable until this afternoon. Today she had shattered their trust and now they would know who the Lord of Raven's Keep was and would obey his commands.

Sensing that only one item remained to make certain of his control and Jamelyn's defeat, Justin called his squire to attend him as he made his way down the stairs. Gibbon came hurrying forward, a light film of ale foam still on the fuzz he called his mustache.

"Bring McDougal from the dungeon. I would speak with him," Justin said as he settled his large frame in the chair at the head of the table.

A short while later Shawn stood before the master of Raven's Keep. He blinked rapidly against the light after his long incarceration in the dark bowels of the castle. Deep lines imbedded with grime from the dungeon formed about his green eyes as he squinted uncertainly at Justin, who rose from the chair and faced him.

"McDougal, I have had you brought forth for only one reason, and that is to determine your fate. The fief is now secure and I have time to deal with its one remaining problem—you."

The muscles across Shawn's firm belly contracted tightly as he drew in a deep breath. He would accept his death with

courage. Stalwartly, Shawn braced himself for the Englishman's next words.

"You may swear allegiance to me as Lord of Raven's
Keep and the cohort of the heir of Cregan or you may choose
to die. Your fate is your decision," Justin proclaimed.

Shawn's bushy, reddish-gold brows lowered over his green
eyes in confusion. Giving a slight shake of his shaggy red
head, Shawn tried to clear his hearing. He could not believe
he had heard the black knight correctly. Wetting his dry lips,
Shawn asked hoarsely, "Cohort to the Cregan heir?"

Watching the burly Scot's reaction with keen interest,
Justin nodded. "Aye, yesterday Jamelyn of Cregan was
married to me. She is now my wife and I would have your
decision, Scot."

Shawn's breath left him in such a rush it seemed as if
a large fist had hit him squarely in the middle of his stomach,
knocking the wind from him. Dumbfounded, he stared at
Justin, his mouth agape at the Englishman's disclosure. It
was too much to comprehend: his Jami married to the enemy.

Justin could see the conflicting emotions playing over
Shawn's flushed features and briefly wondered what type
of relationship existed between his mannish wife and the
Scotsman McDougal. Could he be more to her than just her
loyal vassal? Nay, Justin thought as he perused the older
man from head to toe, not even this rough Scotsman could
be attracted to such a skinny wench.

Justin's gaze came to rest once more on Shawn's ruddy
features. He could read the doubt in the man's eyes and it
irritated him. The thought of the Scotsman questioning his
word annoyed Justin to an unusual degree. With his lips
narrowing into a thin line and his eyes coldly calculating,
Justin said, "I care not whether you believe it or nay. I only
want to know if you will swear fealty to me as the Lord of
Raven's Keep or choose the gibbet."

Shawn's steady gaze never left Justin's determined face.
He did not like the only true choice left to him. If he chose
the gibbet, Jami would be left alone to face this enemy, and
he knew his young friend would need him even more now,
having been forced to marry Lord St. Claire. Shawn's lips

were set in a grim line as he slowly nodded his head and said, "I will swear fealty to you, my lord."

A slight, caustic smile touched Justin's lips. He had expected no other answer from the Scot. It seemed these people's loyalty was not as firm as his wife would have him believe. To save their lives they would swear their vows of loyalty to anyone. Justin did little to hide his contempt for the Scot. "Then tonight you will give me your pledge." Turning to Jacob, he ordered, "Take him and make him bathe. He stinks to high heaven, as do all the Scots I have met."

Justin settled his sinewy frame once more in the chair as the prisoner was led away. Stretching out his long, muscular legs in front of him, Justin braced his hands behind his head and relaxed. A triumphant smile lifted the corners of his beautifully molded lips as he watched the flames in the grate. Tonight would assure that all, including his firebrand of a wife, knew that he was Lord of Raven's Keep.

After today, Jamelyn St. Claire would realize she was no longer in command of the fief. Though her obstinate nature would make it hard for her to accept, she would also learn to obey her master.

Justin's thoughts turned to King Edward, and he wondered if his monarch had realized exactly what his marriage to Jamelyn would do. Nay, he thought, Edward hoped to keep the people peaceful through their loyalty to the Cregan heir. He never dreamed it would turn them against her.

The Scots were a thorny lot. They would not forgive Jamelyn easily for marrying the Englishman. To them her rule ceased to exist when the vows were spoken. A scornful smile crept across Justin's full, sensuous lips. The villagers would have praised her in song and legend had she died by refusing the match. Now, because she still breathed, they did not feel she deserved their loyalty.

It would take time for him to gain the loyalty the serfs had bestowed upon Jamelyn, but it would come. By governing fairly and seeing that all went well for them, Justin would earn what he sought. He knew the workings of the peasant mind. Much depended upon their bodily comforts.

If their stomachs were kept full and their bodies warm during the cold of winter, the people of Raven's Keep would accept him as their rightful lord.

Tonight would remove the last obstacle in his path. McDougal's oath of fealty would assure that all would be secure, and soon Justin would be able to return to London and the court of Edward III. With that thought came the image of Anne of Chester. He could feel his loins begin to respond to the vivid recollection. Ah, my beautiful and sensuous Anne, Justin mused, shifting uncomfortably in the chair to ease the swelling ache. It will not be long before I have you once more in my bed.

Jamelyn paced her chamber like a caged beast. With her slender arms folded over her chest and her delicately-shaped lips pressed grimly together, she experienced a wave of depression that her frustrated movements could not dispel.

Her mind was burdened with the knowledge that she had failed her people after vowing she would always see to their welfare. Knowing they believed the same did not help ease her troubled thoughts. It tore at her already battered pride, rendering its frazzled edges nearly irreparable. Had it not been for Shawn, Jamelyn knew she would have faced death rather than submit to Justin St. Claire and forfeit her people's trust and loyalty.

Shawn, Jamelyn thought as she halted her furious pacing in front of the narrow window. Her eyes swept over the granite walls to the bright splashes of color brought forth in the trees beyond by the coming of autumn. At least I still have your loyalty.

Laying her forehead against the cool stone, Jamelyn continued to look at the vivid red and gold of the oak and beech. Autumn was usually Jamelyn's favorite season, but this year it brought her little joy. Her mind was filled with too much turmoil to enjoy such a simple pleasure.

Her depression deepened as she reflected on the past weeks. She had held fast to the knowledge that she had not been totally defeated because she still possessed the love and loyalty of the inhabitants of Raven's Keep. Today had severed that slender bond. Shawn was now her last anchor against the bitter defeat that threatened to sweep away her courage. Her friend had always been there to give her support and to insure all went well since her arrival at Raven's Keep. Tenaciously, Jamelyn's mind clung to that strong image.

The squeak of the iron hinges that bound the oak door broke Jamelyn's reverie. She swung abruptly about, ready to do battle if the intruder was her husband. Instead, she was surprised to see the two auburn-haired girls, Nora and Maille. The two sisters gave her sheepish grins, their healthy cheeks flushing becomingly as they dropped an awkward curtsy.

Nora, the more vocal of the two, spoke. "My lady, we have come as instructed."

Disconcerted for a moment, Jamelyn stared at the two pretty girls. At last she said, "I can well see that, but why?"

The girls glanced uncertainly at each other, wondering at Jamelyn's strange behavior. The look on their young mistress's face when they first entered the room had sent shivers down their spines. Now her confusion about their presence further served to make them think something had happened to her mind. Blushing from Jamelyn's intense gaze, Nora said, "My lord told us to serve you."

Exasperated at her own lack of memory, Jamelyn ran her fingers through her short curls and released a long, disgusted sigh. She had been too absorbed in her problems to consider the main reason for their visit to the village.

Vexed at having someone to serve her, Jamelyn stared at the two girls, wondering what they were supposed to do. She was mystified at the idea of having to delegate duties to servants. During the past ten years, Jamelyn had cared for herself, neither expecting help nor wanting it from servants.

Jamelyn's quandary increased by the moment as she stood helplessly puzzling over her problem. A silent sigh of relief escaped her as Jacob entered the room, his arms loaded with more material. With as much bravado as she could summon, Jamelyn haughtily ordered, "Jacob, instruct Nora and Maille

in their duties, since it was Lord St. Claire's desire for them
to serve me."

Turning on her heel, Jamelyn gave them her back as she
crossed once more to the narrow window. She hoped her
actions gave the impression that she was irritated with her
husband's high-handed manner rather than her own lack of
knowledge about dealing with menials.

Her hope was realized. Jacob and the girls thought nothing of her actions except what Jamelyn had intended. They
would have been shocked to know that Jamelyn's stomach
tied itself in knots because of the uncertainty sweeping over
her, and that her air of assurance was only a facade to hide
behind for protection against the unknown.

Jamelyn squeezed her feathery lashes tightly together as
she listened to Jacob give Nora and Maille their instructions.
She knew she had to regain control of herself. It was not
like her to experience such feelings of inadequacy. She had
faced fierce warriors in battle and had never encountered
such doubts about herself. Suddenly sensing the root from
which her dilemma stemmed, Jamelyn's eyes flew wide with
surprise. She knew how to behave like a man but had learned
nothing of what women were supposed to do.

Never a coward, Jamelyn drew in several deep breaths
and tried to quell the anxiety that seemed to creep up from
the soles of her feet to travel over her entire body. She
bravely faced the problem head-on, but found that approach
did not serve her in this instance. Recognizing this, Jamelyn
clenched her teeth as she tried to suppress the urge to scream
out her ire at the devious tricks of nature. She knew she
would not be facing this new predicament had she been born
a man. Had her obstinate pride let her voice her feelings of
inadequacy, it would have served Jamelyn much better and
caused her less suffering.

Jacob had to repeat, "My lady," several times to draw
Jamelyn's attention, she was so absorbed in her thoughts.
Letting out a long breath, she turned to face the Englishman
as he continued, "If you would tell the girls which material
you prefer, they can begin with your gown."

Jamelyn eyed the pile of fabrics with open animosity, as

if she blamed the inanimate objects for finding herself lacking. "Let them choose. I care little about such nonsense," Jamelyn said as she once more hid behind an air of disdain. Her perverse pride would not let her speak of her inadequacies for fear they would be presumed a form of weakness.

Seeing the stubborn set of Jamelyn's jaw, Jacob knew he would receive little help from the mistress of Raven's Keep. Picking up a shimmering piece of satin, he handed it to the bashful Maille. "The green will do. See that my lady has a suitable gown by tomorrow." Glad to have the matter settled, Jacob quickly left the three young women to finish the task. The battle-toughened soldier felt distinctly uncomfortable in his new role as chatelaine. It suited him ill to see to Lady St. Claire's servants and the ordering of her wardrobe.

Nora and Maille quickly set about laying out the shimmering piece of satin and gathering the necessary sewing accessories. When that was finished, Nora approached Jamelyn, a long piece of twine in her hand to take the measurements needed before they could begin the construction of her gown. The expression on the young servant's face reflected the uncertainty she felt about disturbing the quiet figure by the window. She glanced at Maille for reassurance and saw her sister give a slight, nearly indistinguishable nod. Taking a deep breath, she said, "My lady, we will have to know your size before we can cut the gown."

Jamelyn's irascible mood was further irritated by the girls' constant use of the term "my lady." Turning on Nora, she spat, "Damn me, Nora. I am your friend, if you have forgotten. I am Jami, not my lady."

Nora lowered her eyes nervously to her work-roughened hands, her fingers fidgeting with the twine as she bit her bottom lip and shook her head. "Nay, ye are now my lady."

A stricken look crossed Nora's face as she glanced in her sister's direction and then proceeded with the work at hand. She sensed the pain she had given Jamelyn with her words but could do little to help it. Her father had given both girls strict instructions before they left their small, thatch-covered cottage. He could not refuse Lord St. Claire their services in the castle, but they were to have nothing to do with the traitorous Lady of the Keep. The friendship the three had shared over the years must be forgotten; the one they called friend no longer existed, except as the Englishman's wife.

Subdued by their father's order, Nora and Maille worked silently at their chore. The only sound in the still room was the fabric as it gave way beneath the sharp edges of the scissors. The girls did not like what they had to do. It was not as easy for them to turn away from their lady as it had been for the other people of the village, because they had been close friends to Jamelyn. However, it was not within either of them to disobey their father's order.

Jamelyn noted the absence of chatter between the two girls. That in itself indicated much to her. In the past Nora and Maille had kept up a constant prattle. Their silence revealed their discomfort over this situation in which they found themselves pulled in two different directions. Jamelyn was not delighted with it any more than they were, but there was nothing any of them could do to change matters. They could not erase anything that had transpired since the English had come to lay claim to Raven's Keep.

Settling herself in a chair near the fireplace, Jamelyn stared moodily into the leaping flames as she reflected upon what had happened to her and her people. Things might have been different if Lord Cregan had not died at Halidon Hill or if she had had more men to fight the English, but that had not been the case. One could always look back and see the ifs in the past, but that did little good for the present. With the thought of her men, Jamelyn glanced at the two girls busily working on the emerald satin. Having had no contact with anyone from the outside during the past weeks, Jamelyn had not heard any news concerning her men. Several of them had family in the village and if anyone knew anything about them it would be Nora and Maille, for the two girls had a nose for gossip and heard nearly everything that went on in the hamlet.

"Nora," Jamelyn said, and watched the girl's hand pause

in her cutting. "Have you heard how my men are? Have any of the villagers received any messages?"

Nora glanced at her sister and swallowed nervously. She knew Jamelyn was anxious about her soldiers' welfare but was afraid to answer because of her father's orders. Seeing Maille's nod, Nora turned to Jamelyn. "Aye, they are safe, my lady."

Relieved, Jamelyn settled back in her chair. The girls' hesitancy to speak of things concerning her people quickly reminded her of their feelings. She would press them no further for information.

To their credit, Nora and Maille worked swiftly. The gown was cut and they had begun to stitch it together when Justin's knock sounded on the door and he entered without waiting for his wife's permission.

Jamelyn watched with a certain wry amusement as the two girls seemed to shrink in their effort to go unnoticed by the tall, handsome knight. However, that was not to be as Justin strode across the room to observe the work in progress. He nodded his satisfaction before turning to Jamelyn. "We will dine in the main hall tonight, my lady."

Without arguing, Jamelyn rose from her chair by the fire, her small chin in the air as she faced her husband. "As you wish, my lord." Without further comment, she turned on her heel and left Justin staring at her small, slender back, amazed by her easy acceptance of his order. Jamelyn had reached the top of the stairs before Justin collected himself and caught up with her. Taking her arm, he was again surprised to find no resistance, and he escorted Jamelyn down to the great hall.

Upon their entrance into the vaulted chamber, Anthony left the group of Justin's vassals and came to greet them. He gave Jamelyn a warm smile as he bowed elegantly. "My lady, it is a pleasure to have your company this evening."

Her emerald eyes swept haughtily over the handsome blond knight, but Jamelyn did not condescend to speak. She walked past and seated herself upon the long wooden bench at the rough-hewn table without comment.

Justin could not suppress the smile Anthony's bewildered

expression aroused. His friend was not used to women resisting his good looks and charming ways. Slapping Anthony sympathetically on the shoulder, Justin strode past and took his seat at the head of the table in the intricately carved chair reserved only for the lord of the manor. With a slight nod of his head, he indicated that his vassals should be seated. They filled the benches on each side of the long table as the cooks served their supper.

Jamelyn ate her meal of stew and haggis in silence. She listened to the lively banter that surrounded her but caught only parts of each conversation. Her attention was drawn to Justin and Anthony as they discussed their plans for the following day's hunt. Though her husband and his friend spoke with animation, she sensed an underlying tension in the hall. She noted as the meal neared its end that Justin's vassals began to grow more subdued, and she wondered at it.

Once replete, Jamelyn let her gaze wander about the hall that had been her heritage. Nothing had changed visibly, but to her all was different. It was no longer the safe haven where she had spent so many happy evenings listening to her uncle's vassals as they told her stories of their bravery and daring in battles of the past.

The great hall seemed to already possess the characteristics of its new lord. Fresh rushes covered the floor, their scent wafting through the air. No growls or snarls were heard when a morsel fell from the table, as the hounds had been exiled to the kennels, where their fights would not disturb Justin's meals.

So absorbed in her thoughts of the events that had taken place within the great hall in the past, Jamelyn failed to note the silence that fell over the assembly. Her attention was drawn back to the present by the sound of Justin's chair scraping the floor.

Jamelyn watched as Justin rose from his chair, towering over all those present. She glanced at Anthony as if he might explain the heavy tension that had come into the chamber with Justin's action. Seeing the direction of the blond knight's gaze, Jamelyn's own followed it to the entrance. Her eyes widened at the sight that met them. Shawn McDougal, cleanshaven and dressed in fresh clothing marked with her husband's colors, stood before them. Her smooth brow creased with worry as an uneasy feeling swept over her. Seeking some answer to the multitude of questions that flew into her mind, Jamelyn looked at Justin.

Noting her confusion, Justin said, "Bring the man here."

Jamelyn held her breath as Shawn crossed the room to stand before Justin St. Claire. The Scotsman's gaze briefly touched her face before he knelt in front of Justin.

At his action Jamelyn's eyes widened in shock and she came to her feet, her hands still gripping the table's edge, her knuckles white as the meaning seeped into her brain. Hoarse words were torn from her paralyzed throat, inaudible to all except Justin as she said, "Nay, Shawn."

Justin glanced down at his wife's ashen features, her wide, emerald eyes the only color in her pale face. Her strangled denial confirmed Justin's suspicions that a special bond existed between the two, but he did not believe it was that of lovers. It was rather that of a leader and a devoted follower. From the first, he had suspected Shawn's affection and loyalty to the young woman as well as hers to him. By forcing Shawn to swear fealty to him, Justin would accomplish exactly what he had set out to do. For a moment pity stirred within his chest for the valiant young girl as she faced her final defeat at his hand. Choking this strange emotion in the bud, Justin looked at the Scotsman. "Shawn McDougal, I have brought you here to swear your allegiance to me as Lord of Raven's Keep. Do you so vow?"

Shawn lifted his newly-groomed head and looked squarely at the English knight. The expression in his eyes held a mixture of defeat and regret. Taking a deep, steadying breath, Shawn said, "Aye, me lord. As Lord of Raven's Keep ye are my liege and I vow my loyalty and sword arm to ye. I will protect all that ye possess with my life."

Jamelyn had turned away from the spectacle and was staring with unseeing eyes at the soot-blackened walls, so she did not see the fleeting look Shawn gave her as he spoke the last words. Her nails dug into the rough undersurface of the table as she realized this was to be her final defeat at the Englishman's hand. He had planned well and now had taken all. With that thought, Jamelyn's stubborn pride resurfaced, pushing aside the vanquished feelings Shawn's actions had aroused. With her small chin set at an obstinate angle and her eyes sparkling, she looked at her husband and thought, Nay, you do not have all, you English bastard. You do not have me.

Justin's voice echoed loudly through the silent chamber, his tone firm, verifying his command as he said, "Then rise, Shawn McDougal. I accept your homage. Serve me truly and you will be rewarded." Glancing briefly at the silent figure of his wife, Justin's gaze returned to the redheaded Scot, his meaning clear as he said, "Dishonor your vow and all you hold dear will be forfeit."

Understanding Justin's warning, Shawn bowed his head in submission. "As a vassal to the Lord of Raven's Keep, I will honor my vow." The Scot's shoulders sagged as he rose to his feet and without looking at Jamelyn's shocked face, left the hall as swiftly as his weak and trembling legs would carry him. Lord St. Claire had shrewdly thwarted his plans before he could put them into action. Shawn was now free of the dungeon, but he was not free to help Jami.

The Scot's large body trembled visibly as he stepped out into the cold night air. His whole being rejected what he had been subjected to and his stomach churned as a sense of impotent fury swept over him. He rushed across the bailey and leaned weakly against the stable wall as his stomach gave up the gall that choked him. He remained for a long while in the shadows, too ashamed of his helpless position to be seen by anyone. The very act he had hoped would be of help to Jamelyn had only succeeded in hurting her.

Jamelyn forced her features to reflect none of the turmoil that squeezed her insides like a vise. Regaining control over her turbulent emotions, she faced her husband calmly as if she had not been touched by the proceedings of a few moments before. Her tone was flat and emotionless as she said, "May I now return to my chamber?"

Justin regarded his wife thoughtfully for a short while and then nodded his consent. He watched Jamelyn walk from the chamber with head held high, reflecting none of the defeat she had received from Shawn's vow of fealty. He was not surprised by her actions. Jamelyn St. Claire rarely did as he anticipated.

Once out of sight, Jamelyn fled up the stairs to her chamber and slammed the door behind her. Leaning against the solid oak, she clenched her hands until her nails bit into the flesh of her palms. Her green eyes scanned the chamber and she was relieved to find that Nora and Maille had finished their chore and had gone. The room was silent, the only break in it being Jamelyn's heavy breathing. Her chest rose and fell rapidly and she tasted the sweetness of her own blood as she bit into her lower lip in her fury.

Jamelyn's eyes narrowed dangerously. They seemed to dance with flames as her rage grew against the English knight who thought he had bested her. He had the power to force her into marriage and to turn her loyal subjects against her, but that did not mean he had conquered Jamelyn, herself.

A derisive smile curled the corners of her shapely lips as she thought, I outwitted you about our marriage night, English dog, and I will outwit you again. Feel safe and secure in your triumph, for it will be short-lived. I promise you that, Justin St. Claire.

Still fuming, Jamelyn crossed to the bed and grabbed the green satin gown. Throwing it to the floor, she stamped upon the fine fabric, wishing with all her heart that she was treading upon the man who sat gloating over her total defeat.

Chapter 5

A sharp smack on her rounded bottom startled Jamelyn from her troubled sleep. It had been near dawn before she had closed her eyes to finally drift into a restless slumber. Her mood was black as she rubbed her stinging posterior and rose with a curse upon her lips to face her assailant. Her jeweled eyes narrowed and a dangerous gleam shimmered within their sparkling depths as she looked at her husband.

Justin stood with his arms folded casually over his wide chest and a smug smile tugging at the corners of his sensuously molded lips. He leaned at ease against the tall post at the foot of her bed and looked down at her as if his presence in her chamber was nothing out of the ordinary. "My lady, 'tis time to arise. The hour grows late, and if you plan to join us you had best hurry."

For the first time Jamelyn noticed Justin's clothing. He wore a deep brown leather tunic and chausses, a quiver of arrows slung over one brawny shoulder, and a long hunting knife sheathed at the wide belt around his waist. Tiny furrows creased her brow as a bewildered expression dimmed the angry glint in her eyes. "I am to join you on the hunt today?"

Justin's cheek twitched with humor at the perplexed look on his wife's face. "Aye, I thought you might prefer hunting the boar to staying here to see to your wardrobe."

Jamelyn eyed her husband suspiciously, wondering at the game he now played. His pleasant demeanor did nothing to ease her distrust. She had learned the hard way that she could put little faith in his show of good humor, for each time she had made that mistake in the past she had been dealt a stunning blow. However, this morning she was in no mood to discover what devious schemes ran about in Justin's handsome head. The thought of the hunt was too exciting for her to question his motives.

Sliding her long legs from the bed, Jamelyn quickly retrieved her boots and slipped them on. She had not bothered to undress the previous night before falling into bed to lie staring up at the dark ceiling. Pulling the red and black tartan from the chest at the foot of her bed, Jamelyn wrapped it about her thin shoulders and then ran her fingers through her short, tousled curls. Turning to Justin, she said, "I am ready."

A bemused smile curved Justin's lips at his wife's lack of concern about her appearance. That was one thing he did not think he would ever grow accustomed to. She seemed oblivious to the fact that women did more than run their fingers through their hair to attend to their toilets.

While Jamelyn buckled the wide belt about her waist, Justin surreptitiously studied her slender form. It came to his mind again that Jamelyn would not be unpleasant to look upon if she gained a little weight to take away the sharp edges, and took a few pains with her toilet. Her bone structure was good, her features delicately sculpted, but Justin's gaze was drawn to her vivid green eyes, which contrasted boldly with the thick, feathery lashes that fringed them.

Justin also took note of the riotous auburn curls that now framed her small face so charmingly. The silken strands shimmered with copper highlights as the morning sun streamed through the window, gently caressing them. How would she look attired as a lady? Justin wondered.

With that thought in mind, his gaze fell upon the crumpled fabric at his feet. He bent and picked it up. As he straightened, his gaze met Jamelyn's, a defiant gleam coming into her eyes.

Laying the partially finished gown upon the bed, Justin said, "Then let us go."

Justin did not comment upon Jamelyn's treatment of the gown. He knew from the stubborn look on his wife's young face that an argument was sure to ensue if he did. Today Justin did not want to have any dispute with Jamelyn. He planned to try to ease the hostility between them. If he ever hoped to return to England, all had to be secure within the fief—including his recalcitrant, unorthodox wife.

The hounds raced ahead of the hunting party, sniffing the crisp morning air for the scent of the quarry. Justin, Jamelyn, and Anthony rode in the lead until the dogs picked up the trail and bayed. The dogs were soon out of sight, and all the hunters kicked their mounts in the side, urging them forward in their rush to keep up with the hounds.

The hunters charged into the dense forest in hot pursuit. Jamelyn lagged behind until they disappeared from view. She reined her mount to a halt and listened to the hounds. They were following a path that she had found only a short while before the English came. The boar had dropped its spoor, marking its domain. Jamelyn knew the animal would take this trail in trying to elude the hounds. Determined to be the one to take the boar, Jamelyn urged her horse in the opposite direction. She would await the fierce beast instead of tiring her mount in the chase.

Without a backward glance, Jamelyn rode swiftly, lying low over the steed's neck to avoid the low-hanging limbs. She could hear the hounds and knew by the sound that they had already changed direction and were traveling toward her. There was little time to reach the small clearing where the boar would break free from the dense undergrowth and take a stand against the pack.

Jamelyn knew that if she was fortunate, she would have time to reach the clearing before the animal and have her lance ready as the beast came charging in. Kicking Red Devil to a faster pace, Jamelyn pushed a low branch from her path without thought and then let it go as she passed. A great "Oof!" reached her ears as the limb swished through the air, and she looked around to see Justin flying backward over his saddle from the force of the blow to his middle.

Justin landed with a great thud upon the hard, leaf-strewn earth. The impact knocked the breath from him and left his senses dazed. A smile of pure delight curved Jamelyn's delicate lips at the sight of the English knight lying flat on his back on the ground. Reining Red Devil to a halt, she nonchalantly perused her husband's still form as she crossed her arms over the pommel of her saddle. Jamelyn knew from the deep breaths he took in his effort to clear his rattled senses that he had not broken his neck as she would have hoped.

The sound of the baying hounds nearby drew Jamelyn's attention away from Justin. She knew the boar would soon come charging down the well-worn path. Her eyes scanned the forest for help to see to the Lord of Raven's Keep; there was none. Jamelyn realized the rest of the party was behind the approaching hounds. It was up to her to either help her husband or let the boar have him.

Jamelyn's inborn sense of justice overrode her hatred for the English. The man lying before her was her enemy. Had she faced him in battle she would not have blinked an eye at his death, but she could not let the wild animal rip him to pieces with its large tusks. With that thought in mind, Jamelyn slid from the saddle and grabbed the barbed metal lance from its holder. She had no time to try to help Justin from the ground to safety. His life depended upon her having enough strength to slay the boar that was now tearing through the dense underbrush.

Jamelyn had only enough time to brace her lance against the ground before the beast came charging forward. It leaped toward her in its wild frenzy. Jamelyn felt the spear sink into the beast's chest as the force of its charge knocked her backward. The boar squealed with pain and rage as it thrashed about, trying to regain its feet to charge at her once more. Hot blood spattered Jamelyn's tunic and chausses as she grabbed the end of the lance and tried to force it further into the beast. She had missed its heart, only wounding it, and her strength was not enough to hold the huge animal down. The lance broke in her hands as she grappled with the strong animal and she was thrown against the bole of a large oak. The force of the blow knocked the wind from her lungs and she gasped for air. A pair of wild, beady eyes fixed upon her as the boar pawed the earth, readying to charge once more.

The ground was crimson with the boar's blood as Jamelyn withdrew from its sheath the sharp hunting knife Justin had given her before they departed the keep. It would be of little use against the huge animal, but it was the only weapon at hand. Standing transfixed, her heart beating rapidly within her breast, Jamelyn awaited her fate. She gazed into the mad, red eyes and knew she faced certain death.

The boar snorted and pawed, throwing dirt several yards behind it. The hounds grew closer. Hearing them, the animal let out a squeal of outrage and charged toward Jamelyn.

Justin had regained his senses as Jamelyn fought her desperate battle with the boar. Seeing her dilemma, he quickly retrieved his lance and ran forward, bracing it on the ground and placing his weight against it as the animal lunged forward. Justin's aim was true; his spear pierced the boar's heart. Its great body fell instantly to the bloody earth, trembling in the throes of death.

Breathing heavily, Justin turned to his wife to find she had not moved a muscle. She stared down at the carcass of the animal, then slowly replaced the knife within its sheath. No trace of fear etched her young, blood-spattered features. The only indication that she had been affected by the events of the past minutes was the slight tremble of her hand as she put her weapon away. Justin marveled at her calmness. His own heart hammered against his breastbone as he ran his long, tapering fingers through his raven hair and brushed away the leaves that clung to it. "Are you all right, Jamelyn?" he asked, watching her face intently.

Taking a deep breath, Jamelyn drew her eyes away from the dead boar and nodded. "Aye," she said, her voice steady.

In that moment, Justin's esteem began to grow for his young wife. She had shown courage that few men possessed in confronting a wild boar. He knew she had saved his life by her quick actions. Justin also realized that it would have been just as easy for her to ride away and leave him to be savaged by the beast. In his dazed state, he would not have survived. The boar would have torn him to shreds with its large, yellowed tusks. But Jamelyn had chosen to risk her own life in her effort to save him. Placing one hand on her shoulder, Justin looked down into her small face as he took her hand with his other and brought it to his lips. He kissed the grimy, blood-caked tips of her fingers as he gazed into the unfathomable green depths of her eyes. "You saved my life, my lady, and I thank you."

Jamelyn drew in a quick breath at the strange, tingling sensation that passed through her fingers to her hand and then ran like hot flames up her arm. Shocked by the odd feelings his touch aroused, Jamelyn jerked her hand free as she said, "We are even, my lord. You also saved mine."

Justin let his hand drop to his side as his men rode into the clearing, the hounds barking and snapping at the dead animal. Anthony's blue eyes bulged with surprise as he spied his friend and his lady standing amiably together. "Ho, Justin. You have made the kill," he said, as he reined in his mount and climbed from the saddle.

A wry grin curved Justin's lips as he said, "Nay, Anthony. Jamelyn was the first to spear the beast. She saved my life."

A look of stunned disbelief flickered across Anthony's handsome face and he arched one blond brow as he looked at his friend. Justin's pride was apparent in the tone of his voice, and Anthony cast a questioning glance at Jamelyn. He was again surprised to see something on her face that he never dreamed of seeing, a faint blush tinting the young woman's cheeks. Anthony's boyish face crinkled into a smile. "Then we are all grateful to Lady St. Claire."

A mischievous gleam entered Justin's eyes as he grinned at his friend and slapped him on the back affectionately. "Then you will not mind seeing to the beast while we ride back to Raven's Keep." Without waiting for Anthony's answer, he turned and took Jamelyn by the arm to escort her to her mount.

Anthony released a long, disgusted breath as he glanced down at the carcass of the large boar. It would take all of them to make it ready to take back to the castle. Mumbling under his breath, he withdrew his sharp hunting knife to begin. "She should have let him have you," he said irritably as he bent to the distasteful task. Pressing his lips firmly together, he plunged the knife into the boar's fat belly.

For the first time since their violent meeting, Justin and Jamelyn were able to be near one another without venting their hostility. Together they had faced a common enemy and from that experience a slender bond of camaraderie had developed between them. Neither could say it was friendship, but during those desperate moments in the forest, a mutual respect had grown.

No words passed between the two as they rode over the softly rolling meadows that lay before the keep. Each contemplated the strange turn of events. Justin's speculative gaze rested upon his silent companion. A new facet to her personality had been revealed to him during the past hour. A pleased smile tugged at his lips as he studied her delicate profile. His wife fought like a man and acted like a man, but from her reaction to his kiss, Justin suspected that somewhere deep within Jamelyn St. Claire dwelt a woman.

Jamelyn felt Justin's gaze upon her but refused the temptation to look at him. She could not forget the strange feelings his kiss had stirred within her and was embarrassed to have let the man have such an effect upon her. Not understanding the unusual stirring that had made her cheeks brighten, Jamelyn in her naïveté presumed her feelings stemmed from her relief at being rescued from certain death.

Shawn McDougal saw the two riders enter the gate; at the sight of Jamelyn's blood-spattered figure, the breath caught in his throat. Rushing forward, he took the bridle of Jamelyn's horse and looked anxiously up at her. Deep lines of concern etched his cleanshaven face as he said, "Are ye all right, Jami?"

Shutting out the emotions that swept over her at the sight of Shawn's worried face, Jamelyn's face was a cold mask as she dismounted. "Aye, I'm fine." Her words were curt, cutting off any further comment from Shawn. Turning her back on her longtime friend, Jamelyn strode briskly into the hall.

Justin had watched the scene between Shawn and his wife. Pity for the brawny Scotsman welled in his chest at the sight of Shawn's misery-filled face. Trying to ease his new vassal's feelings in some small measure, Justin slapped him on his thick shoulder. "Your mistress will soon see that you have done the right thing, McDougal, and will forgive you."

A woebegone look crossed Shawn's ruddy features as he shook his red head. "Nay, Jami is as stubborn as they come. She'll not forgive me easily."

"Your Jami, as you call her, has a quick mind for all her obstinate nature. It will take time for her to overcome her hurt, but in the end she will recognize you had no choice in the matter. She would not expect you to give up your life so easily."

Feeling somewhat better, Shawn nodded. "Aye, she be a keen lass." His pride and love for Jamelyn was very apparent in his tone. "They say she was born at the midnight hour and it tells in her ways. 'Tis said the midnight born be different from the rest of us."

Justin could agree fully with the Scotsman's perceptions. His wife was certainly dissimilar to any woman he had ever met in his entire life. "You were not at Raven's Keep when Jamelyn was born?"

"Nay, she was born in the highlands. Lord Cregan was given charge of her when she was but a wee lass of only eight years."

As Shawn spoke, Justin realized that he knew very little

of the woman he had married. His curiosity aroused, he asked, "Does she still have family in the highlands?"

A gleam of suspicion glowed within the green depths of Shawn's eyes at Justin's question. It was not his place to inform Lord St. Claire of Jami's past. If he wanted to know more he should ask her himself. "Nay, Lord Cregan was all that was left of her family," Shawn finally answered.

The look on the Scot's face and the tone of his voice indicated to Justin that the subject was closed. However, the bit of information he had gleaned intrigued him. He would have to learn more of Jamelyn St. Claire; by doing so, perhaps he could come to understand her.

Releasing Shawn to go about his duties, Justin strode into the great hall. The only occupant of the vaulted chamber was his wife, who stood drinking a tankard of ale by the huge fireplace. She wiped the foam from her lips as he came forward. "'Tis good to quench one's thirst after a hunt," she said as she set the tankard upon the hearth.

Justin smiled. It was the first time his wife had ever spoken to him politely. "Aye, my mouth still tastes of the dirt I ate from my fall."

At the memory, Jamelyn's soft laughter pealed through the chamber, her eyes glowing with mirth as she looked up at Justin. Then, realizing her foolish behavior, she slapped her hand over her mouth and looked away from her husband's intense gaze.

Cocking his raven head to one side, Justin regarded the young woman before him. The sound of her laughter had been purely female. It was the second feminine trait he had seen in her that day, and from her expression, she realized it. Perplexed that she should want to rid herself of all that spoke of her gender, Justin tipped up Jamelyn's chin so that he could gaze directly into her eyes. "Why do you stifle your joy? This is the first time I've heard you laugh."

Jamelyn was vexed that she should have behaved in such a manner in front of Justin. The mirth died in her eyes as she returned his gaze. "I have had little to laugh about since you came, Englishman."

Seeing her icy expression, Justin knew he had blundered.

His hand fell to his side and he turned to fill a tankard with ale. "Aye" was all he said before downing the cool, foamy brew. He stared into the flickering flames, his hand clenched tightly about the handle of the tankard as he listened to Jamelyn's brisk steps fade from the hall. He did not try to stop her.

A startled gasp was drawn from Nora and Maille at Jamelyn's sudden entrance and her savage slamming of the door. Their identical blue eyes rounded with something akin to fear at the expression playing over Jamelyn's features, and they did not argue with her curt order to leave her. They quickly gathered their things together and fled the room, relieved that their lady had not vented her rage upon their heads.

Jamelyn slumped into the chair before the fire and propped her elbow on the chair arm. Resting her chin against the palm of her hand, she crossed her slender, gartered legs. A bitter smile lifted the corners of her delicate lips as she glanced down at her bloodstained clothing and mused, I would prefer it to be the Englishman's blood instead of that fierce beast's.

Sullenly, Jamelyn stared at the dancing flames as she thought of Justin St. Claire. Since the English knight had come to Raven's Keep her life had turned upside down. She felt that she did not truly know herself anymore. Her emotions seemed to veer from one extreme to the other. Pursing her lips petulantly, Jamelyn had to admit she had enjoyed the hunt and the quiet ride back to the keep. That she could find even a small measure of pleasure in the company of the foreigner in itself surprised and irritated her. Something had changed when she and Justin had faced death together, but for the life of her, Jamelyn knew not what.

Her piquant features reflected her wonder at how easily her husband's name had come to her mind, instead of the vile terms she usually associated with him. Rubbing her temples with the tips of her fingers, Jamelyn shook her head. She could not understand what was happening to her. Justin was her sworn enemy and she was the chieftain of the Clan

Cregan; it confused her to have such strange feelings running rampant within her when she thought of him.

Leaning her head against the chair back, Jamelyn stared up at the soot-blackened beams. She needed someone to explain the new and frightening feelings she was experiencing. At that thought her mind traveled to Shawn McDougal.

The brawny Scot had always been the person Jamelyn could turn to for any explanation her young, inquisitive mind craved. A forlorn little smile briefly touched Jamelyn's delicate lips as she remembered the time when she was twelve and had begun her woman's cycle. It had frightened her. She thought she had been wounded while jousting with her uncle's pages. Severe cramps had doubled her over and Shawn had carried her to her chamber. As she stripped away her soiled clothing, Jamelyn had seen the bright blood and had cried out in alarm. Shawn had been near and had come quickly to her aid. Jamelyn could remember well the ruddy hue of his complexion as he grinned sheepishly at her and explained her body's functions. She had never seen the old warrior blush again since that day.

Jamelyn squeezed her eyes tightly together to stem the burning sensation behind her lids. Last night had proven to her that she could no longer turn to Shawn. He was now the vassal of Justin St. Claire. She was alone now and had to depend upon her own abilities to solve the problems that faced her. It was up to Jamelyn to come to understand the new sensations that made her heart flutter so erratically within her breast when the Lord of Raven's Keep came near.

A tap on the door interrupted Jamelyn's introspection and she looked up to see Nora and Maille lugging the heavy brass-bound tub into the chamber. After several trips, they had it filled with hot water. Their task completed, they left Jamelyn without a word.

Jamelyn eyed the tub distastefully and wondered at her husband's obsession with bathing. Slowly she rose from her seat, releasing a long, resigned sigh, and then began to remove the stiff, blood-stained tunic. She knew it was useless to fight the silent order. If she did not obey, Justin would probably drown her this time. Stepping out of the soiled chausses, Jamelyn kicked them into the corner as a small sign of defiance and then eased her slender body into the steaming water.

Relaxing back against the rim of the tub, Jamelyn let the hot liquid ease her tired muscles. Until that moment, she had not realized the fight with the boar had been that exhausting. She seemed to ache from head to toe. The warmth of the water soothed the soreness that had begun to tighten her muscles. After so many weeks locked away in her chamber, Jamelyn had been unprepared for the strenuous activities that she had endured that afternoon.

Taking the scented bar of soap, she lathered it between her palms and realized with a start of incredulity that she was enjoying the feel of the water and the sweet fragrance that emanated from the soap. She sniffed it appreciatively. Its scent brought back a memory Jamelyn had thought long buried in another life and time. The lavender reminded her of the purple and pink bushes that had grown in her mother's garden. The recollection was vivid.

A grey shadow seemed to pass over Jamelyn's features. Since coming to Raven's Keep she had tried to avoid such memories. The little girl who had been petted and pampered had died the day she entered the black granite walls of Lord Cregan's keep. She had been forced to change her entire life in order to gain the love she so desperately craved after losing her family.

Absently, Jamelyn rubbed the lather over her thin shoulders and down across her full, white breast. Her hand touched the ridge of the red scar from the wound Justin had given her. It had healed but her side was still tender. With gentle fingers she followed the path of the mark from her shoulder down to her small waist. Aye, Jamelyn mused, that child grew into a warrior.

With memories of her earlier life still intruding upon her mind, Jamelyn wondered how her life would have been if the plague had not taken her family and she been reared as a woman. Would she now have a family of her own and be content to let a man rule her and make all the decisions?

Without realizing that the sigh that escaped her seemed to hold a measure of regret, Jamelyn shook her curly head, a defensive note springing into her voice. "Nay, I'd not be content to have someone rule me. Nor will I ever be," she said aloud.

Pushing the memories back into the locked compartment of her mind, Jamelyn quickly finished bathing and stepped from the tub. She dried her slender body with a coarse linen towel and then retrieved her soiled clothing. With a moue of disgust, Jamelyn looked at the filthy garments before letting them fall back to the floor. Her clean body felt too good to wear the dirty clothes. In a quandary, she wondered what she could wear. All of her own apparel her been torn to shreds, leaving her with nothing to put upon her back.

Jamelyn tapped her pursed lips with one finger, her small foot beating a rapid tattoo on the floor as her gaze scanned the chamber for a means of solving her problem. Her eyes came to rest upon the satin gown. Maille and Nora had completed it while she was hunting. Crossing the short space to where the gown lay spread in shimmering glory across the bed, Jamelyn tentatively fingered the soft fabric, not at all certain about the idea of wearing it. Picking it up, she held it against her and could not stop herself from admiring the beautiful material. Its silken texture felt so different against her bare skin—not at all like the wools used in her tunics and chausses.

Intrigued, Jamelyn slid the satin gown over her head. With clumsy fingers unused to women's garments, she finally managed to fasten the tiny clasps down the back. With her curiosity fully aroused, Jamelyn stepped across the chamber to view her reflection in the polished metal mirror.

Thick black lashes touched the soft skin beneath her delicately arched brows as her eyes widened at the sight that met them. The girl who looked back at her was totally female. Jamelyn's mind warred with itself. She had fought to gain recognition as a man and after much hard work, had succeeded. However, she could not keep herself from experiencing a certain amount of pleasure as the soft satin caressed her bare flesh. Jamelyn gazed at the image with eyes the same emerald color as her gown and realized with even more surprise that it was the first time she had looked upon herself and not hated her body for its gender.

Curiously, Jamelyn stepped closer to the shining mirror. She touched her face with the tips of her fingers as she perused her features. Like a blind man trying to see, she followed the path of her sculpted cheekbone to the bridge of her slender nose. From there the tips of her fingers traveled its narrow length down to her shapely lips. Her own actions amazed her.

For some reason Jamelyn could not fathom, she wondered if her features were pleasant to look upon. Her wide, black-fringed eyes reflected the conflicting emotions these new thoughts aroused. She had seen her image many times before in the mirror and in still ponds as she bent to drink, but for the first time in her eighteen years she was conscious of her appearance and what others might think of it.

As her fingers touched her lips, Jamelyn's mind traveled to Justin and the odd tingling sensations his lips had aroused when they touched her skin. Suddenly aware of the direction of her thoughts, she screwed up her face in disgust that she was even thinking of her husband and enemy. She made a horrible face at herself before turning her back on the image in the mirror. The training of the past years resurfaced and her lips firmed into an angry line at her own stupid female folly. She had no time for such nonsense. It was useless to her. She was the Cregan heir and only weak, vain women worried about their appearance.

Striding briskly across the chamber, Jamelyn pulled on her boots and ran her fingers through her short, gilded curls. She glanced down at the gown and gave a mental shrug. It would have to do until she could find something more suitable to wear.

The skirt hindered Jamelyn's steps as she strode to the door. Without thought of the impropriety or immodesty of her actions, Jamelyn lifted the awkward skirt so that it would not impede her movements. Her lips curled at the thought of what her hardened warriors would say to see their Jami dressed in such feminine finery. The smile still teased her delicate lips as she descended the stairs and entered the great hall.

With their backs to the fire, Justin and Anthony were enjoying their tankards of ale as Jamelyn appeared. Their conversation halted in mid-sentence as Lady St. Claire strode across the vaulted chamber with the shimmering satin of her gown held nearly to her knees, exposing her riding boots beneath. They glanced at one another, their eyes glowing with mirth, but they staunchly suppressed the laughter that threatened.

Justin could have hit his friend as Anthony rolled his eyes heavenward and quickly downed the last of his ale. It collided with the bubble of laughter in his throat and he sputtered and coughed. Though Justin was having his own trouble holding back his laughter as he slapped Anthony on the back to help him regain his breath, he was suddenly aware for the first time of Jamelyn as a woman. The sight of her clothed in feminine raiments made Justin realize that his wife would be very becoming with the proper grooming. Pushing the thought from his mind, Justin scolded his friend, "Control yourself, man. She is not a lady of court who is knowledgeable of fashion."

Anthony nodded as he wiped the tears from his eyes and took a deep breath. He gathered as much dignity as he could muster with his mind in its present state and bowed gracefully to Jamelyn. "My lady is lovely this evening," he said, and had to bite his lip to stem the twitch of a smile. Glancing up at Justin to see his lips give a suspicious tremble did little to help Anthony. He hurried on to keep from choking again. "Does she not, my lord?"

Justin swallowed hard and nodded. "Aye, you are right, Anthony. My lady does look lovely."

Their compliments confused and embarrassed Jamelyn. A blush tinted her pale cheeks becomingly as she awkwardly accepted the two men's flattery. "Thank you, sir, but this was all I had to wear. I'm afraid Master Gibbon's clothing is the worse for wear."

Justin's eyes twinkled and he quickly busied himself by pulling out the bench for Jamelyn to be seated, hoping desperately that some action would help alleviate the laughter that threatened to suffocate him.

Jamelyn raised the gown higher and stepped over the bench as she had done all her life. Her mannish actions combined with her boots and gown were nearly too much for Anthony. He quickly refilled his tankard and turned to Jacob, speaking rapidly of anything that came to mind. He knew if he was not careful he would burst into laughter and that could only insult the young woman who sat so naively unaware of her appearance and actions.

Justin glowered at his friend before taking the chair at the head of the table. "The gown is lovely, Jamelyn. The color compliments your eyes. I assume you were pleased with the materials in the chest?"

Jamelyn nodded as she lifted the tankard of ale Nora nervously set by her plate. The two servants were still frightened and awkward in the presence of the Englishmen. "Aye," Jamelyn agreed, "they will do, but I'm afraid they will not last long if made into tunics and chausses."

Justin's hearty laughter sounded through the great hall. He could not control it at the thought of such fine fabrics cut into men's garments. "I'm afraid you are right, but I have no intention of letting them be used in such a manner. The materials are much too beautiful. They are only suitable for a lady's gowns."

Jamelyn's smooth brow knit into a puzzled frown as she considered his words. "Then what shall I wear? I have nothing more."

Justin leaned back in his chair, a smile curling his lips as he chuckled. "My lady will wear what is expected of the mistress of Raven's Keep."

Annoyed, Jamelyn quickly lowered her eyes to keep Justin from seeing her emotions. Her fingers toyed with the knife beside her plate as she raged inwardly over his edict. She did not want to wear the awkward gowns; they restricted her movements too much. Besides, she could not wear her sword belt if she continued to wear such fripperies as Justin decreed. Grudgingly, Jamelyn had to admit the soft fabric felt good against her skin, but it was too confining.

Fingering the satin fabric of her skirt, Jamelyn abruptly changed the subject as she looked once more at her husband. "I did not know my uncle possessed such things and I am puzzled as to why he did not tell me of them."

Folding his muscular arms over his wide chest, Justin gazed speculatively on her young face. He knew so little of the circumstances of Jamelyn's previous life at Raven's Keep. It was hard for him to imagine that the only young woman of the household never knew of the chest in Lord Cregan's chamber. "Perhaps he feared you would want them if you knew," he suggested, and watched Jamelyn's reaction with keen interest.

She seemed to ruffle like an irascible little bird before Justin's eyes. "Nay, I have never cared for such things," she spat, her tone adamant.

Curiosity glowed brightly within Justin's blue orbs as he asked, "Why?"

Jamelyn's small chin rose haughtily in the air as she squared her thin shoulders and spoke as if such things were beneath her. "They are useless to me. One cannot even walk properly in such a garment as this. I nearly broke my neck coming downstairs only a short while ago." Her expression was serious as she pulled up the skirt to demonstrate her point. She was totally unaware of the looks her action received or the appreciative stares that were directed toward her bare legs exposed to the thighs.

With one swift glance about the chamber, Justin cleared his throat and quickly pushed Jamelyn's skirt back into place. He tried to suppress the grin that tugged at the corners of his mouth and forced his voice to hold a severe note of reprimand. "Madam, you are now a married woman and should not bare your legs so freely to the eyes of every man present. As your husband, I am the only one allowed that privilege."

Startled by her husband's words, Jamelyn gazed over the assembly of Justin's men to confirm his statement. Seeing that it proved true, she quickly gave them her back and nervously smoothed the green fabric of her skirt. "That is another reason I do not care to wear women's clothing. Had

I been wearing chausses, my legs would not have been noticed."

Justin chuckled and shook his raven head in wonder. His wife was not embarrassed because his men had seen her bare legs, only vexed that they had looked at her as a woman. "But you are a woman, my lady. It is only proper for you to clothe yourself as such."

Irritation sparkled in the depths of Jamelyn's eyes. "I may be a woman, but I do not have to be vain and silly or dress like a peahen to please the cock." To indicate her part of the conversation was ended, Jamelyn turned her attention to her plate and began to eat the hot bannocks and crowdie cheese. With no thought to proper manners, she devoured the hotchpotch made with a variety of succulent meats and fresh vegetables. After cleaning every morsel from her plate, she gulped down the last of her ale and released a small belch as she propped her elbows on the table and looked at Justin, to see him staring at her with something akin to amazement on his handsome features. "Hunting always makes me ravenous," she said before wiping the back of her hand across her mouth.

Jamelyn's lack of manners made Justin's insides wince. He had often seen his battle-hardened soldiers do the same thing. It was still hard for a man of Justin's sensibilities to accustom himself to the young woman's complete lack of etiquette. He had been reared in a household where the women were all grace and charm, and they would have suffered the rack before acting as his young wife did. She was totally unaware that her manners better suited his men-at-arms than Lady St. Claire, whose heritage demanded strict rules of conduct in society.

From the record books, Justin had learned that the Cregan clan was an ancient line. As lady of that family, Jamelyn should have been bred as suited her station in life. He could only surmise the old lord must have been mad to have taken a young girl and reared her in such a manner.

Justin's sympathy went out to the unfortunate young woman. It was now left to him as her husband to correct the error that had been made in the past. His tone was gentle as he leaned forward and said quietly, "Jamelyn, a lady does not wipe her mouth with her hand, nor does she gulp her food like a trooper going into battle."

Though the criticism was kindly given, Jamelyn did not take it lightly. Justin's words brought to the fore the feelings of inadequacy she had experienced when faced with her new status as Lady of the Keep. Her pride would not let her deal with it calmly and her only defense was anger. Jutting out her small, oval chin, Jamelyn glared defiantly into her husband's eyes. "Aye, that might be true, but I am no lady who sits and darns her husband's clothing and wipes the noses of his brats."

Stonily, Jamelyn rose and pushed back the bench. Jerking the hindering skirts up to her knees, she stepped over it once more. Her eyes flashed as she thought, "I am Jamelyn of Cregan and I will not bow to this man's idea of women. No one will tell me how to act in my own domain.

She turned on her heel and walked swiftly from the hall with back straight and head held high. With one last glance at Justin she left the room, thinking, For all I care, the whole lot of them can be damned.

Jamelyn's brave charade lasted until she reached her chamber. When the door closed behind her, she leaned against it as a sense of her own ineptness swept over her. She knew so much about her own world, but little of that which existed beyond the walls of Raven's Keep.

The swish of the satin gown against the floor drew her attention. Clenching her jaw, she tore at the clasps of the gown and swiftly slipped it over her head. Throwing the offending object to the floor, Jamelyn strode across the chamber naked and climbed into bed. At that moment she wanted nothing to do with the things Justin St. Claire considered the mark of a lady. He would accept her as she was or nay. It mattered little either way, Jamelyn told herself.

Pulling the muslin sheet up to her chin, she blinked her eyes rapidly to stay the unusual moisture that burned behind her lids. Angered unreasonably by her own reaction, Jamelyn flipped onto her stomach and violently vented her rage upon the defenseless pillows. She beat them with her balled fist as she railed, "Damn you, Englishman, why did you have to come? My world was peaceful until your handsome face invaded it."

Exhausted, she finally lay still, her chest rising and falling rapidly, her pulse beating visibly in her throat as she clutched a pillow tightly to her breast. The image of Justin's mocking features fluttered through her mind like the black wings of ravens and she squeezed her eyes tightly shut to try to rid herself of it.

He feels so superior, Jamelyn mused as her eyes slowly opened, the thick lashes shadowing their emerald depths as her eyelids narrowed. Seething inwardly because Justin looked down at her for her lack of knowledge about things of his world, Jamelyn thought determinedly, I will learn, Justin St. Claire, and then you'd best beware.

At that moment Jamelyn forgot that she was a warrior, forgot all she had striven so hard to accomplish. Her thoughts were filled with the fact that Justin considered her some crude Scottish wench who could not measure up to the English. She would show Justin St. Claire that she was as much a lady and a woman as any weak, sniveling English female. Then he would rue the day that he had ever set eyes on Jamelyn of Cregan.

Chapter 6

The flames popped and crackled, sending sparks up the chimney as Jacob threw another log into the roaring fire. The daylight hours of the late October days had grown short as winter approached the lowlands. Raven's Keep contained little warmth; its stone walls only seemed to exude the cold. The men huddled close to the large fireplace, trying to receive what heat failed to escape up the ill-constructed chimney.

Jamelyn sat under the great hood of the fireplace wrapped in her tartan as she, too, tried to avoid the chill of the great hall. The blue wool gown Nora and Maille had sewn for her made Jamelyn long for the warmth of her old clothing. At least wearing the thick material of her tunic and chausses provided some protection against the cold, while the soft, thin wool of the gown did little to relieve her discomfort in the chilly keep. Pulling the red and black plaid about her, Jamelyn was grateful that Justin had not refused her the use of the thick woolen tartan.

At the thought of Justin, Jamelyn's emerald gaze swept

over the hall, seeking out the tall figure of the man she had so often held in her thoughts recently. He was not among the group of English soldiers who tried to escape the bitter weather inside the confines of the ancient keep.

Strangely, the great hall seemed empty without his presence. During the past weeks Jamelyn had grown accustomed to the sound of his rich, masculine voice as he spoke to his men or with Sir Godfrey.

As if her thoughts had drawn Justin's friend to her side, a delicate smile crept to Jamelyn's lips at the sound of Anthony's vibrant voice.

"'Tis colder than a witch's tit outside," Anthony said as he strode in, flapping his arms about his body, trying to warm himself.

Jamelyn looked up at Anthony's cold-reddened face. Of late Sir Godfrey had extended his hand in friendship to her. At first Jamelyn had been wary, thinking the man could not truly offer friendship to the person who had nearly slain him. However, after a while his innate charm began to break through the barrier Jamelyn had erected about herself.

Anthony blew on his nearly frozen fingers and rubbed them viciously together before propping his foot upon the hearth. "I can well understand Justin's hurry to return to England. We have nothing like this bitterness there."

Startled by Anthony's disclosure, Jamelyn managed to suppress her gape of surprise before Anthony could see it. A faint hope flared into life. The Englishmen were leaving Raven's Keep. Jamelyn quickly looked into the flames to hide the sparkle such a bright prospect brought to her eyes. Trying to repress the joy that was sweeping over her, Jamelyn asked calmly so that Anthony would not suspect her feelings, "You are going back to England?"

Anthony's arms rested on his knee as he leaned forward, a frown knitting his blond brows over the bridge of his straight, aquiline nose. "Nay, only Justin and a small guard will go back to England."

The glimmer of hope died before it had gained birth. Jamelyn's shoulders sagged. A rueful expression touched her delicate features as she mused, I was a fool to even imagine the invaders would give up their holdings so easily.

Seeing Jamelyn's woebegone look, Anthony placed one well-groomed hand comfortingly on her shoulder. "Don't look so sad, my lady. I will be here to see that all goes well in your husband's absence."

Irritated by Anthony's presumption that she needed someone to care for Raven's Keep and herself, Jamelyn jerked free of his touch. "I care not if Justin remains or leaves. I only wish all of you would return to England with him."

Anthony feigned an injured expression at Jamelyn's abrupt words. His lower lip protruded into a sad little pout and his eyes reminded Jamelyn of a lost puppy as he said, "My lady, I had hoped we had become friends during recent weeks. I now see that you still hate all of us as your enemy."

Unaware of his jest, Jamelyn was quick to respond to the crushed look on his boyishly handsome face. "Nay, I do not hate you, Anthony. I only wish to possess again what is rightfully mine."

Settling himself on the bench beside her, Anthony held out his cold hands to the blaze. "You are still mistress of Raven's Keep, Jamelyn. Nothing has changed that."

Her green eyes reflected the uncertainty of her precarious position of Raven's Keep. In a sudden burst of honesty, she said, "Nay, Anthony, I am not mistress of this fief and have never been. I know nothing of such things. I am a woman, true, but I am also a soldier. I am much more a prisoner as its mistress than if I had been thrown into the dungeon."

Jamelyn's candor touched Anthony. In that moment of truth, he realized that she recognized her failings as a woman. She was like an old warrior who had been retired from the field of battle and knew not what to do with himself. When the keep had fallen, it had taken everything Jamelyn had ever achieved away from her and she had been relegated back to the role of a woman. Now she was flopping about like a beached salmon, not knowing how to return to the life she knew, yet not wanting to admit defeat.

Intuitively Anthony sensed Jamelyn felt as if she fell far short of what was required of her and her pride had suffered greatly. In her role as a warrior she knew instinctively how to react and did so adroitly. But as mistress of Raven's Keep she found an entirely new world and was baffled by it, though her pride would never let her admit it more than she had already done.

Anthony's strong hand covered hers as he looked down into her somber little face. "I'm your friend, Jamelyn, and if you need my help, I will freely give it." He watched as her expression changed; she quickly hid her uncertainty with a look of contempt. "I need no one's help, Anthony."

He understood her reaction, though she probably did not comprehend it herself. If she accepted his offer, Jamelyn would be admitting defeat and her perverse pride would not let her submit that easily. At present her knowledge of her failure was like an open wound. In time it would heal and then perhaps she would seek him out. Giving her hand a final squeeze before releasing it, he smiled. "So be it."

The tautness left Jamelyn's muscles as Anthony concluded the subject that always made her uneasy. She relaxed visibly as she stretched her feet out to the fire. "When will Lord St. Claire return to England?"

An obtuse smile lifted the corners of Anthony's mouth as he saw the gleam of curiosity glow in Jamelyn's eyes. "At the end of the week. That is the reason he is late tonight. He took a small squad of men to the village to hear the serfs' grievances and to make certain all shall go well with them during the coming months of his absence."

A fleeting expression crossed Jamelyn's face that Anthony could not understand as she looked directly into his blue eyes and asked, "He will be gone all winter?"

Anthony's attention was drawn to the tankard of hot, mulled wine that a servant brought to him. "Aye, that is his plan," he stated absently, before taking a deep drink of the warm, ruby liquid. He could feel his muscles relax as the wine took some of the chill from his body. His stomach rumbled and he cocked one jaunty brow at Jamelyn. "My lady, the Lord of the Keep seems to think nothing of our stomachs. Shall we partake of our evening meal?" With fluid grace, Anthony rose and bowed to Jamelyn as he proffered his arm gallantly to her.

The corners of Jamelyn's mouth twitched as she accepted his arm as if she were a great lady of the court of King Edward. "Aye, my stomach has been gnawing at my ribs this past hour." Jamelyn's regal gesture was destroyed by her speech.

Anthony took a sharp breath, his face reddening as he tried to suppress his laughter, but failed. He threw back his blond head and roared. The sound of his mirth drew several interested glances from the soldiers huddled in the great hall as well as engaging the attention of the tall, handsome man who strode through the entrance, stamping the first snowflakes of winter from his boots.

Justin's gaze scanned the chamber, seeking out the source of such jocularity, and came to rest upon his wife and Sir Godfrey. His smooth-planed brow furrowed thoughtfully as he tossed his fur-lined mantle to his squire. The rogue was up to his old tricks, Justin surmised as he observed the pleased expression on Jamelyn's piquant face. Knowing his friend's penchant for the ladies, Justin determined he would have to speak with Anthony to insure he kept his hands off Jamelyn while he was in London.

Anthony and Jamelyn were already seated at the long, rough-hewn table as Justin strode forward to take his own seat. Settling his lean frame in his chair, he said, "I'm glad to see that I did not miss the evening meal. I am famished." Before the words were completely out of his mouth, Maille hurried forward to serve him a steaming plate of venison with potatoes, black bread, and cheese. She filled his tankard with wine and then scurried away like a frightened mouse.

Slicing a piece of the tender meat, Justin placed it in his mouth and chewed slowly, savoring the delicious taste. For all Lord Cregan's faults and miserly ways, he had provided Raven's Keep with excellent cooks to see to his meals. Swallowing the juicy morsel, Justin glanced at Jamelyn as he sipped his tankard of wine. His fingers absently traced a path on the bright surface of the vessel as he said, "I assume Anthony has told you of my plans?"

Jamelyn did not look up from her plate as she said, "Aye," and continued to eat.

Piqued by his wife's lack of interest, Justin set his tankard abruptly on the table. He was the Lord of Raven's Keep and it should be of some concern that he would be absent for some time. For one brief moment his speculative gaze rested upon Anthony before he once more turned to Jamelyn. "I have seen to the squabbles of the villagers and to their welfare during the coming months. There is enough grain and meat in the storage larders to see their stomachs well-filled through the winter. No problems should arise that will need your attention."

Startled by Justin's words, Jamelyn's head flew up, her surprise and confusion reflected in her eyes as she looked at Justin. She could not believe she heard her husband correctly. He was speaking to her as if she were the true Lady of Raven's Keep instead of the defeated enemy.

Noting her expression, Justin smiled. "Should there be anything more to attend, Sir Godfrey will be here to offer his assistance if necessary."

A glow of pleasure began to creep over Jamelyn, warming her and causing a blush of rose to brighten her cheeks. Her bruised pride swelled within her breast as she gazed into the lean, handsome countenance of her husband. He was leaving Raven's Keep in her charge. For the first time in months, Jamelyn did not feel like a prisoner as she said, "I will do my best to see that all goes well."

A sparkle of triumph flashed in Justin's eyes and he smiled inwardly. The last of his plans had fallen into place. Jamelyn of Cregan would fight to her death to see the fief kept safe for his return. His small gesture of trust would be rewarded tenfold.

With hands clasped and elbows propped on the table, Anthony observed the scene being played out in front of him. He watched as Justin manipulated Jamelyn to his desires. She was too young and innocent of the world outside of Raven's Keep to realize Justin had actually left him in charge of his holdings. His friend had worried over his rebellious wife's behavior in his absence and had finally found a means of insuring her loyalty. Justin's planned gesture had the desired effect. He had been unable to make her obey by force, so now he used a different method of achieving his goal. He was using Jamelyn's own stubborn pride against her.

The day of Justin's departure dawned bright and sunny. The light sprinkling of snow had melted beneath the sun's warm rays. Justin's men and Shawn McDougal sat patiently mounted and ready to make their way to London.

Jamelyn dressed quickly, throwing on the blue wool gown and running her fingers through her lengthening curls before speeding down the corridor to say her farewell to her husband. Holding the skirt high so it would not impede her rapid steps, she raced to the head of the stairs and started to descend when Justin's voice halted her. "Anthony, I expect you to behave toward my wife as a gentleman and a knight of the court of Edward Third. Jamelyn is young and impressionable. I do not want you to take advantage of her because of it."

A warm, tingly, happy feeling swept over Jamelyn at Justin's concern for her welfare. Her heart fluttered rapidly within her breast as she placed her hand on the wooden banister and took one step before she heard Anthony's voice raised in anger. Sensing the dissension between the two friends, Jamelyn felt it was not the time to make her appearance. She retraced her steps to wait in the shadows of the landing. Pressing her back tightly against the cold stone wall to keep from being seen, Jamelyn eavesdropped on their conversation.

Anthony's tone was cold with fury as it filtered up to Jamelyn in her hiding place. "Justin, if you are so worried about leaving your wife, then I suggest you take her with you."

Jamelyn slapped her hand over her mouth to stifle her gasp of protest. She did not want to go to England. However, Justin's next words quelled any such thoughts and chilled her to the bone. The fleeting warmth she had felt only moments before turned to frost on a winter's morn. "Take her with me? Anthony, I know your words are meant in jest, for you know as well as I that I can't take Jamelyn to London. She has the manners of a peasant and the crude actions of a man-at-arms. I would be the laughing stock of all at court if anyone suspected the kind of wife I possess. Besides, you know Anne awaits my return."

Anger forgotten for the moment, Anthony laughed. "True, and you could not bed Anne of Chester as easily with a wife underfoot."

Jamelyn cringed and bit down on the hand that had formed into a tight fist as she listened to the two men discuss her. She wanted to flee their ridicule but could not make her legs move. Pressing her eyes tightly shut, she swallowed the constriction that welled in her throat as she listened to the two friends slap each other on the back and bid farewell.

For some strange, unfathomable reason, Justin's words cut deeply into Jamelyn's breast, constricting the muscles until she could not breathe. Fighting down the ache that rose so suddenly in her, she took several deep breaths to still her quaking limbs before putting her chin into the air and squaring her thin shoulders. The anger that had faded over the weeks ignited once more as she descended the stairs.

Determinedly she crossed to the wide double doors. She was no coward and would not let the English dog see her hide away like a beaten cur. She would bid her husband a gracious farewell, letting him think he had won the day as he rode back to London and his Anne.

Then I will plan my revenge, Justin St. Claire, she thought. And if I succeed, I will be free of you and Raven's Keep will once more belong to me. She pulled the door open and stepped out into the bright sunlight.

With back straight and head held regally high, Jamelyn crossed the frozen earth of the bailey. She squinted up at Justin, who sat mounted on his black destrier, her green eyes sparkling with suppressed rage. "Farewell, my lord," was all that would pass from her tight throat.

Justin gave Jamelyn a slight bow from the waist. "Farewell, my lady. I hope all goes well with you."

Jamelyn's eyes seemed to smolder with embers of fire as she said, "It shall, my lord."

It had been many weeks since Justin had heard Jamelyn use that tone of voice with him. Quirking one dark brow, he wondered what had aroused the devil within the vixen. However, it was too late for him to worry over the matter. They must ride if they planned to reach London within the week. Anthony would have to handle his ill-tempered wife as best he could. Giving a mental shrug, Justin ordered, "McDougal, see to the pack horses," as he put the matter from his mind.

Shocked for the moment out of her anger at the mention of Shawn, Jamelyn scanned the group of men until her gaze rested upon her redheaded Scot. Her anger against Shawn had faded, but now she would be unable to tell him. She had hoped Shawn would once more be at her side if and when she needed him after her husband departed. Now that would be impossible. Curiosity burned in the depths of her eyes as she looked once more at Justin and asked, "Why do you take Shawn?"

Justin paused to bring his thoughts back to the present. His mind had already been on the journey ahead. Looking down into the little, upturned face, Justin knew he could not tell his wife he took Shawn because he did not trust him to remain behind with her. His answer was curt. "I need his services." He did not wait to hear Jamelyn's reply, but spurred his horse forward to the head of the group.

Vexed by her husband's abrupt manner, Jamelyn stood with hands braced on her slender hips and eyed his retreating figure until the jingle of a harness nearby drew her attention. Shawn reined in his horse as he looked down at his Jami, his green eyes trying to convey his explanation of his previous actions. With only the merest of nods, Jamelyn silently assured her friend that she understood. He was forgiven. A flush of happiness deepened Shawn's already ruddy features as he returned the gesture and then urged his mount to follow the Lord of Raven's Keep.

Jamelyn watched the procession until it was out of sight. With her jaw set at a pugnacious angle and arms folded over her breast, she tapped her small foot irascibly against the hard-packed earth. She suspected Justin's motives for taking Shawn to England. It was to ensure Raven's Keep did not fall once more under her control. A grim smile tugged at the firm line of her lips as Jamelyn's eyes narrowed thoughtfully. Lord St. Claire might take Shawn, but that does not guarantee the fief as his domain, she thought.

One delicately-boned finger tapped lightly at her full bottom lip as she gazed distantly across the bailey and considered the options left to her in her effort to outwit her husband. She had to admit the few that sprang into her mind were not feasible. Suddenly, as if the sun had just come out from beneath a dark cloud, an idea bloomed in her mind. The only person who could help her obtain her goal was the enemy who had caused all of her troubles, King Edward III. She had to petition the king to have the pope annul her marriage and reinstate her heritage.

At that thought Justin's insulting remarks rushed back like a black cloud over her hopes. King Edward would not accept her any more than her husband had, Jamelyn realized. She did not possess the grace and etiquette the Englishmen seemed to prize so highly. Puzzled by this new dilemma, Jamelyn glanced down at the blue wool gown, her hand absently fingering the soft fabric as she tried to solve her problems. There was only one way in which she could succeed, Jamelyn knew. She must become a lady.

Jamelyn's green gaze swept over the bailey, seeking out the only person who held the key that would unlock the weapons she could use against her husband: Anthony Godfrey. He was Jamelyn's only hope of securing her desire.

Spying the object of her search, Jamelyn crossed the bailey to the stables. What she had in mind was a devious scheme and it chafed against Jamelyn's innate honesty. However, Jamelyn knew it was her only chance of regaining what was rightfully hers. She tried to suppress the qualms of her conscience with that argument and adamantly told herself that Justin had used unfair tactics to gain Raven's

Keep. To regain the fief she would have to use any means at her disposal to retaliate against Justin St. Claire, for he was an expert at using underhanded methods to secure his desires.

The ground had begun to thaw near the stables, making it a muddy sea that Jamelyn had to cross to speak with Anthony. She hesitated at the edge of the quagmire and watched the blond knight as he knelt and ruffled the ear of a shaggy puppy that scampered in delight about him. Jamelyn's hesitation was not caused by the quagmire that faced her, but by a sudden uncertainty about her own decision of moments before.

Pushing away her doubts, Jamelyn squared her shoulders, took a deep breath, and stamped determinedly through the mud to Anthony's side. Hunkering down without thought, she pulled the blue wool skirt to her knees, layers of the lovely fabric draping between her thighs to the wet ground.

Anthony's lips twitched at Jamelyn's unladylike position as she clicked her fingers to the puppy to draw its attention. Glancing into her set little face, the laughter died in his throat. Something lay heavily upon Jamelyn's mind for her to seek him out. Sensing her momentary need for silence, he held his peace and waited for her to be the first to speak.

The furry little body of the puppy leaned into Jamelyn's fingers as she scratched its back. Its pink tongue flopped from its mouth and curled at the tip before it bestowed an affectionate lick upon the source of its enjoyment. Jamelyn patted the small head as she looked thoughtfully up at Anthony. "We should not pet him or he will not make a good hunter. It will spoil him."

Anthony slapped his thigh and the puppy scampered to him, jumping and yapping happily at all the attention. "All of us need a little tenderness at times. I'm sure we will not ruin him because of it."

An enigmatic expression played over Jamelyn's features as she gazed down at the small, furry beast. Jamelyn could not understand the battle that was taking place within her. Anthony had befriended her and now she would use it to her advantage. It lay ill upon her mind to employ such trickery, especially with the one who had shown her kindness.

"It will gentle him and that is a weakness. He will become timid and not have the courage to hunt," Jamelyn said, as if her words would help ease the war of wills within her.

The corners of Anthony's mouth lifted as he shook his blond head. "Nay, gentleness is not a weakness, Jamelyn. I have seen gentle women who have a backbone of steel. I have seen knights who are fierce in battle, yet they have a gentle spirit. Nay, Jamelyn, gentleness is a form of quiet strength that most of us do not possess."

The sunlight shimmered upon her gilded curls as Jamelyn cocked her head to one side and studied Anthony as he continued, "It takes a brave person to chip away the rough edges until they are well-honed. It is not an easy task for man or woman. With courage it can be accomplished, Jamelyn."

Seeing her expression grow thoughtful, Anthony suspected he had struck upon Jamelyn's dilemma. Her reaction pleased him. It showed that the old wounds were healing. If she could put the past years behind her and accept her role as a lady, then her life with Justin would go much easier. He would gladly offer his help, but Anthony knew he could not do so until asked.

Jamelyn's gaze strayed into the distance, past Anthony and the small confines of Raven's Keep. It was as if she was seeing another world, one that would take time and much learning for her to enter. Slowly she turned once more to Anthony, her voice low, no more than a whisper as she asked, "Will you help me, Anthony?"

A wide, pleased grin spread his shapely lips as he nodded, "Aye." Taking her small hand within his own, he gave it a reassuring squeeze. "Be brave, my fine lass, and you will become the true Lady of Raven's Keep. Then no one can find fault."

Guilt swept over Jamelyn at her culpability. Involuntarily her eyes misted and she blinked rapidly to stem the burning moisture that threatened.

Tenderly Anthony's hand came up to caress her pale

cheek. "This will be your first lesson, Jamelyn. It is not shameful to cry."

She sniffed and wiped her eyes with the back of her hand as she gave Anthony a wobbly smile. "Aye, but it will take time for me to learn all that you may teach. My mind battles against it, but deep within me I know I must learn. I am a warrior at heart, Anthony, and I'm afraid that will never change," she replied honestly.

Anthony rose and pulled Jamelyn to her feet. Placing a comforting arm about her slender shoulders, he walked with her companionably back to the keep. As they entered the dim interior of the castle, he turned her to face him. Placing his hands on her shoulders, he looked down into her piquant face. "You do not have to change, my fierce little Scot. We have only to hone away your rough edges, as I have said. You need not go against nature to have strength. I believe there are none as fierce as the women I have met in Edward's court. They may not carry a sword about their waists, but there is no man alive who can stand up against them. With soft words and gentle ways they rule the world. During the past weeks I have watched you, Jamelyn, and have come to believe you are a gem of incomparable value. Once we chip away the outer layers, I think we will find a diamond beneath the crude surface."

A diamond is cold and hard, Jamelyn thought as she looked up into Anthony's kind face. It was a correct description of how she felt at using him to further her own means. Though she did not like it, it was all she had to use in her defense. She did not have the physical strength to fight Justin, but if she learned all that Anthony could teach her, she might best him in the future.

The pale winter sun did little to illuminate the great hall through the waxed, parchment-covered windows. The chilled air within the castle was cold enough to form Jamelyn's breath into visible vapors as she tried once more to descend the stone stairway. The small, flat board balanced upon her head trembled precariously with each step and finally fell with a loud thump before clattering down the remaining stairs. Vexed beyond endurance at her own clumsiness, she stamped down the last steps and braced her hands on her narrow hips, prepared to do battle. "I can never do this. 'Tis foolish to parade about with a piece of wood upon one's head."

Anthony could see the tempest brewing but could not suppress his mirth at the sight of Jamelyn's irritated expression. He threw back his head and laughed, the sound of it echoing throughout the castle. Finally bringing his mirth under control, he admonished her, "If you are to be a lady, you have to learn to walk gracefully and not go charging about like a wild boar."

Anthony's laughter shredded the last slender bond Jamelyn had placed upon her temper. Infuriated, her emerald eyes narrowed and her chin jutted out angrily. "Boar? I don't see anything wrong with the way I walk. I get to where I want to go. This business of trying to be a lady is sheer torture." As an example, Jamelyn grabbed a handful of fabric from the skirt of her gown and held it up. "This is the problem. It keeps hindering my steps by wrapping about my legs. Anyway, I've decided I don't want to be a lady if I have to suffer such foolishness."

Dropping the offending object back into place, Jamelyn folded her arms over her chest as she fumed to herself, I'll face Justin with my sword instead of proceeding with this absurd plan.

Anthony's lips twitched again but he managed to keep the impulse to chuckle under control. It was the same each day. Jamelyn had little patience. She would become disgusted if she could not accomplish the task he set for her within the first few attempts. Over the past months Anthony had learned how to maneuver around her outbursts and did so again as he said indifferently, "Then we will forget about it. I just thought Justin—"

His sentence was cut off before he could complete it as Jamelyn stormed, "Justin! Aye, I think he left you here to torture me. I would wager he is laughing with all his elegant ladies about the fate I am suffering at your hands. 'Tis all

planned. He could not defeat me, so he chose a subtle
method of torment and hopes to drive me mad."

Angry, unshed tears shimmered on Jamelyn's thick lashes
as she looked up at Anthony. Her indignant little face touched
his heart. Without considering his actions he reached out
and pulled her resisting little figure into his arms. His hand
soothed the curls that were now growing into a gilded mane
that lay about her shoulders. "Nay, Jamelyn. You are the
one who asked me to teach you. Justin is unaware of our
actions. He will be totally surprised when he returns to find
you an elegant lady."

Jamelyn took several deep breaths to regain control over
her temper. The thought of Justin returning to the fief as its
lord quelled her anger as if a bucket of ice water had been
poured on it. Anthony's words renewed her determination
and she tried to make amends for her outburst. "I apologize
for the things I said, Anthony. Would you only ask me to
mend an armor or joust with one of your knights, I would
not hesitate. What you do ask of me I find the hardest task
I have ever tried to master."

Cupping Jamelyn's face within the palms of his hands,
Anthony tipped her chin so that he could study her features.
His feelings for his lord's lady had grown deeper than friendship. At first he had thought it only admiration for her hard
work, but something along the way had changed his feelings
for her. Perhaps it was her determination to become a lady.
Few people would even attempt to alter their lives so drastically. Anthony could not be certain what had made his
emotions become more deeply involved with Jamelyn when
he knew nothing could come of it. She was Justin's wife
and Justin was his best friend. Resignedly, he pushed his
feelings away as he said, "You are brave, Jamelyn, and will
not let something so trivial hinder you from achieving your
goals." Placing a brotherly kiss upon her brow, he stepped
away and picked up the board. Handing it back to her, he
said, "Now try it again."

Jamelyn wrinkled her nose in distaste and stuck out her
small tongue at Anthony, but took the board and retraced
her steps to the head of the stairs. With her small jaw

clenched tightly and her lips pressed into a firm line, she balanced the object as she descended the stairs. The board remained in place until she reached the landing.

Anthony clapped his approval and she preened under his praise until he picked up the board and handed it back to her. "Now try to do it without looking like you are going to the gibbet."

"Damn you, Anthony," Jamelyn said as she once more climbed the stairs.

The warm breath of spring tenderly caressed the cold landscape of the lowlands, bringing forth the first young blossoms from their winter's sleep. The heather greened and burst into a profusion of purple and pink blooms, making the Scottish countryside a wonderland of color.

Jamelyn St. Claire also blossomed like the heather. Much had changed about the young woman since Justin's return to England. It would have been hard to imagine that the skinny, boyish girl could have been transformed so drastically in such a short period of time. The inactivity of the cold winter months had added weight to her once angular body. It had rounded into soft curves, giving full evidence of her sensual female form. Her short curls had grown to lay about her creamy shoulders in ringlets of reddish gold, reminding one of newly minted copper. Her sharp cheekbones were delicately sculpted and touched with rose, as were her beautifully molded lips. The imp had disappeared to be replaced by a ravishing woman.

Anthony sat silently watching Jamelyn as her slim fingers plied a needle through the material on her embroidery frame as if she had done so all her life. Tiny lines crinkled about his blue eyes as he remembered the first time Jamelyn had made the effort to learn this ladylike pastime. She had threaded her needle deftly and then pushed it through the fabric, only to screech in pain as she stuck her finger. Her face had screwed up in pain as she pushed the embroidery frame violently away from her and sucked on her injured hand. Her green eyes had narrowed dangerously as she regarded Anthony, daring him to comment on her awkwardness. He had remained silent and after a few minutes, she had shrugged her slim shoulder and pulled the embroidery frame back to her. Her delicate mouth pouted peevishly but she resumed her efforts.

Anthony was still amazed at the metamorphosis that had taken place before his eyes. Now looking at Jamelyn, it was hard for him to associate her with the girl who only a few months before had wielded a sword in defense of her castle and had come close to taking his life.

Ruefully, he had to admit it had not been an easy task. He had suffered her abuse daily as she railed at him. At times he had feared he would not succeed or that Jamelyn would take his sword and slay him in one of her fits of temper. The last big battle between them had been only the week before when Anthony had decided it was time to correct Jamelyn's abhorrent table manners. He had been completely surprised by her violent reaction to his criticism. At the time he had not remembered Justin's earlier comments about her table manners, but was soon reminded of them.

The evening had begun peacefully. Jamelyn had entered the great hall, gracefully crossing to the table and seating herself with as much aplomb as any lady of Edward's court. Everything had gone smoothly until Nora had served them. Jamelyn had been extremely hungry from her hard day's work and had forgotten everything else except satisfying the ache in her belly. She had begun to gulp the crowdie cheese and black bread, washing it down with a hearty swig of ale, when Anthony commented that ladies did not eat in such a manner.

Jamelyn seemed to freeze for a moment, forcing the last bite down her throat as it constricted with fury. Anthony's words only served to remind her of Justin's criticism. Abruptly she stood, her knuckles white as she clenched the handle of the tankard of ale. "Damn you, Anthony. You are just like Justin. You can never be satisfied with me. Can I not at least enjoy my meal in peace without your constant reprimands?"

Used to Jamelyn's outbursts, Anthony did not realize the extent of her anger as he said, "Cool your temper, Jamelyn.

A lady does not devour her food like a man-at-arms, no matter how hungry she may be."

Jamelyn's cheeks flushed a deep rose and her emerald eyes sparkled like jewels as she spat, "That is what Justin said also and I'll not have his criticisms thrown at me again. I have worked hard to do all you have asked over the last months. My fingers are poked full of holes from the needle, my feet ache from learning to dance, and I cannot move about freely because of these stupid gowns. I am weary to the bone of being a lady. Perhaps this will dampen your appetite for criticism." With that she picked up the tankard and poured the ale over his head.

Anthony sat dumbfounded, the ale dripping down his face, as he looked up at Jamelyn and realized his mistake. He had quickly apologized and finally, after much cajoling, had managed to cool Jamelyn's temper.

Looking at her now, he knew his efforts had been worth all the trials and exasperation he had endured through the long winter days.

A mischievous twinkle brightened his eyes and his lips curled into a devilish grin at the thought of Justin's reaction when he returned. The man would probably go into shock when he saw Jamelyn. Justin's wife could easily outshine any beauty at court. Jamelyn St. Claire was a beautiful, alluring woman.

The twinkle dimmed at the thought and Anthony released a silent sigh of regret. It was his ill luck to have fallen in love with his friend's wife. He could no longer deny the fact and it troubled him to a great extent. Had it not been for his relationship with Justin, Anthony knew he would have no compunction about seducing Jamelyn to his bed. In the past months he had dreamed often of such an event. However, his love for Justin had made him staunchly push his feelings aside.

Anthony's musings were interrupted by the sound of heavy boots upon the rough-hewn floor. Forcing his thoughts and gaze away from Jamelyn, he looked up and his eyes widened in surprise to see Gibbon and Jacob striding across the hall. For a moment he searched for the tall figure of his friend.

Upon not seeing Justin, one sandy-blond brow arched quizzically over his blue eyes as he asked, "Gibbon, has Lord
St. Claire returned?"

Gibbon bowed to Sir Godfrey and shook his head. "Nay,
my lord. I have come only to bring a missive from him."
Handing the rolled parchment to Anthony, Gibbon looked
at Jacob. "The ride has created a great thirst within me. Do
you think Maille might find a bit of ale to quench it? 'Twould
be well received."

As Gibbon spoke his gaze was drawn to the beautiful
lady sitting serenely at the embroidery frame near the fire.
A knowing gleam brightened the squire's brown eyes as he
glanced once more at Sir Godfrey. The man's reputation
was well deserved and Gibbon envied him his prowess with
the opposite sex. At eighteen he was still shy around women
he found attractive, though he would not have admitted it
to a living soul. He desperately wanted to be like Sir Godfrey
and Lord St. Claire. They never lacked in feminine com-
panionship. The lady was a fine example of that. If there
was a fair maid even in this godforsaken land, Anthony
Godfrey would find her.

Jacob's hearty slap on the back brought Gibbon's attention once more to his friend. "I think that can be arranged.
Nora will see to it unless 'tis Maille you prefer to serve
you." Gibbon's young features brightened with a blush and
the two friends laughed at the innuendo as they made their
way to the long table across the hall.

Slitting the wax seal with his dirk, Anthony unrolled the
message. His usually affable expression altered as he read
the instructions enclosed. Torn with conflicting emotions,
Anthony glanced up to find Jamelyn's eyes resting speculatively upon him. Rolling the parchment once again, he
released a long breath as he tapped it against his knee.
"Justin has ordered me to return to England."

Jamelyn's hand paused briefly before she stuck the
scarlet-threaded needle once more into the fabric. "How
soon do you leave? I know you are anxious to return to your
home."

Anthony did not feel the urgency Jamelyn suggested. He

was loath to leave Raven's Keep and its mistress. A bond had formed between them over the past months and it gave him little pleasure to think he would not see Jamelyn for some length of time. "I am supposed to leave tomorrow. Justin needs my assistance in a mission King Edward has assigned him. There have been disturbances from raiders along the border of late and Justin wants me to join him in his effort to catch the scoundrels."

Jamelyn lowered her thick lashes over her eyes as she looked away from Anthony's intense gaze and back to her embroidery. She picked up the needle and pushed it through the fabric as she tried to hide the jubilation that was sweeping over her. Once Anthony was gone she could put her own plan into action. She had worked too hard to let anything mar it now. Even the very needle within her hand was proof of her efforts. She had sat for many tedious hours over the embroidery frame trying to master the art and could admit with some pride that she had managed to do it acceptably well.

Strangely, though, Jamelyn felt a little bereft at the thought of Anthony's departure. He had befriended her when everyone else had turned their backs on her because of her marriage. Staunchly, Jamelyn pushed those feelings from her mind, remembering that she could not let anything interfere with her plans. If things ever were to return to normal in the fief, she must be free of Justin and have control of Raven's Keep.

Forcing her voice to remain calm, Jamelyn said, "I wish you a safe journey, Anthony."

Anthony's hands balled into tight fists on the arm of the chair as the muscles contracted across his velvet-covered chest. Jamelyn did not deserve the treatment Justin was meting out to her. It would serve him right if someone stole her away, Anthony fumed to himself. Reaching across the short space that separated them, he stayed the rapid movements of her fingers. "I do not want to go, Jamelyn," he said, his voice echoing his emotions.

Jamelyn's heart beat furiously in her breast, its movement visible in the rapid pulse at the base of her creamy throat.

If Anthony should not obey her husband's command, all would be lost. Striving to keep her voice even and her meaning clear, she looked into Anthony's blue eyes. "You must obey Justin, as must I as his wife."

Her words served to remind Anthony of his position and that of the beautiful woman whose hand felt so warm and tender beneath his own. Only friendship could ever exist between them. Releasing her hand, he leaned back in his chair. His long fingers rubbed his smooth-shaven chin as he regarded her. "Aye, I must obey, but I want you to come with me."

Jamelyn seemed to freeze as every muscle within her tensed. She had feared that request. Her voice was as cold as the chill that crept up her spine as she said, "I can't go to England."

"Why?" came Anthony's soft reply.

Jamelyn worried her soft lower lip as she sought an explanation to appease Anthony. Her fingers fidgeted nervously with the fabric of her gown. "Justin does not want me there, as you well know. He is ashamed of me."

Suddenly, as if a bright candle had been brought into a dark room, Anthony thought he fully understood the reason behind all of Jamelyn's endeavors. Even after all that had transpired between them, she still wanted to please her husband. She still considered Justin her enemy, but he had also touched some distant part within Jamelyn that she did not fully recognize at the present time. Thoughtfully, Anthony reflected over this new development. He knew Justin could come to love his wife if he were given the chance. If he could only see her as the elegant lady she had become instead of the unmannered waif he had left.

"You are coming to London with me, Jamelyn."

Adamantly, she shook her gilded head. "Nay, Anthony. That I will not do. Raven's Keep is my home and here I will remain no matter what you say. You cannot force me to go with you. You know Justin would have your hide nailed to the stable wall if that were the case. I will remain at Raven's Keep until your return. Rest assured all will be well in your absence."

Frustrated that he would not have the opportunity to bring together the two people he cared for most in the world, Anthony said, "Is there nothing I can say to sway you? Justin will be pleased with all you have accomplished. You will not shame him, Jamelyn."

Again she shook her head. "Nay, Anthony. I will never travel to London unless it is to the benefit of Raven's Keep." Jamelyn did not add that that would be her reason for venturing into enemy territory as soon as Anthony was safely on his way.

Chapter 7

Justin's vassals relaxed before the fire as night enfolded
Raven's Keep within its peaceful arms. Replete from the
hearty repast of roast boar and cool ale, all within the castle
sat quietly enjoying the stillness that time of evening afforded
when stomachs were filled and daily chores completed. At
the sudden sound of a moan all eyes turned toward the
mistress of the keep, who clutched her stomach and leaned
forward in agony.

Jacob paled at the sight and rushed forward to offer
assistance. Kneeling at Jamelyn's side, his face reflecting
his worry, he asked, "Are you ill, my lady?"

Jamelyn gave Jacob a trembling smile as she leaned weakly
back into her chair and placed one hand to her brow. "I feel
a little feverish and my stomach pains me." Her eyes misted
as she once more clutched her stomach and looked beseechingly up into Jacob's weathered face.

"My lady, let me take you to your chamber." Without
waiting for her consent, Jacob lifted Lady St. Claire in
his arms and strode from the hall, at the same time bel-

lowing for Nora and Maille to attend their mistress. Jamelyn leaned her head on Jacob's shoulder, hoping to hide the guilty expression that she knew was playing over her features. Jacob's concerned face had aroused her treacherous conscience once more. She had hoped that after Anthony was gone she would have no more such qualms, but now discovered that one more Englishman had found a special place in her heart, and it pleased her little to deceive kindhearted Jacob. But as with Anthony, Jamelyn's determination and thirst for revenge won out over her emotions as Jacob carried her up the winding stone stairway to her chamber.

He kicked the door open and crossed to the bed, where he gently laid her upon the soft down mattress. She smiled gratefully up at Jacob, the gesture faint and her lips pale. "I'll be fine in a short while, Jacob. I'm sure it must be something I ate that does not agree with me."

Jamelyn's words did not convince Justin's vassal. Deep lines of worry etched about his firmly-held lips as he gazed down at Lady St. Claire. She was now his responsibility since Sir Godfrey had left him in charge of the fief in his absence. Jacob knew it would go ill with him if something should happen to the Lady of the Keep while his master was away. Needing to vent some of the frustration such a thought aroused, he eyed Nora and Maille, causing them to fidget nervously with their aprons. His voice held something akin to a threat as he said, "Care for your lady and if she should worsen, call me at once."

With gentle fingers, Jacob touched Jamelyn's brow and was relieved a tiny bit at finding it cool. He tried to give a reassuring smile as he said, "You do not seem to have a fever, so I will leave you in the care of your maids. If you need anything further you have only to send one of the girls and I will see to it immediately."

Jamelyn bit the inside of her lip to keep herself from smiling at the anxious expression on Jacob's craggy features. She nodded in answer. At that moment it would have been impossible to speak without revealing her ruse.

Jacob patted her hand comfortingly like an old mother

hen before leaving her alone with her servants. As the door closed behind him, Jamelyn threw back the covers and sat up. Crossing her legs beneath her, she smothered an impish giggle behind her hand and motioned for Nora and Maille to join her on the soft bed.

Nora and Maille could not suppress their mirth as easily and laughed as they plopped down beside their mistress, their weight bouncing the three conspirators about the bed. All three girls leaned weakly against one another until their fits of laughter passed.

Jamelyn was the first to regain her composure and wiped the dampness from her eyes. "Shhh . . . we have to be quiet or they will hear us. I'm supposed to be ill and not giggling like some silly chit."

With eyes glowing mischievously, the three huddled in the center of the large bed and discussed their plans. Nora glanced furtively over her shoulder, her eyes searching for any eavesdropper as she said, "'Tis working as you said it would, my lady."

Jamelyn nodded sagely, her movement making her auburn curls tumble in wild disarray about her shoulders. "Aye, now that Jacob thinks I am ill it will be only one more day before I can leave Raven's Keep."

Always the more sober of the two sisters, Maille looked dubiously from her mistress to the excited face of her sister and then back to Jamelyn. "My lady, 'tis afraid I am that your plan will'na work. What if Jacob insists on seeing you?"

Jamelyn's delicate lips curled impishly, a shrewd glint sparkling in the depths of her eyes as she said, "I have thought of that. You will tell him I have come down with a severe case of the fever and fear it might be the plague that you have heard has caused many deaths in several villages to the north. That should insure he keeps his distance. After a week or so Nora can put on one of my gowns and be seen near the window by the guards. That way no one will suspect that I am not within my chamber."

Nora could not stop the giggle of delight that escaped her at the thought of wearing a fine gown. She wrapped her arms about herself and stared dreamily up at the soot-darkened ceiling as she mused, "If only Gibbon could see me wearing such a fine gown, he then might find me pretty."

Her sister's lips pursed angrily as Maille's jealousy rose. She gave Nora a light shove to bring her out of her day-dreams. "'Tis I who he should see and not you, Nora McPherson. I'm the one he has eyes for, and you had best remember it."

Sensing a battle nearing between the two sisters, Jamelyn quickly interrupted, "If all goes as we have planned, then you both will have a beautiful gown as your reward."

With mouths slightly agape at their mistress's generosity, the two girls looked at Jamelyn in wide-eyed wonder and said at the same time, "It shall, my lady." The enticement of the gowns added to their determination to see their mistress accomplish her goal.

At their awestruck expressions, Jamelyn grinned and hugged her two friends. It had not been so long ago that they had turned away from her. It felt good to have their friendship once more. It had taken months for the two girls to set their grievances aside and Jamelyn hoped fervently that the rest of the inhabitants of the fief would do the same in the near future when she was once more in control of Raven's Keep.

Things do change, Jamelyn thought with confidence. Nora and Maille are proof of that. They now see Gibbon as a handsome young man instead of one of the hated English. Considering her own thoughts, Jamelyn realized she had also altered her feelings to a certain degree. She no longer considered Jacob and Anthony the enemy but now looked upon them as friends. Still, there was Justin to be dealt with. Jamelyn felt all would be well if she succeeded in her quest and sent a silent prayer heavenward that her plan would not fail.

"Nora, did you borrow the clothing from Gibbon's chamber as I instructed?" she asked.

Smiling triumphantly at Maille, Nora said, "Aye. I sneaked in just after he and Sir Godfrey rode out of the gates this morning. I found you a pair of chausses and a leather jerkin with a tunic and linen chainse. I also took the liberty of borrowing one of this capes as well as a woolen tam to cover your hair."

Jamelyn climbed from the bed and strode across to the narrow window to view the darkened bailey. Against the blue velvet sky, the darker silhouettes of the guards were visible as they kept watch on the turrets to insure the safety of Raven's Keep. She thoughtfully regarded their movements for a while before turning once more to the maids. "Good. Now all I need is to find my weapons." Jamelyn's gaze rested upon Maille. "I need you to distract the guard at the armory until I can secure my sword and dagger. Do you think you can do it?"

Still vexed that it had been Nora who entered Gibbon's chamber, Maille cocked her head saucily to one side and raised her chin in the air. "Aye, 'twill be a simple task. The man who keeps watch has been eyeing me recently."

"Then 'tis settled. We must convince Jacob of my illness and then we will see to my weapons. If all goes well I should be able to leave the keep tomorrow night."

The warm rays of the sun had barely begun to evaporate the morning dew when Jacob's fist pounded against Jamelyn's door. Nora had remained with Jamelyn through the night and quickly opened the heavy oak portal, allowing Jacob only a glimpse of Jamelyn lying on her bed, tossing and turning in her feigned illness.

Pressing one finger to her lips to impress upon Jacob the need for quiet, she whispered. "My lady's fever has risen."

Jacob's brow furrowed as he peered into the chamber and put his palm against the flat surface of the door to push it open, but Nora held firm and shook her head. "Nay, you cannot enter."

Brusquely, Jacob ordered, "Out of my way, wench. I'll see to the lass."

Nora stood steadfast, all of her small weight pressed against the solid oak as she shook her head rapidly from side to side. "Nay, I'll not let you come in. It has the look of the plague. 'Tis best that only Maille and I see to our lady in case it is the dread disease. That way it will not be spread to the rest of the people of the fief."

Jacob's usually ruddy complexion turned ashen. He seemed to freeze at Nora's dire prediction. If it was the black death the maid was correct in refusing him entry. Nervously, he stepped back and rubbed his hand over his stubbled chin worriedly before nodding his assent. Jacob could only pray the girl was wrong, but it was best not to take chances. "I'll send word immediately to London to inform Lord St. Claire of his wife's illness."

Jacob turned to go but Nora's words halted his steps. "Nay, I'd not do that now. We are not certain it is the plague. 'Tis foolish to cause Lord St. Claire worry if it is only a brief bout with the fever."

Nora held her breath as she watched indecision flash across Jacob's weather-beaten face and then relaxed visibly as he nodded. "You are right. I'll wait until we are sure. Keep me informed of any changes."

Nora smiled gratefully at the Englishman. "Aye, I'll do that. Maille and I will not let anything happen to our mistress. Rest assured of that."

Closing the door, Nora leaned weakly against it as she looked at her mistress, who sat silently applauding her success. "You have a quick mind and a persuasive tongue, Nora McPherson. I fear the one you set your heart on will not have a chance against them," said Jamelyn.

Nora's eyes sparkled with devilment as she walked saucily across the chamber and posed with one hand behind her head and the other resting on her hip. "Then Master Gibbon had best beware."

Jacob came several times during the day to check on his lady's progress. Each time Nora gave him the same answer. Jamelyn's fever was still high and it was best that he did not enter the chamber until they could be certain that it was not contagious.

As night descended across the Scottish lowlands, Jamelyn dressed in Gibbon's clothing and sent Maille to seduce the guard away from the armory door.

Slipping on the linen tunic and woolen chausses, Jamelyn

scratched absently at her thigh where the coarse fabric made
her itch. Crossing to the metal mirror, Jamelyn gazed at her
reflection. The old Jamelyn faced her. It seemed as if all
the previous months had been wiped away with the ease of
only changing her clothing. Though the satin gown had been
soft against her skin, it felt good to be free of the restrictions
placed upon her limbs by the feminine garments her husband
had dictated that she wear.

Jamelyn eyed her reflection, her chin rising in the air as
a surge of self-confidence swept over her. Her lips curled
at the corners and her emerald eyes glowed with pleasure
at the sensation of freedom she experienced.

Striding briskly across the chamber, Jamelyn felt as if
she was again Lord Cregan's heir. Picking up the wool tam,
she pulled it down over her auburn hair and stuffed the loose
curls beneath it. Throwing the cape about her shoulders,
she glanced one last time at her image in the mirror before
crossing to the door and easing it open to peep warily into
the corridor. It was empty.

With the dark cape held close to her and every nerve
alert to any sound, Jamelyn stealthily crept from her chamber and followed in Maille's wake. She descended the
servant's stairs on silent feet and crossed to the scullery
before taking the corridor that led to the armory. Holding
her breath, she eased along, pressing her back against the
cold wall, and peered into the small circle of light provided
by the lone torch upon the wall. To Jamelyn's relief, Maille
had succeeded in luring the unsuspecting guard away from
his post. They stood some distance away from the door
so that it posed no problem for her to enter unseen.

As silent as the fog rolling across the moors, Jamelyn
crept into the large chamber and without trouble found the
objects of her desire. Her hand closed about the hilt of her
sword and gripped it tightly as a sense of power seemed to
flow through her veins. Hefting the shining weapon toward
the heavens in offering to the ancient gods, Jamelyn vowed
she would succeed in reclaiming her heritage as well as
ridding herself of the husband she did not want. With her

weapons in hand, all that was left for her to do was to make her way to England and see the king.

From the corner of her eye, Maille saw Jamelyn's furtive movements as she slipped from the armory and disappeared into the darkness of the corridor. The guard's confusion was reflected in his puzzled expression as the girl coolly rebuffed his advances and abruptly decided it was time to return to her duties. He tried to delay Maille and steal a kiss, but the fingerprints left on his cheek by her slap halted any further attempt to seduce the young woman. Rubbing his stinging jaw, the guard grumbled about the fickleness of women as he watched Maille's quick retreat.

All was quiet within the castle as Jamelyn stuffed the green gown into a leather pouch along with the cheese and black bread Nora had brought her earlier. She hugged her two friends fondly good-bye and then made her way to the tunnel through which her men had escaped from Raven's Keep. She prayed silently with each step down the narrow stone stairs that Justin had not found the escape route and ordered it closed.

Finding no obstruction in her path, a thankful sigh of relief left her lips and was echoed by the stone walls. The sound sent a chill of alarm up Jamelyn's spine and she glanced furtively in the direction in which she had come as if her small sigh would draw the attention of Justin's men. Jamelyn veered to the right of the passageway, knowing well the dangers that lay in the opposite direction. Had she not known that the deep, silent river that flowed toward the sea lay only a short distance down the other path, she might not have recognized the low, stirring sound of the water. Her ancestors had constructed Raven's Keep upon a slight hill riddled with subterranean caverns and had used them to their advantage by excavating one until it opened above ground some distance from the castle. The rest led to watery peril. Swatting the cobwebs out of her face, Jamelyn made her way cautiously along the dark passage.

Emerging from the black tunnel, she looked up at the

star-studded sky, savoring the sense of freedom that swept over her. A bubble of laughter formed in her throat at the sensation and she wanted to raise her hands to the black velvet night and dance with the joy of knowing she had outwitted the Englishmen.

Caution soon overrode her impetuous emotions, causing Jamelyn to creep with shoulders bent low into the nearby woods. Upon entering the safety of the shadows, Jamelyn straightened and turned to take one last look at the huge, dark shape of Raven's Keep. Her chest constricted with the emotion the sight brought forth; there lay her heart, and it would remain in those dark walls until she returned free to claim it once more. Swallowing back the sudden rush of feelings, she turned on her heel and staunchly made her way toward the thatched cottages of the hamlet. She needed a mount to carry her the great distance to England. Red Devil was stabled comfortably within the keep's walls, making his use an impossibility. Jamelyn would have to borrow one of the shaggy Scottish ponies the serfs used for their labors.

It took all the stealth and cunning she had been taught over the years to catch one of the shy animals. The hour was growing late when she finally managed to capture one and bridle it with the rope she had brought in her pouch. The ride would be uncomfortable without a saddle, but Jamelyn thought little of the inconvenience. She had no time to consider her personal comforts; it was imperative she put as many miles between herself and Raven's Keep as possible before dawn. If she dawdled, she might encounter a hunting party or some of the serfs from the village. Word would spread rapidly back to the keep that she was not ill and had fled the watchful eyes of the Englishmen.

With her pouch slung over her back, Jamelyn threw her leg over the pony's bare back and kicked the short, shaggy beast in the side as she urged it into its fastest gait. The pony's stocky legs lacked the speed of her beloved Red Devil, but as the hours passed the steady drum of its hooves ate up the miles. By dawn they were well away from Raven's Keep.

The hard pace Jamelyn set tired the pony as well as its rider. Its lathered sides indicated that it could not go much further without rest. Feeling secure that she was far enough away from the keep to give herself and her mount a much-needed break, Jamelyn reined in the animal in a densely forested area and slid wearily from its back. Her bottom ached unbearably and she rubbed it absently before stretching her tired limbs, easing the tautness of her sore muscles. The past inactive months had taken their toll. She had exercised little during her recent endeavors to become a lady and now the pain gave evidence to the type of lifestyle she had been leading.

Securing the pony near several clumps of new spring grass so that it could replenish its strength, Jamelyn yawned widely as she took her pouch from her back and dug out the cheese and black bread. Tearing off a hunk, she devoured it quickly and settled her tired body against the trunk of a large oak. The huge boughs draped nearly to the ground, making a peaceful bower for her exhausted slumber. She felt secure in the green, leafy tent that surrounded her, but only meant to close her eyes for a short while. Jamelyn yawned again and her thick, feathery lashes fluttered over her eyes. She slept deeply as the sun rose high in the sky and slowly crept westward.

A soft neigh from the pony awoke Jamelyn with a start. Abruptly she sat upright, rubbing the sleep from her eyes as she searched the quiet glade for any sign of danger. Her heart beat rapidly in her chest until she oriented her senses and realized what had caused her to wake up. Taking a deep breath of relief, Jamelyn looked up at the flickering shadows made by the late sun's rays through the thick foliage. Her eyes widened in surprise when she realized she had slept the day through. Her stomach rumbled hungrily as she stretched her arms over her head and shook the last traces of sleep from her mind. She rubbed the hollow ache just below her ribs before once more digging out the cheese and bread. Her dry meal made her thirsty, but there was little Jamelyn could do about it until she found a stream to quench her need. At last, her appetite appeased, she remounted and set out in the direction of England.

Twilight deepened into the dark shadows of night as Jamelyn rode along the narrow road. The moon's first rays were just spreading over the horizon when she heard the distant sound of running water. She had tried to keep her mind off her parched throat but at the sound of the water, the full impact of her thirst hit her. Eager to taste the cool liquid, Jamelyn urged her mount off the road and entered the dark forest. It was a mistake Jamelyn realized too late.

Engrossed with the thought of appeasing her thirst, Jamelyn failed to keep alert to the ever-present danger of those traveling alone. The instincts she had honed to a keen edge had been dulled by the past months and she did not hear her attackers until it was too late to save herself from being knocked from the pony's back. The impact stunned Jamelyn as she hit the hard forest floor. Her senses reeled and were dazed as the breath left her in one great *whoof*. Gasping in great gulps of air, she shook her head in an effort to clear it.

As the world began to slow its rapid spinning, Jamelyn managed to focus her eyes, and the sight that met them made them widen in shock. The first thought to cross her mind was *Justin*. She froze as she looked up at the tall, dark image standing astride her. The shadows hid his features, but few men possessed the stature of her husband. She had been found.

Leaves rattled and twigs snapped as the giant was joined by several men in the small clearing. "Ho, Royce, the blasted pony took flight, but I see ye have caught its rider."

A sudden sense of relief swept over Jamelyn as she realized the man towering over her was not her husband. But it vanished as quickly as it had come. She had been waylaid by bandits.

From the corner of her eye Jamelyn saw the dim outline of her sword lying near her and without thought of anything else beyond her own survival, instinctively scrambled to retrieve it. Her efforts were stayed by the heavy foot of her captor. With crushing pressure he placed it without mercy upon her outstretched arm. "Hold, or you'll regret it, me lad."

Jamelyn could do little else but obey. Her arm felt as if it would splinter into a thousand pieces from the man's weight. The searing pain made her bite her lip to keep from crying out in agony. She clenched her teeth tightly as she strove to remain quiet.

She felt the deep chuckle that rumbled from the huge man's chest in her numbing arm as he looked at his comrades. "I caught the wee thing, but 'tis only a boy."

"Then do ye plan to crush the life from the puny lad with yer foot, Royce?"

As if remembering where his boot rested, Jamelyn's captor moved it. She released a long, shuddering sigh of relief. Her fingers tingled as the blood rushed back into them. Tentatively, she moved them to regain use of her hand. Slowly she could feel the strength returning and as one who never submitted easily, she tried once more to reach her weapon. However, before she could accomplish the feat, her captor kicked the sword away and growled, each word vibrating with a life of its own, "Lad, ye do try a man's patience. If ye want to keep yer scrawny life, then I would suggest ye try no more foolishness." The man's voice seemed to come from the very depths of his being and with a swiftness that elicited a startled half cry from Jamelyn, he reached down and jerked her to her feet before him.

She strove to regain control of her composure as she faced the giant. She had to keep a cool head so she would be able to react quickly when the time was right to try to escape the brigands.

"It seems the lad has more spirit than size. What do ye plan to do with him?" Thomas McFarland asked the younger man.

Royce eyed Jamelyn cynically as she pulled the cape more securely about her to obscure her gender. "We'll take him back to camp and if he possesses nothing of value, then I guess it will be the end of the wee mite."

At the giant's words, Jamelyn began to struggle in earnest

as his large hands descended on her. Her efforts were futile. He grasped her roughly by the nape of the neck and shoved her before him through the dense undergrowth until they came to another clearing. Her feet barely touched the ground, making it impossible to flee. The man's strength amazed Jamelyn, for he handled her as if she weighed no more than a feather.

A fire blazed in the center of the area where Royce finally released his iron grip on Jamelyn and she stumbled to the ground. Several men watched the scene with interest as Royce towered above her with legs spread and arms akimbo. "Thomas, see what's in the lad's pouch."

Jamelyn watched with bated breath as Thomas held up her pouch and unlaced its fastenings. The flickering light from the fire emphasized the older man's craggy features and revealed his confusion as he dumped the contents upon the ground at his feet. He eyed the green gown momentarily and then looked toward Royce for an explanation of the women's clothing.

Warily Jamelyn turned her head up to gaze at the man towering above her. For the first time she could see his features clearly and stared at them with something akin to awe. She had not expected to find such sculpted cheeks and hawk-like nose on a brigand. The man's face would have been devastatingly handsome had not a hideous scar marred the once smooth surface of one cheek and his intelligent forehead. A black patch covered the area where the slash crossed under his dark brow, indicating his loss of one eye. However, Jamelyn's gaze was drawn to the other keen, sapphire eye that stared intently at her.

Time seemed suspended. Nothing moved within the camp as the raider curiously studied his captive. Suddenly, his sensual lips curved upward at the corners and a great bellow of laughter issued through the still night. With one swift motion, Royce pulled Jamelyn to her feet and jerked the cape from her shoulders before she could prevent it. Next his large hand captured her woolen tam and threw it off, letting her long, gilded mane stream across her shoulders.

"Here is your answer, Thomas. 'Tis not a lad but a lass we have caught this night."

Royce chuckled at Jamelyn's vain attempt to retrieve her cape as he dropped it casually at her feet. He hindered her efforts with one large hand upon her shoulder and pulled her to his side as his men eyed her trim form appreciatively.

For the first time in her life, Jamelyn had the urge to cringe as the men's heated gazes ran over her body. Jamelyn did not realize what a charming picture she made in Gibbon's clothing. The extra weight she had put on during the winter months made the young man's hose cling to her shapely legs and his leather jerkin strain across her full breast. She was only aware of the sudden vulnerability she felt under their probing stares. Staunchly she suppressed her first instinct, to hide, and raised her small chin in the air, her eyes sparkling with contempt as she bravely ordered, "Unhand me, oaf."

Another chuckle rumbled from Royce's broad chest at Jamelyn's bravado. He boldly traced the sleek curve of her obstinate little jaw with one long, tapering finger. "The wench has spirit, but I have ways of taming her." Before Jamelyn realized his intent, Royce swept her into his arms, bringing her small frame snugly against his own lean form. "Would you like for me to show you my methods? 'Twould cause no hardship on me and you might find it enjoyable."

Jamelyn eyed the raider coldly, her green eyes reminding Royce of shards of ice as she pressed her lips firmly together and refused to respond to his forward suggestion.

As a man used to having women put up little objection to his charms, Royce thought he had everything well in control. He relaxed, enjoying the lovely features of the woman in his arms. He did not feel Jamelyn tense as she readied herself to spring to freedom and was unprepared as she abruptly dug her elbow into his stomach and shoved with all her strength against his wide chest. The blow caught Royce just below his ribs and knocked the breath from him momentarily. His arms fell away from his captive and she turned to flee. Laughter erupted from Royce's men at the surprised expression that crossed their leader's face before he started after his cunning captive.

Jamelyn's dash to freedom came to an abrupt halt as she looked for an opening through which to escape. To her bewilderment, she was surrounded on all sides with the huge raider hot on her heels. Knowing she had to stand and fight, Jamelyn withdrew the jeweled dagger and turned to face her pursuer. Her lips curled back in a snarl as she said, "Lay another hand on me and it will be your last. Come no closer."

Royce paused and realized his foolishness for not having searched the vixen in the first place. The firelight flashed on the polished steel, making him wary of the one he had thought would give him no trouble.

Thomas spoke up from behind him. "Beware, Royce, she looks as if she can use the dirk."

The sound Royce emitted could not be construed as a chuckle, for it held no mirth. His keen gaze took in Jamelyn's stance and knew Thomas was right in his assumption. The girl had been trained to use the deadly dagger. It would not be a simple matter to take it from her, but take it he would. With a swiftness belied by his size, Royce tried to grab Jamelyn's wrist but instead received a long, bloody scratch down his forearm from the tip of the dagger as it ripped into his sleeve.

Withdrawing to a safe distance, Royce studied his young adversary. Dark lashes lowered over his blue eye, concealing the dangerous gleam that sparkled in its depths as he absently rubbed his stinging arm. A trickle of blood ran down his hand and across his wide palm. Angered more by the insult than the wound, Royce's lips curled into a snarl, revealing his even, white teeth as he said, "Wench, you will pay dearly for that mistake. No man or woman marks Royce McFarland without suffering the consequences of the deed."

A small spark of trepidation crept up Jamelyn's spine at the sinister tone in the raider's voice. She watched as he unconsciously fingered the livid scar along his cheek; she sensed that the feel of the rough skin reminded him of the past and his vendetta against the person who had placed the hideous mark upon him.

Jamelyn did not realize how close to the truth she was. At that moment Royce was staring at her but did not see her, as memories rose up from the past to haunt him. He had been twelve years old when Thomas McFarland had found him roaming the countryside in a state of feverish delirium. Had it not been for that good man's care, Royce would have died. He had taken the boy to his small holding in the north of Scotland and had helped him over the fever that ate away at his young body. After his recovery, Royce had been unable to remember any of his past and Thomas had adopted him as a son. Strangely, Royce could remember his age and a vague image of a crest. But he could not recall how he had received his wound nor why. Since that time, he had suffered nightmares and from them he knew his enemy had been English.

Royce had tried to put his bitterness away until the English soldiers had come and taken Thomas's small holdings. That act had released all the hatred that had built up over the years within him and he now retaliated by raiding the estates along the borders and attacking any traveler suspected of being connected with England.

Royce's lips quirked into a derisive grin at the thought of the English soldiers who hunted his small band of raiders without success. He had hidden in the dense forest and watched as King Edward's favored knight, Justin St. Claire, led his men on the futile mission. Royce felt triumphant at the sight. He knew his efforts to harass his enemy were proving fruitful if the English king sent one of his most valued knights to seek him out.

Though Royce was not privy to the English court gossip, he had learned much of Justin St. Claire. Royce had been intrigued when he had seen him in London on one of his many trips to the city to sell the items of value the Scots raiders took in their raids. The sight of the handsome knight with his entourage of squires and pretty ladies had aroused Royce's curiosity and he had made it his business to learn all he could about his adversary. He had found it easy, for

Justin St. Claire was well known for his bravery in battle and for the respect King Edward held for him. People loved to talk about his heroics.

Royce could not suppress the envy the man aroused within him. Justin St. Claire possessed all the things that he and his friends had been denied. It made his revenge all the more sweet in knowing Justin St. Claire was failing to accomplish the mission his king had commanded. To Royce it felt as if he had defeated the brave knight on the field of battle.

A tingle of fear traveled up along Jamelyn's spine as the silence lengthened and she watched the expressions play over Royce's scarred features. She fought back the sensation, knowing well that if she gave way to it, she would be lost. Her breath was coming in short, uneven gasps as she gained the courage to break the stillness that surrounded her and brazenly spat, "'Tis you who make the mistake, vermin. Lay another hand on me and you'll take the low road to join your ancestors."

Jamelyn's heart fluttered in her breast as Royce's eagle gaze centered on her pale face. A wicked grin spread his shapely lips as he said, "We shall see who has made the mistake." With that he lunged at her, his great weight knocking her to the ground. Her breath left her and the dagger flew from her grasp into the underbrush. Jamelyn struggled to regain her feet as she fought against the large form of her captor, but all her efforts failed.

With ease, Royce captured her hands and pulled them over her head, halting her attempt to do him damage. She could feel the warm stickiness of his blood as it ran from his arm to her own.

"Vixen, cease this moment or I'll have you tied to a tree and stripe your back with the whip," Royce ordered. "Feel lucky I have given you a choice. You deserve much worse for your foolish actions."

Jamelyn's green eyes flashed with loathing as she glared up at Royce. "A choice? You coward. You will not fight me like a man but use your great size to defeat me because I'm a woman."

Royce tried to suppress the smile that trembled on his lips at the irony of her statement. "True, I do not fight you like a man, for you would already lie dead if I had done so. Feel grateful for my mercy."

"Mercy?" Jamelyn spat. "I see no mercy in your attack upon my person."

Royce's good humor was restored at the sight of Jamelyn's defiant little face. She looked like a spitting kitten. He eased his body from hers and pulled her to her feet. "Thomas, tie the vixen up until I decide what to do with her."

Thomas managed the task while suffering every invective known to Jamelyn's man-at-arms vocabulary. It was with great relief and a certain amount of satisfaction that he tied the squirming vixen's hands behind her back. He had just straightened and was dusting his hands together, a smug look crossing his face, when the sentinel ran into the clearing. "The English are nearby. Douse the fire or they'll see it."

The raiders sprang into action, quickly putting out the fire, leaving the area in darkness. After several hushed orders from Royce, his men blended into the shadows, leaving an eerie silence in their wake. Forgetting about his hostage, Royce turned to make his own escape, but Jamelyn's words halted him, taking away the precious moments he needed to gain safety. "Do not leave me here."

The urgency in her hushed plea puzzled Royce as he knelt at her side. "I would think you would be pleased to be rescued."

Jamelyn's low voice was laced with venom as she spat, "I've no love for the English. It will go hard on me if I am found. Give me the mercy you have spoken of, Royce McFarland, and do not leave me here."

Royce cut Jamelyn free. He had not time to argue or to question her reasons, for there were few moments left in which to make their escape. Already the sound of horses hooves vibrated through the still night. Lifting Jamelyn's light form within his arms, Royce hurried in the direction of the stream. Knowing the terrain well, he waded across the small brook and climbed the moss-covered bank. Jamelyn's weight did little to impede his swift progress as he silently made his way through the dense forest until he spotted the shelter he had been seeking. Royce moved through the brambles concealing the opening of a small cave which lay beneath an outcrop of granite. Jamelyn winced as the sharp thorns pricked her tender skin, but Royce paid no heed to her discomfort as he crouched low enough to enter the opening. The cave was tiny, only large enough for Royce and Jamelyn if they were pressed closely together.

Jamelyn was uncomfortably aware of the huge male form pressing her against the sharp stones at her back. She could feel Royce's hot breath upon her neck as he turned his head and whispered, "I am in the vixen's den."

Beneath the hand that rested upon his wide chest, Jamelyn could feel Royce's silent chuckle and her heart fluttered strangely within her breast as his silky voice filled their dark refuge once more. "Do you not feel I deserve a reward for my services?" Without waiting for her reply, Royce's lips captured Jamelyn's. She could not free herself from the hard, suffocating kiss. Her back was firmly entrapped against the stone wall while Royce's lean form immobilized her from the front.

Jamelyn was helpless to prevent Royce's actions as his lips pressed against her own trembling mouth. His tongue caressed the tender flesh, seeking an entrance to the sweetness beyond, but to his surprise he found no response. He ceased his quest and leaned away from Jamelyn as much as the tight confines would allow. His eyes sought her features, but the total darkness obscured her from view. He could hear her rapid breathing and sensed her innocence. Experienced in the ways of women, Royce knew from her reaction that Jamelyn was unaccustomed to a man's touch. Taking a deep breath to calm the desire that raced along his veins in rapid, searing currents, he asked, "Who are you and why do you fear the English?"

A knot formed in Jamelyn's stomach and she swallowed nervously, wetting her dry lips with the tip of her tongue. Royce's advances had frightened her more than facing him with her dagger. She drew in a deep, ragged breath and her voice trembled slightly as she said, "I was Jamelyn of Cregan until the English came to Raven's Keep."

The light touch of Royce's fingers upon her cheek startled Jamelyn, her heart pounding against her breastbone until Royce spoke. His voice was tinged with regret. "'Tis sorry I am to have mistreated you, lass. I knew Lord Cregan. He was a brave man to die beneath the English sword." Taking Jamelyn's small hand within his own huge grasp, Royce continued, "Why are you not at Raven's Keep?"

Jamelyn was thankful for the darkness, which obscured her features from view. So concealed, she could speak freely without Royce seeing her hurt and humiliation. "I am on my way to England to seek King Edward's favor."

Royce's fingers tightened hurtfully about Jamelyn's hand and she recoiled from the pain. "You jest. Lord Cregan's niece would not go to our enemy."

Finally managing to free her hand from Royce's painful hold, Jamelyn moved her fingers to restore the circulation as she said, "Months ago that would have been true, but not now. If I am to regain my heritage I must seek out the English monarch. He is the only one who can free me from an unwanted marriage and restore my land to me."

"Marriage?" Royce stuttered, dumbfounded because of his lusty thoughts of only moments before.

"Aye, I was married by Edward's order to Lord Justin St. Claire."

Royce threw back his raven head and his laughter seemed to tremble the stone walls. He clapped his hand over his mouth to stifle his mirth and to keep it from alerting their enemies. Royce took a deep breath to regain his composure, his voice still trembling with humor as he said, "My lady, 'tis your husband we have just avoided."

"What?" Jamelyn gasped, appalled at her close encounter with disaster.

"Aye. The soldiers who now search for us are led by Justin St. Claire."

Jamelyn leaned weakly against the cold stone of the cave wall. She needed its support, every muscle within her body trembling at the thought of Justin discovering her. It would have been the end of all her plans.

The sound of horses and the low voices of their riders penetrated their hiding place. Royce's large hand covered Jamelyn's mouth to insure her silence. His own breath caught in his throat as he waited for the group of soldiers to pass. It was unlikely the soldiers would see the entrance to the cave, but Royce prepared himself to do battle if they stumbled over it by accident.

Gradually the sound became indistinct as the group moved away from the fugitives' refuge and Royce released his hold upon Jamelyn. "They have gone," he whispered before easing his large frame closer to the cave's entrance. Warily, he peered out into the dark night. A smile lifted the corners of his sensual lips as he turned back to Jamelyn and gave her his hand. "We have eluded them once more. King Edward will not think so highly of your husband when he returns to London without his quarry."

Jamelyn took Royce's hand gratefully and let him pull her from the tight little cavity. She had begun to feel like a fox hiding from the hounds. She brushed away the dirt that clung to her clothing, her voice reflecting all the pent-up anger she held against her husband as she said, "I care not what the king thinks of Justin. All I want is Raven's Keep."

Pushing back the sharp-needled brambles, Royce led Jamelyn from their hiding place. The moon came from behind the clouds to illuminate her beautiful face and for the first time Royce realized the true loveliness of the woman who had come so abruptly into his life. Gently, Royce placed one wide-palmed hand against her smooth, lightly tinted cheek as he gazed down into her eyes. "Lass, what you seek will not be easy to gain."

Jamelyn moistened her dry lips with the tip of her tongue as she looked up into the scarred, handsome face. "Aye, that I know. But I will not surrender my claim upon my heritage easily, either. Raven's Keep is all that I have and I will not see it trampled beneath the boots of the foreigners."

Royce tried to stem the hot current of blood that rushed through him in response to Jamelyn's lovely, determined face. "How do you plan to see the king? Your husband is one of his favored knights. Do you think he will listen to one young girl?"

Jamelyn's thick lashes lowered over her emerald eyes and she worried her full bottom lip with her even white teeth as she considered Royce's words. "I will ask for an audience," Jamelyn stated, innocently unaware of court procedure.

Royce felt the stirrings of sympathy within his chest as he slowly shook his dark head and smiled at her naïveté. "'Tis not so simple, lass. You must know someone at court to gain entrance to the king's chamber. Do you think your husband will let you see Edward when he realizes why you have come to London?"

Jamelyn stepped away from Royce and turning her back to him, stared off into the moonlit night. "He will not know. I must present my claim to the king before Justin knows I'm at the palace."

Royce placed his hands on Jamelyn's slender shoulders and turned her to face him once more. His intense gaze reflected his doubt of her success. "You need help, lass, and I owe Lord Cregan a favor from long ago. I can repay my debt to your uncle and also see that you get yourself into no more trouble along the way."

Jamelyn shook her auburn hair, the light from the moon shimmering silver on her copper-streaked mane. "Nay, you cannot travel to London. It would be too dangerous and I cannot ask that of you."

Royce's chest rumbled with a deep chuckle as his fingers tightened about Jamelyn's shoulders. "You need not ask. It is a debt that will be paid. There will be no danger for me, for I have friends in the city. Edward's men seldom look beneath their noses for the game they seek. Come, we will tell Thomas and then be on our way. We must ride swiftly if we are to arrive before your husband."

Royce's determined tone indicated it would be fruitless to argue. Jamelyn accepted his offer gratefully. At this time of her life, Jamelyn of Cregan needed a friend.

Chapter 8

The sun was a bright orange ball upon the carpet of a cornflower blue sky as Jamelyn and Royce rode through the gates of London. Jamelyn was exhausted from the rapid pace they had set during the past days, but her fatigue was forgotten at the sight of the city. At midday the streets were crowded with pedestrians, sedan-chairs for the rich who did not want to fight their way through the crowds on foot, and carts in which the middle class moved their goods. She stared in wide-eyed amazement at the throngs of people.

As she tried to take in all of the new sights, Jamelyn did not realize she and Royce were as much a curiosity to the city dwellers as they were to her. The sight of the huge man with an evil-looking patch over one eye and his beautiful companion in her wrinkled satin gown drew many eyes as the two rode along the cobbled streets.

The thriving city both frightened and excited Jamelyn. London with its population of forty thousand throbbed with life. Her senses were assaulted from all sides by the sounds and smells of the metropolis. She was fascinated by the many shops displaying all manner of goods in their windows, but her nose wrinkled in distaste at the rancid odors that emanated from the streets, where chamber pots had been emptied and refuse had been thrown. It was a far cry from the sweet, clean air of Scotland. Her eyes widened in shock at the sight of a harlot brazenly soliciting customers by displaying her mammoth breast to the men who passed her on the sidewalk.

This was London, England's capital. In it one could find everything to suffice all manner of tastes and vices. On its streets elegantly dressed ladies went about their daily business with pomanders held to their noses to keep away the foul odors, while prostitutes hawked their services to one and all. Pickpockets and cutthroats eyed the crowds, seeking their chance to take the unwary victim. All manner of humanity existed within the city, and to Jamelyn it was a world far beyond anything she could have dreamed.

She glanced at the wide shoulders and strong back of her companion as he led the way through the crowds and was thankful that she had met the border raider. Had it not been for Royce, Jamelyn knew London itself would have frightened her to such an extent that she would have been unable to seek out the king. As her uncle often said about an enemy who retreated, she would have "tucked her tail and fled" back to Scotland. But the sight of Royce's huge frame moving so easily through the streets without concern or fear reassured her.

The crowds began to thin somewhat as they turned toward the king's Westminster Palace. Royce reined his mount to a halt before the palace that had been occupied by the monarchs of England since the year 1054. Letting his reins go slack, he leaned on his pommel and looked up at the magnificent structure with its hammer-beamed roof added by Richard II, before turning to the woman at his side. "The king's banner is not flying over the palace, so he is in residence at Windsor. That castle is favored by Edward."

Jamelyn's delicately-shaped mouth was agape in awe at the sight of the huge palace. Her wide-eyed expression reflected her apprehension at entering such an imposing place, and she seemed to relax visibly at Royce's words. The sight of Westminster Palace made Jamelyn feel small and insignificant. Forcing this strange new feeling away, she looked up at Royce. "Then should we not ride to Windsor?"

He had watched the fleeting expression pass over Jamelyn's face and sensed somewhat her trepidation at venturing farther into enemy territory. "Aye, that we should, if you have not changed your mind about your foolish scheme." He waited, hoping to hear Jamelyn say she had decided against this venture, but knew as he watched her chin rise in the air and her spine imperceptibly stiffen that she had not.

Jamelyn cocked her head to one side as she looked up at him, her emerald eyes sparkling with the challenge as she renewed her determination. "I have not changed my mind."

Royce's lips curled at the corners and his eyes glowed with pride as he looked at Jamelyn. During the past days his admiration for the young woman had grown, for her will to succeed matched that of any man he had ever encountered.

"I did not think you had," he chuckled as he urged his horse in the direction of King Edward's favored residence, Windsor Palace, dominated by its massive round tower. It was the largest inhabited castle in the world.

The sun was sinking below the horizon, the evening sky a multicolored panorama of vivid gold, splashed with rose and lavender, as Royce halted his mount before the Duke's Inn. In the distance, the setting sun made Windsor Palace look as if it were made of gold, its multitude of windows, diamonds that studded the magnificent jewel that rested along the steep ridge above the north bank of the Thames. The king's banner swayed gently in the evening breeze over the round tower, indicating Edward's presence. The sight relieved the weary travelers.

Jamelyn's muscles ached as she climbed from the saddle and turned to gaze at the castle. There lay her goal. It was so near, yet so far away. Tomorrow she would lay her pride at Edward's feet and pray that he would not trample upon it as his troops had done Scottish soil.

At the feel of Royce's arm draped comfortingly about her shoulder, Jamelyn gazed up at her friend. He, too, stared at the imposing castle in the distance as he said, "Lass, you still have time to change your mind." Absently his hand came up to touch the scar upon his cheek, and from that small action she sensed his anxiety over her safety. His tone also conveyed his concern as he said, "I'll be unable to help you after I leave you at the gates, Jamelyn."

She looked down at the large, powerful hand resting upon her shoulder and placed her own over it before her gaze returned to the palace. "Tomorrow I see King Edward, Royce. You have nothing to fear for me. I am still Lady St. Claire and that will insure my safety."

Royce's fingers curled about Jamelyn's shoulder and gave it a reassuring squeeze. "I pray that will be so, lass." With that, he turned toward the inn and escorted Jamelyn into its dim interior, which smelled of stale wine and ale. He acquired two rooms for the night and then ordered a hearty meal of roast beef and ale. After appeasing their appetites, they retired to their rooms to seek the sleep their tired bodies craved.

Jamelyn welcomed the warmth of the small fire and the feel of the rough sheets against her bare skin. She had missed the comfort of her own bed during the last week. Her bones were weary from having to sleep on the hard earth. Snuggling down into the straw-filled mattress, she tried to sleep. Though her eyes felt in their weariness as if the straw from the bedding was beneath her lids, she could find no rest. Her mind kept turning over the events of the coming day. So much rested upon the English monarch's decision. He held her whole life in the palm of his greedy hand.

At last Jamelyn's exhaustion overcame her anxious thoughts and she slept. However, her sleep did not go undisturbed. She dreamed of the indigo-eyed knight who had taken everything from her. She tossed and turned as the moon crept across the horizon to give way to the approaching dawn.

Jamelyn awoke as the first rays of the sun peeped through the grimy window, seeming to give life to the dust motes that danced in slow rhythm in the bright splash of light. Stretching her arms over her head, she hoped to relieve some of the soreness in her still tired limbs. She felt as if she had not slept more than a few minutes. Dark circles tinted the delicate skin beneath her eyes as she blinked against the bright sunlight that filled the room.

Throwing back the thin wool blanket, Jamelyn slid her gracefully slender legs to the edge of the bed and sat up. She shivered from the early morning chill as her bare feet touched the rough planking of the floor. Pulling the blanket from the bed, Jamelyn wrapped it about her nude body as she padded to the small window and rubbed a clear spot in it with the ball of her palm, her gaze going immediately to the castle on the hill.

Though the morning was still new, with the dew glistening upon the blades of grass along the roadside, the merchants were already at the palace gates to do their daily business. Fishwives carried their heavy baskets beneath their arms, with their hands braced against wide hips, while others carted fresh produce and meats up the winding road so the English king would feast well that day.

From her vantage point, Jamelyn was able to survey the activity surrounding the gates. She noted the guards posted at the entrance, keeping watch with a keen eye over all who entered Windsor. All but the merchants were stopped and questioned. Some were permitted to enter, but others were turned away. Jamelyn leaned her brow against the windowpane as she tried to think of a way to pass the guards unhindered. Royce had been right in his assumption that it would be hard for her to gain admittance to Edward's presence, and now she had to find a means to overcome her first hurdle.

For long moments Jamelyn's piquant face screwed up thoughtfully, her smooth forehead furrowing with tiny lines as she brooded. Suddenly, her eyes brightened and a mischievous smile tugged at the corners of her soft, rose-tinted lips. Dropping the blanket to the floor, she hurried across the chamber to the green satin gown and slipped it on. Tugging on her boots, Jamelyn grabbed her pouch and then rushed from the room as if the devil was upon her heels. In her excitement, she sped the few steps to Royce's room and pounded on the door. Without thought to the consequences, she did not wait to hear Royce bid her entry, but pushed the door wide in her eagerness to tell him of her plan.

Jamelyn's rapid steps halted in midstride at the sight that met her eyes. Her cheeks turning crimson, she quickly turned away, very much aware of the naked masculine form rising from the bed. She had glimpsed the broad, hairy expanse of Royce's bare chest and his narrow hips before averting her eyes in embarrassment. Her own reaction added to her discomfort. Jamelyn had often seen the male body unclothed, but during the past months she had begun to view men differently since she had become aware of her own sex to such a degree.

She heard Royce's deep chuckle and could feel the heat rise in her cheeks even more with the knowledge that he knew of her discomfort. Turning to the fireplace, she knelt and busily rekindled the glowing coals. Clearing her throat, she said, "I'm sorry to have disturbed you, but I know how I'll get into the castle."

Royce settled his large frame once more upon the bed and pulled on his hose and tunic. "You did not disturb me, lass. But 'tis dangerous to burst into a man's room. I might have been occupied in other matters or I could have throttled you before I was completely awake, thinking you the king's men."

Jamelyn's cheeks flamed again at his innuendo as she poked at the dry wood she had placed on the flames. "It was foolish, but I have little time to waste. I must go at once to the castle if I'm to see Edward."

Scratching his dark head and yawning widely, Royce stood, his tousled curls falling boyishly about his chiseled features as he said, "What reckless scheme is now running rampant in that pretty head?"

Slowly Jamelyn rose to her feet and cast one surreptitious glance in Royce's direction before facing him. "I will enter with the merchants and then seek Edward out after I am past the guards."

Royce's craggy cheeks puffed out as he blew a long, silent whistle beneath his breath and shook his head. "Lass, it will never work. 'Tis best you tell the guard who you are and then ask for an audience with the king."

Brushing back a stray, gilded curl from her face, Jamelyn braced her hands on her hips and said, "Royce, look at me and you will see the reason that I cannot do as you suggest. Do you think the guards will believe I am Lady St. Claire? I know my plan sounds foolish, but it is my only hope to gain entry to Windsor."

Royce glanced at Jamelyn's rumpled attire before he picked up his sword belt and strapped it about his lean waist. Proffering his arm to her, he said, "Then we had best go. I know it is useless to argue with you. Jamelyn, you possess more stubborness even than I do, and once you set that pretty head on something, then woe be unto the one who tries to deny you."

A smug smile touched Jamelyn's lips as she raised her chin in the air and placed her hand on Royce's arm. "I am Jamelyn of Cregan. My uncle taught me well."

Royce's bronzed hand covered Jamelyn's affectionately and squeezed it. "Maybe so, lass, but it is a dangerous course you have set. If you need me, I will be here for two days. After that you can always send a message to the priory at Selkirk and I will receive it."

Misty emerald eyes met Royce's dark gaze. "I will remember, and if all goes well you are welcome at Raven's Keep, Royce McFarland. I have need of friends such as you."

Royce and Jamelyn waited at the edge of the village until a group of merchants began the short trek to Windsor. Their carts were loaded with fresh produce and wheat for the kitchens of the castle. Jamelyn and her border raider walked a short distance behind the merchants until the gates lay only a few yards away. Slowly, without raising suspicions, they moved closer to look as though they belonged with them. Royce gave Jamelyn's hand a reassuring squeeze before he dropped back and disappeared into the forest along the roadside.

Alone, she gazed nervously up at the high stone walls that surrounded the palace grounds. She sent up a silent prayer that the guards would not question her as she entered the gate. Her heart pounded furiously within her breast and her knees quaked so badly that she feared the movement would be noted beneath her wrinkled gown. She placed her hand on the side of the cart to gain much-needed support and to give the illusion she was one of the merchants. Her breath caught in her throat, the last few steps seeming like miles, as she and the small band of merchants passed through the portal onto the wide, spacious grounds of Windsor Palace.

Jamelyn breathed a deep sigh of relief as she realized she had gained entrance to the palace grounds. One minor hurdle had been crossed, but now ahead of her lay the major obstacle to her plans; she must find a way into the palace without being seen. She followed the group along the graveled drive that led to the kitchen entrance, her gaze scanning every crevice of the castle with the hope of spying some means to accomplish her aim. As the merchants haggled and bickered with the cooks over the prices of their goods, Jamelyn saw what she desired. It was a small door several yards away from the kitchen that would have gone unnoticed by anyone else.

Satisfied with her find, she wanted to scream in vexation at the length of time it took the cooks and merchants to conclude their dealings. After what seemed an eternity, the merchants gathered their empty baskets and turned to leave. Watching closely to see she went unobserved, Jamelyn lingered behind and then made a dash for the door. Without looking back, she darted into the dim interior and leaned against the rough stone wall until her eyes became adjusted to the inadequately lit entrance. Beads of perspiration moistened her soft upper lip as she looked about her and realized she had entered the laundry.

It was a large chamber with several open fire pits that were insufficently ventilated, so the atmosphere was constantly thick with smoke. Huge caldrons steamed on the fire while the laundry maids bent over large wooden tubs and pounded and scrubbed the linens of the royal household. The scent of lye filled the air and stung Jamelyn's eyes, making them water.

With a hand that trembled slightly from her own daring, she wiped away the moisture from her face as she gazed at the sweating servants. They paid no heed to her intrusion but kept up their methodical labors, knowing well there was little time to squander or they would suffer the consequences. The head laundress felt her authority and used it often by laying the whip to their backs or dismissing them from their jobs. There were too many small mouths to feed in their homes for the laundry maids to pay any attention to the auburn-haired beauty in the wrinkled satin gown.

Relieved that no one questioned her presence, Jamelyn forced her legs to move at a slow but steady pace across the chamber to the door she suspected would lead her into the castle. With a calmness she did not feel, she opened it and walked into the corridor beyond. Lit by only a few torches placed at long intervals along the stone walls, the passageway was even darker than the laundry. She paused to ascertain in which direction she should travel. There were several corridors that joined the one in which she stood and she did not want to choose the wrong one. A rash decision could only lead her into trouble.

Jamelyn turned to the stairway she could see a short distance away. She still was uncertain whether she had chosen the right way, but she knew she could not stand about until someone noticed that she did not belong in the king's household. The sound of giggles alerted her in time for her to dash into the shadows of the stairwell before two young maids descended, their arms laden with trays of silver and china that contained the remnants of the morning meal. Jamelyn held her breath and pressed her back tightly against the wall as she heard one of the maids say, "His Majesty was ravenous this mornin', Megan. His spirits are high from what that young squire told me."

Her companion's high-pitched laughter echoed down the corridor. "Now, be off wit' you, Bess. That young squire doesn't know of things that pertain to 'is Majesty. 'E's not much more than a groom, so 'e don't know the doings of the king."

"Yer wrong there, Megan. Roland—" the maid giggled at the use of the young squire's name—"knows more than ye give him credit for. 'E says the king 'as been in much better spirits since the Lady Anne came to court."

Jamelyn listened to the maids' inane gossip from her hiding place and waited until they were completely out of hearing distance before she stepped from the shadows. With one furtive look in the direction in which they had gone, Jamelyn silently made her way up the winding flight of stairs to come to a door a few feet beyond the landing. Taking a long, steadying breath to give her the needed courage, she touched the latch with her fingers and slid it silently back. Stealthily, she eased the door open and peeped into a long, plush-carpeted corridor. To her great relief she saw no one. Only the suits of armor that rested below portraits of past generations occupied the long, dark-paneled hall. Had Jamelyn's thoughts not been centered so intensely on her reasons for being in Windsor, she would have gaped in awe at the rich, gleaming wood of the walls and the ornate, gilded frames that surrounded the portraits of England's previous monarchs.

Cautiously, Jamelyn made her way along the portrait galley, the thick carpet silencing her footsteps as she crept forward, alert to any sound that might indicate she had been found. But all was quiet as she came to another flight of stairs. She took several tentative steps and then froze at the sound of voices coming in her direction. Rapidly, her eyes scanned the gallery for a place to hide and came to rest upon the long, velvet drapes that covered one tall window. With the agility of a frightened mouse, she sped back down the steps to the window, secreting herself behind the thick fabric. The voices came nearer and then passed as Jamelyn tensed for discovery. Her fingers trembled as she eased the velvet back and peered with wide, searching eyes from her refuge as the voices became indistinct. She breathed a sigh of relief as she found the corridor once more empty. Without further hesitation she ran up the flight of stairs and silently passed along another carpeted hall. However, luck was not with her on this venture. She rounded a corner and collided with two uniformed guards.

"Ho, what have we here?" one guard said as his large hand clamped down on Jamelyn's shoulder, halting her flight. His companion eyed her briefly, his eyes filling with contempt at the sight of her rumpled appearance. "It looks as if the wench thinks to visit the king."

Annoyed by the man's tone, Jamelyn raised her chin in the air and squared her shoulders as she looked at her captor haughtily. "I have come to see the king. Now, if you would be so kind as to show me to him, I would appreciate it."

The guards laughed in unison; with a smirk on his face, her captor said, "I'm sure you would appreciate it, wench, but 'tis not our duty to show every beggar or prostitute their way to His Majesty. The only place you are going is to the gates."

Insulted by his remarks, Jamelyn forgot how she had entered Windsor as she resisted his heavy hand. "Nay, I have come to see King Edward. Release me this moment."

To give aid to his comrade, the second guard clamped his beefy hand about Jamelyn's other arm and the two tried to drag her away. Digging her heels firmly into the soft carpet, she rebelled, her own anger erupting at their rough treatment of her. "Release me, oafs," she commanded, but the two men paid no heed to her words.

The first guard's fingers bit brutally into the flesh of Jamelyn's upper arm as he said, "Wench, it would be best for you to cease this foolish struggle. If you persist your back will feel the bite of the whip before you are thrown through the gates."

A group of men dressed for the hunt halted at the sight of the struggle between the palace guards and the young, auburn-haired woman. One pair of light blue eyes widened in shock as their owner recognized Jamelyn. Anthony Godfrey sent a silent prayer heavenward that his neck would not feel the bite of the rope before nightfall. Swallowing the tightness that formed in his throat, he turned to the dark-haired man at his side and gave an elegant bow. "Your Majesty, if I have your permission I will see what has caused this disturbance."

Edward's carefully groomed, bejeweled hand waved Anthony away without a word. Anthony quickly crossed the short distance to the struggling threesome. "Loose her. I will be responsible for the lady."

A perplexed expression crossed the face of one of Jamelyn's captors as he gazed from the nobleman back to the still-squirming hostage. "The wench has slipped into the palace, my lord, and we were only doing our duty."

Anthony nodded, wishing at that moment that he had gone straight to join Justin when he found out his friend had already set out to the borders after the bandits, instead of deciding to rest a few days and enjoy Edward's hospitality. Irritably he said, "Aye, I know that, but the lady will cause no trouble. You have my word on that."

The guards gave Anthony a skeptical look as they released Jamelyn, then bowed to him before withdrawing. They glanced one last time at the nobleman and the young woman, uncertain that one man could handle such a wildcat. Then, shrugging, they went about their business.

Before the guards had passed from view, Anthony turned on Jamelyn. "My God, what are you doing here?"

She brushed her tousled curls from her face and her small chin jutted out defiantly as she said, "I've come to see the king."

Anthony ran his fingers through his hair, astounded by Jamelyn's rash actions. At that moment he could have placed both hands over his handsome face and wailed in anguish at his own foolishness for not seeing the reasons behind her desperate need to learn to be a lady. "The king? Jamelyn, have you lost your wits?" Anthony finally got out as he took her arm to lead her away. He had forgotten, however, that his sovereign was only a few feet away.

Edward's voice quickly reminded Anthony and the knight's complexion turned to a pale shade of grey as Edward said, "Sir Godfrey, is this any way to treat one of my subjects?"

Anthony swallowed convulsively as he turned to face his king and sought desperately for an answer. His fingers tightened their grip upon Jamelyn's arm as he envisioned his own execution. Nervously he ran one finger beneath the gold-embroidered collar of his tunic, imagining the feel of the rough hemp against his skin.

Edward noted the young man's discomfiture and smiled as he wondered what devilment young Godfrey was now scheming. "Sir Godfrey, I'm afraid that I do not have all day. Would you kindly explain this person's reason for being in the palace?"

Sooner than she had expected, Jamelyn faced England's monarch. Forgetting her mission, all her thoughts centered on the fact that before her stood her enemy, the man who had caused all of her suffering. All her pent-up anger surfaced, causing her to ignore the etiquette Anthony had taught her as she faced Edward III. With her chin high, she stared unflinchingly into his dark eyes. Her own eyes sparkled with fire at the cold, imperious tone he had used when he spoke of her as though she was something less than human.

Seeing her look, Anthony rolled his eyes heavenward, knowing his fate had been sealed. His voice shook and he had to clear his throat several times before he could say, "Majesty, may I present Lady St. Claire."

Anthony tensed even more as Edward's dark gaze swept over Jamelyn from the top of her tousled, copper-streaked head to the tips of her riding boots. A smile curled the corners of his thin lips as he met Jamelyn's stare once more. "Damn me, the lady would slay her sire with her green barbs." Extending his hand to Jamelyn, Edward continued, "Come forth, my lady, and let there be peace between us."

Anthony held his breath as he waited for Jamelyn's reaction. He released an audible sigh of relief as she accepted

Edward's hand and with head held high walked beside England's king. Anthony followed, dumbfounded by the turn of events.

The intricately carved doors of the audience chamber swung silently closed behind them as Edward escorted Jamelyn to the chair at his side and personally seated her. "Now, my Lady St. Claire, what brings you into my palace like a thief in the night? Surely you know that you and your husband are always welcome at my court?"

At the thought of being welcomed by her enemy, a scathing retort sprang to Jamelyn's lips, but she swallowed it back. Remembering her reason for coming to Windsor, she strove to make use of all the instructions Anthony had drummed into her head during the long winter months. "Majesty, please forgive my behavior. I fear I am sadly lacking in the knowledge of court protocol."

Edward chuckled with pleasure. It was refreshing to hear someone who spoke honestly for a change. "My lady is forgiven. Now, will you tell me your reasons for causing such a fracas?"

Jamelyn hesitated briefly as she glanced at Anthony before plunging directly to the heart of her troubles. "Sire, I have come to ask you to petition the pope for an annulment of my marriage and the restoration of my lands to me as heir of Lord Cregan."

Anthony stifled his moan before it escaped, knowing that if Edward did not slay him for aiding and abetting her, Justin St. Claire would.

The stillness that had invaded the chamber at Jamelyn's request lay over it like a heavy shroud. The silence lengthened as Edward leaned back in his chair and propped his chin on his bejeweled hand. A cold, hostile gleam sparkled in his dark eyes, dimming the warmth he had shown only moments before as he studied Jamelyn's lovely face.

Unconsciously, Jamelyn shifted nervously under the king's intense regard. Sensing that she had handled things badly and in doing so had failed, Jameyln clasped her hands tightly in her lap to still their trembling. The long, agonizing moments passed slowly as she waited for the English monarch to refuse her plea. A knot formed in her stomach and her muscles coiled from tension. From what she read in Edward's expression, the last of Jamelyn's hopes died to lie heavy and cold as a stone placed upon a crypt.

The first emotion to pass through Edward had been anger, but as he watched the lovely woman, a scheme began to form in his shrewd mind. Jamelyn St. Claire was a beauty. Even so, his plan to marry her to Lord St. Claire had failed. The young woman's words had just confirmed it. However, Edward III was not a man to accept defeat easily when he wanted something. And in this matter there were two things England's monarch desired: peace with Scotland so he could turn his attention to France, and Anne of Chester.

Ah, my lovely Anne, Edward thought. If I have my way, you will soon be in my bed instead of longing for Lord St. Claire.

The tip of one bejeweled finger traced the curve of Edward's bearded chin as he thoughtfully regarded Jamelyn before saying, "My lady, I am afraid you ask too much. I need peace with Scotland. Though Raven's Keep is only a small fief, others may see from our actions there that we only want to rule fairly and will lay down their weapons."

Jamelyn's feathery lashes fluttered over her eyes to hide the resentment that flared within their depths. It galled her to have to plead to her enemy, but to regain Raven's Keep she would put her pride aside. "Majesty, I do not seek to do battle with you. If you will consider my request, I will swear fealty to you alone and do everything within my power to see that you have the peace you desire without having to quarter your troops at Raven's Keep to insure it. I will give my word as Clan Chieftain that none in my domain shall raise a sword against England."

Edward's hand rested against the arm of his ornately carved chair, his fingers tapping meditatively against the shining surface of the rich wood. A cunning glint came into his dark eyes as he said, "There are other things to consider beyond peace, my lady."

From the cold ashes, Jamelyn's hope sprang back to life and began to swell within her at the king's unspoken hint that perhaps all was not lost. Her eyes searched Edward's swarthy face. "If it is in my power to remove any obstacles I will do so, Sire."

A predatory look flickered briefly in Edward's eyes. His quarry was falling into his hands. A satisfied smile touched his lips as he said, "I'm afraid there is only one obstacle in my path and that is Justin St. Claire."

Anthony had remained silent during the intercourse between Jamelyn and Edward. He was puzzled as to the direction in which the conversation was leading until Edward mentioned Justin. In that moment the pieces began to fall into place and pity stirred within his chest for the young woman whose face was bright with expectation. Edward was leading her down a garden path to secure his own desires. Rashly, Anthony considered warning Jamelyn but knew he would pay dearly for such disloyalty to Edward. It was best for him to hold his tongue and hope that all would turn out well. Anthony Godfrey had never been a coward, but in dealing with Edward of England it was best for all concerned to be prudent with one's actions. Especially when the king's heart was involved. Since returning to England, Anthony had learned of Edward's desire for Anne of Chester and knew the reasons behind his monarch's actions in ordering Justin to marry. Anthony also knew at that very moment Edward was scheming once more to gain his lady love.

Suddenly a small smile crept across Anthony's sensuous lips as he remembered his own thwarted plan. Perhaps Edward's cunning would serve the same purpose and bring Jamelyn and Justin together.

Unaware of the direction of the two men's thoughts, Jamelyn's smooth brow furrowed as she looked from Edward to Anthony and back again, bewildered. "Justin? I would gladly do battle with him if that is your wish."

Amused at Jamelyn's reply, Edward threw back his dark head, his laughter filling the huge chamber. Tears glistened in his eyes as he tried to regain his composure and weave his web even tighter about Jamelyn. "It it not Lord St. Claire I want you to do battle with, my lady. It is the Lady Anne of Chester. If I consider granting your request, you will have to do two things: you will pledge your loyalty to me to insure peace and then you will seduce your husband away from Anne."

Stunned by Edward's proposal, Jamelyn gaped in disbelief at England's monarch. She was willing to give her loyalty to regain her land, but she had not expected his last request, nor was she able to fulfill it since Justin St. Claire loathed her.

Seeing her look of shock, Edward leaned forward and took Jamelyn's hand in his own. "My lady, is this too much to ask to restore your heritage? I ask only a small thing and afterward you will be free." Edward's voice was low and cajoling as he stared into Jamelyn's pale face, his dark eyes urging her to obey his wishes.

The midday sun streamed through the tall, lead-paned window, making Jamelyn's gilded mane shimmer with fiery highlights as she slowly shook her head. "'Tis impossible. Justin would never turn to me, even if I were willing. He feels nothing for me because I do not possess the charm and beauty of a lady. If I arouse any emotion within him it is contempt."

Edward pressed Jamelyn's fingers to his lips, placing a gentle kiss upon them as he murmured soothingly. "My lady, have you not looked into a mirror? You are beautiful. If Lady Anne did not already hold my heart I would surely grant it to you."

Jamelyn's lightly tinted cheeks deepened in hue and she lowered her eyes away from Edward's intense gaze. She was embarrassed by his unexpected flattery. Shaking her head again, she said, "Nay, I cannot do it. Even if I succeeded in doing what you ask, Justin would never release me from our marriage."

Sensing his near victory, Edward artfully placed the last gossamer-thin webbing about Jamelyn as he said, "He will not know the woman he falls in love with is his wife. From the description he gave of you, I would not have believed one so lovely could be the same person of whom he spoke when he returned from Scotland."

Edward's words stung. The wound Justin had inflicted before leaving Raven's Keep lay open and the king's words were like salt as they burned into Jamelyn's tender pride. Instinctively, her chin rose in the air and her eyes smoldered with green fire as she looked once more at Edward. She pursed her lips angrily as the thought of her husband's mocking disdain. Justin St. Claire deserved to be punished and England's king was giving her the opportunity. If it were at all possible, she would make Justin fall in love with her and then trample that love beneath her boot before she returned to Raven's Keep.

Jamelyn's tone reflected the bitterness that welled within her against her husband. "To regain Raven's Keep, I will try to do as you ask, Sire, but I'm afraid I know little of such things as seduction." She glanced at Anthony, an apologetic smile touching her lips fleetingly as she continued, "Though Sir Godfrey did do his best to teach me how to become a lady."

Edward's smile was triumphant as he looked at Jamelyn. "All that will be necessary will be provided. By the time Lord St. Claire returns, Lady St. Claire will be an entirely different person."

Jamelyn lowered her eyes to her hands so as to appear acquiescent to Edward's statement, but thought, I might look different, but I shall always be Jamelyn of Cregan and you had best beware of that fact.

Chapter 9

Jamelyn was bored nearly to tears. It had been five long, monotonous weeks since she had agreed to do Edward's bidding and she had yet to see her husband. The king had kept Jamelyn secluded in luxurious accommodations in the upper ward of the castle, explaining his sequestering her away from other members of his household as his way of insuring that Jamelyn was properly groomed before being presented to his court.

Jamelyn had to admit that during her stay at Windsor she had not spent her days idly. Nearly every waking hour had been under the instruction of a tutor whom Edward had employed to see Jamelyn's rough edges well honed. From daylight to well into the evening the tutor smoothed and polished Jamelyn from head to toe, from speech to manners, from the way she walked to the way she ate. A lady's maid had also been acquired to see to her physical grooming as well.

Little remained in evidence of the young heiress of Raven's Keep who had entered the palace in a wrinkled satin gown.

She was clothed now in silk and satin kirtles with velvet and damask cotehardies and sideless gowns worn with elaborate hip girdles. Tippets of exquisite embroidery which reached to the floor were attached to her skin-tight sleeves, making one think of a great, plumed bird. The kirtles' sleeves were fastened with dozens of tiny pearl buttons and beneath the fitchets in the front of the skirt a silk purse with gold embroidery hung from a narrow inside belt. Soft leather slippers with pointed toes rested upon her feet; her riding boots had long since been thrown out, for no lady of standing would dare to wear such uncouth things upon her person.

The only difference between Jamelyn's fashionable attire and that of any other lady of court were the higher necklines of her gowns. The mode of the day was a very low neckline, but Jamelyn's scar prevented her from adopting the fashion. Along with the other adornments had come the gold netting that covered her shimmering auburn tresses, which were braided over each ear in the ram's horn style.

Looking upon the elegantly attired young woman, no one could have imagined it had been less than a year since she had abhorred the thought of putting feminine clothing upon her back. Only within the depths of her being, hidden from the eye, did the same Jamelyn of Cregan exist. It was the Jamelyn of old who was vexed at the length of time she had been kept a prisoner within the walls of Windsor.

With a deep, hungry yearning to be free of the restrictions placed upon her, Jamelyn leaned her gilded head against the smooth wood facing of the window and stared out over the eighteen-hundred-acre Great Park of Windsor. Her emerald gaze swept over the thick, deep-green forest toward the distant horizon. Her longing for Raven's Keep gnawed away at her patience. A rueful little sigh escaped her softly tinted lips as she wondered if her foolish behavior would ever allow her to see that precious land again. Over the weeks of strict discipline, keeping her volatile temper under control as best she could while Edward's tutors polished her for his intrigues, Jamelyn's doubts had begun to eat away her resolve to see Justin punished. In her present frame of mind all she wanted was to be free to return to the black granite walls of her home.

Her anger had cooled and now Edward's scheme had become distasteful to Jamelyn's naturally honest temperament. The long wait had given her time to reflect on the monarch's devious politics, and she had come to realize that she was embroiled in nothing more than a petty game of seduction, and that had not been her purpose in coming to Windsor.

She had not worked all through the cold winter months to learn to be a lady in order to help fill Edward's bed with his paramour. If that was the type of life the people of the king's court led, it was not for her. All she wanted was to regain her home.

Revenge still lay simmering within her mind, but she preferred a different method of extracting it. The irony of her situation made Jamelyn's soft lips curve upward in a cynical little smile. She had come to Windsor to petition the king to free her from her husband, only to find that she would have to gain Justin's love to be rid of him.

What he asks is irrational, Jamelyn thought as she turned away from the beautiful view and her stormy green eyes scanned the elegant interior of her quarters. Had I been able to gain Justin's love, I would not be here now.

Shocked by her own betraying thoughts, she began to pace the thick-carpeted floor. Folding her arms over her breast, she firmly pressed her lips together, an angry sparkle shimmering in her eyes as she fumed to herself, Nay, I don't want Justin's love. All I want is Raven's Keep. I need no man's boots beneath my bed to make me happy.

Engrossed with her musings, Jamelyn failed to hear Edward's entrance until he spoke. "By the expression on your face, my lady, I'm glad you do not have a sword close at hand. 'Twould be too dangerous."

Startled, Jamelyn swung about to face the king of England. Belatedly remembering her manners, she made a low, graceful curtsy to the English monarch. "Sire, forgive me, but I did not hear you enter."

Pleased that he could no longer hear the soft Scottish

burr in her voice, Edward smiled as he settled his lean frame in a comfortable chair and crossed his silk-clad legs casually before him. Resting his elbows on the chair, his graceful hands splayed wide, the king tapped the manicured tips together thoughtfully as he studied Jamelyn. "From the look on your face, you would not have noticed if all of my troops had stormed into your chamber. What thoughts bedevil your mind so deeply, my lady?"

With ill-concealed resentment, Jamelyn looked at Edward. Her small chin jutted out petulantly as she said, "I do not like being kept in a silken prison, Sire. I grow weary of my confinement and the wait."

Edward's fingers toyed with his pointed beard, his gaze never wavering from her face as he said, "Then it is my command that you wait no longer. Tonight you will meet your husband and if all goes well, you will receive all that I may grant."

Jamelyn's thick-fringed eyes widened in surprise. "Justin has returned?"

Nodding, Edward said, "Aye, he returned only an hour ago. I was sure you had seen him ride through the gates, but alas, you were too preoccupied with your scheming to be reunited with him to know that your desire was so close at hand."

Edward's humor was lost on Jamelyn. Her misgivings over their planned ruse grew stronger by the moment. With fingers uneasily working the tiny buttons of one sleeve, she moistened her dry lips with the tip of her tongue and took a deep breath. "Sire, please release me from this intrigue. Let me return to Scotland."

An angry light entered Edward's dark eyes and his lips firmed into a narrow line as he regarded Jamelyn with calm deliberation. "So you do not honor your word. Like all Scots I have met, you speak brave vows until you have to face the test of battle; then you cringe as the first sword is drawn. You disappoint me, my lady. I had thought you stronger than that."

Edward's words bit deeply into Jamelyn's pride. Her back stiffened as she squared her shoulders defiantly. Her eyes sparkled with ire. "We Scots have never fled from battle, as the English dead can attest." Jamelyn's words were laced with venom, her anger making her forget the power Edward held over her. Within his bejeweled hand lay her life or death.

A white line etched Edward's tightly-held lips as he looked at Jamelyn. His square jaw grew rigid as he suppressed the urge to throttle her with his bare hands. His temper burned white-hot within him and it took all of his willpower to refrain from violence. Taking a deep breath to compose himself, Edward glared at her, his cold eyes seeming to rivet her to the carpeted floor as he rose from the chair and towered over her. With his fists held tightly clenched at his sides, he strode to the open window and breathed deeply of the cool air to try to calm his rage. He needed this woman if he was to gain his desire, but when he did, woe be unto anyone who stood in his way to see her punished for her impudence. No one spoke to Edward III in such a manner and went unscathed.

Holding his emotions in tight rein, Edward turned once more to face Jamelyn. He smiled, but no warmth could be seen in the gesture. His conciliatory tone and words were belied by a silent threat. "My lady, it is best that we lay aside this vendetta. It has lasted much too long. We are no longer enemies. Out of what I ask of you, we both will gain. Does Raven's Keep and your freedom mean so little to you?"

A chill of apprehension crept up Jamelyn's spine to raise the silken strands of gilded hair on the nape of her neck as she looked into Edward's hostile eyes. She understood the message he conveyed and knew if she disobeyed his wishes, all would be lost, including her freedom. The king would see her locked away in the darkest dungeon. Her shoulders slumped in defeat as she bowed her head and her voice was low as she said, "They are my life."

Edward's lips curled smugly in triumph. "Then I will personally escort you to the ball tonight. The queen is once more large with child and has withdrawn from court affairs until after her delivery. Tonight, my lady, you will grace my arm with your loveliness."

Feeling completely defenseless, Jamelyn did not look at Edward as she answered tonelessly, "I would be honored, Sire."

The scent of perfume permeated the hot evening air as the crowd swirled to the soft strains of music floating down from the minstrels' gallery. Jewels flashed with brilliance in the light from the crystal chandeliers and the swish of satin could be heard as the women twirled about their partners. The sight reminded Jamelyn of a rainbow seen through the shimmering mist over the lochs of Scotland. The human peacocks displayed their finery to the peahens. Like the mating dance of those flamboyant birds, the ladies did likewise as they curtsied before the king's courtiers.

Upon Edward's and Jamelyn's entrance to the ballroom the music ceased and all eyes turned to the English king. The ladies dropped deep curtsies while the men bowed respectfully from the waist and made a graceful leg. Edward smiled warmly at the assembly and waved his hand signalling for the music to resume before he led Jamelyn forward.

Many speculative glances were cast in their direction. Surprise and regret were reflected on many of the women's faces at the sight of Edward's lovely companion. With Queen Phillipa in seclusion awaiting the delivery of her fifth child, they had hoped to draw the monarch's attention. The expression playing over the faces of Edward's courtiers was entirely different as their gazes swept over the ravishing beauty at his side.

The guests stepped back to make a wide circle as Edward bowed to Jamelyn and then led her gracefully through the first set. The shining surface of the parquet floor reflected the images of the handsome king clad in rich, ruby velvet embroidered with golden threads and his alluring companion in a kirtle and cotehardie of vivid emerald green to match her startling eyes. A sideless gown of gold velvet embroidered with emerald silk about the hem and an emerald-studded gold girdle completed her magnificent attire.

At the beginning of the dance Jamelyn felt awkward, unused to the movements required to do the proper steps. However, the soft, lyrical sounds of the music soon soothed her taut nerves and she let it take her mind away from the staring eyes. Her feet moved of their own accord as she became absorbed by the lilting sound and slow, sensuous movements. Enjoying the peaceful feeling it created within her, Jamelyn smiled up at her companion. Edward's breath caught in his throat and his heart seemed to beat erratically for a moment as he realized the true extent of Jamelyn's beauty. Had he not coveted Anne of Chester for so long that she had become an obsession with him, Edward would have eagerly wooed the Lady St. Claire to his bed. But that was not to be, for Anne filled Edward's mind until no other woman could ease his desire. She was like an opiate in his blood and only she could satisfy his craving.

Edward returned Jamelyn's smile warmly. His dark eyes glowed with secret delight. He sensed his triumph would soon be in hand, for he had seen Justin St. Claire pause in his conversation with Anne to watch them dance. Edward's keen eye had not missed the interested expression that crossed his knight's handsome features as Justin's gaze swept over Jamelyn. Edward could not contain his glee and throwing back his dark head, laughed aloud with the pure joy that swept over him.

The last strains of music died in the warm night air as Edward bowed to Jamelyn and with much aplomb led her toward his courtiers. A congenial smile remained on his shapely lips as he introduced Jamelyn as Lady Catherine Michaels from Hindon in Wessex.

Jamelyn could not suppress her own smile at the gallants' eagerness as each pressed forward for an introduction. But the smile froze on her lips and she tensed as her eyes came to rest on her husband and the beautiful, black-haired woman at his side. She knew without anyone telling her that the woman was Anne of Chester. Anne was an extraordinarily beautiful woman. Even from a distance, Jamelyn could see that her complexion was flawless and her cheeks were tinted a delicate rose. Thick, black lashes surrounded vivid blue eyes that narrowed in irritation as Justin's attention was drawn away from her. Her red, bow-shaped mouth pouted peevishly as she placed a possessive hand upon Justin's arm and said something to make him smile and return his attention to her once more.

Knowing well Edward's intention toward the lady, Jamelyn drew in a sharp breath and braced herself for her first encounter with her husband in months. Instinctively, she held her chin regally in the air and straightened her back as Edward extracted them from his eager courtiers and led her across the shining floor to Justin and Anne. Justin bowed as Anne swept Edward a graceful curtsy, the action causing her full breast to come precariously close to spilling from the low neckline of her sapphire gown.

The appreciative glance Justin cast in the direction of the voluptuous view presented to him and the king rankled Jamelyn unreasonably. Though she adamantly vowed she did not want Justin St. Claire, she could not suppress the twinge of jealousy his small action aroused. Irritated by her own reaction, Jamelyn placed the blame on her own feminine vanity, something she would have died before admitting a few months earlier. Silently she cursed her own stupidity. I'm not jealous, she fumed. It is only the men's foolish gawking at such a display that infuriates me.

Edward smiled at his favored knight and gave a regal nod as he said, "Justin, I'm glad you have returned. How did your mission go?" Though he spoke to Justin, Edward's eyes never strayed far from the beautiful Anne.

The pleasant smile faded from Justin's lips. "I'm sorry to say, Majesty, I failed to catch the raiders. Like all vermin they go into their holes when they sense a trap has been set."

Jamelyn's lips twitched almost imperceptibly at the thought of Royce outwitting Justin. She could feel Edward's muscles tense beneath her hand and sensed his annoyance with his favored knight. That added to Jamelyn's pleasure.

Justin did not fail to note the slight movement of Jamelyn's rose-tinted lips. Her expression reminded him of a cat that had managed to lick up all the cream and now stood preening with satisfaction at the deed. He assumed the young beauty was pleased with the honor Edward had bestowed upon her that evening by escorting her to the ball. Nearly every woman at court would have strangled the others for that same privilege. At least this young beauty had not openly flaunted her victory over the other ladies, though her eyes held a glint of smugness in their bewitching, emerald depths.

As if drawn by some magnetic force, Justin's gaze traveled once more to the beautifully molded lips that curved ever so slightly into an enticing smile and with a sudden jolt, he realized he had been imagining the feel of those soft petals of flesh beneath his own hard mouth.

Edward's keen eyes missed little. He noted Justin's interest and chuckled silently to himself. All was going as he had expected. "Lord St. Claire and Lady Anne, let me introduce Lady Catherine Michaels from Wessex. She has just come to Windsor at my invitation."

"It is a pleasure, Lady Michaels. You honor us with your beauty," Justin said gallantly as he bowed over Jamelyn's hand.

Though Lady Anne spoke pleasantly, murmuring polite words of welcome, her attitude was more reserved and her blue eyes flickered with fiery glints. Like those of an animal sensing another encroaching upon its territory, her invisible bristles rose against Jamelyn from the first moment of their introduction. She wanted no other woman at court who could rival her beauty or capture Justin's eye as this young tart seemed to be doing.

She sent a silent, heated message as she looked at Jamelyn, and the battle lines were drawn. Jamelyn accepted the challenge and shot her a haughty glance in return before smiling sweetly up at Justin. To further annoy Anne, she said in a honeyed voice laced with lush seduction, "You are most kind, sir."

The scorching look that had passed between the two women did not escape Edward. Taking Lady Anne's hand, he bowed. "My lady, will you allow me the privilege of this dance?"

"I am honored, Sire," Anne said as her withering gaze swept over Jamelyn, daring her to trespass on her domain in her absence.

Never one to back away when the gauntlet had been thrown, Jamelyn gazed up into her husband's handsome face, her own expression provocative. With the invitation so clear, Justin forgot Anne and proffered his black velvet arm to Jamelyn. Lost in the fathomless depths of her sparkling eyes, Justin felt his voice go husky as he said, "Shall we dance, my lady?"

Jamelyn gracefully accepted his arm and let him sweep her out onto the dance floor. A strange tingling sensation sped along her spine at the touch of his hand about her waist and in confusion, she blushed as she looked up into his intense gaze.

As if mesmerized, Justin could not draw his eyes away from her lovely features. Lady Michaels's vivid beauty overshadowed that of other women Justin had known. Even Anne's sultry loveliness could not compare to the fiery allure Catherine Michaels possessed. He felt himself involuntarily drawn to her like the old adage, a moth to the flame. He was intrigued by the mysterious charm he sensed about her and longed to explore until he knew all her secrets.

Though they had met only moments before, Justin felt as if he had known Catherine Michaels at some other time and place. His dark-winged brows knit slightly as he searched his memory to no avail. The feeling kept niggling at his mind but he knew if he had ever met the beautiful woman before he would have remembered her. After this night he also knew he would never be able to forget her, his attraction was too intense. He had not felt this way about a woman since the first time he had seen Jessica, his late wife.

All of Justin's senses were attuned to Lady Michaels. The feel of her skin, the light scent of lavender that wafted up to his nostrils, sent flickering embers to ignite his desire. The curve of her delicate mouth as she smiled with pleasure at the dance, her graceful movements—all were branded within Justin's mind, simmering his passion for a woman he had known for less than ten minutes.

Justin's silence and intense scrutiny made Jamelyn uneasy. A prickle of apprehension crept up her neck and she missed a step and nearly stumbled. Justin swiftly came to her aid and placed his wide-palmed hand beneath her elbow, steadying her. Nervously she wet her lips with the tip of her tongue as she gazed up at her husband's concerned face. She knew she could not go on without knowing whether or not Justin had recognized her and her voice mirrored her anxiety as she asked, "Sir, why do you stare? Have I offended you in some manner?"

Justin's soft laughter was absorbed within the noise of the chamber. "Hardly, my lady. Forgive me if I stare, but I find it hard to keep my eyes from your beauty."

Jamelyn's cheeks deepened to a lovely dusty rose and she lowered her thick lashes to hide the confusion that swept over her at his compliment. Justin's next movement drew her startled gaze to his face once more as his fingers firmed on her elbow and he led her through the double doors onto the terrace. Her eyes were full of questions and a hint of fear as he continued down the flagged steps and into the rose garden beyond.

Justin's pace did not slacken as he maneuvered her along the gravel path to a small, vine-covered alcove. His action had been so unexpected that Jamelyn was unable to find her voice until they reached their destination. Taking a deep breath, she began to reprimand him, "My lord," but her words were cut off as he pulled her abruptly into his arms and kissed her. His lips devoured the petal softness of her mouth and to her surprise, her lips opened to let him explore the sweet cavern beyond. When Justin's passionate kiss ended, she drew in an unsteady breath and placed her hand above her fluttering heart, breathlessly looking up into her husband's dark features.

A wry smile curved his sensuous lips as he said, "I have been wanting to do that since the first moment my eyes rested upon your delicate lips. Forgive my rash behavior, my lady, but I could fight the urge no longer." Tipping up her small chin with one long, bronzed finger, Justin gazed at Jamelyn, holding her transfixed as he continued, "I know we have just met, but I feel as if I have known you for more than just a short while."

Fear made Jamelyn's breath catch in her throat as he unwittingly hit upon her secret. Swallowing back the nervous tremble in her voice, she said, "I sensed the same thing, my lord."

A hint of humor touched his deep voice. "Justin. I think the last minutes have ended any formality between us, Catherine."

Jamelyn could feel the heat rise to her cheeks and nervously looked away from his penetrating gaze. The full moon's silvery light illuminated her perfect features as she stared pensively out into the lovely spring night. Things had transpired too quickly and she had been unprepared for his advances, which still made her insides quiver so oddly. The touch of Justin's finger as it traced her sculpted cheek before drawing her to face him once more, again sent the strange tingling through her. With her eyes wide and uncertain she gazed up into his concerned face.

"Have I frightened you, Catherine?" he asked.

Jamelyn's voice quavered slightly. "Nay, but I think it is time for us to return to the palace. The king will be looking for me."

Tiny lines etched Justin's smooth brow as he looked down at Jamelyn and placed his strong hands upon her shoulders to impede her possible flight. "Are you telling me there is more between you and Edward than just friendship? Is that your reason for visiting Windsor?"

For a moment Justin's words puzzled Jamelyn. There was no friendship between the English king and herself. She paused before her eyes grew wide as she comprehended his meaning. Her tone was adamant as she said, "Nay, there is nothing between Edward and myself."

Relieved, Justin smiled. He had feared her answer would be different and knew that if Edward had set his mind on Lady Michaels, he would have to put his own feelings aside. "I'm sorry, Catherine, but I had to know. When may I see you again?"

Jamelyn glanced up at her husband uneasily. Very much aware of the touch of his hands, she shook her head as if trying to clear it of all the new and frightening sensations that were running rampant within her. "I do not know."

Leaning closer, Justin peered into her eyes, his breath warm upon her cheek as he whispered, "You feel it, too, don't you, Catherine? Perhaps it is something decreed by fate, but I have to see you again. Say you will come here after the ball is over."

Jamelyn rapidly shook her head. Her heart pounded erratically within her breast; it was too soon and she needed time to sort out the alien feelings Justin's presence caused within her. "Nay, I can't."

Justin's thumbs met at the base of Jamelyn's slender throat and caressed the soft, sensitive flesh there as he gazed into her eyes. "I do not believe in love at first sight, Catherine, but I feel something for you I can't explain. Please do not torture me in this way. There is an excitement between us that we cannot fight. Come to me this night, Catherine. Do not deny me." Justin's voice was deep and husky, as much a caress as his fingers upon her flesh.

The velvety soft tone mesmerized Jamelyn, as did the urgent look within the depths of his blue eyes. A thrill of excitement ran along her slender back to where his hands rested warm and inviting upon her shoulders. Against her better judgment, the words seemed drawn from her, and she nodded. "I will come."

Justin's lips curved with pleasure as he pulled Jamelyn once more into his arms and tipped up her small chin for his kiss. His lips were gentle, savoring each moment to store up until he could taste them again.

The pulse in Jamelyn's throat beat rapidly as Justin released her and took her arm to escort her back to the palace. Before leading her once more through the double doors, he placed a brief kiss upon her temple. The blush that had begun a moment before deepened into crimson as they stepped back into the ballroom and came face to face with Edward and Anne.

A knowing smirk played about the king's lips as he eyed first Jamelyn and then Justin. She quickly looked away from his smug face, only to see Anne's fine features openly hostile. Her blue eyes glittered with malice as she looked coldly at Jamelyn. Her bow-shaped lips were pursed into a tight, angry line as she placed her hand possessively on Justin's sleeve. "I'm afraid I do not feel well, Justin. Will you be so kind as to ask our leave of His Majesty so that I may be excused for the evening?"

Edward gave a negligent wave of his bejeweled hand as he smiled at Anne. "You are excused, my lady. I would not have your beauty marred by illness. You must take care." Edward's tone caressed each word and his gaze simmered as he looked at Lady Anne. To his satisfaction, she bestowed a winsome smile upon him as she curtsied. "You are most kind, Majesty." Anne glanced at Justin to see if he had noted her light flirtation and was further infuriated to find his eyes once more upon Catherine Michaels.

Edward wanted to laugh aloud at the expression on Anne's face, but suppressed the urge as he took Jamelyn's arm. "My lady, would you care to dance?" With that he swept Jamelyn once more out onto the polished dance floor, leaving a fuming Anne and a jealous Justin behind.

Chapter 10

Moodily, Justin drummed his long, brown fingers against
the smooth surface of the chair arm as he watched Anne
pace back and forth across the carpeted floor. Usually the
sight of her voluptuous body so cunningly revealed by her
diaphanous gown would have inspired passion, but tonight
it only served the opposite purpose.

Justin understood the reason for his lack of response to
Anne's sultry seduction. It was branded upon his mind and
his senses: Catherine Michaels. The very thought of that
petite beauty sent his blood rushing in hot currents through
his veins and it was all he could do to remain seated and
listen to Anne's tirade. She was miffed by his lack of ardor
and her beautiful face was marred by her sullen, angry
expression. Justin had tried to remain patient, but as the
minutes ticked by and he thought of the lovely young woman
who awaited him in the moonlit garden, his vexation grew.
Justin did not want to leave Anne in such a state — too many
years of friendship lay in their past — however, he could not
abide much more of her tantrum.

Noting Justin's distant air, Anne ceased her furious pacing. With arms folded beneath her breast to help emphasize their creamy fullness, she turned to him, ready to resume the argument; but before she could open her mouth, Justin held up his hand. Disgusted with himself for listening to her harangue and tired of Anne's possessive behavior, he ran his fingers through his hair as he said, "Enough, Anne. I have listened to your caviling too much already. You do not own me and I will have no more of your proprietary attitude."

Startled by Justin's abrupt command, for he had never spoken to her in such a manner before, she pouted and her blue eyes misted with tears. Sensing all her arguments had not worked, she changed her strategy. Kneeling beside Justin's muscular thighs, she pressed her breast against them, wrapping her arms about his waist, and gazed up at him with glistening eyes. "Justin, I do not mean to seem so possessive. It is only my love for you that causes me to act the shrew. I can't stand to see you with another woman." Anne's voice was soft and impassioned. "I have loved you for so long, Justin. You broke my heart when you took Jessica to wife, but still I wanted no other. After you lost Jessica I thought you might turn to me, but as time passed and you did not ask me to be your wife, I accepted that and was satisfied with having your love without marriage. Then you married that Scottish heathen and once more I have to share you—but I will not also share you with Catherine Michaels."

Justin's fingers were not gentle as he freed himself from Anne's clinging arms and stood. A telltale twitch in his cleanshaven cheek revealed his irritation. Testily, he strode across the room and stared out into the warm night. Anne's words served to remind him that he was not free and could never possess Catherine even if he did love her. His life was already bound to the perverse young woman in Scotland. The image of his wife's stubborn little face floated into Justin's mind and involuntarily he compared her with Anne. Jamelyn would never stoop to tears to sway him, but then, she would never possess the allure of Catherine Michaels.

Justin's gaze traveled over the black rooftop to the star-studded sky as he thought, What I would not give to have a wife with Lady Michaels's beauty and the courage and spirit of Jamelyn of Cregan. The thought only deepened Justin's already black mood. He was resigned to the fact that it would never be and he still had to resolve his problem with Anne. He did not want to hurt her, but neither could he let her demands sway him. Turning, he found Anne standing only a few feet away, her eyes large, liquid pools as her teeth held her full bottom lip to stay its trembling. Justin's expression softened and his voice was calm and soothing as he said, "I have told you, Anne, you do not own me. I am married and I fear Edward will not let me dissolve my marriage. This bond will help bring the peace in Scotland he desires now that he is faced with war with France. It is useless for us to argue over something neither of us can change."

Exasperated that her ploy did not work, Anne's hot temper flared again and she stamped her silk-slippered foot and crossed her arms over her breast. Her blue eyes sparkled with fiery rage as she hissed, "Justin, I will not have it. I have done too much to have your love. You belong to me and must make Edward see your marriage is a mistake. I have tried to be reasonable, but now my patience is at an end. I saw the look in your eye tonight when you gazed at Lady Michaels. I will not share you with her any more than I will with your wife. You have to decide between us, Justin; until you do I will not come to your bed again."

Justin's own simmering temper burst into flames and his eyes were like cold granite as his gaze swept over Anne from the top of her head to the tips of her small feet. His lips narrowed into a thin, angry line and his voice sent an icy chill down her spine as he said, "Is that an ultimatum, my lady? Do you say your love for me rests only in possessing my name as well as my fortune? You know well, sweet Anne, that I do not like to be ordered about."

Sensing her mistake immediately, Anne tried desperately to make amends. Crossing the short space that separated them, she put her arms about Justin's rigid body. Tilting her face up, her lips were only inches from his as she said, "Justin, do you love me so little? I have given up the king's bed to remain faithful to you. If you persist you will force me to turn to Edward. I will have no choice."

Through half-lowered lids, Justin's glacial gaze studied Anne's flawless face impersonally before his fingers curled about her arms and forcibly removed them from about his waist. A bleak, gnawing suspicion settled in the pit of his stomach as he realized the reason behind Edward's command for him to marry. The king wanted Anne and knew he could not have her if Justin was free. Justin's hopes for his future also dimmed. Edward would never let him be released from his marriage.

An intense, burning rage ripped through Justin's gut at the king's duplicity and he wanted to lash out and hurt someone. His lips curled cruelly in a derisive smile, his flinty gaze mocking as he said scornfully, "You could not have Edward's name either if you go to his bed. Will you refuse the man you profess to love and then seek out the king to whore for him to gain his favor?"

Anne recoiled from Justin's cruel words as if she had been slapped. She placed her hand against her cheek as her eyes narrowed. "How dare you speak in such a manner to me after all the years I have given you my love and have received nothing in return except a small pittance of your affections. I have accepted the crumbs of your love for too long. First you take the sniveling little Jessica and now think to have me wait until you appease your wanderlust once more. Nay, I'll not wait for you again."

Justin's face drained of color as his fingers bit into Anne's shoulder and he shook her. "Do not speak of Jessica," he ground out between clenched teeth. "I explained long ago my feeling for her. It is your own foolishness if you think I could ever change."

Terrified by the look on Justin's face, Anne fought against his brutal hold. Freeing herself, she rubbed her bruised flesh, new and real tears glistening in her blue eyes as she backed away from him. "Was it foolish to hope you would finally turn to me once Jessica was gone?" Anne's voice trembled as she looked up into Justin's angry face.

Seeing her fright, Justin's anger vanished as quickly as it had come. He wearily shook his head. "Anne, I have never made you any promises. Had it not been for the murdering Scots I would still have Jessica and this conversation would not now be taking place." For one brief moment Justin's handsome face looked haunted by memories.

Anne could not abide the look and turned her back to keep Justin from seeing the bitterness that welled within her eyes. It was like a sore that had never healed within her heart. Her own memories assaulted her and she pressed her fingers to her temples as if trying to force them away.

Anne had been obsessed with Justin since she was fifteen and had freely given her virginity to him in the hope she could sway him away from Jessica. Her efforts had proved futile and his rejection was like gall in her throat. Its acridity had settled deep within Anne, bringing forth a violent hatred for anyone Justin loved. She had despised Jessica, but had pretended to share Justin's grief so that she could comfort him and further ingratiate herself to him.

Justin St. Claire was the only thing that had been denied Anne of Chester in her life and her obsession for him had deepened over the years. She would do anything to assure that he would be hers.

Justin regretted his brutish actions. Wrapping his arms about Anne, he placed a kiss on her tousled, bowed head and then leaned his own raven curls against her shimmering locks. "Anne, we have been friends far too long and you have always known my feelings. Nothing has changed."

Anne's small hands balled into tight fists at her sides as she slowly nodded. "Aye, nothing has changed." She waited for Justin to speak, but only silence greeted her. She felt another light kiss on her hair and then heard the door of her chamber open and close as Justin left her. Great, angry tears cascaded from beneath Anne's tightly closed lids, making a silvery path down her cheeks. She pressed her lips firmly together to stem the shriek of rage that threatened to engulf her as she thought bitterly, Nothing has changed, Justin, nor will it!

Unware of the turmoil her presence had created between the two people only a few corridors away from her chamber, Jamelyn leaned against the stone balustrade of the balcony and stared up into the twinkling blue velvet sky. Absently, her fingers traced the thin, pink scar that marred the smooth skin of her shoulder just beneath the neckline of her kirtle. Her mood was pensive. She caught her soft lower lip between her even teeth as her gaze traveled to the silvery garden below.

Soon she was to meet Justin. The ball had ended and the time drew near, but she could not force her feet to move in the direction her heart seemed to urge her to. "What is happening to me?" she asked the calm, moonlit night, but no answer came to ease the baffling emotions that swept over her or the tautness of her nerves.

Unable to look at the lovely scene a moment longer, Jamelyn withdrew back into her chamber. Without realizing her own agitated actions, she began to pace the room like a felon who has been sentenced to the gibbet. She felt torn between heaven and hell. She had come to Windsor to free herself from Justin St. Claire and now found herself wanting to run down the winding stairs to fly into his strong arms. Jamelyn's cheeks burned at the memory of his lips upon her soft mouth. A deep, searing heat seemed to center in the pit of her abdomen and quiver there with a life of its own as it sent out urgent messages that said, Go, go to Justin.

Bewildered by the myriad of emotions sweeping over her, her steps faltered and she pressed her tightly clasped hands to her lips as she bowed her gilded head and closed her eyes. She tried to fight the strange sensations that clenched her insides like a vise of steel. "No, I will not go," she said to the stillness of her chamber. "If I succumb to these female stirrings, I will be lost." As the words passed from her lips a small voice echoed in her mind, But it is the king's order. If you do not go to Justin, Raven's Keep will be lost.

The conflicting emotions battled fiercely within Jamelyn

as she again paced across the chamber for what seemed like the hundredth time. The clock struck three tinkling chimes in the distance, and her hand involuntarily reached for her velvet mantle. Tying it securely about her shoulders, she walked from the chamber and down the elaborate staircase. She told herself she was only doing the king's bidding, yet a weakness invaded her body and tiny flaming sparks seemed to ignite her blood as she stepped out into the cool morning air.

The breath caught in her throat as her eyes rested upon the tall silhouette at the end of the graveled path. The moon illuminated Justin's raven head, streaking the blue-black strands with silver. Her heart fluttered painfully in her breast as her emerald gaze took in her husband's wide shoulders and traveled down his sinewy frame, absorbing the pure beauty of his masculine form. Jamelyn had to admit he was the most perfectly formed man she had ever seen. Justin exuded strength from every sinew of his powerful body and against her own will she was drawn to him. She could no longer fight her attraction to him. The warrior in her respected his strength while the woman was fascinated by his masculine sexuality.

On silent feet Jamelyn moved forward and paused a few feet away from her husband. Justin St. Claire was her enemy, her mind told her, but the gentle ache within her belly made her crave things she could not truly comprehend. Staunchly, Jamelyn quelled the feeling. She had a purpose and could not let her feminine body overrule her mind. She had to be strong for Raven's Keep, though she knew her body was weak in its defense against Justin's touch.

The swish of satin alerted Justin to Jamelyn's presence and he turned to face her. The pale light of the moon revealed his chiseled features, highlighting the flat planes of his brow and shadowing the intensity of his eyes. Jamelyn could see the gleam of his white teeth as he smiled and came forward.

He took her hand within his strong grasp and raised it to his sensual mouth. His lips caressed the tender flesh of her palm, sending shivers along her spine, and his words were full of emotion as he murmured, "Catherine, I feared you would not come."

The deep velvet of his voice sent fiery tentacles racing along every taut nerve in Jamelyn's body and she quickly withdrew her hand from his to try to regain some measure of control over herself. "I should not have come." Her own voice was husky from the feelings that constricted her throat and she turned away to avoid his intense scrutiny.

A shock of electricity passed through her as Justin's strong arms encircled her and pulled her back against his chest. "Why, Catherine?" he asked as he inhaled her enticing scent.

Justin's nearness was too much for Jamelyn and she turned within his arms, placing her flat palms against his chest to press herself away from his sinewy body. "'Tis not right. We sneak here like thieves in the night after you have seen Lady Anne to her chamber."

Justin tilted her small chin up with his thumb so that he could gaze into her emerald eyes. "Anne means nothing to me. She is only an old friend."

Jamelyn searched Justin's face, her sparkling eyes anxious to find the sincerity of his words. Seeing nothing to belie them, a swift current of relief swept over her and she lowered her thick lashes over her eyes to hide the joy that surged through her.

Unconsciously a tiny, provocative smile teased the corners of her soft mouth and the temptation was too much for Justin to resist. His strong arms drew her easily against him and his lips captured hers. His kiss was gentle at first, tentatively exploring the honeyed softness, but as his passion caught fire, it deepened, his mouth becoming hard as he devoured her delicate sweetness. At her awkward, trembling response a thrill of pleasure swept over Justin and his arms tightened about her.

Without realizing her own actions Jamelyn's arms crept about his neck, her fingers curling into his raven hair; her body pressed closer, seeking to ease the tender ache that had once more flickered into life within her abdomen.

Some indistinct sound broke through Justin's passion-blurred senses and he released her lips reluctantly. His large hand captured the back of her gilded head and pressed it tenderly to his chest as his gaze swept over the shadowy garden. He saw nothing but he had the eerie sensation that their tryst was being observed with unfriendly eyes.

With a swiftness that drew a startled gasp from Jamelyn, Justin swept her up into his arms and strode from the garden. His elegant quarters lay only a short distance away. Her slight weight hindered his steps little and he ascended the curving stairway to his door, taking the well-worn stones two at a time.

Justin set her once more on her feet as he kicked the door closed behind them. The soft glow of the candles revealed her wide, alarmed eyes as she gazed up at him. A rush of tenderness swept over Justin. Catherine was so small and fragile and her eyes seemed to mirror her soul. He sensed her fright at his abrupt actions and gently placed his wide palm against her pale cheek, his eyes begging for her understanding. "I did not mean to frighten you, my love. All I wanted was to have a moment of privacy away from prying eyes. Forgive my impetuosity, but my chamber lay close at hand and I did not want to give you a chance to refuse my invitation by thinking I had something more devious in mind." Justin's lips curled into a beguiling smile as he tried to reassure her.

Jamelyn's soft laughter filled the room as she relaxed. Justin had touched upon the very thing she had feared. At the thought of her own foolishness a blush brightened her cheeks and she quickly avoided Justin's intense gaze. He chuckled, reading her thoughts, and he smiled at her embarrassment. "My lady, you cut me to the quick, but perhaps my reputation has preceded me. However, I would not like to disappoint you if you prefer I not act the gentleman."

The laughter died between them as Jamelyn's feathery lashes fluttered up and she looked into Justin's smoldering eyes. She swallowed the tightness in her throat and made a small step backward, placing a restraining hand upon Justin's chest. She tried to keep her voice light as she said, "Nay, sir. I prefer the gentleman."

Seeing the wary light flash into her eyes, Justin took the

hand from his chest and kissed the tip of each finger before leading her to a small chaise longue near the fire. Seating her gallantly, he tried to soothe her unease. "Then a gentleman I will remain, my lady." With that he turned to a nearby table and poured two crystal glasses of wine. Handing one to her, he settled his large frame at her side, casually crossing his muscular legs before him as he sipped the sweet burgundy. He did not speak. He wanted to give Catherine time to overcome the shyness he sensed he had aroused by his forward actions. Justin did not mind the peaceful moment. He was enjoying watching the firelight as it played over her fine features and he savored each moment of her loveliness. Her elegant profile seemed to tug at his memory, but he pushed the irritating sensation away. He did not want to think of anyone except the lovely Catherine Michaels.

The silence lengthened, the only sound in the chamber the popping and crackling of the fire in the grate. Jamelyn sipped her wine and kept her gaze upon the dancing flames to avoid looking at Justin. She knew what she was supposed to do but could not bring herself to obey Edward's command. The king had assumed it would not be difficult for Jamelyn to seduce her own husband since she bedded him before, but the king did not know the secret of her wedding night. Jamelyn had never lacked courage, but in this instance she felt timorous. She feared the unknown path her treacherous heart urged her to take. Perhaps if Edward had known of her lack of experience, he would not have asked this of her, but Jamelyn doubted it. The king was determined to have Anne and cared little for the agony Jamelyn was feeling because of his edict. Had anyone warned Jamelyn of the effect Justin would have on her, she would have quickly denied that she could feel anything for her enemy beyond hatred, but she was swiftly learning that her mind could still hate while her body became enthralled with the one her mind cried out against.

Justin's presence was more intoxicating to Jamelyn than the rich, ruby wine. Each moment made her more uncomfortably aware of his lean body. His silk-encased thigh accidentally brushed her leg and seemed to burn through the material of her gown. She drew in a deep breath and glanced uneasily at him to find his intense, smoldering eyes upon her. No words passed between them as he took the wine glass from her trembling hand and set it on the nearby table. Gently he tipped up her chin, the heat of his dark gaze searing into her soul, as his lips came down on hers.

Jamelyn's senses reeled. The touch of Justin's scorching kiss burned through the barrier she had tried to erect against him. It crumbled under the onslaught, releasing her feminine instincts from their prison. Where only tiny roots of sensation had taken sprout before in Justin's arms, they now burst into full growth, the buds flowering into exotic, sensual blooms.

With a volition all their own, Jamelyn's arms crept about Justin's corded neck, her fingers intimately entwining with the silken strands of his raven hair. His scalding kiss made her forget King Edward's order, forget her intention to free herself from Justin, and forget that he was her enemy. All was lost to the burning need Justin's touch aroused within her young body.

The intensity of Jamelyn's passionate nature had always been directed to other channels when she had forced her femininity into the background and strove to be a man. She had hidden the essence of female sensuality beneath a hard veneer, determinedly denying it even existed. Until now the surface had only been scratched, but under Justin's touch it cracked wide and deepened into a cavern that engulfed her.

Jamelyn responded in kind to each of Justin's caresses, innocently unaware that women usually let the men lead in the areas of love. Her heart beat rapidly and her breast rose and fell as her breathing became short. With a moan Justin released her, his own breathing fast as he looked down into her flushed face. Tracing the delicate shape of her rose-tinted lips, now swollen from his kisses, his voice deep and husky, he said, "I want you, Catherine, but I will not force you."

A timid smile touched her lips as she laid her hand against Justin's square jaw, caressing it with her fingers before her hand slipped behind his head to answer his plea. She drew his head down and gave her lips to him once more as evidence of her surrender. Her soft mouth opened to his questing tongue and sparks of fire exploded between them as Justin's tongue played a sensuous game with hers.

He moaned again, but this time it expressed his pleasure as he swept her into his arms and crossed to the large fourpost bed. Gently he placed her on the velvet counterpane before joining her. Raising himself on one elbow, he gazed into her lovely, passion-glazed eyes, their emerald depths sparkling with fiery glints of gold as she returned his look. Her beauty inspired awe within Justin; never had he hoped to find a woman with a passion to match his own.

He wanted to touch all of her and see the total, naked beauty of the body that aroused feelings within him that he had thought long dead. Tenderly, he moved to release her from her gown, his fingers brushing over the rough surface of the scar through the silken material of her kirtle.

Jamelyn froze. The thick lashes that had fluttered down upon her cheeks at his caress, flew wide with fright. The touch of his hand reminded her of the secret she now desperately wanted to hide. If Justin saw the mark he had left upon her, he would know her true identity. The thought made her shiver. If he learned of her deception he would hate Jamelyn of Cregan all the more. That thought tore at her heart. Grasping his hand with her own, she halted his movement and looked up at him, her eyes begging for understanding. "Please snuff the candles."

Mistaking her frightened expression for shyness, Justin smiled. Touched by her innocence, he dropped a light kiss upon her small nose before rising and putting out the light. Her demure modesty only heightened his arousal. He had sensed from their first kiss that Catherine Michaels was inexperienced in the ways of love. He would be her first, and if God granted it, her last. And if it was in his power, he would keep and protect this fragile flower until his death.

Justin released the drapes about the tall four-poster, enclosing them in a dark cocoon surrounded by silk, and reached for her once more. Feeling free to give herself to her husband, Jamelyn soon forgot everything except the feel of his hands upon her skin. She let him undress her and then helped him from his own clothing. Unconsciously, she avoided Justin's touch along the left side of her body as she eagerly responded to his caresses. His lips traced a fiery path along the sleek curve of her neck, pausing briefly to run his tongue over the throbbing pulse in her throat before moving slowly down her creamy right shoulder to find her full breast. His hands blazed a torrid trail along her flat abdomen to the silken flesh of her thighs. His velvet touch increased the tender ache in her belly and her thighs opened of their own volition to allow his questing fingers to explore the soft flesh at their junction. A moan of pleasure escaped her passion-swollen lips as Justin found the entrance to the dark, moist valley of rapture.

Hearing her moan, his hard maleness throbbed in answer against her thigh. Justin knew he could no longer control his own need and captured her lips once more in a hard, searing kiss as he moved between her legs. With a gentleness that would seem foreign in such a battle-hardened knight, Justin came to her. He felt the tight resistance of her maidenhead and knew that to give this lovely woman the true glory of love, he would have to first give her the sting of pain. He thrust forward quickly, trying to prevent as much agony as possible, but Jamelyn only flinched momentarily as her virginity was breached and she became a woman. The stinging soon mingled with a more erotic sensation and was quickly forgotten as she began the ancient ascent with Justin to the paradise of love. The secret given to each man and woman from the beginning of time unfolded within the two as they shared the ecstacy meant by the gods for lovers.

Jamelyn's back arched, pressing her more tightly against Justin as she cried her pleasure. Every nerve within her vibrated and seemed to explode into a shower of searing stardust. Her nails left their mark upon Justin, branding him as her own, but he did not feel the pain. The corded muscles in his neck went taut and he, too, experienced the height of sensual pleasure as his seed spilled forth into the dark womb of life, leaving him gasping for air as each sinewy muscle within his hard body pulsated with gratification.

He lay forward, bracing his weight upon his elbows, as he gazed down at her and kissed her tenderly. He could feel her response as her body caressed his manhood. With care he eased to her side and rested his dark head upon her breast. He could hear the beat of her heart as it slowed to normal and suddenly realized his own heart beat in unison with her. He had known Catherine Michaels for only a few short hours, but he had fallen totally in love with her. Nestled against the soft, full mounds of her breast, Justin savored the knowledge. For so long he had thought he could never love another woman except Jessica. That love still rested in his heart, but he realized it had only been the love of tender youth. Tonight, he had experienced the love of a man who had found a woman to equal him.

Slowly, he raised himself on one elbow and peered down into her shadowy face. The small splash of light revealed her contentment and the love that glowed brightly within the depths of her emerald eyes. Justin's voice held the warmth of a summer's night, sultry and caressing as he said, "I love you, Catherine. I had not thought it possible to feel this depth of emotion for anyone."

Jamelyn's small hand caressed Justin's cheek and he placed a light kiss on the tips of her fingers as they traced the sensual curve of his lips. She swallowed convulsively as her own feelings washed over her in a great tempest. Her voice trembled as she said, "And I love you, Justin." Tears both of regret and great joy mingled to dampen her thick, sooty lashes as she snuggled against his lean body. She lay her head against his lightly furred chest as he wrapped his strong arms about her and contentedly drifted off to sleep.

Sleep did not come as easily for Jamelyn as she lay against the man she loved and realized for the first time that they were now truly married in every sense of the word. Her heart swelled within her and she felt as if it would explode with the pain his avowal of love brought her. Justin loved her but he did not love *her;* he believed she was Catherine Michaels.

Jamelyn had to bite her lip to stem the dry sob that threatened to escape as her misery swept over her. She had come to Windsor to free herself of Justin St. Claire, but now knew that for as long as she lived, her heart would always be bound to the handsome English knight. She tasted her own blood as her teeth broke the soft flesh of her lip. All she wanted to do was to scream out her ire at the tricks fate kept playing on her. The gods seemed never to be satisfied to let her have a moment of happiness without tearing it from her grasp.

Slowly, she eased from Justin's embrace and quietly slipped from the bed. She dressed quickly, pausing only briefly by the rumpled bed where he had enthralled her heart and soul forever. Gazing down upon his peaceful, chiseled face, she longed to place a kiss upon his beautifully molded lips, but stemmed the urge. Jamelyn knew that if she succumbed to the plea of her heart she might never leave his side. She had to get away from Justin long enough to try to sort out her tumultuous emotions. With him so near, she would never be able to think coherently.

Quietly, she left Justin's chamber, her eyes lingering briefly on his smooth, brown, muscular back, as he lay sleeping on his side as though she still lay near him. Stilling the wild beating of her heart that the sight aroused, Jamelyn descended the stone steps to the garden below.

She was unaware of the livid blue eyes that watched her hurried flight. Had she seen the hatred mirrored in their depths, she would have been forewarned of the danger that lurked in her future.

Chapter 11

The first heavy rain of summer battered relentlessly against the leaded panes of Jamelyn's window. The steady downpour had caused Windsor to become a great, chilly cavern as the dampness invaded its elegant halls. Fires blazed in fireplaces as its inhabitants tried to thwart the unusual cold. They huddled close to the warmth of the flames and stayed in their chambers to avoid the drafty halls.

Though Jamelyn remained in her quarters, she paid little heed to the chill that hovered in the damp air. After living so many years within the cold granite walls of Raven's Keep, it hardly affected her. Like the rest of Edward's guests, she sat before the fire, but her mind was not on any bodily discomfort from the weather. With her arms folded about her bent legs, her cheek resting on her knees, Jamelyn stared with unseeing eyes into the jumping flames. Her unbraided mane cascaded about her shoulders, its copper-gilded strands catching the light from the fire and shimmering like burnished gold. The warmth from the flames tinted her pale cheeks a bright, vivid rose as her green eyes brimmed with tears, which sparkled like liquid diamonds as they crept to the tips of her thick lashes and then made crystal paths down her delicately-sculpted cheeks.

Jamelyn's misery was like a physical force. It welled within her, threatening to choke her. With effort she swallowed back the tightness and pressed the heels of her palms against her burning eyes as her mind desperately sought a solution to the predicament in which she had become enmeshed.

It had been weeks since her first night with Justin and she was still far from a solution to her problems. Justin still believed her to be Catherine Michaels and each night he professed his love for her as she lay in his arms. Ironically, she reflected, that was what she had intended to do to Justin from the very beginning in order to avenge herself. Her vow to make him love her had been fulfilled, but now she found she did not want to trample that love beneath her heel. As each day passed and her heart became more deeply involved, Jamelyn sank further into the quagmire of deception.

Every moment in his arms magnified her fear of Justin learning her true identity. She could not endure the thought of seeing the love that was reflected in his eyes turn once more into hatred when he learned Catherine Michaels was in fact the wife he scorned.

Jamelyn spent her nights in sensual bliss in Justin's bed and gave herself up freely to the delights of their love, only to return to her chamber to pace the floor until the first light of dawn could be seen spreading across the horizon.

The burden of her predicament was playing havoc with her nerves. She slept little and of late her normally healthy appetite had vanished. The very thought of food made her ill. In the latter recesses of her mind, Jamelyn suspected the reason for her distaste for food but tried to deny it. However, today she had finally faced the truth. She was carrying Justin's child.

Her shoulders drooped as she pressed her forehead against her velvet-clad knees and rolled her head from side to side. Again fate was deciding against her. The time for keeping her secret had run out. Tonight she would tell Justin the truth and pray that he would not throttle her for her deceit.

With a rueful sigh, Jamelyn raised her tear-streaked face and wiped her damp eyes with the back of her hand. She now knew she would have to take the advice Anthony had given her several days earlier when he had visited her and coerced her into telling him the reason for her wan expression. When she refused at first to disclose the emotions she felt for her husband, Anthony had threatened to go to him with the truth of her identity. Finally Jamelyn gave way and told Anthony of her love for Justin.

The blond knight had been pleased to learn that Justin and Jamelyn loved each other. It had been his fondest hope to see them together. Yet knowing his friend and his hatred for the Scots, Anthony understood the dilemma Jamelyn faced if she revealed her identity. Though Anthony feared the outcome of such a disclosure, he persisted and tried to convince Jamelyn to go to Justin with the truth. She had adamantly refused. Her love for her husband was too new and at that time she could not deliberately destroy the beautiful relationship that had developed between them.

Jamelyn's hand crept to her flat belly and she squeezed her eyes tightly closed. Moisture again shimmered beneath the spiky, black points of her lashes as she imagined Justin's hostile features when he learned the wife he despised carried his babe. Her heart twisted within her chest. Her condition made the decision come too soon. She had as yet to store away all the memories of Justin's love that she knew would need to last her for the rest of her life.

Absently she rubbed the ache in her temple as she got to her feet and crossed to the rosewood armoire. Tonight would be her last evening with Justin and she wanted to look her best for him. She would savor their last moments together with every ounce of her being. Then before she left him, she would tell him all.

Without calling for assistance from the maid Edward had provided, Jamelyn dressed. She chose a pale gold kirtle with a deep gold sideless overgown and a pair of matching, pointed-toe slippers. The color emphasized her dark-fringed eyes that shimmered with tiny flecks of gold. She braided her auburn locks and placed a gold net about them. Eyeing her image in the tall mirror, Jamelyn was satisfied with her appearance. The only flaw that she could see was the distant, haunted look within the depths of her emerald eyes. Pinching her pale cheeks to give them color, she squared her shoulders and raised her small chin in the air. With all the courage she could muster, she left her chamber to face the hardest battle of her life.

Jamelyn's knock was hesitant, reflecting the overwhelming trepidation that swept over her at the thought of what she had to do. Her knees trembled as the door swung wide to reveal Justin, a warm smile playing over his shapely lips and his face glowing with the love he felt for her. For a moment their eyes met, one pair filled with a melancholy light while the other shimmered with happiness.

Without a word, Justin swept her into his arms and pressed a heated kiss upon her delicate lips, revealing the eagerness with which he had awaited the moment that they would once more be together. His strong arms lifted her slight form easily and he carried her to the bed. No words were needed between them. Their lips conveyed the message of their hearts. Each evening began in the same manner. The hot current of passion flamed instantly merely by the touch of their hands. It seemed they could never become sated of one another, their bodies greedy for the ecstacy they received in each other's arms. If Justin did not carry Jamelyn boldly to bed, she would be the one to instigate their lovemaking.

At the touch of his sensuous lips, her mission was forgotten as she gave herself up to the pleasure he aroused within her. Her arms encircled his strong neck, holding him close; she felt the beat of his heart against her breast as she pressed instinctively near his sinewy body.

Justin laid her gently on the bed, reluctantly releasing her soft mouth as he turned to extinguish the candles and close the drapes about the bed. He had learned over the course of their many evenings that she was uncomfortable if the candles remained lit.

The chamber lay in darkness except for the embers glow-

ing in the grate as Justin disrobed and eagerly slipped into
the velvet blackness of their love nest. He lay beside her,
his ardor very apparent as he pressed his male hardness
against her velvet-clothed thigh. The very thought of her
tender flesh pressed against his urgent need sent thrills of
pleasure along Justin's spine, and his lips quickly sought
out her honeyed mouth as his experienced hands removed
her clothing.

He felt her tremble as his hands caressed the secret places
he had found during the hours of erotic exploration of her
beautiful body. He knew well how to arouse her until she
cried out for him to release her from the agony of her own
pent-up desires.

Justin's lips and tongue followed his hands in a leisurely
pace as they flirted maddeningly over her silken flesh to
those sensitive areas until Jamelyn writhed beneath him.
Her thighs spread, offering all for him to devour. Her supple
flesh answered each of his sensuous caresses with a quivering response.

Justin accepted the gift and paid homage to the honeyed
glen with scorching kisses that sent fiery threads of ecstacy
along every nerve in her throbbing body. She moaned with
pleasure as her hands sought to draw Justin back to her so
that they could voyage on the incandescent ship of ecstacy
into the tempest of passionate fulfillment.

Understanding her need, his own seething like white-hot
flames within his veins, he came to her, capturing her lips
as he joined with her until he was deep within the dark,
warm sheath of love. Their bodies moved in unison, singing
together the age-old song of love until the slow canticle
changed in rhythm and the madrigal filled their souls, and
their voices could be heard as they cried out in rapture.

A light film of perspiration glistened on their bodies as
they descended once more to earth. Their heartbeats slowed
as Justin lay on his back and pulled Jamelyn into his arms.
With her flushed cheek pressed against the hard bands of
muscle that crossed his wide, furred chest, she listened to
the steady rhythm of his heart. His long fingers entwined
the shimmering auburn tresses that had come unbound and

curled the silken strands into ringlets of coppery flames. Jamelyn would always treasure that small gesture, for to her it revealed Justin's total contentment as they lay together in the afterglow of love.

She could nearly hear her world shattering about her as reality settled its weight once more upon her slender shoulders. The light flush left by Justin's lovemaking faded from Jamelyn's cheeks as she ran her hand over the flat, muscular planes of Justin's abdomen. Swallowing back the rush of tears that filled her throat, she forced her voice to remain steady as she asked, "Justin, what of our future?"

His fingers ceased their play and his muscles tensed. He took a deep breath as he eased from her and sat up. Running his fingers through his tousled, raven curls, Justin could not look at her as he said, "Our future is what has plagued me for many nights, Catherine."

Jamelyn clutched the covers to her to keep Justin from seeing her scar as he turned a haggard face to her and gently traced the curve of her cheek before he continued. "There is much I have not told you, my love, but now I feel the time has come." He drew back the drapes so that he could see her as he spoke.

Nervously, Jamelyn held the sheet about her and nodded as she tried to gain enough courage to also speak of the things she had kept hidden. "I, too, have much to tell, Justin."

A rueful little smile curled his lips as he placed the tip of one brown finger against her lips to halt her words. "Catherine, I must speak first, though it tears my heart to shreds."

Jamelyn's muscles grew taut and her knuckles turned white from her tight grip on the sheet. Long, agonizing moments of silence passed before Justin said, "It all began so long ago. You were no more than a small girl at the time I first met Jessica." Justin had been gazing into the orange coals of the dying fire until he heard Jamelyn's swiftly indrawn breath. Looking into her startled eyes, he placed a gentle hand upon her shoulder and his fingers moved in a soothing motion as he caressed it. "You have nothing to fear, my love. Jessica was my first love, but you will be my last. You have helped me rid myself of her ghost, which kept my heart deadened to love for so many years."

Confused by his words, Jamelyn said, "Ghost?"

"Aye," Justin said as he turned his face away once more and stared into the dark recesses of the chamber. "Jessica has been dead for over ten years."

The pain Justin suffered from his memories was evident in his voice and Jamelyn wanted to soothe his hurt. Placing one small hand over his, she tried to comfort him. "I'm sorry, Justin. I did not know." Her voice was full of compassion and Justin's expression was tender as he turned to gaze into her beautiful face. "You have nothing to be sorry for, my love. 'Tis the bastard Scots who are to blame for Jessica's death."

Jamelyn's breath caught in her throat and her heart pounded wildly within her chest as she watched the kind, loving expression of Justin's face fade into a cold mask of hatred as he continued to speak. "On that fateful day when the border raiders attacked my uncle's estate, I lost more than my wife; I also lost my younger brother, Richard. At least where Jessica is concerned I do have some peace of mind because they found her body lying near her spaniel with a piece of plaid in her hand. But Richard's body was never recovered. His torn tunic was found on the rocks at the water's edge, so it is presumed that his body was washed out to sea." Justin's voice was icy with venom and his eyes held a distant look as if he could still see his wife's body, lying on the dais in the family chapel, prepared for burial. His hand clenched tightly into a fist, the veins standing taut through the tanned skin, as if he still clutched the small, torn piece of tartan that had been found in Jessica's hand, while he silently vowed to make the Scots pay with their lives.

A deathly stillness hovered over the two lovers as Justin paused. Jamelyn looked into her husband's handsome face and a shiver ran up her spine. Her insides seemed to twist into knots as he brought himself back to the present. "Jessica and Richard are not the reason I now speak, however. I only wanted to explain my reasons for hating the barbaric Scots race before I tell you of the woman King Edward forced me to marry."

Justin's words were like a knife plunging into Jamelyn's heart. She felt it pierced and split asunder within her breast. She now understood her husband's hatred for her and her people, but it did little to ease the agony she was experiencing at the realization that she could never have Justin's love.

He felt her muscles grow taut and saw her face drain of color. Misconstruing her reaction as a sign that his revelation that he could not take her to wife had hurt her, Justin quickly continued, "My love, forgive me for not telling you sooner, but I feared to lose you. I love you too much, Catherine. I want to make you my wife as soon as I am free. Tomorrow I will go to Edward and beg on bended knee for him to petition the pope in Avignon to free me of this bondage."

Jamelyn pressed her hand over her mouth to keep from sobbing aloud. She could not suppress the tears that brimmed in her eyes, turning them into large pools, reflecting the agony that ate at her soul. The crystal droplets trembled on her sooty lashes before cascading unhindered down her pale cheeks. Though she had known of Justin's feelings all along, deep within her Jamelyn had secretly hoped that when he learned the truth, he would forgive her and accept her as his wife and the mother of his babe. It had been a foolish dream and now those hopes withered and died, leaving behind a large gulf that was filled with misery.

Through a mist of liquid diamonds Jamelyn gazed at Justin, seeing the deep lines etched about his shapely lips as he anxiously awaited her response to his disclosure. The dark, shining depths of his eyes seemed to hold a plea for her understanding, begging her not to turn away from him. That look severed the last slender threads binding her heart.

An excruciating pain twisted within Jamelyn's breast, making her gasp. Earlier in the afternoon she had thought her time had run out because of the child she carried, but it had been too late for Jamelyn before she ever came to Windsor. There was only one thing she could now do for

the man she loved. She would see King Edward and arrange
to give Justin the freedom he desired. It was her last gift
to him, the only act of love she could show the man who
had been hurt so deeply so many years before.

Unconsciously, Jamelyn's hand rested protectively over
her belly. Her eyes mirrored her misery and despair. She
knew it now to be useless to reveal her identity and her
condition. All that was left to her was to return to Raven's
Keep and bear Justin's son without his knowledge. His
hatred for the Scots was too deeply ingrained and he could
never love her, nor the child she carried. Jamelyn feared
his loathing would only be magnified if he knew the truth
of her scheming and deceit.

Without a word, Jamelyn slipped from the bed and
dressed. She paused briefly, her hand resting on the latch
of the door, and gazed once more into Justin's hurt, confused
face, knowing it would be the last time she would ever see
him. His handsome features shimmered through the cloud
of tears that flooded her eyes before she fled back to her
own quarters. He did not try to halt her, his own misery
gnawing away at his insides with the knowledge that his
fear had been realized and he had lost the woman he loved.

Behind the locked door of her own chamber, Jamelyn
let the weakness that had been creeping over her have its
way. She sank to her knees on the soft carpet and with arms
wrapped about her waist, leaned forward until her forehead
touched the floor. Great, racking sobs shook her slender
form before she lay prone, covering her head with her arms.
She wept openly for the first time in years. Tomorrow she
would give Justin his wish and knew at that same moment
that her heart would lay forever like a cold stone within her
breast.

When her tears were spent and nothing but dry sobs still
closed her throat, she curled into a ball and stared across
the chamber at the dying embers of the fire. She wrapped
her arms about her belly, holding the only thing she would
ever possess of the man she loved. His child would grow
within her and she would nourish it with her body and her

love. However, the passion she had shared with Justin would be like embers in the grate. It would lie cold without him to kindle it with his touch. The mother's love within her she would give his child, but the woman's love Jamelyn could never give to another man.

Justin had not moved from the side of the bed since his lover had left him. He sat with head bowed and hands hanging limply between his muscular thighs. He had found love once more but the Scots had again succeeded in taking it away from him. Bitterness surged through him with renewed vigor and he angrily slammed his fist against the hard wood of the four-poster. The pain in his hand did little to relieve him of the knowledge that he had lost Catherine Michaels because he had been forced to wed the skinny bitch at Raven's Keep.

With his jaw rigid and his lips curled back into a snarl of rage, Justin grabbed the crystal decanter of wine and smashed it against the fireplace. The alcohol flamed as it spattered into the coals. Like his rancor, it blazed hot and intense.

A black, deadly mood settled over Justin as he rang for a servant to bring more wine. When his wish was fulfilled, he did not bother to use a glass, but drank directly from the decanter, gulping down the contents as he silently cursed the fates that had brought love once more into his life and then abruptly taken it away. Draining the ruby liquid from the crystal decanter, he ordered another and proceeded to drink himself into a stupor in the hope of quelling the empty ache within his chest.

The sky was still heavily overcast when Jamelyn's thick lashes fluttered open. Her limbs were stiff and sore, for she had made her hard bed upon the floor. With a grimace she stretched and then pushed herself upright, rubbing her aching muscles. Jamelyn managed to gain her feet as the maid tapped on the door and then entered with her breakfast of toast and tea. The events of the previous evening combined with the effects of sleeping on the floor did little to improve

Jamelyn's disposition and she quickly sent the maid away without the warm smile that usually accompanied her orders. Her stomach churned with nausea as she eyed the food distastefully. She had no appetite for the light brown bread and golden tea, nor for what she must do.

Jamelyn dressed with care for her meeting with Edward and hoped that after this day she would never have to see the English monarch again. A lump rose in her throat, but she swallowed it back and blinked rapidly to stem the new rush of tears that burned her eyes. She clenched her teeth and determinedly squared her shoulders as she looked at the wan image reflected in the mirror. She would cry no more; tears did little good because nothing could be changed. She would face the future stoically, having learned well the perfidy of fate. Though her resolve was valiant, the shimmering brightness of her eyes and her ashen complexion revealed the inner turmoil of her emotions more than words could ever do.

Taking a deep breath, Jamelyn tried to gain the courage she would need to face Edward. She had to put forth a brave front and not let the English king see the vulnerability she felt. Her love for Justin had breached her defenses and she had no weapons left to use. They had all been destroyed as the walls of her heart crumbled under his touch.

Jamelyn recognized her own defeat and turned from the mirror. Her gaze swept over the luxurious accommodations of her chamber. She had learned that there were more methods of torture in this elegant prison than in the darkest dungeons. Gathering her few belongings, she stuffed them into her leather pouch. When she left Windsor she wanted no reminders of her time spent within the castle of Edward III.

A cynical little smile touched her pale lips as her eyes came to rest upon her hand tightly clasped about the gold girdle over her abdomen. True, she would leave all the elegant gowns Edward had given her, but she would always have one reminder of her nights in Windsor Castle.

Without a backward glance, Jamelyn picked up her pouch and slowly walked from the room. Her feet felt weighted with heavy iron manacles as she made her way through the marble and tapestry-lined halls to the king's audience chamber. Each step took her farther away from Justin, and it was by sheer force of will that she made her feet move.

Though it was only a few minutes that Jamelyn had to wait to see the king, it felt like hours before the huge, ornate double doors swung wide to admit her. Instinctively, she stiffened her back as she walked regally into the chamber. With fluid grace she sank into a low, perfect curtsy before England's monarch and waited until he acknowledged her. "Rise, my Lady St. Claire, and tell me what has brought you to see me so early this morning."

Hiding the trembling of her hands within the folds of her gown, Jamelyn looked at Edward, her chin high and her emerald eyes sparkling with resolution. "Majesty, I have come to seek your release from my marriage and the return of my land. I have accomplished the mission set for me and now want to return to Scotland."

Edward lounged back in his chair, his long fingers twirling the tip of his pointed beard as his lips pursed thoughtfully. One dark brow arched over his keen eyes as he gazed at Jamelyn. The memory of the English monarch was long and he had not forgotten the insults he received from her delicate lips. When he spoke, his voice was tinged with casual disinterest, as if the conversation was not important to him. "I'm afraid that will not be possible."

Edward's words were so unexpected that Jamelyn was stunned momentarily until their full impact sank into her mind. Her brow puckered as tiny lines etched across it like streaks of lightning and her eyes narrowed, deepening into a greenish grey like the ocean before a storm. Her fury built into a tempest, but she managed to retain a small measure of composure as she said calmly, "Sire, I have done as you requested and I have seen that you have gained your desire with Anne of Chester. That was the only stipulation of our agreement."

Edward's dark eyes were like cold granite as his lips curled derisively at the corners. "My Lady St. Claire, it is time you learned that I am the one who applies the stipulations to any agreement I make. True, I now have Anne, but if I free Justin I might not be able to have her in the future. Regrettably, she still thinks herself in love with your husband."

Jamelyn was no longer able to contain the loathing that swept through her, and her eyes flashed as the old hatred for the English resurfaced. The fresh wounds upon her heart were forgotten as Jamelyn's warrior instincts came to the fore. All her attention was centered on the man who had used her as a pawn in his wicked game of lust. In Edward's mocking eyes, Jamelyn saw her own gullibility and clenched her fists tightly at her sides to keep from flying at him with claws bared. Her rage bubbled through her veins in white-hot currents. Desperately she strove to maintain her composure and swallowed back the contemptuous words that rose to her lips. It would do little good to rage and storm her protest, she realized, for Edward possessed all the power and her battle would be lost by a few ill-chosen words. She had to make Edward realize that freeing Justin would not affect his relationship with Anne. "Sire, you do yourself an injustice. Surely you cannot believe Anne would choose a mere lord over the king of England?"

With a nonchalance that further infuriated Jamelyn, Edward flicked the soft fur that edged his velvet mantle as he said, "Perhaps you are right, my lady, but I prefer not to find out. Your request is denied."

Jamelyn's temper exploded. "Majesty, is this the way all Englishmen keep their word? I have done as you bid and now you do not uphold your promise to return my land and petition for an annulment of my marriage."

Edward's eyes narrowed as he leaned forward and glared at Jamelyn. His knuckles were white as he gripped the arms of the chair and his lips firmed into a hard line. "You are insolent, Lady St. Claire, but I will let it pass for the moment. I have other need of your service. I will agree to let you return to Raven's Keep instead of putting you into irons for your impudent behavior. I feel it will be much better for you to oversee the harvest at the fief."

Edward's lips quirked at one corner at Jamelyn's puzzled

expression and he paused, letting his words sink in, before he revealed his true motives. "Since things have not gone well with France, I need all of the supplies I can muster to feed my army. You will see to it that two barrels of grain out of every three are sent back to London for that purpose. Do you understand?"

The blood drained from Jamelyn's face. Edward's intention was to bleed Raven's Keep dry of its very life. Her people would starve over the winter months if she did as he commanded. Resolutely, Jamelyn squared her shoulders and bravely faced Edward. "Sire, I'm afraid that will not be possible. Raven's Keep is a small fief and only produces enough to insure the well-being of her own people."

Edward slammed his bejeweled hands down upon the shining dark wood surface of his chair as he hissed, "Is it not better for your serfs to feel the slight gnawing of hunger rather than the cold blade of steel, which will be their lot if you do not obey me? Get yourself back to Scotland, my lady, and tempt fate no more. I will soon send your husband to see that my wishes are carried out."

Jamelyn had little doubt that Edward would carry out his threats. She had seen his power before and knew she had no choice but to obey. However, she did not want Justin to return to Raven's Keep and find that she was Catherine Michaels. She had seen only a glimmer of Justin's animosity toward his Scots wife the previous evening and did not want to experience the full extent of his hatred when he learned the truth.

Her knees grew weak at the thought and she sank to the floor in submission to Edward's command. Her emerald eyes looked up at England's sovereign beseechingly. "Majesty, I will do as you ask if you will only keep my husband from returning to Raven's Keep."

Edward's voice was cold with hostility as he said, "Again you add stipulations, my lady. I am your sovereign and will judge when and where to send my vassals. 'Tis best you learn that lesson well. My word is law. Now rise and take yourself back to your barren land. I will see you have an escort. Wait in the antechamber until it is time for you to leave." Edward waved a hand in the direction of the door, and as Jamelyn turned to leave his words stopped her in midstride. "My lady, beware of rash acts against us in the future. I will not be so lenient again." With that the king turned his attention to other matters of state, ignoring Jamelyn's subdued exit.

Absorbed in her own tumultuous thoughts, Jamelyn did not note the silent figure who quickly slipped through the curtained exit at the rear of the chamber. After her confrontation with Edward, her nerves were strung taut and her anger again seethed. She could not wait patiently for the escort the king had promised. To quell the urge to reenter the chamber and slay the English monarch with her bare hands, she began to pace the small room. Her moment of weakness had passed and she reflected on the events of only minutes before. Her eyes became a deep forest green with fiery glints of gold as she folded her arms over her chest and silently fumed, My word is law! Beware of rash actions. I will not be lenient.

You say your word is law, Edward of England, she thought furiously, but if it is in my power, you will never see the benefits of Raven's Keep. Rash actions indeed! The only rash action I have committed was believing in you. But I have learned my lesson well. I will beware of your deceit in the future.

A gruff voice startled Jamelyn from her angry musings. "My lady, we have been sent to escort you from Windsor."

Without question she followed the two rough-looking men down the winding stairs at the rear of the palace and across the paved courtyard to the stables. A small roan mare had been readied for Jamelyn and she threw her pouch over the back of the saddle and climbed onto it. Her eyes strayed briefly toward the windows she knew to be those of Justin's quarters before turning her back and urging her mount to follow her escorts' lead.

An eerie, tingling sensation crept up Jamelyn's spine and raised the silken strands of hair on the nape of her neck. She sensed her exit did not go unobserved, but suppressed the urge to look once more at the castle. She did not want to look at Windsor, nor be reminded of all that had transpired within its vaulted chambers. She had to look forward—toward the future—and try to find a means with which to thwart Edward III.

Had Jamelyn looked back, she might have seen the cold eyes that glittered with malice as they watched her ride through the gates. She would also have noted the satisfied curl of a pair of full lips.

Chapter 12

Loud, angry voices awoke Justin. He moaned as he rolled over on his stomach and covered his throbbing head with a pillow. He tried to thwart the agony the sound caused his head by pressing his hands, palm down, against his ears, but the loud banging on his bedchamber door made him peep from beneath his haven to see Anne as she strode briskly to his bed and unceremoniously plopped down at his side. Her action jarred another moan from Justin.

Squinting up at her through bloodshot eyes, he tried to shield them with his hand against the grey light that filtered through the tall windows. Wetting his dry lips, he cleared his throat, but his voice was still hoarse as he said, "For the love of heaven, Anne! Are you trying to slay me while I am still abed? Can you not see I'm in misery?"

Anne placed her graceful fingers on Justin's temples and gently massaged them. A sweet, enchanting smile curved her full lips as she said, "My love, you know I would never have disturbed you if I did not have something of import to tell you."

Pushing away Anne's hands, Justin raised himself on one elbow and rubbed his dark-stubbled chin. "At the moment, Anne, there is nothing that important to me. All I want is to be left alone so I can die in peace."

Anne's sultry laughter pealed through the chamber, further adding to Justin's misery. He fell back upon the pillows and threw one strong arm over his eyes as she said, "Justin, you have never been able to hold your wine. But that is not what I have come to speak with you about."

Without looking at Anne, Justin murmured irritably, "Then say it and be gone. I find your humor at my expense lacking in its usual charm."

With an air of smug satisfaction, Anne settled herself more comfortably on the soft down mattress, spreading the skirts of her gown about her with the tips of her fingers as she said, "I have seen your wife."

The stillness that followed Anne's words was a silence like that found in a crypt. Finally Justin's wide chest expanded, his muscles tight bands of iron as he drew in a deep, resigned breath. "Where did you see my wife?" His eyes were dull and forlorn as his arm dropped away from his face and he stared at Anne.

She fluffed the material of her skirt before looking at Justin. As their eyes met she could not conceal the glint of triumph that flashed into hers as she said, "In the anteroom of the king's audience chamber."

Abruptly Justin sat up, the sheet falling away to reveal more of his masculine torso to Anne's appreciative gaze. Her blue eyes raked his broad chest down to his lean hips, only partially covered by the soft muslin. The sight made a tender ache form between Anne's thighs and her blue eyes glowed with a predatory glint, mirroring her hunger for Justin. Forcing her gaze away from the intoxicating sight, she looked once more into his face. The sight quelled her burning desire as he glared at her malevolently and his voice was harsh as he said, "No more of your games, Anne. tell me all you know."

Anne's flawless features seemed to glow with cunning malice as she raised her chin in the air and cocked her lovely raven head to one side. "'Tis what you should have said to Catherine Michaels."

With the speed of a striking serpent, Justin's fingers closed over Anne's arm and jerked her to him as he glared down at her. "What has Catherine to do with the fact that my wife is at Windsor?"

Anne's smile mocked Justin as she freed herself from his brutal hold and absently rubbed her stinging flesh. "Much, I would say, since they are one and the same."

Dumbfounded momentarily, Justin stared at Anne before throwing back his tousled head and roaring with laughter. He fell back on the pillows and wiped the moisture of his mirth from his eyes. He swallowed back several more bursts of laughter before regaining control of himself. His lips still curled at the ridiculous idea as he said, "My dear Anne, you have ever been the one to play the jest. For a moment I thought you were serious. It is good to know we are once more friends. For a time I had thought you had begun to hate me."

No longer able to control her urge to touch Justin, Anne ran her hand across his bare chest, savoring the feel of the crisp curls that furred it. "Justin, you know I could never hate you. I only turned to Edward after you chose Catherine to warm your bed. And it is for that reason that I have come to you now. I do not jest when I say I have just left the room where your wife awaits her escort back to Scotland."

At Anne's words Justin's face grew solemn, all previous mirth vanishing as if it had never existed. His features were like granite as deep grooves etched the corners of his sensuous lips and his thick-lashed eyes narrowed. "Anne I'm in no mood for more of your folly. My head throbs and my mouth tastes as if I have dined off the stable floor."

Exasperated, Anne spat, "Justin, you are the fool that Edward and your wife have played you for. I overheard them talking. Edward wanted me and your wife agreed to seduce you away from me to regain her land, and freedom from you!"

Justin felt his heart contract as the razor edge of Anne's words cut into it. He shook his head to try to force them away but they pounded into his brain, echoing there like a death knell. Numbly, he said, "Catherine and Jamelyn—the same person. No, it cannot be. I would have recognized my own wife."

Angrily Anne flounced from the bed and braced her hands on her hips as she looked down at him. "Then you are a fool, Justin. Surely you saw some mark that you recognized?"

Justin's smooth brow knit as he considered Anne's words. He could not honestly say he had ever seen Catherine completely naked. She had been so adamant about the room being in total darkness when they had made love. Suddenly, as if the sun had come from behind the dark clouds to illuminate the overcast day, Justin realized the reason behind her modesty. If Anne spoke the truth, then Catherine would have carried the scar from his own blade. He had seen Jamelyn's mark when he bathed her and she would have known Justin would instantly recognize her because of it.

The veins on the backs of Justin's strong hands stood taut as he balled his fist. His jaw clenched and a muscle twitched in a telltale sign of the rage that engulfed him. Without a care for modesty, he threw back the covers and stood naked before Anne. He began to pace the chamber, his movements sleek and agile, each sinew tense with the fury that possessed him. He reminded Anne of the caged lion she had once seen at a fair. His anger excited her, as did the sight of his well-rounded, muscular buttocks, which rippled with each movement. Anne's desire grew, and she wet her lips as she imagined clasping that firmness in her hands as Justin thrust violently within her. Her heart beat rapidly and her breathing became uneven as she forced her eyes away from the part of his anatomy that always excited her.

"Justin," she said, her voice husky, but he paid no heed to her. "Justin," Anne said again as she placed her hand on his arm to halt his rapid movements. Her touch seemed to bring Justin back from some distant plane and he paused as she continued. "Justin, you cannot let this upset you so. You now know the truth and can deal with it accordingly."

He pulled away from Anne's touch and took his velvet robe from the bed. Draping it about his wide shoulders, he said, "Aye, I can deal with it. I will see Raven's Keep leveled to the ground before I am through."

Frantically, Anne shook her head from side to side as her fingers gripped Justin's sleeve, biting deeply, but Justin paid no heed to the pain. "Nay, Justin. Edward is still king. You cannot anger him. Forget about Raven's Keep and your wife. We can still be happy together, as we were before all of this transpired."

Justin shook off Anne's hand and strode across the chamber to gaze out over the Windsor park. The green of the trees reminded him of Catherine's eyes. No, damn it, Jamelyn's eyes, and he was fool enough to be duped by her trickery. Justin's thoughts made his rage smoulder anew. Slowly, he turned back to look at Anne and a shiver passed over her at the cold, hate-filled eyes that gazed at her. "Nothing can ever return to the way it was until I am free of that Scottish bitch."

Fear etched tiny lines across Anne's smooth brow and marred her flawless features. She hastened to Justin and wrapped her arms about his lean waist. Pressing her pale cheek against his chest, she could hear the angry drum of his heart and could nearly smell the rage he exuded from every pore. Breathlessly she pleaded, "Justin, soon you will be free of her. Do not anger Edward and lose all because of it. Perhaps she will have a fatal accident before she reaches Scotland."

Justin's hands were not gentle as he took Anne's shoulders and pushed her away from him. "The bitch had best hope she does, for if she survives I will make her life hell on earth." With that he strode from the chamber, his voice loud with anger as he called for Gibbon.

Anne perceived that Justin's common sense would make him do nothing to anger his king; her fear faded and a pleased smile curved her lips. Patting the loose strands of raven hair that had escaped the gold netting that bound her blue-black tresses, she gazed toward the distant horizon as she thought victoriously, Sooner than you think, you will be free of her, my love.

With his cheek resting on his fist, Justin sat scowling into space as Gibbon laced his boots and attached the gold embroidered garters about his muscular calves. His mood was black, more so than the heavy clouds that hung ominously over Windsor.

Sensing his master's ill humor, Gibbon remained silent and did his work efficiently. When Justin's abrupt command came, he jumped nervously. "Send Sir Godfrey to me." Very much aware of Justin's stormy temper, Gibbon swiftly obeyed, not wanting to provoke his lord further. He found Sir Godfrey in the stables overseeing the grooming of his favorite steed. Gibbon nervously relayed Justin's command and uttered a brief warning about his master's mood.

Perplexed, Anthony went directly to Justin's chamber to find that Gibbon had correctly judged Justin's temperament. Almost with a snarl, Justin said, "What in hell took you so long?"

Anthony's blond brows arched in surprise at Justin's harsh words. His blue eyes scanned the chamber to make sure it was to him Justin spoke in such a surly manner. Confused, Anthony rubbed his smooth-shaven cheek as he looked once more at his friend. "I came as soon as I received your message, Justin. What on earth has got your temper up this early in the morn?"

The cold steel gaze of Justin's angry eyes seemed to pierce Anthony. "I thought you were my friend. Now I find you are like our good king, no friend of mine."

Bewildered at Justin's ridiculous statement, Anthony wondered about his sanity. "I am your friend, as is Edward. Surely you know that by now."

A cynical smile curled Justin's lips. "So I thought, until I find you and Edward have betrayed me."

Anthony knew Justin's statements were untrue. Exasperated at the veiled innuendos, his temper beginning to heat, Anthony said, "Now, 'tis my time to ask, what in hell are you talking about? Have you lost your wits?"

Justin released a small, mirthless laugh and shook his head. "Nay, I think I have just found them. I know now who I can trust to be my friends."

A muscle twitched in Anthony's jaw and his blue eyes glittered. "Damn it, do you expect me to understand your riddles? Cease this prattle and tell me what is on your mind."

Justin leaned back in his chair, his eagle gaze sweeping over Anthony. "If that is your wish. I know about the little deception planned by the king and my wife."

Anthony dropped his eyes from Justin's hostile gaze. He could no longer look at his friend as his anger faded. "When did you find out?" The words were softly spoken, lightly touched with regret.

"So you do not deny it? I did not think you would. If nothing else, Anthony, you have always been honest with me. Damn it, man! That is what puzzles me now. Why did you let them do it?"

Pleading sapphire eyes met cold indigo ones as Anthony looked once more into Justin's set face. "To be honest, I had hoped you would fall in love with Jamelyn. But even if I had opposed Edward's scheme, I could not have told you or he would have had my head."

Justin shoved himself abruptly from his chair, towering over the younger man with fists tightly balled at his sides and knuckles white from the pressure. "You got your wish, Anthony. I fell in love with her, but I did not know she was my wife. How was I to suspect the beautiful Catherine was the skinny, boyish wench I had left behind in Scotland? There was always something about her that tugged at my memory, but I pushed it away. Now I know why. You, Anthony, more than anyone else, should know I can never love that Scottish bitch. Too much anger and deception lies between us and this little episode only confirms it to me."

Anthony's wide shoulders drooped with Justin's words. "Would it help to know she did not want to do it?"

An unreadable expression flickered over Justin's angry countenance before he drew in a deep breath and spat, "Nay, it matters little what she did or did not want. She is like all of her race—they will do anything to achieve their aims. They murder and lie without a thought."

Ruefully, Anthony shook his head and placed a comforting hand on Justin's shoulder. "Nay, Jamelyn is not like that."

Shaking off Anthony's hand, Justin turned from him, his resentment rekindling. "By your tone, Anthony, I would think you, too, have fallen for her allure. Did she let you come to her bed to keep your tongue silent? She feigns passion very well, so it would be no hardship on her, I'm sure."

Anthony's anger exploded at Justin's insult. Blue flames seemed to shoot from his eyes as he glared at his friend's back. "Justin, you go too far. I will not have Jamelyn's honor, nor my own, maligned. If you were not my friend and I did not know how you now suffer, I would call you out for the offense. Damn it, Justin! Can you not see Jamelyn is a lady who could give honor to your name? Are you going to let your hatred of the Scots ruin the rest of your life?"

Justin's harsh, mirthless laughter again filled the chamber as he swung abruptly to face Anthony, his narrowed eyes showing the contempt he felt for all Scotland. "Honor by deceit? Is that what you mean, Anthony? I have found little honor among her race and I have a right to hate them. I have a long memory. You should know that fact well. I will not easily forget what my wife has done, nor will I forget that you and Edward conspired with her. Now leave me. I cannot go against my king, but I do not have to keep a viper at my breast as a friend. You are released from my service."

Anthony's breath left him. He was stunned. His throat constricted and he felt a burning sensation in his eyes. He and Justin had been friends for more years than he could remember. Now he had ruined that friendship only by wanting what he thought would be best for Justin.

Anthony's insides twisted with conflicting emotions. He was angry at Justin for his lack of understanding, but he was also hurt. He did not want to lose Justin as a friend. He wanted to shake Justin to try to make him see that Jamelyn was worth his love, but he clenched his fist tightly at his side to stem the urge. "Damn it, Justin!" was all Anthony could say before he spun on his heel and left the other knight to brood once more in silence. He had to put as much distance between them as possible or things would be said to make their parting irreconcilable. Anthony slammed the door on his way out, relieving some of his own vexation, but he silently prayed that in the near future Justin would see that he was still his friend and always had been so, no matter how stupidly and rashly he had acted on his behalf.

The black clouds predicted rain, but it did not begin until the three travelers were some distance from Windsor and then it came down in a heavy, steady drizzle, dampening them to the skin. The chill of the afternoon made fog swirl about the horses' legs and turned the landscape into a grotesque, mist-shrouded realm. Its eerie tendrils brought forth all the imaginings that were usually suppressed during the waking hours.

Wrapping her cloak tightly about her to ward off the damp and cold, Jamelyn paid little heed to the direction in which her escorts traveled. She was absorbed in her memories of the past weeks and thought of little else as the miles passed beneath the horses' hooves. She did not pull her thoughts away from the man she had left at Windsor until the steady drum of soft earth changed to the sharp, clipped sound of cobbled streets. Surprise mingled with confusion as she looked about and found herself once more in London. Turning to the man riding at her side, she asked, "Why have we come to the city? 'Twould have been better to go directly north."

In the dim twilight of the rainy afternoon, Jamelyn could not see her escort's features because of the hooded cloak he wore against the elements, but she heard his brusque reply, "'Twas our orders, my lady."

Jamelyn's emerald gaze scanned the tall buildings and deserted streets as she wondered at Edward's command. Her brow knit in bewilderment as she turned once more to her escort. "Why would the king order us to London?"

The man chuckled and a chill went up Jamelyn's spine as he said, "'Twas not the king's orders, my lady, but Lord St. Claire's."

Stunned, Jamelyn could find no more words. She stared ahead into the gloomy twilight, a cold, numb feeling creeping up from the pit of her stomach to settle heavily in her breast. Why did Justin order his men to bring me to London? she asked herself, but that question was soon answered when her escort grabbed the bridle from her hands and began to lead her down a dark alley. Suspecting the worst, her thoughts turned frantic: My husband has learned of the deception and now plans on ridding himself of me.

Jamelyn's escorts halted their mounts in front of a shabby, two-story building, the upper floor of which leaned dangerously out over the cobbled street. Her actions focusing on her own survival, Jamelyn kicked out at the man who tried to pull her from the saddle, but his companion quickly came to his aid. They jerked her roughly to the wet ground and with hands clamped firmly about each of her arms, pulled her toward the dark cavern of the door. She squirmed to free herself and wished fervently she could reach the dagger she had strapped about her thigh earlier. However, their coarse, callused hands thwarted her attempts to reach her small weapon to defend herself.

One large hand pounded on the unpainted surface of the oak door, while the other ensured that Jamelyn could not escape. The portal squeaked open, a thin line of light outlining the dark head that peeped around the edge of the door. "What ye wanting here?"

"We be here to see the Dirk. We've got business to discuss with him," Jamelyn's captor said as he placed a flat-palmed hand against the wood and shoved it roughly open so they could enter.

A voluptuous woman faced them. Her eyes flashed as she braced her hands on her wide hips and threw her head back to glare at the intruders. "Ye ain't got no business here. Now be gone with ye."

The larger of the two guards, whom Jamelyn had begun to call Rat because of his sharp, pointy features and beady eyes, said, "Wench, we have business with the Dirk and intend to see him. We're soaked to the skin and our balls are nearly frozen off from the cold. We won't leave until our business is concluded and we can find a warm wench and ale to take away the chill. Now tell your master we're here."

The woman's lips pursed and her large breasts nearly tumbled free of their confinement with each breath she took. Her eyes glittered maliciously as they swept over the three at her door before she spun on her heel and huffily stamped down the darkened corridor to the rear. It was only a moment before she returned. Her deep-set eyes traveled the length of Jamelyn's trim form before she said, "Dick will see you but be warned, he don't like to be disturbed during his evening meal."

Rat chuckled as he pulled Jamelyn along in the woman's wake, eyeing her swaying hips appreciatively as he said, "The Dirk won't mind us disturbing him when he sees our business."

The woman smirked up at the two men as she opened the door and stepped aside for them to enter. "He's in the throne room so mind yer manners. The King expects his due."

Before Jamelyn could comprehend the woman's words, she was roughly jerked into the room. She blinked rapidly, trying to focus against the bright light.

The woman plopped down on an overstuffed couch and propped her feet up to expose her legs to the thighs. "They're here, Dick," was all she said before picking up a plate and settling it on her knees to finish her meal.

Jamelyn's eyes rounded in amazement as they traveled over the chamber. From the dilapidated appearance of the foyer and the exterior of the building, she would never have suspected such luxury existed within. Soft carpets silenced their footsteps as they moved to stand before an ornate chair inlaid with gold. The walls were hung with silk that would have made many of the wealthy noblemen of England give a sigh of envy. The furnishings were equally extravagant, as was the throne of the King of the Gutter. Heavily carved tables boasted services of gold and silver in this underworld kingdom. Gold candelabras lit the room. However, it was not the trappings of the chamber that held Jamelyn's attention, but the man who sat upon the throne.

He was clothed in dark burgundy velvet edged with fur of miniver about the hem of his cotehardie and sleeves. His surcoat was padded at the shoulders and inset with jewels. Around his narrow waist he wore a heavy belt of gold encrusted with rubies and upon his slender legs, hose made of silk and held up with garters bejeweled with diamonds. Jamelyn realized with a start that had she seen him in another setting she would have thought him the king of England.

Though the man's attire drew the eye, it was his arresting features that made Jamelyn look closer. He was not a handsome man; his deep-set eyes and overly large nose, along with his narrow lips, negated that possibility. But the light that glowed in his eyes made a tiny shiver creep up Jamelyn's spine as she gazed into their penetrating depths. At first glance his small mouth gave the illusion of weakness, until one looked into the piercing depths of those eyes. They projected all the power the man possessed in his small kingdom.

Dick the Dirk's gaze flickered briefly over the two men and then settled speculatively on Jamelyn. He studied her from her small feet to the top of her copper-streaked head before stopping at her lovely, pale face. A semblance of a smile passed over his thin lips as he said, "Guinn told me you had business with me. Have you brought some quality goods or only this tasty wench with you?"

A large hand at the small of her back gave Jamelyn a rough shove and she stumbled forward to fall to her knees before the throne. She brushed the loose curls from her face as she glared up into the smoldering eyes of Dick the Dirk, the King of the Gutter. Unaware of how the man had gained his name, Jamelyn spat, "They have brought me here against my will. I order you to release me at once."

With one long finger against his cheek and a thumb bracing his chin, Dick lounged negligently on one elbow as he looked down at Jamelyn. "I assumed it was against your wishes, my lady, but that is of little import." His cold gaze turned once more to Jamelyn's escorts. "How much do you want for the wench?"

Jamelyn gasped at the indignity as Rat spoke. "She be a feisty wench, yer lordship, and should do well in bed with her spirit. I would say ten shilling would not be too high a price."

With careless disregard of Jamelyn's stunned expression, the Dirk fumbled briefly at his waist to pull away a small leather pouch. He tossed it to Rat. "The bargain is sealed; now be off with you."

Rat caught the bag and weighed it in his hand before tucking it into his belt. A wide, satisfied grin spread across his rodent-like features as he bowed to the Dirk. "'Tis been nice doing business with ye, my lord." With that Jamelyn's escorts left her at the feet of London's underworld king.

Before Jamelyn could find the words to protest the transaction, Guinn came to her feet. Her hands were braced angrily on her full hips and her lips narrowed as her dark eyes showed her rage. "Wha' do ye mean by doing tha'? Ye can't mean to keep the skinny wench?"

Menace glimmered in the Dirk's eyes as he turned to look at the woman, pinning her to the spot on which she stood. "Do you think to order me about, Guinn? Have a care that you do not rile me."

Sullenly, Guinn dropped her eyes away from the Dirk's and seated herself once more. Under lowered lashes she cast black looks at Jamelyn as she murmured, "'M sorry, Dick. I forget me place sometimes, love." Guinn well knew her role in the Gutter King's household and would not abuse it. The Dirk's reputation was not unjustly bestowed upon him. He was known for his easy and vicious skill at slitting a gullet with his dirk. It was also known that no one crossed him without feeling that deadly blade at his throat. He would kill without remorse, no matter what relationship existed between him and his victim. Dick the Dirk had already rid himself of two wives and both brothers. Guinn did not want to be the third wife to meet such a fate.

Dick's narrow upper lip curled in contempt at Guinn's

meek acceptance of his order. He felt nothing but scorn for her and her lot. They all obeyed without complaint. Dick expected obedience from his followers, but it took away his pleasure when none showed enough spirit to give him reason to wield his power in a manner that would please the darker side of his depraved nature.

Guinn's cowering position disgusted Dick and he turned his heavy-lidded eyes to more interesting game. He liked his women with more spirit than the sow sitting on the couch. He could feel his mouth fill with saliva as his eyes rested on Jamelyn. A fiendish light glimmered in the malevolent depths of his eyes and his thick tongue licked his lips in anticipation of seeing her naked. On her slender body he would mete out all the exquisite tortures he had found to give him the most pleasure. A smile curved his thin lips at the sight of her flashing eyes. Amused, he thought, Ah, my beauty, you'll not be as malleable as poor Guinn and I'll receive more pleasure from it.

Dick wanted to laugh aloud at the look the young woman gave him as he rose and towered over her. Had she watched a snake approach, her green eyes could not have been filled with more loathing. Dick extended his bejeweled hand to her with all the grace of a gentleman born at court and smiled sweetly down at her. "Rise, my lady."

His voice was soft and cajoling but Jamelyn refused the hand proffered to her and scrambled to her feet under her own power. She faced the Gutter King with her chin high in the air. "Sir, I insist you free me instantly."

Dick chuckled at her bravado and the sound sent a tremor of apprehension racing through Jamelyn. She fought back the fear that urged her to turn and flee before it was too late. Instead she squared her shoulders and gazed directly into the Dirk's hard, black eyes as he closed the space between them. She managed to suppress the urge to cringe as he ran one finger along the curve of her pale cheek. "Ah, my fine beauty, they were right; you do have spirit. Tonight you will please me well. And perhaps if you do well enough I will consider keeping you. Does that not suit you, my lovely?"

Eyeing the Dirk with distaste, Jamelyn stepped away from him with calm deliberation, her movement expressing her disdain. Her voice was cool and aloof as she said, "I'm afraid I will have to disappoint you. I have no intention of sharing your bed tonight or any other night. For your own well-being I suggest you release me before the wrath of King Edward comes down on your own pretentious head." Unaware of how her words added to Dick's excitement, she tried to brazen her way out of the situation.

Dick's eyes seemed to smolder like glowing embers from hell. "I am not afraid of Edward, wench. He has his kingdom and I have mine. There are few who are brave enough to come into my realm. Come, my beauty, to bed."

Dick turned away, expecting his command to be executed without question. But Jamelyn's adamant refusal halted his steps in midstride. "Nay, I'll not go with you."

A wave of pleasure swept over Dick and he could feel his loins begin to swell as he slowly turned to Jamelyn. Leisurely, as if his intention was nothing out of the ordinary, he drew back his hand, his wide palm striking her hard across the cheek and knocking her to the carpeted floor. Dick expected to see her cower like all his women did, but the auburn-haired vixen surprised him. He caught only a flash of long, shapely legs as Jamelyn jerked up her gown to retrieve her small, sharp dagger. In the next instant she had rolled away from the Gutter King and regained her footing. She bent low, bracing herself for his attack, her own words a low snarl as she spat, "Lay another hand on me and it will be your last act. Now I will leave this vile place to you and your host of vermin." Jamelyn began to back toward the door, warily watching Dick for any movement to indicate his attack.

Enjoying himself, the Dirk threw back his head and his evil laughter filled the chamber as he rubbed his hands together in anticipation. It reminded him of the days of his youth when he cornered the wild alley cats that lived in the refuse-strewn streets of London. They always spat and hissed until his hand closed about their furry necks and snapped the life from them. His hands were still scarred from their

claw marks and he treasured the scratches. The red marks
had turned white over the years and he wore them as a
symbol of his power over life and death. It was in those
early days that he had begun to savor the death throes of
his victims; their agony was his joy.

A dribble of saliva beaded his lips and he licked it away.
A predatory glint brightened his mad eyes as he began to
advance on Jamelyn. The thought of the pleasure he would
receive from the beautiful creature with the eyes of a cat
throbbed through his veins, making him forget any danger.

Jamelyn waved her dagger threateningly at Dick, trying
to keep him at a safe distance, but her action did little to
repel him. Pain was not a new experience for the Dirk and
he savored it as much as he enjoyed inflicting it. Determinedly, he kept moving forward, though Jamelyn had
knicked him in several places and red drops ran down his
hands.

"Come no closer," Jamelyn warned him. "You have only
tasted the tip of my dagger, but if you insist I will have to
end your vile life."

The Dirk's eyes glazed with sadistic passion and his
breathing became heavy. "Inflict your worst, my beauty,
but I'll have you now beneath me." With that Dick lunged
at Jamelyn but she quickly side-stepped him, ripping his
velvet sleeve to the shoulder as she cut a thin gash along
his extended arm. Behind them, Guinn gasped.

Dick paused and clasped his arm to stem the flow of
blood. He grinned at Jamelyn. "You play the game well,
wench, but I will be the victor." Forgetting his wound, he
threw himself at Jamelyn, his weight knocking her to the
floor and taking her breath away with the impact. He grabbed
her wrist and twisted viciously until she released the dagger
from her tightly-clenched hand. Dick's fingers closed about
Jamelyn's slender throat and slowly tightened until her eyes
were wide and her face red from lack of air. "I'll have you
now, wench." His voice was husky as his lips came down
brutally on hers. She could taste her own blood as his pressure broke the delicate flesh of her tender mouth. She tried

to struggle but found the Dirk's body pinned her to the floor so that she could not move.

With his free hand, Dick began to tear at Jamelyn's gown, his fingernails leaving burning scratches on her tender breast as he tore at the material. In the distance, Jamelyn heard Guinn whimper, but knew she could expect no help from that quarter. Her head seemed to vibrate with a heavy pounding that she thought must be her heart; she briefly wondered if she was going to faint until a loud "Ah-hum" made her realize that her humiliation had been seen by another besides the Dirk's wife.

The sound also made Dick pause in his savage mauling and turn to glare up at the intruder who dared to interfere with his lust. His lips drew back in a snarl as he hissed, "Out with you. Can't you see I've a wench to pleasure?"

The Dirk's body shadowed the identity of his victim from Royce's view, but he did not like the animalistic way the man was treating the woman. It mattered little to Royce if she was a slut from the gutters, he could not condone such brutality.

Aware of the Dirk's well-earned reputation, Royce knew he could not interfere directly on the wench's behalf. He was in the Dirk's territory and had to go warily if he was to help the woman and not lose his own life in the process. It was too dangerous to openly defy the man without having the support of more than his own blade to aid him. All the Dirk had to do was to call out and the room would be filled with the vermin he controlled.

"So be it, then," Royce said casually, and acted as if he was turning away. "I can see you are willing to forfeit the gold that the treasure I have would bring. Perhaps the gent on King's Street will be more interested." Royce hoped the Dirk's greed outweighed his sadistic lust and his hope was fulfilled as Dick ceased his fondling of Jamelyn's bare breast and began to get to his feet. It was the mistake she had been waiting for.

Seeing her moment as the Dirk braced one hand on the floor to rise, Jamelyn brought her knee sharply upward, catching him in the groin. The Dirk howled with pain and clasped his injured member as he rolled away from her. In that same instant she scrambled to her feet, her breast heaving with exertion as she panted for air. Her frightened green eyes traveled to the man who had interrupted the Dirk's attack and widened as she recognized Royce McFarland. Without thought of how her impulsive need of protection would affect their situation, she flew across the room to press her face tightly against his hard chest. The feeling of relief made her tremble as Royce's muscular arms enfolded her within their strong embrace.

Royce was as surprised as Jamelyn to find her the victim of the Gutter King. In shock his arms automatically wrapped about her and held her close as he said, "What in the name of all that is holy are you doing here?"

Trying to regain a small measure of her composure, Jamelyn gazed up into his scarred face before her eyes traveled once more to the Dirk, who had managed to regain his feet and limp awkwardly to his throne. "My husband had his men bring me here and sell me to that loathsome creature."

Jamelyn felt Royce's muscles tense and glanced uneasily up to see his face set in a rigid expression, his one sapphire eye flashing with fire. Before she could speak further the Dirk said, "It seems you know the wench, McFarland. Did you have it in mind to have her for yourself?"

Sensing the imminent danger presented by the Dirk, Royce let his arms fall away from Jamelyn and set her roughly from him. A smile curved his shapely lips as he swaggered forward to stand before the Gutter King. He forced his voice to remain steady and filled with disinterest. "Aye, I know her. She hails from Scotland, too, but I'm not interested in having her. I like my women with more meat on their bones, like your Guinn. Now that's a nice piece of flesh."

Bewildered, Jamelyn looked up at the man she had considered her friend. Now he acted as if she meant nothing to him and his friendship lay with the Gutter King. Her shoulders slumped and she swallowed back the rush of tears that formed in her throat. Her world had totally turned upside down. Justin had sold her into slavery and Royce had now abandoned her in her hour of need. Tears stung the backs of her lids and she blinked rapidly to dispel the threatening dampness. She bowed her head to keep from looking at Royce and his vile companion. She would not give them the satisfaction of seeing her misery.

Royce sensed Jamelyn's hurt and had to quell the urge to draw her once more into his arms and give her the comfort and assurance she needed. If he gave way, it would be a fatal mistake.

Satisfied with the Scot's explanation, Dick smiled amicably as he relaxed back in the chair. "Enough talk of women. The wench will get what she deserves after we conclude our business. Now what have you brought that is of such great value?"

With agile fingers, Royce withdrew a dazzling diamond necklace from his pocket. The light from the candles caught the gems, bringing their brilliance to life. They sparkled in Royce's hand, throwing a rainbow of color across his wide palm as he held out the jewels upon it to show the Dirk.

Dick's tongue greedily flicked over his thin lips as he reached down to touch the necklace, only to find that Royce's strong fingers had once more enclosed it within their grasp.

"It is best we bargain first," Royce said. "These are too valuable to leave my person until the bargain is struck and the gold lays neatly within my own pocket."

The sound that emanated from the Dirk's throat was tinged with evil mirth as he propped his elbow on the chair arm and leaned back. "You will never change, Scot. You know well I could easily have them taken from you, but I would hate to end our profitable relationship so sadly. How much do you want for the bauble?"

Royce held the jewels up to the light and watched the flashing fire within their depths as if to consider their value before returning them to his pocket. "The necklace is worth well over a hundred pounds, so I would think fifty would not be too high a price."

The pleasant expression vanished form the Gutter King's face as he observed Royce through half-closed lids. "You ask too much. I'll give you ten."

Royce patted the leather tunic over the necklace and his blue-black hair shimmered from the light of the candles as he shook his head. "Nay, I'll keep the stones before I'll give them to you for that. It will be fifty or nothing."

The Dirk's mouth thinned into a red slash across his face. He glared angrily at the Scot, then shifted his perusal to Jamelyn. An idea glimmered to life within his cunning mind. He wanted the wench more than he had wanted any woman in a long time, but his greed overrode his lust, for he wanted the necklace more. "I'll give you twenty and the wench. That is my final offer."

Casually Royce's gaze traveled to Jamelyn, but he exhibited little interest in the Gutter King's proposal. He knew if he accepted too readily he would be playing into the Dirk's hands. With a feigned sigh of regret, his tone reflecting boredom, Royce looked at the Dirk. "True, she could keep me warm at night, but that will not put food into the bellies of my men. I'll have to decline your offer."

Jamelyn's startled cry of dismay drew the two men's attention. She crossed the short space to Royce and knelt at his feet. "Accept his offer and I will give you the rest of the gold you need for your men," she pleaded. Her eyes misted with tears at the thought of her former friend leaving her at the mercy of the vile Gutter King.

Royce's heart twisted within his chest at the sight of his valiant Jamelyn kneeling at his feet, begging for his help. Without revealing the turmoil her actions aroused within him, he staunchly turned his back to her as he said, "The wench makes the offer more tempting."

The Gutter King sat rubbing his palms together, anticipating the feel of the diamonds within his grasp. "Do you accept?"

With calm deliberation, Royce considered the proposal and then nodded. "Aye. Twenty pounds from you and the wench to warm my bed until I receive the rest from her. It is a bargain."

The Gutter King ordered Guinn to bring his strongbox. He did not want to chance the Scot changing his mind on the deal. The Dirk wanted to laugh out loud at the ridiculous idea of the wench being able to give McFarland the remaining sum. Scot, he thought as he counted out the gold coins, you have been played the fool this night. Securing the sum agreed upon in a leather pouch, he tossed it to Royce. "It is always a pleasure to do business with you, McFarland. I look forward to our next meeting; I am always richer for them."

Royce withdrew the necklace from his pocket and tossed it to the Gutter King before tucking the gold-filled pouch within his tunic. "'Tis always nice to feel the weight of my labors near my heart." He patted the bulge against his chest as he turned to Jamelyn, his expression concealing his urgency to be gone from the den of thieves. "Now, wench, we'll be about our business and leave the King to his. You still have your end of the bargain to keep and I warn you, you had best please me well."

Wrapping his strong fingers none too gently about her wrist, he jerked her to her feet and pulled her from the Gutter King's luxurious domain. As the door closed behind them, Dick's laughter reached their ears as he bragged to Guinn about truly besting the Scot this time.

Leading Jamelyn to his mount, Royce hoisted her up into the saddle and mounted behind her. Wrapping his mantle about her to keep the chilly dampness at bay, he urged his horse into a gallop toward the gates of London. He wanted to be far away from the city before the Dirk realized the necklace was of far less value than he had claimed.

Hurt by Royce's actions with the Dirk, Jamelyn remained stiff and unyielding in front of her rescuer. She would not lean against his wide chest and give him reason to believe she would eagerly fall into his bed. Her position was uncomfortable and the night air was cold but she determined to keep as much space between them as possible on horseback.

Sensing her feelings, the border raider said nothing as they traveled north. The rapid pace he set left little room for conversation and he felt it in their best interest to place as much distance as possible between them and London before he tried to make Jamelyn understand his reason for acting in such a manner toward her.

Knowing Dick the Dirk, he would soon have his cut-throats scouring the countryside for the man who had tricked him out of his gold and the woman. Royce's lips curled into a caustic smile as he looked down at the rigid little back in front of him. Jamelyn of Cregan did not realize what this night's work had cost him. To save her he had severed the only contact he had for selling the items they took in their raids. It would not be easy for him and his men in the future without some middleman to give them gold enough for their goods to fill their bellies.

Dawn was creeping over the horizon as Royce pulled his horse to a halt near a swiftly flowing stream. Without asking permission, he grasped Jamelyn about the waist and set her on the ground before turning to see to his horse's welfare. As if remembering their own need for nourishment, he said, "There is cheese and bread in the saddlebags. Take it down to the stream and we'll eat there."

Jamelyn eyed Royce's broad back hostilely and crossed her arms over her breast, making no move to obey him. She'd be damned if she would go from one type of slavery to another.

Tying the bag of oats about his horse's head, Royce turned to find her standing as he had left her. Giving a rueful shake of his dark head, he smiled. "You're still angry at me, aren't you, lass?"

She turned her face away, refusing to answer. The touch of Royce's fingers beneath her chin as he turned her face once more to him startled her, but she could not step away from his large form, for he held her imprisoned by his strong fingers. His voice was soft as he said, "I'm sorry, Jamelyn, for the way I had to act, but it was my only chance of getting you out of that hellhole. Forgive me, lass, and let us be friends once more."

Jamelyn wanted desperately to believe Royce, but suppressed the tiny lift of her heart that his words aroused. She would not let herself be fooled again into believing in his friendship. Her eyes sparkled with resentment as she said coldly, "Nay, Royce. You're no friend to me. Your kind words will not make me come to your bed without force."

At the stubborn set of her little face, Royce threw back his dark head and his laughter silenced the birds in the nearby trees. "Lass, at least you have not changed since I last saw you. Put away your anger and let that keen mind work clearly without your temper coloring your thinking. Had I not bargained for you like that, you would still be with the Dirk and now I must take up valuable time trying to make you understand. Can't you understand, lass? The necklace was worth less than half the gold the Dirk gave me. I gambled with our lives to get us free of the Gutter King. Had the Dirk realized it . . ." Royce ran one finger across his throat to indicate their fate.

Jamelyn's eyes widened and her soft lower lip fell agape at his words. Suddenly her face brightened and she threw her arms about his corded neck. "Forgive me, Royce. I should have understood."

His strong arms wrapped about her and held her close as he chuckled, "I understand, lass. Were I in your position I would not trust anyone either. Now tell me how you came to be at the Dirk's."

A shadow flickered over Jamelyn's features, dimming the glow of her happiness of a moment before. "'Tis a long story, Royce."

Releasing her, he retrieved the cheese and bread from his bags and then draped his arm comfortingly about her slender shoulders as he led her toward the bubbling brook. "Then we had best get comfortable and fill our stomachs while you tell me."

Settling herself on the lush, green grass, she took the food Royce offered, but her appetite faded as she began the story that led up to her incarceration in the Gutter King's dilapidated palace. It was hard to speak, but with Royce's gentle encouragement, Jamelyn finally managed to tell him all that had transpired between the king of England, Justin, and herself while at Windsor.

Royce's long fingers curled about her hand, trying to give her some measure of solace by his touch. Jamelyn hesitated only briefly before she told him of her love for Justin and that she carried his child back to Scotland within her. She could feel Royce tense and hear the angry hiss of his rapidly expelled breath as she spoke of Justin's plan to rid himself of her. At last her tale ended and the silence lengthened between them.

Royce folded his muscular arms over his bent knees and stared off into the distance, chewing the last of his bread and cheese. Swallowing the mouthful, he brushed the crumbs from his leather tunic and looked solemnly at Jamelyn. "Lass, you have been through much since I last saw you. What do you intend to do now?"

With her hands lying limply in her lap, holding the black bread that she could not eat, Jamelyn considered Royce's words and shook her gilded head. "I know not. The only thing left to me is to return to Raven's Keep and bear my babe. At present I do not seem to possess enough strength to fight. My love for Justin and the child seems to have robbed me of much."

Royce's blunt-tipped fingers rubbed his furrowed brow in annoyance at his own inability to come to her aid. A muscle twitched in his craggy face beneath the patch as he said, "I would defend you if I were able. But as a reiver there is little I can do except offer my protection until you reach Raven's Keep."

Suddenly her expression changed. The look of the old Jamelyn of Cregan, who had faced the English so bravely, flickered to life and added a new vitality to her features. Her cheeks glowed with excitement as the corners of her lips curved upward. "Royce, that is the answer!"

Puzzled, his dark brows knit over the bridge of his narrow nose and he eyed her suspiciously, sensing from the look on her face that some mischief lay at hand. "What is the answer?" Royce's voice was cautious, knowing well the trouble she had brought down on her head from the last scheme that had taken root in her mind.

Jamelyn clapped her hands in glee and her green eyes sparkled with secret mirth. "You are a reiver and *can* help me. Edward expects his tribute from Raven's Keep, but I do not want the English dog to have one grain of produce from its fields. My people will starve if I do as Edward has ordered. However, if I do not, he will come with his troops and kill them. That is where you can help."

Royce shook his dark head in confusion. "I don't understand, lass."

Like a small child, Jamelyn scrambled to her knees before Royce and laughed. "I will pretend to do as Edward has ordered, but you will steal all the grain back for me. In that way he will never suspect what has actually happened."

Crossing his arms over his wide chest, Royce considered Jamelyn's plan before throwing back his dark head and roaring with laughter. "Aye, that would work. In that way your people will not starve and Edward cannot say you are going against his wishes."

The laughter died in Royce's face, though a small twinkle still remained in his sapphire eye as he tipped up Jamelyn's small chin and gazed down at her. "Lass, I think you have not lost all the strength you assumed. You are still the stubborn Scottish lass I met that dark night dressed as a lad."

Jamelyn regarded Royce thoughtfully as she rose to her feet. His words were unraveling some mystery that lay concealed in the back of her mind. Royce is right, she thought, studying his handsome, scarred face, I have not changed. I have only pretended to be someone else for so long I have forced myself to believe it also.

Jamelyn straightened her back and squared her shoulders, her chin lifting confidently once more as she said, "Aye, I'm still Jamelyn of Cregan. During the past months I have been so overcome by everything that I briefly began to believe otherwise, but now I know exactly who and what I am."

Suddenly the breath caught in her throat as the riddle solved itself. Briefly she paused to consider her words, her brow furrowing before her eyes widened in amazement. It was as if someone had drawn a heavy curtain away from a window, letting the bright sunlight of reasoning spill into her mind. It flooded her with wonder as she gazed up at Royce. "All of my life I have pretended to be one thing or the other to try to gain favor in the eyes of others. Now I

have to please no one except myself. I am a woman, Royce."
Jamelyn's tone reflected her own surprise at finally accepting herself without pretense.

Her chin inched higher with pride and her emerald eyes
glowed with a new radiance as she said, "I have my child
and my people's welfare to consider and I accept both
responsibilities. Just because I was born a female does not
mean I am weak and can be used as I have been in the
past."

A small, contented smile crept over her delicate lips.
"Don't you see, Royce? I am a woman and have at last
realized that I have always been so and have had nothing
to be ashamed of. I can be the heir of Raven's Keep and
the chieftain of the Cregan Clan without lying to myself or
anyone else. I do not have to subjugate my feelings any
longer or despise the ones that are natural to me.

"I can ride, fight with my sword, or preen before a mirror
without having to feel I am betraying someone. I have finally
come to understand that I *am* all I pretended in both facets
of my life, and that makes me a complete woman." Jamelyn
laughed aloud with the joy of her knowledge. It swept through
her with a tingling rush of freedom as she loosed the mental
bonds that had bound her over the years. Exuberant, she
threw her arms about Royce's neck and danced a gay Scottish
jig on tiptoe before him.

Astounded by her long speech, Royce blinked several
times as he watched Jamelyn's antics. A bemused expression
played over his scarred face as he shook his head and placed
both hands on her shoulders to stay her movements. "Lass,
I could have told you all that if you had only asked."

Jamelyn's white teeth flashed in the sun as she laughed
up at Royce. "Aye, you could have, but I would not have
believed you until now. It has taken nineteen years for me
to learn this lesson, Royce, but it is one I will not forget
in the future. Let us be off to Raven's Keep so I may show
everyone that I am a woman who cannot be taken as lightly
as Edward and Justin have presumed in the past."

Chuckling, Royce picked Jamelyn up in his strong arms

and strode back to where his mount was tethered. Lifting her into the saddle once more, he thought, I'm afraid the king of England and your Lord St. Claire will be much surprised at the woman in you, Jamelyn of Cregan.

Chapter 13

The jingle of harness and the creak of leather stilled as Justin raised his gauntleted hand to halt the squad of men in the forest before Raven's Keep. It had been nearly a year since he had seen the dark granite walls of the fortress, and from his vantage point Justin could see that nothing had outwardly changed about the imposing structure. But he felt that much would be different within its thick stone ramparts because he now knew the true extent of deceit practiced by the woman who resided there.

Though his heart lay like one of the stones from those towering walls, cold and heavy within his chest, a burning anger still seethed in his mind against the cunning woman known as his wife. His knuckles grew white beneath the leather of his gauntlet as he gripped the pommel of his saddle. During the past three months he had tried to forget Jamelyn and the deception she had played against him. He had hoped never to have to return to Raven's Keep and face the woman who had trampled his heart beneath her boot and fled before his wrath could come down on her. However,

Edward had commanded him to return to his holdings. Since the harvest had begun, the tithe Edward had levied against Raven's Keep had failed to reach its destination in England because of border thieves. It was Justin's mission to find the culprits who had stolen the much-needed grain for Edward's army and see them punished.

A grim smile of satisfaction curled the corners of his lips as he turned in the saddle and looked at the entourage that followed his men. It appeased his sense of justice to know that Anne of Chester had traveled with him. Edward had ordered him back to Scotland never suspecting Anne would follow, and in that Justin had gained a small measure of revenge against his king.

At first Justin had refused to allow Anne to accompany him, but then decided it would do his wife good to see he had been little affected by her sham. He had vowed that Jamelyn of Cregan would never know of the pain he had suffered because of her.

His cold gaze turned once more to the castle. Aye, he thought, much has changed, Jamelyn. No longer will you find me the peacemaker nor the kind, gentle lover. I will rule this fief with an iron hand.

Scanning the surrounding area, he was satisfied to see all had gone well in his absence. He noted the village had grown by one thatched cottage, indicating that one of the serfs had married and would serve Raven's Keep well in the future, to see that the bellies of his family did not go empty.

The heat of the day made beads of sweat form on Justin's brow and he removed his helm, pulling back the linen hood beneath to catch a small bit of the breeze that stirred the changing leaves overhead. Propping his helm on the pommel, he crossed his arms over it, his gaze focusing once more on the lowered gate of the keep. His men stationed in the castle had recognized the St. Claire banner and now awaited his entry. However, Justin did not urge his mount forward. He knew the delay was useless, but he needed more time to try to gain control over his turbulent emotions.

Jamelyn was only a short distance from him, and at that

thought he could not stop the erratic beating of his heart as the memories of those wonderful nights spent with her in his arms came flooding into his mind and senses. He could almost feel her satiny skin beneath his hand. The morning breeze seemed to hold the very scent of her to tantalize his nostrils. Damn her to hell, he thought as he violently kicked his destrier in the side and galloped toward Raven's Keep.

Nora came scurrying into Jamelyn's chamber; her eyes were wide and her usually rosy complexion was pale. She told Jamelyn that her husband had been sighted by the guards on the ramparts and was now approaching the castle.

Jamelyn's stomach seemed to do a flip-flop at Nora's news, but she forced herself to stand. Gathering all of the courage she possessed, she adjusted the silk netting over her braids and pinched her ashen cheeks to bring color into them. She would not face Justin like a pale, frightened mouse. He could do his worst to her, as he had tried to do before, but she would not let him see her cringe. Straightening her cotehardie of turquoise damask, Jamelyn was grateful for its fullness, which concealed her condition. She was also thankful that she had not gained a great deal of weight like other women did during their pregnancies. The only evidence visible to the eye when she was clothed was the extra fullness that had come to her breast and the translucent glow her complexion held when she was not upset. Satisfied that her secret was safely hidden, she walked slowly from her chamber and down the shadowy corridor to meet once more with her enemy—her husband.

Jamelyn stopped at the foot of the stairs and waited with her back stiff and chin held high. She heard the horses as they entered the bailey and came to a halt before the entrance of the castle. Taking a deep breath to quell the quaking that had begun in the pit of her stomach, she prepared herself to face her husband. She did not have long to wait. The huge doors swung wide to reveal Justin and his entourage. Her eyes were fastened to her husband's handsome face as he strode into the foyer, throwing his helm and mantle to his squire. Jamelyn savored the sight of the arrogant tilt of his raven head and his sculpted features, until a feminine voice broke the trance that had come over her.

"Justin, you don't mean this is where we are to stay?" Anne said as she sniffed disdainfully and looked about the almost barren hall. As her blue eyes swept the chamber, they came to rest upon Jamelyn standing silently at the foot of the stairs. Anne remembered the strong vexation she had felt upon learning that Justin's wife was in residence at Raven's Keep, having somehow managed to escape the Gutter King.

Anne's blue eyes narrowed briefly, reflecting her annoyance, before her lips curled into a malicious little smile. She had failed in one endeavor but would not do so again. She would put the bitch in her place once and for all. She would show Jamelyn St. Claire who held Justin's affections.

Possessively draping her arm through Justin's, she pressed her ripe breast against his muscular arm as she leaned toward him and said, "It seems the lady of the manor has come to welcome us, my love." Her icy gaze traveled once more in Jamelyn's direction.

Justin's eyes followed Anne's to come to rest coldly upon Jamelyn. His features were set in a hard mask, tiny lines etching his beautifully molded lips as they firmed and narrowed, a small twitch of irritation visible in the muscle of his clenched jaw. Taking Anne's hand, he brought it to his lips before leading her forward and halting in front of Jamelyn. "My lady, I would like to present Lady Anne of Chester. I'm sure you remember her from your brief interlude at Windsor. She will be my guest while I am in residence at Raven's Keep. See that she has all the comforts this meager fief can offer."

Each word was laced subtly with venom, but Jamelyn refused to cower before the man who had sold her into slavery. She faced him bravely, her own features void of any expression, hiding the turmoil that Justin's presence created within her. Her eyes were the only thing about her face to mirror any emotion and she could not stop the glint of hurt and anger that flashed into them. Lowering her lashes, Jamelyn said, "All will be seen to, my lord."

"Then have wine brought to us immediately." Placing Anne's hand back through his arm, Justin turned from Jamelyn as though she no longer existed. He led his mistress toward the blazing fire at the end of the great hall. Anne cast one triumphant glance in Jamelyn's direction before following Justin's lead.

Jamelyn's fingers curled into claws at her sides. The sight of Anne's elegantly gowned back made her long to rush forward and tear the woman's raven tresses out by the roots. Taking several long, deep breaths, Jamelyn managed to quell the urge. Her throat constricted with the curses she wanted to fling at Justin's head, and it took every ounce of her willpower to curtail the ire that bubbled within her as the green-eyed monster raised its head. With her mood black and her eyes the deep grey-green of storm-tossed ocean waves, Jamelyn turned her back on the scene and went to send Maille to bring her husband and his guest refreshments.

After giving the servants their orders, Jamelyn quickly escaped the hall and sought out the privacy of her own chamber. As the door closed behind her, she leaned weakly against it, her lips trembling and tears shimmering against her sooty lashes as she gazed about her haven. Wiping away the moisture with the back of her hand, Jamelyn held back a new onslaught of tears as she crossed to the window and gazed through misty eyes at the land beyond. No! she thought, I won't let you upset me like this. Too much is at stake, Justin St. Claire, for you and Anne to ruin it all.

In the distance Jamelyn could see the coppice of trees where she met with Royce each time to arrange another raid. She longed to place the white cloth in her window as a signal for Royce to meet her. At that moment she needed the comfort of his friendship to protect her against the agony that had renewed itself with Justin's return to Raven's Keep. Her knuckles were white as her nails bit into the wood of the windowsill. She could not chance jeopardizing all they had accomplished because of a fit of jealousy.

Resigned to dealing with her own problems herself, she turned from the window and slumped down into the leather chair. Covering her eyes with her hands, she tried to concentrate on other matters of importance. She sat up with a start at a tiny butterfly motion within her belly and a look of wonder crossed her face as she placed her hand over her rounded abdomen. Her babe had moved. Her fingers spread protectively over the sensitive area, feeling the soft stirring of her babe for the first time. All else was forgotten except the miracle of nature. A thrill of pure joy pierced Jamelyn's soul as the full impact of her condition hit her. A life grew within her womb. Her child, her flesh and blood and the future heir to Raven's Keep, moved within her.

Jamelyn's first instinct was to rush downstairs and tell Justin, and in her excitement she had nearly risen from the chair before she realized it would do little good to tell her husband of the child. It would only serve to remind him of his hatred. Justin detested her and all she represented. His feelings were implacable toward the Scots; his action of selling her to the Gutter King was proof of that.

Sinking down into the chair once more, she closed her thick lashes over her tear-bright eyes as she wearily laid her head back and let her hand rest again on her swelling belly.

The fluttering movement beneath her palm made Jamelyn realize that the love she had tried to expel from her heart was still deeply rooted. She had tried to give Justin one last gift of love by freeing him from the marriage he despised, but had failed in that effort. Now his child moved within her womb, reminding her of the love she could never possess. The intensity of emotion that welled within her threatened to choke the breath from her.

Justin St. Claire was her enemy, her husband, the father of her babe, and the man she knew she would always love. His cruel retaliation after finding out about her charade tore at Jamelyn's heart, yet the tenderness and love he had given her before knowing the truth was more deeply embedded in her soul than all else.

She had heard the men who served her uncle speak of a woman's heart as being very capricious. She had to agree with that sage observation if it meant being able to love and hate at the same time. She could deny neither emotion. She hated Justin vehemently, yet love overrode its opposite when she looked into his penetrating blue eyes and remembered his tender caresses as they lay entwined in the darkness of his chamber. Beneath her hand lay the living reminder of those sensuous times and her mind warred with her heart.

Engrossed with her thoughts, Jamelyn was unaware of the passage of time. She remained in her chamber until the last light of day had grown into the mauve glow of twilight. She pondered her conflicting emotions but failed to come to an understanding of either. She could no more solve her dilemma than she could explain why the seasons changed.

Jamelyn was abruptly drawn from her morbid reflections by the sound of her chamber door crashing open upon its hinges; she looked up with wide, startled eyes at the tall figure lounging in the doorway. A cynical smile crooked Justin's lips as he strode forward and bowed to Jamelyn. "My lady, I have come to escort you to the great hall. You have a guest to serve this evening. I will not have my household embarrassed by the rudeness of its mistress." Justin's words were spoken with such sarcasm that they made a travesty of her position at Raven's Keep. His mockery combined with an afternoon of mental turmoil released the only defense Jamelyn could use against her husband— anger. She felt it begin as a burning sensation in her cheeks. From the delicately-sculpted line of her cheekbone, her softly tinted skin deepened to a bright rose hue that traveled downward. The anger surged along every nerve in her body. Green flames danced in her eyes as she stood and faced her husband. Without conscious thought, Jamelyn braced her hands on her slender hips, ready to do battle as she said, "I'm afraid, my lord, that you have forgotten I am not a servant to dance attendance at the whim of your guests."

Justin's cynical expression hardened into open hostility as he gazed down into Jamelyn's defiant little face. His eyes narrowed and a telltale muscle twitched in his jaw as he said, "Nay, I have forgotten nothing, wench. You will serve as I dictate. I am master of this fief and I will say who is the servant or nay. Do you understand?"

With a calmness she did not feel, Jamelyn lifted her chin

in the air as she spat, "You may be master of Raven's Keep but not of me, my lord."

Justin's chest rose and fell rapidly as he tried to maintain control over his own anger. "You try me too far, my lady. I will be obeyed or you will suffer the consequences."

Tears burned Jamelyn's lids and she blinked to stem their flow as all the hurt came rushing forward to engulf her. She wet her dry lips with the tip of her tongue and swallowed as she said, "Aye, I know much suffering at your hand, my lord."

Justin balled his fist tightly at his side to keep from strangling her. His lips thinned into a hard, narrow line as he thought, You know nothing of suffering until your heart lies cold and dead within your breast, as mine does. However, Justin did not speak his thoughts, nor did he see his own hurt mirrored in the green depths of Jamelyn's shimmering eyes. "My lady, you are not the only one who will suffer from your disobedience. As master of this fief I have the right to use your servants as your surrogate. I need not touch one silken strand upon your lovely head but can use Nora or Maille. Will you enjoy their pain as much as your own?"

Jamelyn gasped, "You would not!"

Calmly Justin nodded. "If need be, then I will. It seems the love you have professed for these poor Scots is as shallow as that you proclaimed for me. Will you see their backs opened with the lash or will you obey my commands?"

Justin's words were like a physical blow to Jamelyn and she had to grasp the arm of the chair for support to keep her knees from giving way beneath her. Slowly her gilded head bowed and she nodded. Her words were no more than a soft whisper as she said, "I will obey, my lord."

Justin had to lean forward to hear Jamelyn's soft-spoken reply. It was a mistake. The scent of her filled his nostrils and quickened his blood and he had to force himself to keep from reaching out and drawing her into his arms. He turned away abruptly to break the bewitching spell and said as he strode briskly to the door, "Then I will see you downstairs within the half hour." With that he slammed the door to leave Jamelyn defeated once more at his hand.

Her limbs trembled uncontrollably as she sank into the chair to keep from falling. Justin's cold, granite features were emblazoned upon her brain as she stared at her tightly clasped hands without seeing them. The severe man she had just faced was not the man she had left in Windsor the night he had pleaded for Catherine Michaels' understanding and love. He was a stranger whose hostility was like a physical force that battered her already bruised emotions mercilessly.

Is my whole world made of illusions? Jamelyn asked herself as she pressed her fingers to her aching temples. But she had known of Justin's cruelty before, when his men had taken her to the Gutter King. A tiny voice within her heart cried, Then why does it hurt?

Jamelyn knew the answer but refused to acknowledge it. She would not accept the love she felt for him. It was better to feel hatred instead of the pain caused by loving him. She could defend herself and her child if she was not vulnerable to the callings of her heart. Justin had let his hatred override the love he had professed for her and she would do likewise.

She crossed to the metal mirror and squarely faced her pale reflection. During the past months she had resolved to see to the welfare of her people and she would not let herself sink into the quagmire of emotions that dwelt within her heart. She could not be so selfish; too many people depended upon her as the Clan Chieftain. She would proceed as planned and pray with each day that the pain would lessen and eventually disappear.

The sound of laughter greeted Jamelyn's ears before she entered the great hall. She paused on the threshold, her green eyes sweeping the chamber until they came to rest upon the wide back of her husband and the raven-haired beauty sitting on his right. Anne of Chester sat in the chair reserved for the mistress of the manor. The sight rankled. With her lips pressed firmly together, Jamelyn strode across the hall and began to help Nora and Maille serve the evening meal.

Jamelyn received several strange looks as she served

Justin's men their trenchers of hard bread and tankards of ale, but no one commented on her actions. After all were served, she stood silently with the other servants until Justin motioned her to take the seat several spaces down from his own. She did as he bade and sipped the cool ale and nibbled at the roast venison as she listened to the men's conversations around her.

Stoically, she kept her eyes away from the head of the table, where Anne's laughter could be heard at some small quip Justin made. The sound made Jamelyn tense and she let all pretense of eating fall away. She sat with fists balled in her lap and eyes staring straight ahead, firmly vowing she would die before letting Justin know she was affected by his preference for Anne.

Jamelyn shut out the words around her, the conversations becoming a steady drone that soon lulled her into relaxing. However, the mention of Anthony Godfrey drew her attention once more and she leaned forward to hear what Jacob said. "'Tis a shame Sir Godfrey could not have come with you, my lord. He would certainly enjoy putting a noose about the bandits' necks when we catch them."

Jamelyn glanced down the table at her husband to see his face darken. The bright blue of his eyes dimmed as his jovial mood faded and his face became like hard granite. "I'm afraid Sir Godfrey is no longer welcome at Raven's Keep," was all he said as his steely gaze traveled in Jamelyn's direction. It settled upon her with such an intense expression of dislike, she could nearly feel his antagonism like fingers about her throat. Fearlessly, she returned his gaze. The open hostility between them seemed to clash like two battle-axes, making all fall silent around them.

Annoyed that Jamelyn had finally gained her husband's attention, Anne placed her hand on Justin's arm and broke the lethal silence as she said cajolingly, "My lord, we were speaking of the bandits who have been taking the goods meant for Edward. Do you think it will take you long to capture them?"

A sigh of relief seemed to hover in the air as Justin turned his attention once more to Anne. "Nay, it will not take long to find the scoundrels. They will rue the day they stole from my fief."

Jamelyn quickly lowered her sooty lashes over her eyes to hide the gleam of triumph that flashed into them. Sipping her ale, she mused, So that is the reason for Justin's return.

Casting a furtive glance in her husband's direction, Jamelyn had to bite the inside of her lip to hold back a smile. It will be a cold day in a very hot place, Justin St. Claire, before you capture Royce McFarland, she thought as she watched Justin speak with Anne. You will not bleed Raven's Keep dry of its livelihood for your deceitful king. My child will not be paupered because of the greed of the English, she vowed silently as she sat and waited for the meal to come to an end.

When at last the hearty appetites of Justin's men had been appeased, they began to leave the table to enjoy an evening of games and dice. Jamelyn remained seated until Justin gave her permission to leave the table. With as much dignity as she could summon in front of her husband and his mistress, she rose and walked from the great hall. Free of prying eyes, she sped the rest of the way to her chamber, latching the door behind her to make sure no one entered as she placed the white cloth in the window to signal Royce.

Tonight, while Justin was satisfying himself with Anne and his men were celebrating the end of their long journey, Jamelyn would sneak from the castle to meet Royce. She would wait until she was sure Justin's men were well into their cups after renewing old friendships with the comrades they had not seen for nearly a year. When the hour arrived to join Royce in the coppice, it should be safe for her to leave Raven's Keep.

Jamelyn changed from the velvet cyclas and soft kirtle into a dark tunic with soft woolen chainse and slipped the old pair of Gibbon's braies over her slender legs before settling down to await the hour of midnight. The silvery light of the full moon was all that broke the total darkness of her chamber. Propping her heels on the seat of the chair, she folded her arms about her knees and rested her head on them, listening to the sounds of the castle. The hours ticked by and gradually the noise abated as everyone else within the keep settled down for their night's rest. At last the nighttime stillness crept over the castle, enfolding it in silent arms.

Jamelyn watched the silver ribbons of light grow shorter as the moon rose higher in the blue velvet sky and knew it was time. She moved with the stealth of a stalking cat, her green eyes warily scanning the shadows of the corridor as she crept down the winding stairs and made her way through the cellar to the secret passageway. The path was well worn, for she had used it often since her return to Raven's Keep and needed no light to show her the direction she should take.

At the end of the tunnel, Jamelyn hesitated, peering out into the darkness to insure that she would go unobserved as she ran into the thick underbrush nearby. Speeding across the small clearing, she was as fleet as a fawn and found the path that would lead her through the trees to Royce.

Her footsteps were light, making no sound as she entered the shadowy glade where only tiny threads of silver penetrated. Pausing, she looked about but could see no one, and she nearly let a startled cry slip from her lips as two large hands touched her shoulders. She spun about to find Royce's large frame directly behind her. "Lass, I had been wondering when I would see you next. I have watched for your sign for well over a month."

Taking a deep breath to steady the pounding of her heart, she said, "I would have come sooner had there been a reason, but Jacob decided it was best to await the last of the harvest before sending more to England."

Royce stepped back into the shadows, crossing his suede-covered arms over his wide chest and bracing himself against the trunk of a huge oak, with one foot propped against the rough bark. "But the end of the harvest is not due for another week. Why have you come so soon?"

Peering into the shadows so that she could try to see Royce's face as she spoke—but failing—Jamelyn said, "I have come to warn you. Justin has returned to Raven's Keep to find the thieves who have taken Edward's goods."

Royce's chuckle sounded like no more than the breeze ruffling the leaves. He stepped forward and placed his hands on her shoulders. A wry smile curved his lips as he gazed down into her moonlit face. "'Tis nothing to worry your pretty head about, lass. I have outwitted Edward's men before."

Vexed that he took her warning so lightly, Jamelyn shook free of Royce's hands. Crossing her arms over her breast, she eyed the tall raider as her boot tapped the soft, leaf-strewn earth with irritation. "Royce, you should heed my warning. Justin is not a man who will give up the chase easily. Too much depends on our success. Winter is coming and if you are caught, my people will starve."

Sensing Jamelyn's inner turmoil, Royce said, "You are not worried that I will fail, lass. There is more here than you are telling me. What else troubles you over your husband's return?"

Unable to face Royce's searching gaze, Jamelyn turned her back to him. "There is nothing else. All that concerns me is your safety and the welfare of my serfs."

Closing the space between them, Royce turned her to face him once more as his gaze took in her lovely, pale features. "Does it hurt that bad, lass?"

Her chin quivered as she looked up into the shadowy face of her friend. "I don't know what you mean."

He leaned close to look into her tear-bright eyes. "I think you do. You forget you have told me of your feelings for your husband and of the child you now carry. Can you truly say his presence has not affected you?"

Jamelyn gave a small, pathetic shake of her gilded head as her lips trembled and great crystal tears brimmed in her eyes before cascading down her delicately-boned cheeks. The sight touched Royce's heart more than he would have imagined. Instinctively he pulled her against his hard chest, his hand caressing her copper-streaked hair as her cheek pressed against the sinewy muscles over his heart.

Feeling his comforting caress, Jamelyn at last gave way to the misery that had been building in her since that afternoon. She wept openly, her tears dampening the leather of Royce's tunic.

He remained silent, giving her time to release all her pent-up grief. He held her tenderly until she could cry no more and sniffled like a small child.

"Lass, oh my beautiful lass." Royce murmured soothingly against her bowed head. "I wish I could ease the pain in your heart."

Jamelyn's eyes glistened in the moonlight as she took a deep, trembling breath and looked up into his compassionate face. His feelings were reflected in his one sapphire eye. He cared for her and in that moment she needed someone to care, to love her, to make her forget the husband who now lay within the arms of Anne of Chester. Deliberately, Jamelyn's arms crept up around Royce's strong neck and her fingers curled in his dark hair as she pulled his head down to her.

Royce remained still as she pressed her lips against his. Though his loins cried out for him to possess her and take what her small, flickering tongue offered, he did not respond to her heated kiss. He sensed the heartrending reason behind her action and knew he cared too deeply for Jamelyn to abuse her already battered emotions further. If he let himself respond to her soft, sensuous lips, all would be lost. He had to keep a tight control over his emotions for her sake.

Had it been anyone else, Royce would not have hesitated to take what was so freely offered, but this was Jamelyn of Cregan, the woman he had grown to love. His heart and his throbbing body cried out for him to lay her upon the soft earth and thrust deep within her lovely warmth, yet he could not. Jamelyn did not love him. She had given her heart to the scoundrel who had returned to Raven's Keep to wreak more havoc upon her. It took all of Royce's willpower to reach up and unclasp her hands from about his neck and put her at arm's length from him. "No, lass," was all he could force from his tight throat.

Stung by Royce's rejection of her, Jamelyn stood silent,

her eyes misting with hurt as she wet her dry lips and finally managed to whisper a shaky, "Why?"

Every lean muscle in Royce's body was taut from his desire for her as he ran his long fingers through his dark hair and shook his head. "You know well the reason, lass. You do not love me. You only want to use me to make you forget. Go back to the castle, lass, before I forget that your heart belongs to Justin St. Claire and you carry his babe within your belly."

Jamelyn turned her sparkling eyes to glance at the dark structure outlined against the velvet sky before she once more looked at Royce's tormented face. Her voice was quiet and forlorn as she said, "Why should I not seek out another's arms when my husband now lies within those of his mistress?"

Royce's brow furrowed as he asked, "Mistress?"

An icy chill seemed to creep over Jamelyn and her lips narrowed into an angry line as she spat, "Aye, his mistress. He brought Anne of Chester to Raven's Keep to warm his bed. I am now relegated to the position of servant in my own castle. Anne sits at Justin's right as the lady of the manor." Jamelyn's voice was filled with all the bitterness the thought aroused within her.

Hearing the hurt that she failed to keep out of her voice, Royce tentatively raised one hand to draw Jamelyn to him, but it froze in midair. He could not touch her again or he would not be responsible for what would happen. Letting his hand fall, Royce said, "Did you tell him of the child?"

Jamelyn shook her gilded head violently from side to side. "Nay. His hatred of me would only grow if he knew of my babe."

"Are you so sure about that, lass? Perhaps all would be well if you told him."

Jamelyn's green eyes traveled once more to the castle. "Nay, Justin will not know of my babe. It is mine and I will see to its welfare. He will be the future heir of Raven's Keep and I'll not let Justin or anyone else take that from him. That is the reason we must not let my husband succeed in stopping the raids," she said, her voice reflecting the resolution she had made earlier. "That is why you must be wary, Royce. Justin will be as determined to catch you as we are to foil Edward's plans."

Confidently, Royce looped his thumbs in his wide belt and nodded. "Aye, he will try to catch us as he has done in the past, but he will fail in the attempt. I'll not let you or what you hold dear be destroyed by the English, Jamelyn. He will gain no glory at the expense of Raven's Keep. Lord St. Claire does not know he has a spy within his camp and that will work for us."

Chapter 14

The silence of the great hall was shattered as Justin and his men strode through the huge double doors. "Damn!" the tall knight said as he tossed his gauntlets to Gibbon. "How can the entire shipment have disappeared without a trace?"

Jacob removed his helm and laid it aside as he shook his head. "That I do not know. The bandits vanish, it seems, into thin air. Even when their trail is so hot we can nearly hear their horses, they seem to become invisible."

Justin removed his own helm and pulled back the coif before rubbing his hand across his stubbled chin. They had been searching for the reivers since before dawn, but to no avail. The thieves has succeeded once more in taking the tithe meant for King Edward. Justin had found his men bound securely to a large oak, but the shipment of grain and pack horses had vanished, as well as the tracks that would have led Justin to the bandits.

It had been the third shipment to disappear within the month. The thieves seemed to be able to read their minds and to know when and where Justin and his men would be

at any given time. Their cunning exasperated his already
bruised ego. In all his experience in war, he had always
been able to come out the victor. Now a miserable bunch
of thieves were succeeding in outwitting him where all other
enemies had failed. His vexation mounted daily at his inability to deal with such a trivial situation.

Deep lines traced a craggy path about his shapely lips
and fanned his dark eyes as he turned from his men and
took in the occupants of the great hall. The sight did little
to lighten his grim mood. Lady Anne sat by the huge fireplace on a stool with her feet tucked in demurely, embroi-
dering, while Jamelyn and Nora cleaned the ashes from the
hearth. His wife's cheeks were smudged with soot and he
was reminded of the first time he had seen her small, defiant
face. Jamelyn of Cregan had changed little since that first
day. She might now possess the manners of a lady, but
beneath that polished exterior dwelt the stubborn vixen he
had first met.

The proof of that lay before his eyes. He had not meant
for her to take the role of servant, but since their argument
the day of his return to the keep, she had stoically remained
in that position. At first it had pleased his vindictive nature,
but now the sight nettled him more than he cared to admit.
Jamelyn worked like a slave while Anne sat beautifully
gowned, idling her time away. Jamelyn was his wife and
not Anne, and it was an insult to him for her to act as a
servant. It was time she became aware of the fact.

Over the past weeks some of his bitterness and anger
against Jamelyn had eased. He had watched her as she
moved about the hall and could not stop the quick rush of
blood in his veins at the sight of her rounded bottom as she
bent over the pot at the fire. Nor could he stop himself from
admiring the fluid grace or soft laughter that came so easily
when she talked with the servants or his men. In those
moments it was hard for him to remember his resentment
toward his wife and all she represented to him.

Anne noted the heat of Justin's intense gaze as he strode
forward and sensed his intention. She had seen his eyes
stray toward his wife during the last weeks and was deter-

mined to keep Jamelyn in the position in which she now served. Laying her embroidery aside, Anne smiled seductively as she stood and went to meet Justin, halting his steps in his wife's direction.

Throwing her arms about his neck, she kissed him before saying, "My lord, I'm so glad you have returned. It has been such a dull day without you. But let me cease this prattle. You must be tired." Holding onto Justin's arm possessively, she looked at Jamelyn and her words were curt as she ordered, "Bring my lord wine and then see that his bath is readied." With that she looked sweetly up at Justin. "Be seated, my lord, and rest until the servant has your bath heated."

Justin noted the flash of fire within Jamelyn's emerald eyes at Anne's command. At present it was best to let everything remain as it was. Her temper and his own were not on the best of grounds at the moment. He decided he would speak with Jamelyn later in the evening when there would be no one to interrupt them. Settling his large frame in the chair, he let Anne prop his feet upon the small stool before she curled up like a contented cat at his side. Had the room been entirely quiet Justin was sure he could have heard Anne purr.

He accepted the wine Jamelyn brought without comment and watched as she returned to the fire and lifted the heavy iron caldron over the blaze to warm the water for his bath. Anne curled her fingers in the silken hair at the nape of his neck, caressing him intimately as she asked, "My love, did you catch the villains today?"

With a feeling near to disgust, Justin pulled Anne's hand away from his neck and placed it in her lap as he said, "Nay, the scoundrels again escaped." Though his gaze rested on Jamelyn's trim back, he failed to see the slight smile that touched his wife's lips as she continued to stoke the fire.

Jamelyn found small things to keep her busy near Justin and Anne so that she could listen to their conversation. Over the past weeks she had accepted her role as servant for only one reason; to eavesdrop on Justin's plans for Royce's capture. They were not suspicious of her and talked freely of their problems in her presence. It had made it much simpler to keep Royce alerted to their movements.

Only one man suspected anything amiss in Jamelyn's meek actions—Shawn McDougal. The redheaded Scot was wary of his young mistress's docile behavior and had watched her closely since their return to Raven's Keep. He had seen the triumphant gleam in her eyes when Justin had returned to the keep without succeeding in his quest to capture the border thieves. That was when Shawn's suspicions had begun to grow that there was more afoot than anyone surmised.

Hoping to find a clue to answer the question that niggled at him, Shawn had gone to the village and asked the serfs if they had any knowledge of what was transpiring at Raven's Keep. They had all been very closemouthed to him and his curiosity was magnified by their refusal to tell him anything. It was further aroused when he learned by accident from Nora that no new marriage had occurred in the village to account for the cottage that had been constructed. At last all the pieces of the puzzle fell into place one night when he had gone secretly to the village and had searched the new dwelling. There he had found several barrels of grain marked for the king of England.

Now Shawn knew for certain that his Jami was helping the thieves. It was his duty to report his findings to Lord St. Claire, but he could not betray Jami again. He had done so once by swearing fealty to Justin and it had taken her a long time to forgive him. Shawn was not willing to chance losing again the friendship he so treasured.

Shawn respected Jamelyn for the courage it took her to defy the king's edict and secretly applauded her daring. For a short while he had thought the Jami he had known and loved was lost to him, but he now realized nothing had changed. She was still the Jamelyn of Cregan the old lord had raised to see to the welfare of the people of Raven's Keep.

Shawn could only watch and pray that Jamelyn's cunning would go unnoticed by those who held her less dear to their hearts. At that thought, his gaze came to rest upon the raven-haired woman at Justin's side. Jami, he thought, be careful, my brave lass, or the witch will have the noose about your neck.

Justin's eyes never left the sleek curve of his wife's back as he said, "Tomorrow will be the last shipment of grain to England. My men will follow only a short distance behind the pack train, while I will take a small squad and leave at dawn so that we can travel ahead and scout the area to make sure it reaches its destination." Taking a long sip of the wine, he wiped a stray ruby drop from his lips with the back of his hand before he continued. "Hopefully, we will catch the bandits by surrounding them before they have time to escape."

Jacob propped one foot on the hearth and rested his elbow on his knee as he leaned forward. "Do you think they will suspect a trap?"

Justin shook his blue-black head. "Nay; if we ride out as if we were a hunting party, they should not be wary of our motives."

Anne's eyes were wide and shining with excitement as she gripped Justin's arm and said, "You must let me come with you. If they see a woman among your party they will never suspect you are setting a trap."

Without making an obvious movement, he eased his arm away from her clinging hands as he considered her words. His gaze rested momentarily on her beautiful face before once more traveling to the slim figure at the fire. "I see no reason why you and Jamelyn could not join us. There should be no danger even when we overtake the bandits."

Two sets of startled eyes looked at Justin, one blue and one emerald green. Both women were astounded by his words, but for different reasons. Anne was first to recover her speech. "I'm sure Jamelyn would not find it amusing to be among the men who hunted some of her beloved Scots."

A slow, easy smile spread Justin's lips as his eyes challenged his wife to accept his offer. "What say you, Jamelyn?

Would you rather stay here than enjoy the fresh morning air and a brisk canter through the woods?"

Jamelyn rose from her place at the hearth, her hand automatically going to the small ache in her back. She rubbed it absently as her own eyes defied Justin's. "I would prefer the brisk ride, my lord, but in other company."

Justin chuckled, delighted to see the sparks once more in her eyes. Deliberately, he reached for Anne's hand and his thumb caressed its smooth, white surface before bringing it to his lips. His eyes sparkled with devilment as he placed a light kiss upon his mistress's hand before saying, "So I would imagine, but I'm afraid you will not get your preference, my lady. You will ride with us at dawn."

To further pique Jamelyn's temper, he rose and placed Anne's hand intimately through his arm to escort her from the hall. Pleased with his attention, Anne cast one smug, victorious glance at Jamelyn before letting him lead her up the stairs to his chamber.

Jamelyn turned abruptly back to the fire. Her eyes glowed with anger, reflecting the heat of the flames, as she took the poker and released her rage upon the charred logs.

Sparks popped and crackled as they showered up the chimney and fell into the open caldron of water hanging over the flames. Shawn watched as Jamelyn stoked the blazes higher until the heat brightened her cheeks to a deep rose. Sensing her rage, he placed a calming hand upon her shoulder. "Have a care, lass, or you'll burn the keep to the ground. Let your anger cool, as well as the fire in the grate. You will lose all if you do not gain control of yourself."

Jerking free of Shawn's hand, Jamelyn faced him with her eyes flashing. Vindictively, her words rushed out in a hiss. "Hopefully, if I do, the witch will be burnt to cinders along with it."

Shawn's lips crinkled at the corners as he thought, Aye, my lass still has spirit. But he said, "Don't let the green-eyed monster ruin everything for you, Jami. You have accomplished much for your people during the last months. Let your temper cool; all will be well in the end."

Jamelyn's hand clenched about the iron poker. Her

knuckles grew white with the strain as tiny lines formed about her delicate lips. "How did you find out?"

Shawn chuckled as he took the poker and placed it once more against the stone hearth. "Did you think to keep the secret from the man who knows you best in this world, Jami? I have watched you grow from a wee mite into a keen, courageous woman. We Scots are a canny lot and are not easily duped by one of our own."

The grimy smudges of soot stood out starkly against Jamelyn's ashen cheeks and her voice was faint as she asked, "Will you tell Justin?"

A rueful expression crossed fleetingly over Shawn's ruddy features. "Nay, lass. My first allegiance has always been to you and Raven's Keep."

Jamelyn looked quickly away from his solemn face. His loyalty touched her deeply and her throat constricted with emotions she could not express in words. Her eyes burned with tears and she brushed them away with the back of her work-roughened hand as she swallowed the lump in her throat. A small, tentative smile then played over her lips. "It seems the smoke has gotten into my eyes."

Feeling the same tightness within his own throat, Shawn also tried to lighten the somber mood. His lips quirked at the corners as he nodded. "Aye. It isn't any wonder with the way you have been flailing the fire. 'Tis lucky I know your temper is not directed at me, lass."

Shawn scanned the hall warily to ascertain whether Jamelyn's actions had gone unobserved. "But it is also fortunate no one else saw your show of ill humor or they would know the vixen has been playing a game with them."

She blushed under his reprimand as her eyes followed his about the chamber. "Aye, you are right, Shawn McDougal," she said, placing her hand on his strong arm. Their eyes met and both knew instantly they were in accord. "'Tis good to have you home," Jamelyn whispered before turning once more to her duties. She picked up the ladle and filled a kettle with steaming water before hurrying from the great hall.

Shawn's arms were akimbo with his hands braced on his

hips as he watched her scurry up the stairs toward her husband's chamber. 'Tis good to be home, Jami, he said to himself before picking up his tankard of ale and downing its contents.

The door to Justin's chamber was not latched securely and swung open easily under Jamelyn's touch. The sight that met her eyes did little to cool the temper that had been at the boiling point since before her husband and his mistress had come upstairs. Justin was seated before the fire with Anne curled up on his lap like a velvet feline. They kissed passionately, unaware of Jamelyn's presence until she clanged the kettle down upon the hearth. The noise startled Justin. Instinctively he came to his feet, unceremoniously dumping Anne to the floor as he rose, ready to defend himself if necessary. Many years of hard training had honed his reflexes to a keen edge and he reacted without conscious thought.

Anne let out a shriek of pure rage as she landed on the hard floor. "Damn you, Justin, can you not see that it is only a servant with the water for your bath?"

Jamelyn's lips curled provocatively at the sight of Anne's predicament. Her smile further infuriated Anne as the dark-haired woman clambered ungracefully to her feet without Justin's assistance and eyed Jamelyn spitefully. "How dare you laugh at me? Get out this instant before I have you whipped."

Before Justin could intercede between his wife and his mistress, Jamelyn braced her hands on her hips, her eyes sparkling with challenge as she spat, "Have me whipped? My lady, I'm afraid you have forgotten you are only a small bit of fluff to warm my husband's bed. I am mistress of this keep."

Anne's flawless features flushed a violet red and she sputtered with rage as she turned to see Justin's eyes gleaming with mirth. "Are you going to let her speak to me in this manner? I demand you have her punished for such behavior."

The humor faded from Justin's eyes. "My lady, cease this prattle. I'll not have such caterwauling within my household. Anne, it is time you returned to your chamber; and Jamelyn, finish filling my bath. I have no time or patience for such trivial matters."

The two women eyed each other hostilely for a fraction of a moment before doing as he had bade. Still enraged, Anne stamped her foot before leaving Jamelyn alone with her husband. She slammed the door violently behind her. The action seemed to make the stout timbers tremble.

Justin noted the pleased expression that flickered over Jamelyn's face as she resumed her duties. Settling himself once more in the chair, he crossed his muscular legs before him and interlaced his fingers across his hard stomach as he said, "My lady, Anne is a guest at Raven's Keep and as such, I expect you to show her courtesy."

Resentment rippled along every nerve in Jamelyn's body, but she refused to let Justin know his words affected her in the least. "Aye, my lord" was all she said as she poured the hot liquid into the wooden tub and went to fetch more water. When she had the tub nearly filled to the brim, she turned to leave him to his bath, but his words halted her.

"My lady, I would have you scrub my back."

Taking a deep breath, Jamelyn slowly retraced her steps to the side of the tub. Her lips were set in a grim line as she waited for her husband to disrobe. She kept her lashes lowered to keep from viewing his unclothed body. With her hands clasped tightly before her, she tried desperately to hold back the heat that rose in her cheeks as he sank into the steaming water.

Justin smiled at the sight of her set features. He wanted to laugh aloud at the blush that crept up the ivory column of her neck to brighten her cheeks as he slowly descended into the tub. A sense of pleasure swept over him with the knowledge that Jamelyn was not as unaffected by the sight of his naked body as she would have him believe.

He bathed himself leisurely, enjoying her discomfort to the hilt. He lathered the crisp mat of black curls upon his hard chest and then proceeded to do the same with his long, shapely legs. At last, when he could find nothing more to prolong his bath, he leaned forward and tossed the bar of soap to Jamelyn. "Scrub my back." He watched her face intently and was well satisfied by the slight tremble of her hand as she touched his tanned, smooth skin.

The feel of Justin's wet flesh beneath her hand made Jamelyn forget the resentment she had felt only a short while before. It had been many months since she had felt his powerful muscles ripple beneath her touch. His body stirred her own senses and a tingle of pleasure surged through her. For a few exquisite moments, she pretended to be his beloved wife and enjoyed the sensual pleasure she felt as she massaged the broad expanse of his back.

Her fingers moved tantalizingly from the small of his back to his wide shoulders, working gently at the sinewy flesh. She could feel the tension leave his muscles under her tender ministrations and heard him release a long, relaxed sigh as his hand came up to halt her own. Gently he drew her to face him, his keen blue eyes searching her lovely features before his fingers eased to the back of her neck and pulled her down to meet his own sensuous lips.

Justin's kiss jarred Jamelyn to her very core. With the intensity of a lightning bolt splitting the stormy sky, it ignited the passion she had tried too hard to forget. Breathless, she drew away, her emerald eyes brimming. Her heart cried out for the things she could never have as she gazed down into his smoldering eyes. With her heart pounding against her breast, she turned and fled the chamber before she could succumb to the pleas of her body.

Jamelyn's reaction surprised and bewildered Justin. He stared at the vacant space where only a brief moment before she had stood. Her expression of pain was branded upon his brain and he could not understand it. What he had seen upon her lovely face might have made him believe she suffered as much as he did from their tumultuous relationship, if he had not known better.

Running his fingers through his damp hair, Justin leaned back in the tepid water. He leaned his head against the rim of the tub, closed his eyes, and tried to reason out the emotions sweeping over him.

Jamelyn of Cregan is a deceptive bitch, he thought as he

tried to quell the blood rushing through his veins and the heat that had built in his loins. But damn it, I still want her!

Startled by the honesty of his own thoughts, he bolted upright, his eyes flying wide as he realized the truth. No matter how he argued with himself, he still wanted Jamelyn. She seemed to ferment his blood like a heady wine. He had wrestled with the fact that she was one of the hated Scots; she was devious and had been forced upon him without his consent—yet he could no longer deny his desire for her. She held some mysterious quality that drew him to her against his will. No other woman had held that power over him before.

Abruptly Justin stood and dried himself roughly with the linen towel, his sudden actions reflecting the turmoil of his thoughts. I will get you out of my blood, Jamelyn, he vowed to himself. You are my wife and I have no reason to flagellate myself with wanting you. I have the right. Stepping from the cool water, he strode purposefully across the chamber to the rich burgundy velvet cotehardie and soft linen chainse laid out on the bed for him. He slipped them on and smoothed the silk hose over his sinewy thighs without calling for assistance to dress. He was in no mood for Gibbon's fumbling on this night. A grim light of determination glimmered in the dark blue depths of his eyes as he strapped his gold girdle about his hips and then strode briskly from the chamber and down the corridor.

Anne was already seated at the long table as he entered the great hall. She noted his brief pause as his gaze traveled over the assembly until it rested upon Jamelyn's small figure at the hearth. From long experience Anne recognized the fleeting expression that crossed Justin's face before he joined her. The heat in that one look ignited Anne's already volatile temper. She seethed inwardly as her own sultry gaze turned to Jamelyn. Bitch, she thought maliciously, you will not have him again. I see the heat in his eyes when he looks at you and I'll not be second choice again. I have waited far too long.

As Justin settled his large frame into the chair at her side, Anne hid her hatred well beneath a charming smile as she said, "I can hardly wait until tomorrow. I will be the envy of every lady at court when they hear of my exciting adventure."

Justin had to make a strong mental effort to draw his thoughts away from Jamelyn and back to the present. "Aye, it will be much more so if we capture the villains."

With her lips curling seductively, Anne ran one perfectly manicured nail along Justin's velvet sleeve. "Have you ever failed with anything you set out to do? I cannot remember a time when you have not eventually gotten your desire."

At Anne's words Justin's eyes traveled once more to his wife's small form. Absently, he raised Anne's hand to his lips and placed a casual kiss upon its smooth, white surface. Distracted by Jamelyn's trim figure, he murmured, "That has always been true in the past and hopefully will continue to be so in the future."

Further irritated by his abstractedness, Anne no longer tried to hide her vexation. She jerked her hand away so abruptly, it startled Justin.

A wry smile touched his lips as he arched one raven brow quizzically in her direction. Seeing the blue flames in her eyes, he said, "Pray tell, my lady, what has ruffled your fine feathers this eve?"

Anne's full breast rose and fell as she breathed in deep, angry breaths. Her lips pouted as she spat, "How dare you kiss my hand while ogling that wretch!"

Justin's smile mocked Anne. Her arrogance teased his own temper as he said, "Wretch, Anne? I see only my wife. Be satisfied you sit on my right while she serves my men. I have told you before I do what I please. Now let us finish our meal in peace. I've suffered enough of your ill humor this day."

Aware that she had once more let her unruly temper overstep its bounds, Anne feigned an expression of penitence. Her blue eyes misted and her full lower lip trembled slightly as she looked up at Justin. "I'm sorry, my lord. 'Tis only that my heart tears into shreds when you look at another woman, even when she carries your name."

At Anne's expression, Justin's annoyance faded. Though

her constant possessiveness nettled him, he could not brush her aside easily. They had been too much to each other over the years. He knew he had been her first lover and it was she who had always been there when he needed someone. For all her faults, Anne had been the only truly constant thing in his life. Contrite, he took her hand once more within his own strong grasp and placed a light kiss upon it. "We have been friends far too long to argue over such a small matter. I will admit Jamelyn holds an attraction I do not understand, but I have vowed to rid myself of it. Give me time, Anne; that is all I ask."

Anne's white teeth flashed in the candlelight as she bestowed her most captivating smile upon him, thinking, You will be rid of her sooner than you think, Justin. But aloud she said sweetly, "I will be patient, my lord."

Relieved to see her smiling again, Justin squeezed her hand before kissing it again. "Thank you, Anne."

As the evening progressed the talk turned once more to the next day's search for the thieves. Jamelyn sat and listened to all that was said, absorbing each bit of information to relay to Royce after all slept within the castle.

Tomorrow the last of the grain would be shipped to England and that would be the final raid for Royce and his men. They had been successful during the past months and Jamelyn wanted to insure that their mission would end with as much success as it had begun. At last it will be over, she thought with a silent sigh of relief. Her people would be well fed during the hard, cold months of winter and Royce would no longer be put into jeopardy because of his friendship to her.

Feeling a tingling sensation at the nape of her neck, Jamelyn looked up from her wine to see three pairs of eyes on her. One was malevolently blue and filled with hate. The other pair of indigo eyes held an expression Jamelyn could not read, but it left a warm sense of anticipation in her belly. Drawing her eyes away from Justin's, she met the last pair of eyes with her own as Shawn McDougal smiled and raised his tankard slightly to her in a silent toast to her future success. A light blush tinted her cheeks as she quickly looked down at the ruby liquid in her goblet.

"Do you think you can be ready to leave at dawn, Jamelyn?" Justin's direct question startled her and she jumped in her seat as her eyes flew to her husband's smiling face. Wetting her dry lips, she nodded. "Aye, I can be ready."

Placing both palms on the table, Justin rose and looked down the long expanse at his men. "Then it is all settled. My group will leave at dawn and scout ahead to insure the safety of the pack train. We will take the bastards unawares and see them hanging from the gibbet before sunset." With that he proffered his hand to Anne, drew her to her feet, and escorted her from the hall.

Justin's announcement drew murmurs of approval from his men. They were tired of the constant galloping about the countryside in search of an invisible enemy. It nipped at their pride as much as their leader's to be outwitted by a bunch of thieves. All present but Shawn were eager for the raiders' demise. If all went as Lord St. Claire planned, the morrow would end the hunt and they could once more resume their normal routines.

Jamelyn listened to the men discuss the coming day's events as she finished her evening chores. She was tired to the bone and the ache had returned to needle irritably at the small of her back. But her work for the night was not over when she finished clearing the table and banking the coals in the hearth. She still had to alert Royce to Justin's plans.

The soldiers had settled down early for their night's rest. Their snores were already drifting in the air when Jamelyn sent Nora and Maille off to their pallets and made her way wearily up to her chamber.

Her actions were lethargic as she lit the candle and moved to the window. The white cloth lay folded on the sill and she set the candle alongside it as she draped the material so it would be visible from Royce's vantage point in the trees.

Jamelyn curled herself into the chair and settled down to wait until all was quiet within the castle. Folding her arms over the padded arm rest, she gave way to the lassitude that had come over her and lay her head upon the cushion of her arms. Her sooty lashes fluttered down over her emerald eyes as the warmth from the fire and her fatigue took their toll. She meant to only rest for a few moments, but soon drifted into sleep.

She awoke with a start, her mind disoriented from the vivid dream she had been experiencing. In the whimsical fantasyland of sleep, Justin had come to her. It had been so realistic, Jamelyn's skin tingled from the kiss he had placed upon her cheek. Pushing herself upright in the chair, she stretched her cramped legs as she rubbed the sleep from her eyes and yawned widely before looking about her. Then her eyes widened in surprise. Justin stood quietly watching her, an expression of unrestrained passion playing over his face as he gazed down into her sleep-softened features. Bemused by her dream, she did not resist as his strong arms went about her and he lifted her from the chair to carry her to the large bed.

Mesmerized by the intense heat in the depths of his eyes, she did not protest as his long fingers began to undress her. When his strong but gentle hands removed the last of her garments, they moved to her braided mane of auburn hair, freeing it from its confines and spreading it upon the white pillow. Jamelyn lay naked, resembling a porcelain doll with a halo of copper fire fanning about her on the counterpane. As Justin's hot eyes swept over her, she felt vulnerable in the candlelight, for it exposed all of her secrets to his keen gaze. She moved instinctively to extinguish the candle he had set on the bedside table. In the darkness she would be able to savor her husband's love without revealing her condition to him. She did not want reality and all the old hatreds to encroach upon this moment within his arms. She longed to prolong the fantasy that seemed to consume them, bringing their love once more to life.

Justin's hand stopped hers before she could reach the flame and his voice was husky with emotion as he brought the tips of her fingers to his lips and whispered, "Nay, I want to see all of you."

Fear of discovery clouded Jamelyn's eyes, but he continued, "You are beautiful, Jamelyn. Over the past months the thin young girl has bloomed into a ravishing, voluptuous woman, more desirable than ever, with your flawless complexion tinted the color of a spring rose and a body that has matured to a fullness that pleases the eye. Do not hide from me; let me have all of you without reservation."

Her emerald eyes glowed with hope and she sent a silent thank you to heaven as she looked into her husband's handsome face and realized he did not suspect her condition. Her delicate lips curled at the corners in a provocative little smile of relief. Justin thought nothing unusual about the changes in her body and she prayed her babe would remain still beneath his sire's hand.

Jamelyn lay back on the bed, presenting her body to Justin's view. She was grateful that she had not gained a great deal of weight, for her belly was only a small mound. But she had no need to worry; his eyes never left her face as he rose from the bed and began to disrobe.

She could not speak. Her heart beat rapidly, her breathing became short and uneven, and all thoughts left her with the exception of his nearness and the beauty presented to her eyes. She was awe-struck by the sight of his naked body and stared unabashedly. The light from the fire made his muscular frame gleam like molten gold and her breath caught in her throat from the desire that swept over her in a violent wave. A tingling excitement filled her and she had no power to object as he joined her on the down mattress. No thoughts of the past or future existed within her mind; she lived only within that erotic moment of time as she stretched her arms toward him, encircling his corded neck and drawing him down to her eager mouth.

The barriers Jamelyn had erected about her heart against Justin crumbled as his lips captured hers in a hot, devouring kiss. She responded to his touch like the desert sands to a rare rain. Her fertile passion blossomed. She could not get enough of him as her hands roamed over his sinewy frame, savoring the rich feel of his masculine flesh. Her fingers curled the dark hair on his chest, then explored the resilient, bronzed skin of his wide shoulders and the corded column of his neck before twining themselves in the blue-black curls of his hair. Her tongue met his in erotic battle, and she relished the taste of the fine wine he had consumed before entering her chamber. Her body was like malleable clay beneath his artistic hands as he caressed it and molded it against the hard length of him, sculpting her to his desire.

No words were spoken between the two lovers. None were needed. Each responded instinctively to the other's passion, consumed with the desire to give as much pleasure as was received. At last Jamelyn could stand no more of the exquisite torture of Justin's hands and mouth. Her thighs spread, her hips beckoning, as her nails dug into the hard muscles of his sensuous buttocks, bringing him to her for fulfillment. She moaned her pleasure aloud as his hardness entered the moist passage and she arched her back to receive all of him, abandoning herself to the raptures of their union.

Too long their bodies had been denied this exquisite plea-sure. Their love burned with the intensity of a searing inferno, making their joining as fierce as a midsummer's tempest. They soared together upon the raging winds of ecstasy, traversing the furor of their volatile passion until they reached the calming hurricane's eye of sensual bliss.

Jamelyn clung weakly to Justin's glistening body as wave after wave of rapturous pleasure rippled through her body. Tears of happiness crept from beneath her lashes to gently trickle down her flushed cheeks.

Justin felt the dampness of her tears on his cheeks as he eased from her to lie at her side. Tenderly, he bent and kissed the shimmering droplets away before wrapping his arms about her and pulling her against his chest. He ran his fingers through her gilded tresses, enjoying the feel of their silken texture as he held her lovingly within his embrace. Too many emotions filled him to be able to speak. He could find no words to express the feelings that had erupted within him in the past moments.

Feeling Jamelyn's warmth against him, he watched the dancing shadows upon the black-beamed ceiling as he reflected upon his earlier intentions. When he had come to her chamber, he had been determined only to use her body to rid himself of his desire for her. Yet as he had looked down at her lovely, innocent face as she slept, those thoughts had been erased from his mind. Justin knew he should have had the strength to turn and leave Jamelyn to her sleep, but he could not resist touching her smooth, delicately tinted flesh. It was that small touch that had been his undoing. It brought back all the memories of the nights they had spent within each other's arms. His throat was filled with the things he wanted to say, but he could not force himself to voice them. His mind defied the urgings of his heart, reminding him of the treachery he would leave himself open to if he gave way. Her previous deception still lay like a red-hot iron in his mind, burning away the peace and pleasure he found with her.

Justin now realized his mistake too late. Taking Jamelyn to bed had not eliminated his desire for her. Instead it had the opposite effect. No matter what she was or what she had done, he knew he still wanted her. It was madness and he wondered at his own sanity as he lay holding the woman who was like a poison he could not resist, though it would mean his own demise.

Wrapping her more tightly within his embrace, he smelled the heady scent of her fragrant hair and buried his face in the shimmering strands, forcing his worries away. He would face those realities during the day, but for now he would savor her warm body as she lay sleeping beside him. Giving way to the languor left by their lovemaking, Justin drifted into a contented sleep, one he had not experienced since Jamelyn had left Windsor.

All was quiet in the chamber beyond the solid oak door as Anne leaned against the cold stone wall. Tears burned her eyes and ran unchecked down her cheeks. She had heard the moans of ecstacy that had escaped the two lovers and her hand was marked with the print of her teeth where she had bitten it to keep from crying out in rage and pain. It had taken all of her self-control to keep from storming the chamber and tearing Justin from the bitch's arms.

Anne could nearly visualize the two lovers entwined within

each other's embrace as they slept in fulfilled serenity. The thought infuriated her. Damn you, Justin! I have tried to be patient far too long and I will not tolerate more. I will see you free of the bitch once and for all! she fumed in the darkness of the corridor.

Crouched in deep shadows, she tried to think of a means to rid herself of her rival. It would not be as easy as before. Jamelyn St. Claire was now in her own domain and Anne knew she would have to move with care to insure Justin never suspected her of his wife's demise.

A small sound drew her attention from her devious thoughts. Alert, she peered into the darkness and listened as the latch on Jamelyn's door was drawn slowly back. Her curiosity aroused, Anne pressed further into the shadows and waited to see who crept so furtively from the room. As the door swung open, the light from the fire illuminated Jamelyn's slender form as she quickly and silently closed the door behind her before making her way down the corridor.

Intrigued by Jamelyn's secretive movements, Anne wanted to find what led her away from her husband's side after their intimate interlude. With as much stealth as the other woman had used, Anne silently followed her down the servants' stairs to the wine cellar. Anne's brow furrowed as she wondered why Jamelyn would sneak to the cellar to retrieve a bottle of wine when a servant could easily have been sent. Blending quietly into the darkness, she watched as the mistress of Raven's Keep lit a small candle and then moved several stones. A door swung open to reveal the black cavern beyond. At that sight a malicious smile played over Anne's lips as she thought, So, you give yourself to Justin and then creep away to meet someone else. Bitch, you will rue the day you lay in Justin St. Claire's arms. As Jamelyn disappeared into the blackness, Anne did not hesitate to follow. Without knowing it, her enemy had given Anne the weapon she had been seeking to use against her.

The image of Justin's sleeping face floated into Jamelyn's thoughts as she made her way along the tunnel to meet

Royce in the coppice of trees. The soft glow of the candle
she carried bathed her, as did the warm radiance left by
their lovemaking. Her features reflected the languor that
possessed her, her lips still slightly swollen from Justin's
kisses and her eyes heavy-lidded with satisfaction. She
wanted to warn Royce of Justin's plans, but an urgency
burned within her to return to her husband's arms.

Blowing out the candle, she set it near the entrance before
making her way into the underbrush and hurrying to meet
her friend in the clearing.

Royce stepped from the shadows, and as Jamelyn swung
to face him he noted her soft expression and his heart froze
within his chest. He had seen that look many times on the
women he had bedded. Jamelyn's slightly flushed cheeks
and shining eyes gave away the events of the previous hours.
Swallowing back the ache the sight aroused within him, he
said, "What news have you?"

Jamelyn noted Royce's brusque tone and grim expression
but did not question the reason behind it. "Justin and his
men are setting a trap for you tomorrow. He will leave at
dawn and ride ahead of the pack train to lie in wait for you
to attack."

Folding his arms over his chest, Royce turned to stare
at the dark outline of Raven's Keep. He could not endure
looking into her face as he said, "Tomorrow will be our last
raid, Jamelyn. Have you decided on what now lies in your
future?"

Jamelyn's delicately-arched brows knit over her slender
nose. Royce's question confused her. "My future?" she asked.
"It is as before. I will remain at Raven's Keep to insure my
people do not suffer."

Royce swung to face her and with a swiftness that caused
a startled gasp from her, reached out and drew her into his
arms. His fiery gaze delved into her eyes, searching for
answers he wanted desperately to hear. "Come away with
me, Jamelyn," he breathed hoarsely. "Your people will not
suffer under St. Claire's rule. If nothing else, he is a just
man to govern your fief. You have no worry there. It is
your own welfare that concerns me."

The feelings Royce had tried to hide surfaced at the sight of Jamelyn's sensually satisfied expression. Her face shredded the hard control he had previously managed to keep over his emotions where the lovely Scottish lass was concerned. Before Jamelyn could answer Royce's question, he captured her lips with his own, placing a scorching kiss upon them, trying to erase those he knew her husband had given her only a short while earlier.

From her hiding place Anne could not hear their words, but could see well what transpired between Jamelyn and the tall man with the black eye patch. A cunning gleam sparkled in her blue eyes as she thought, Justin will be mine before the morning light creeps across the horizon! When he learned that Jamelyn had left his bed to fly into the arms of her lover, Justin would finally cast his wife aside and would have grounds besides to have the marriage annulled.

Anne's musings were interrupted as her attention was drawn back to the two in the clearing. She saw Jamelyn place her hands against the man's wide chest and push herself out of his arms. Puzzled by the new development, Anne stealthily moved nearer, hoping to hear their conversation.

"Royce, I cannot leave Raven's Keep. I am the last of the Cregans and will not avoid the responsibilities placed on me as such. It is my home and I love it."

"'Tis not the only thing you love at Raven's Keep, is it, lass? 'Tis your husband, the one you profess to hate so adamantly, who holds your heart. I can see it in your face. You love Justin St. Claire," Royce said, the pain in his own heart making it hard for him to speak.

Jamelyn's face mirrored the turmoil of her own emotions as she gazed up at her friend and said softly, "Aye, I love him, Royce. I carry his child within my womb as proof of that love. I have tried to fight it but can no longer do so. If it is possible, I will also try to gain his love. I think he feels some small measure of warmth for me, but so much has happened in his past that it is hard for him to accept it."

Royce's wide hands cupped Jamelyn's chin as he gazed

down into her eyes. "I wish it was otherwise, Jamelyn."
His words held the futile wish that had grown in his heart
over the past months.

Tears of regret and gratitude dampened her long, spiky
lashes as she looked up into his handsome, scarred face. "I
did not seek my love for Justin, Royce. However, I can no
longer evade it. I know the path before me is uneven and
I may lose my way along with my heart, but I think I have
the strength to face what lies ahead. Even if Justin does not
come to love me, I will have his child and that will be
enough."

Anne could not make out all of their words, but her breath
caught in her throat as she heard the last sentence. Her eyes
narrowed and her full lips thinned into a hard line, turning
her lovely features into a cold mask of hatred. Jamelyn's
statement changed her plans entirely. She could not go to
Justin now and tell him of Jamelyn and her lover. Justin
would never turn his wife away while she carried his heir.
Anne knew she would have to find another means—and
quickly—of ridding herself of his pregnant wife. He must
never learn of the child Jamelyn carried.

Afraid of being seen, Anne slowly backed away from
the clearing. When she felt secure that she could not be
heard, she ran back to the passageway and felt along the
dark tunnel until she reentered Raven's Keep. Her heart
pounded furiously in her chest as she made her way through
the keep to the sleeping area of her own men. With the toe
of her pointed shoe, she awoke the sergeant of her personal
guard. Placing a finger against her lips, she motioned him
to silence and gestured up the stairs to her chamber. Anne
wanted no curious ears to overhear her plans.

The moon slowly slipped behind the trees as Royce and
Jamelyn spoke, completely unaware that they had been seen
by an enemy worse than any either of them had ever faced
in battle; a jealous, obsessed woman.

When he at last realized he could not sway Jamelyn from
the course she had set, Royce shook his dark head. "Lass,
you know I care for you, but I also know where your heart

lies. If there is ever a time when you need me, I will be here."

Rising up on her toes, she kissed Royce's scarred cheek. "I know, my friend, and I thank you. This will be the last time we will meet here. I hope things will change in the future and you can come openly as my friend to Raven's Keep. Take care tomorrow, Royce. You also mean a great deal to me."

Royce wrapped his strong arms about Jamelyn, clasping her to his chest as he laid his cheek against her shimmering tresses. "I will, lass. I pray all goes well with you." With that he dropped a light kiss upon her auburn head and then swiftly blended into the dark shadows of the night.

Thoughtfully, Jamelyn remained where Royce had left her. No sound penetrated the stillness of the glade as she stood quietly, her mind on the two men who meant the most to her in the world. Were it not for Justin, I could love you easily, Royce McFarland, she thought. Her sigh of relief that the morrow would see her plans complete mingled with one of regret that she would not see her friend again for a long while.

Casting one last glance about the silent, moon-filled glade, Jamelyn turned back to the path that would lead her to Raven's Keep and Justin St. Claire.

Chapter 15

The predawn chill invaded the keep and Jamelyn snuggled closer to Justin, seeking the warmth of his body as she dreamed at his side. Her movements woke her husband and for one brief moment Justin was surprised to find himself in his wife's bed with her nestled against him in sleep. But as the grogginess cleared from his mind, he remembered the hours of ecstasy they had spent together.

Without moving he looked down at the copper-gilded head resting on his shoulder. Jamelyn was especially beautiful in repose. Her shimmering curls framed her lovely face and her delicate lips, slightly parted as she breathed, seemed to beg for his kisses. Her thick lashes cast shadows on her tinted cheeks, bringing a mysterious quality to her features. Those sooty lashes did hide the secrets of her soul, for when they were open Justin sensed he could see into the very depths of her being.

His long fingers curled through the silken strands of her hair as he looked up at the shadowy ceiling and reflected on the events that had transpired between himself and his wife. After the hours spent within Jamelyn's arms, he had to admit to himself that he still loved her and had always loved her, but he wondered if he was again playing the fool. How could he keep loving Jamelyn when he did not trust her? But even her past schemes he could accept more easily than her nationality. Nothing would ever change the fact that she was one of the hated Scots.

Restlessly, he pulled his fingers free of her hair and moved away from her. She mumbled a protest in her sleep as she snuggled into the warm spot he had vacated a moment before. She did not awaken as he sat staring down at her, his expression mirroring the turmoil that churned his insides. Rubbing his hand across his stubbled chin irritably, he still could not decide how to deal with this confusing situation. He loved Jamelyn, but she stood for everything he despised.

She had deceived him once making him believe in her love. Perhaps last night had just been another game to her. But something deep within him quickly denied that accusation. The very thought twisted his heart.

Annoyed, he stood, his gaze once more sweeping over her beautiful face. The very sight of her excited his body and he could feel himself begin to respond. Turning quickly away, he began to dress, knowing he must get away from his wife or he would end up making love to her again— and that would only serve to perpetuate his dilemma.

Pulling on his woolen chausses over his lean, muscular legs, Justin forced himself to think of the duties that lay at hand instead of the warm, soft flesh of his wife. It was not an easy chore, but he knew that at the present time and in his state of mind, he could do nothing else.

He strapped his sword belt about his waist as he finished dressing and strode toward the door. His steps halted at the foot of the large four-poster and before he had time to consciously stop himself, he went to Jamelyn's side and placed a light kiss upon her brow. Straightening, he thought, *After this business with the bandits is settled, I will tend to matters here, one way or the other. But until then all will remain as it has been.*

* * *

A dawn chill permeated the air as the dark blue sky
lightened to mauve. The jingle of harnesses and the rattle
of armor broke the stillness of the early morning quiet.
Jamelyn pulled her tartan closer about her slim form to
thwart the cold's attempt to creep beneath the warm wool.
Red Devil moved restlessly beneath her, anxious to move
his strong muscles into a gallop. She kept a firm hand on
the reins to keep the impatient horse still while Justin gave
his final orders to the men who would ride with the pack
train.

A sense of well-being surged through Jamelyn as she
watched her husband move about, readying the group to
depart. She admired the command he possessed and her lips
curved slightly at the thought that it had not been so long
since she had detested him for that same quality. Her heart
swelled with pride as her gaze raked Justin's sinewy frame
from the top of his blue-black head to his supple leather
boots. In her loving eyes, he was magnificent. He was
endowed with strength and courage that her battle-trained
mind respected, yet he was a gentle, passionate lover, and
all of her feminine instincts responded to him. The very
sight of his broad shoulders and lean hips made her heart
flutter erratically within her breast.

Embarrassed by her own lusty impulses, Jamelyn forced
her eyes away from her husband. Her cheeks bloomed a
light rose from her thoughts as she turned to meet the gaze
of the woman sitting upon the white mare at her side.
Jamelyn's cheeks deepened in hue as she realized Anne had
seen her admiring Justin.

The cold, flinty look her rival bestowed upon her made
Jamelyn's skin prickle with unease at the nape of her neck.
She had known of Anne's hostility since the first moment
they had met at Windsor, yet the look Anne sent in her
direction now bore an almost insane hatred.

Jamelyn turned away. She did not want anything to ruin
the soft glow that still lingered from the previous night. The
sight of Anne's rancor-filled eyes made her remember all
of the insecurities she had experienced over the past months
in her relationship with Justin. On this morning she wanted

no reminders; her acceptance of her love for her husband was too new and fragile. Before last evening her heart had been like a fortified bastion, sealed against her enemy— Justin. Jamelyn vowed not to let Anne's malice destroy the tender peace she had found within her husband's arms since the gate to her heart had been newly opened to him.

The sound of Justin's deep voice penetrated her thoughts and she urged Red Devil forward to follow the group from Raven's Keep. Satisfied that all would go well, she enjoyed the morning ride through the crisp fall air. It had been several months since she had ridden and the feeling of the wind on her cheeks, ruffling the fringe of her tartan, made her spirits soar.

In a sense today would be Jamelyn's birthday, for it would be a new beginning. Royce would once more disappear into the rugged Scottish countryside to go about his own business while she settled down at Raven's Keep as its true mistress. There would be much for her to do, but the first item on her agenda was to try to make Justin truly love her.

She felt her babe stir within her womb and placed a comforting hand over her slightly rounded stomach. Her gaze swept over the group of men until it found the tall leader at the head of the squad. Justin, she thought, our child grows within me. How will you feel when you learn of it?

A tiny frown of uncertainty puckered her smooth brow and she glanced at the beautiful woman at her side. As though Anne was able to read Jamelyn's thoughts, her ruby lips curled into a mocking smile and she gestured at Jamelyn's belly. Venom laced Anne's words as she bent toward her rival and spat, "He will hate the child you bear, for he despises anything connected with you Scots." With that she gave a scornful laugh and kicked her horse to a faster pace, urging it to the head of the group and Justin's side.

Jamelyn's fingers clenched about the reins until her knuckles were white. The blood drained from her face, leaving her ashen, as she realized Anne knew of her condition. No one except Royce and the loyal Nora and Maille had known about her babe. How had Anne learned of it?

Questions flittered like bat wings through Jamelyn's mind. What other secrets does Anne know of me? she asked herself as Justin ordered them to halt in a thick coppice of trees near the edge of a small clearing with a babbling brook gurgling merrily nearby.

"From here the women will not travel with us," Justin said as he glanced at his mistress and then at the pale figure sitting so quietly near the rear of the group. "I will leave your men here to protect you, Anne," he said.

Anne's full lower lip pouted sullenly as she looked up at Justin. "But I wanted to see you capture the thieves."

He shook his head and smiled, as if appeasing a young child. "That I cannot allow. 'Tis far too dangerous. You will be much safer here and can enjoy the beauty of the glade over the wine and cheese I ordered packed for your repast."

Anne quickly lowered her thick lashes over her eyes to hide the guileful expression in their depths. Her lips trembled with the urge to laugh, for all was going as she had hoped. Feigning resignation, she pulled off her soft leather riding gloves and gave a slight shrug. "If that is your decision, then I will abide by it. I'm sure we will enjoy our day while you bring the villains to heel."

Surprise mingled with relief in Justin as he took Anne's smooth, white hand and dropped a light kiss upon it. Her meek acquiescence to his wishes was unexpected. Anne had always wanted to be in on the kill at the hunt; he had surmised that she would want the same now, and had been prepared for further argument.

Though he had agreed to let the women come along, knowing the ruse would work much better with their presence, it still did not sit easily on his mind, for they could be placed in danger. Glancing about the glade, he felt satisfied that at least here they would be out of harm's way and would have the protection of Anne's men. Without having to worry about Anne and Jamelyn, he could give his full attention to capturing the thieves.

Grateful for Anne's lack of protest, Justin squeezed her hand fondly. He wondered briefly why he had never fallen in love with Anne of Chester. She was a lady from one of the oldest and wealthiest families in England and had shown her devotion to him in more ways than one. But there was something that made Justin withhold his affections from her. He could not put a name to it, nor could he explain his reasoning, but some second sense warned him against giving his heart to the lovely Anne.

Then his gaze traveled toward the slender figure sitting on Red Devil at the rear of the line of soldiers. There sits another mystery I have not the time to analyze, Justin mused, before turning his mount and ordering his men to follow.

The black mood Anne's words had caused in Jamelyn was intensified by the sight of Justin kissing the woman's hand and then riding away without so much as a by your leave, my lady, to his wife. A cold, dull feeling crept up her spine to invade the glowing warmth that had filled her. It snuffed her happiness like a candle in a brisk breeze. Numbly she let Anne's sergeant at arms help her from the saddle and stood rigid by her mount as her doubts bloomed anew. Have I been completely misled by my own passion for Justin? The question hovered in her mind like the shadow of a great black bird swooping down on its frightened victim.

Jamelyn worried her full lower lip with her teeth as she absently stroked the roan's neck and watched as Anne slid gracefully to the ground. Something in Anne's demeanor as she spoke with the sergeant aroused Jamelyn's curiosity. She could not hear their hushed discussion, but the sly glances cast her way made her sense she was the subject of their conversation. The skin at the nape of her neck prickled a warning but she did not heed her instinct to flee. She staunchly pushed the foreboding away and reprimanded herself silently. Now I'm seeing ghosts in broad daylight, she thought. This is Raven's Keep and nothing will happen to me here.

Jamelyn tied Red Devil to a low limb before gathering fresh grass for him. The sound of horses entering the clearing made her pause in her endeavors and she looked up to see several men bearing the Chester colors enter the glade and quickly dismount. They bowed to Anne and waited for their orders.

Mystified by Anne's furtive actions, Jamelyn strained to hear what was being said. The effort was useless, for at this distance the conversation was indistinguishable. But a moment later Jamelyn learned the thrust of their words. The hatred on Anne's face as she turned to face her made her realize she should have heeded her instincts. The expression on her rival's face bore no good for the young Lady St. Claire.

Intuitively, Jamelyn grabbed the reins of Red Devil and climbed into the saddle, but before she could put her heel to his side, Anne's sergeant at arms dragged her roughly from the roan's back. She struggled with the powerfully built man but was soon subdued as he wrapped his muscular arms tightly about her. Like bands of steel, they dug into Jamelyn's slender frame, cutting off her air if she moved against them.

Anne's laughter trilled through the glade as Jamelyn ceased struggling in her captor's embrace and eyed the other woman, her green eyes flashing fire as she asked, "What do you mean by this, Anne?" Jamelyn had to gasp for air to speak.

Nonchalantly, Anne smoothed the velvet of her riding skirt and flashed Jamelyn a winsome smile. "'Tis the only way to be rid of you. Justin is much too kindhearted to do away with you once he finds out about the child. He may despise you and the babe, but he could not bring himself to be rid of you because of it. He will feel obligated to let you remain his wife, and I cannot allow that to happen. I love Justin and after you are gone he will turn back to me as he did when Jessica died."

Jamelyn paled under Anne's verbal assault. Would Justin truly stay with her out of obligation to her and his child? Could Anne be right? The very thought seemed to crush the breath from her more than her captor's tight grip. Seeing a look of triumph flash in Anne's blue eyes, Jamelyn bristled. Anne's words might prove correct in the future, but she would never let the witch know how they hurt her now. Anne might kill her, but she would never allow her the knowledge of her victory. "You're mad!" Jamelyn spat. "Justin has left me in the care of your men. How will you convince him you are not the culprit of the vile crime you are planning?"

Jamelyn's words seemed to sever the thin threads veiling Anne's insane obsession. Her eyes glimmered with the bright light of madness as she laughed. "Crime? There will be no crime. You have run away with your lover who carries the scar on his cheek."

Every muscle in Jamelyn's body grew tense, as if she had heard the ring of the death knell. Anne knew of Royce. Her heart pounded against her chest as she swallowed back the fear that clogged her throat; she tried to face the Englishwoman boldly, with the hope of finding out how much she truly knew. "I have no lover," Jamelyn spat brazenly.

Anne shrugged her elegantly gowned shoulder. "You can deny it, but I saw you in his embrace only last night in a thicket of trees near the keep. All I will have to do is to tell Justin your lover followed us and took you with him. Of course, we will have tried to fight, but my men will have been outnumbered."

"Justin will not believe you," Jamelyn said, but her voice was weak as her hopes of making Anne see reason and release her faded.

Anne flashed Jamelyn a derisive smile, her blue eyes scorning her for being so naive. "Oh, he will believe me when I show him the passageway you took to meet your lover. You forget, Justin does not love you, nor does he trust you. You think because he has bedded you long enough to put his seed in your belly that he automatically loves you and has forgotten all your devious schemes. Justin is no fool. I am wise enough to realize that much and if you think otherwise, then you are the imbecile for deluding yourself in such a manner."

The truth of Anne's words cut deep, reopening all of Jamelyn's old insecurities. Her knees grew weak and she sagged against the iron-hard arm that held her. "What do you intend to do with me?"

"Oh, do not worry, you will be seen to. You will not be so fortunate as to escape like the last time."

Puzzled, Jamelyn said, "The last time?"

"Aye," Anne smirked. "You escaped Dick the Dirk after my men took you there, but do not fear—you will not escape again. I won't leave your fate in the hands of an inept guttersnipe this time. My men will take you far away from Raven's Keep before you have taken your last breath. I have given them permission to enjoy what they want of your charms. It is part of their reward for being so loyal."

Jamelyn paled even more at the description of the brief future Anne had planned for her. "Why not just kill me now?" she asked, preferring a quick death to slow torture and degradation before she died.

Anne shook her raven head, the sun glinting on its blue-black tresses, as she said, "I'm afraid that will not be possible. It would be much too easy for you if I just slit your throat. I want the satisfaction of knowing you have suffered, as I did each time Justin took you in his arms and made you moan with pleasure." Turning away, as if Jamelyn's life meant nothing more to her than an insect's, she said, "Take her from my sight. She sickens me."

The sergeant at arms carried the squirming Jamelyn to her mount and roughly propelled her into the saddle. He tied her wrists to the pommel and brought the rope back around her waist to the candle of the saddle, where he secured it once more to prevent any attempt of escape. A heavy cloak was thrown about her shoulders, the hood securely fastened over her auburn hair to keep anyone from recognizing her if they spied the travelers on the road. Unaware of the significance of her clan tartan, the soldier balled it up and threw it to the ground. With one swift kick from his foot, he knocked it beneath a bush.

Knowing it was useless to protest, Jamelyn watched in numbed silence as Anne tore at her own clothing and hair and then allowed her men to tie her to a small tree. The two men who were to take Jamelyn away likewise trussed their comrades.

Anne had planned well. When Justin returned to find

Jamelyn missing and his lovely mistress disheveled and bound hand and foot, he would believe all of her lies. Jamelyn's shoulders sagged at the thought. With all her bright hopes for the future now fading into blackness, she accepted her defeat at Anne's hand. She had fought many battles against strong men, but at last it would be the devious hand of a woman that beat her.

The thought galled Jamelyn and a spark of the old spirit burst back into life. She struggled against her bonds, determined not to be defeated until the last breath left her. With her eyes flashing fiery glints of anger, she looked at Anne through narrowed eyes. "I vow you will pay for this."

Anne leaned her tousled head against the bole of the tree and looked up at Jamelyn. Her mad laughter pealed through the quiet glade. "Tonight I will lie in Justin's arms to comfort him over his loss. Remember that when you lie beneath my men before you die." Her laughter continued to ring in Jamelyn's ears as the two guards led her mount from the clearing and onto the road that led to England.

The clash of metal against metal rang eerily in the noonday air. Justin had come upon the raiders just before they were ready to attack the pack train. The battle that ensued was violent, but his hardened soldiers had the upper hand within a short span of time. The raiders lay dead and dying about the roadway and in the surrounding woods, where a number of them had fled Justin's men. However, their efforts to escape were futile and they were cut down in their flight for freedom.

Now only two combatants were left: Justin St. Claire and Royce McFarland. Both men were of the same height and stature and were evenly matched in this game of life and death. They fought fiercely, sweat running down their heated brows, the salt from their own bodies stinging as it touched their eyes, but the two paid no heed to the discomfort. Their energies were focused on their own survival and the demise of their enemy.

Time after time their heavy battle swords clashed, sending sparks into the air with the force of each blow. The advantage changed hands several times and both men's followers held their breath to see who would triumph.

Royce fought fiendishly against the man who had become like an evil talisman in his life. He no longer saw Justin just as the English enemy, but also as a rival for the affections of the woman he had grown to care for a great deal. He knew that his life was forfeit in any event, for he could not expect to succeed after his men had been cut down. But he did not slacken his effort to cut down Justin St. Claire. If he killed the English knight, at least Jamelyn would have Raven's Keep to herself once more. She might love this black English knight, but Royce did not believe the man could bring her happiness. If it was his fate to die, at least he would do his best to take Justin St. Claire with him.

Breathing heavily from his exertions, Justin parried Royce's blade, the shock from the force of the blow tingling up his arm and making his tired muscles quiver. He had seen the look on his opponent's face and knew that one of them would not leave the field of battle alive. Justin was determined that it would not be he. Sensing the Scotsman's hatred for him, it only magnified his own animosity. He fought with the experience of long years, his blade singing through the air as it moved with lightning speed toward his enemy. The Scotsman narrowly avoided the razor-sharp edge of death as his own blade sliced through the air toward Justin, who countered. The sound of steel rang loudly in the stillness of the roadside battleground.

At last, when the onlookers thought both men would succumb to fatigue, Royce took a step backward to brace himself against another powerful blow from Justin's sword. It was the mistake Justin had been waiting for his opponent to make. He took advantage of the situation as Royce's foot slipped on the wet, blood-soaked grass. The broad side of Justin's sword crashed down on Royce's head in a shattering blow. It stunned the Scotsman and he was unprepared for the quick flash of steel that filled the sky and then entered his shoulder. For a moment a befuddled expression crossed his pale features as he looked from the long blade of Justin's sword to the man still grasping the hilt, then collapsed at his conqueror's feet.

Royce's blood beaded on the polished surface of Justin's blade as he freed it from his enemy's supine body. Sticking the sharp point into the ground, he removed his gauntlets and then pushed back the black visor of his helm. Wiping the sweat from his brow, he stared down at the crumpled form of the Scotsman and had to admit the man had been a worthy adversary. It was seldom Justin found any man who could withstand such punishment for long, and the Scots bandit had proved his merit as a rival by his swordsmanship. Though the man had been his enemy, Justin could not help but admire his courage and ability. It was a shame that such accomplishments could not be put to better use, he mused as he turned to look at the group surrounding him.

"Care for the wounded and then take the thieves back to Raven's Keep," Justin ordered, before mounting his own black destrier to go to escort Jamelyn and Anne back to the castle. Glancing one last time at his men and the scene of carnage, he turned his mount in the direction from which they had come.

His spirits were high as he neared the clearing. He could hear the small brook bubbling merrily in the distance as he approached. The day had gone well and he was satisfied. He had finally snared the culprits in the act and now looked forward to setting his personal life in order. Tonight, he thought, we will celebrate. However, those thoughts were erased from his mind by the sight that met his eyes.

Anne sat on the ground tied securely to a tree and apparently in a faint, while her men were scattered about the clearing, also bound hand and foot. Justin's gaze scanned the area for the small figure of his wife, but to no avail; his heart sank within his chest. His blood ran cold as he took in the scene and quickly dismounted. Bending, he lightly patted Anne on the cheek and unbound her. When her thick lashes fluttered open, he asked, "What has happened? Where is Jamelyn?"

Great tears welled in Anne's blue eyes as she rubbed her

bruised wrists. "She . . . she . . . Oh, Justin, we tried to stop her!" Anne cried, her voice trembling dramatically for effect.

Justin took Anne by the shoulders, his face hardening, his eyes growing deathly cold as he asked, "What are you jabbering about? Speak up, Anne."

Anne sniffled and wiped her nose with her hand as she said, "She left with her lover, Justin. He came with a group of men right after you left and took her with him. My men tried to stop them, but you can see we were outnumbered and were unable to prevent it."

A telltale muscle twitched in Justin's lean jaw and through clenched teeth he spat, "Who was the man?"

Anne's voice quavered as she shook her tousled head. "I know not his name, but he wore a patch over one eye and had a scar on his cheek."

Deep lines furrowed Justin's forehead as his brows knit across the bridge of his nose. "Are you sure of the description, Anne?"

A new rush of tears cascaded down her cheeks as she nodded. "Aye, I'm sure. I was so frightened. I will never forget that awful face. Look what they did to me. We are lucky they didn't murder us." Anne held up her reddened wrist as proof of her words.

Justin knew the man of whom Anne spoke. He now was on his way to Raven's Keep's dungeon bleeding from the wound he himself had inflicted. However, something was not quite right about it all. A niggling suspicion flickered into life in Justin's mind, but it was quickly pushed aside as Anne fell against his chest and wept piteously. "Oh, Justin, hold me. Take me away from this place so I won't have to remember the horror of it anymore."

Justin's fingers were gentle as they smoothed her raven hair back from her pale face and he placed a comforting kiss upon her brow. "I will, Anne. Hush now, it is all over. You are safe and the culprits responsible for this will pay, that I can assure you."

Justin helped Anne to her feet and onto her mount before freeing her men. They rode silently back toward Raven's Keep, each too occupied with his own thoughts to converse

with the other. Anne was busily making plans for her future
as Justin's wife, while his thoughts lingered in an entirely
different direction. He wondered if there could actually be
two men who would fit Anne's description of the man with
whom Jamelyn had fled.

All tenderness fled upon this new deception from his
wife. Again the walls went up around Justin's heart, sealing
out his love for Jamelyn. He vowed Jamelyn St. Claire
would return to Raven's Keep, but she would suffer the
agonies of hell this time. He had been generous and fool-
hardy, but that was in the past. He would find her and then
petition the king to release him from his marriage vows. If
that did not free him from the woman, then she would spend
her life in the depths of Raven's Keep, as would any traitor
to him.

Anthony Godfrey heard the sounds of hooves in the distance and quickly urged his horse into the dense growth
along the roadside. It was much safer for a lone rider to
hide than chance meeting a band of highwaymen intent on
thievery and murder.

From his hiding place he could view the roadway clearly
and waited as the riders approached. At the sight of Anne
of Chester's colors, one blond brow arched over his keen
blue eyes. A satisfied smile curved his shapely lips at the
sight of the hooded figure on the roan. At least he would
not have to contend with Anne's snide remarks when he
faced Justin. She would not be at the castle to try to come
between them as she had always done in the past. Anne did
not like anyone who was close to Justin, whether male or
female. It was a relief to see her pass by headed for England.
Anthony did not need her near to prick the already uneasy
situation with her claws of jealousy. Things would be hard
enough without that type of interference.

Anthony dreaded the encounter with his friend. Though
he still loved Justin as a brother, he knew Justin no longer
felt the same for him. The past months had been an unhappy
experience for Anthony, for he had always enjoyed the close
bond between Justin and himself. At first he had been angry,

but he could well understand Justin's feelings of betrayal, especially by his closest friend.

Anthony also knew that had Justin's heart not been involved, he would not have reacted so harshly at his withholding the knowledge of Jamelyn's identity from him. Justin would have understood that Anthony had no recourse against Edward's wishes if he wanted to maintain his own position at court and stay in Edward's favor. It did no one any good to go against England's monarch. The man had been involved in court intrigues all of his life and knew how to manipulate his courtiers to his own advantage at all times. Justin himself was prime example of that fact, but he had refused to acknowledge it.

Anthony only hoped that after so much time had elapsed, Justin could see the issue more clearly. The sight of Anne traveling once more to England encouraged his belief that Justin might now be receptive to him. It was with that slim prospect in mind that he had asked to be the messenger of Edward's missive to Justin.

Urging his mount back onto the road after the yellow and black colors had disappeared from view, Anthony kicked his horse into a gallop, anxious to reach Raven's Keep and put to rest the animosity between Justin and himself.

Recognizing the boundaries that marked the land belonging to the fief of Raven's Keep, he knew it would not be long before he reached the castle. His mind dwelt upon that fact as he rounded the bend where the battle between Justin's vassals and the border raiders had taken place. Startled by the scene of carnage, he reined his mount to an abrupt halt.

A frown marred his handsome forehead as his blue eyes scanned the roadway. Vultures circled overhead, angry that they had been disturbed from their feast. Anthony's nose wrinkled in distaste at the scent that emanated from the bodies that lay scattered about. The warm afternoon sun made the once peaceful roadside reek with the smell of death. As a sign of warning to anyone who trespassed against Justin St. Claire, the bodies of the thieves had been left where they had fallen to give evidence of what would happen to the next man who sought to go against the Lord of Raven's Keep.

Anthony had heard from an irate Edward of the troubles that had beset Raven's Keep. The message he now carried pertained to that very problem. Edward was enraged because Justin had failed to capture the men who dared to take what the English monarch considered his just due from his conquered foe. The king was commanding Justin to handle the situation promptly or he would send his own men to see the mission done at Justin's expense. That had been another reason Anthony had wanted to come to Raven's Keep. He had meant to offer his assistance to his friend before it was too late and Justin lost Raven's Keep once more to the crown.

This scene of death convinced Anthony that his help would not be needed. By the proof before his eyes, Justin had finally succeeded in doing his king's bidding. The burden of the message he carried lifted somewhat from Anthony's shoulders as he turned his horse from the road to take the shortcut through the forest to the castle.

The sound of swiftly flowing water drew Anthony's attention. Though he was near Raven's Keep, he decided to give his mount a rest. He had traveled hard all day and the beast needed a fresh drink of water before the last short leg of the journey. Reining his horse to a halt at the stream, he dismounted to stretch his own tired limbs. The horse gulped noisily as Anthony lifted his arms over his head, his movement halting in midair as his eye was caught by a bright splash of color across the glade. His curiosity aroused, he left his horse to drink and crossed the clearing. He knelt and pulled the black and red wool from beneath the bush. A puzzled frown creased Anthony's brow as he held it up and recognized Jamelyn's tartan. He had seen the fiery lass wear her badge of honor often enough when she wanted to proclaim her position to all the world.

Sensing something was terribly wrong, Anthony forgot his mount's need of rest as he threw the tartan across his shoulder and raced back to his horse. Mounting the animal, he kicked it swiftly in the side and headed for Raven's Keep, a deep foreboding gripping every fiber of his body. Jamelyn of Cregan would never forget such a precious item as her tartan. That woolen symbol meant too much to the Scots to be left carelessly behind.

Several hours after his ill-fated encounter with the Lord of Raven's Keep, Royce's thick lashes fluttered open in the dark confines of the castle's dungeon. His senses were groggy and disoriented as he regained consciousness. In his fog-shrouded mind he did not remember his wound until he made the effort to move. The pain that seared across his chest, nearly taking his breath, quickly reminded him of his injury—but he could not totally recall the exact circumstances that had caused it. His shoulder throbbed as his blood-caked fingers tentatively touched it and an involuntary moan escaped his dry lips. Swallowing back the pain that seemed to clog his throat, he explored his shoulder with trembling fingers. He found that a bandage had been pressed over the sword slash, its dampness indicating even to his cloudy mind that the gaping wound still bled. With another moan, he tried to raise himself on his elbow. The effort was too much; he collapsed back onto the rotting rushes that lined the damp stone floor.

A sound nearby drew Royce's rapidly fading senses and he peered into the darkness as it came closer. He tensed as a hand came to his face, touching his wide forehead and then the patch that covered his eye before tracing the outline of his scarred cheek. Though Thomas McFarland's voice was weak from the loss of blood from his own wounds, it held all the joy he felt as he said, "Royce—oh, me lad, you're not dead. The saints be praised."

Royce felt his adoptive father smooth back his dark hair that lay matted on his brow. He wanted to speak to Thomas to reasure him, but he could find no power to do so. He felt himself slipping into a dark tunnel, void of any thought beyond the relief from pain that the blackness offered. Giving up the fight to remain conscious, he let himself sink into the shadowy depths that obscured all rational thought.

The sound of heavy boots and the rusty scrape of metal

as the key turned in the lock of the cell seemed to pull Royce once more from his dark world. The door swung wide and several guards entered the cell. Agony tore through Royce's head as their rough hands dragged him from his vermin-infested bed. He moaned as a searing pain shot through his shoulder and along his arm as his wound reopened.

Thomas watched in impotent, anguished silence as he, too, was led from the black dungeon of Raven's Keep and up the cold, slime-covered steps to meet the fate Justin St. Claire had decreed for them.

The afternoon sun was severe in its intensity upon the eyes of the two men as they were propelled roughly through the main entrance of the castle. Accustomed to the total darkness of the dungeon, Royce's and Thomas's faces mirrored the new anguish inflicted upon them by its brightness. They could not see the wooden structure erected across the bailey as they staggered along under the brutish force of their guards. It was a mild reprieve that lasted only until they stumbled into the shadows that lay beneath the gibbet.

A snarl of protest issued from Thomas as he was forced to mount the solid oak steps behind the silent Royce. The agony in Royce's head made him oblivious to everything else.

The two prisoners' hands were bound behind them as they faced the assembly of English soldiers. Royce shook his dark head to try to see, but his blurred vision could only focus on the yellow and black Chester standard flying over Anne's small squad of men.

Like a bolt of lightning searing across a storm-ridden sky, the sight brought forth a vision in Royce's pain-numbed mind. The years dropped away. Gone were the solid stone walls of Raven's Keep and his years spent as a border raider. Royce was once more a young boy, playfully helping his sister-in-law gather wild flowers for her chamber at Clairemont. Jessica preferred the delicate blooms to those grown in the well-tended garden. He could still hear her gentle laughter as he romped with her pet spaniel, Prince.

"Jessica," Royce moaned as his knees threatened to give

way beneath him, but his cry went unnoticed by his guards, for the Lord of Raven's Keep was mounting the steps.

Justin's deep baritone carried to the assembly as he stood beside the two men who would soon swing from the rough hemp noose that swayed gently in the afternoon breeze. "The fate of these two men was decided by their own actions against the crown of England and the Lord of Raven's Keep. Unlike their villainous comrades, they were unfortunate enough to live so that they could be punished, as will be all who go against Edward of England. As vassal to my king and lord of this fief from which they have stolen precious grain that would feed the English troops, it is my duty to see them hanged from the neck until dead. Their bodies will not be interred within holy ground, but thrown into the charnel pit as those of any animal." Turning to the hangman, Justin commanded, "Proceed."

A hush fell over the group, who watched as the dark-haired man was dragged more than led to the noose and it was placed about his neck. The hemp rope burned Royce's skin as the hangman tightened it about his throat, but he did not flinch, for his mind was still in the past.

The seconds ticked by as Justin raised his gauntleted hand to give the signal to let the trap door drop from beneath the bandit's feet. A strangled sound halted the movement of his hand and it froze in midair at the name that reached his ears. "Jessica, run!" It was the voice of a frightened youth and a cold hand seemed to grip Justin's heart as he looked upward to face the leader of the border raiders.

The scar stood out as a jagged, red slash against Royce's ashen features. His strength was fading quickly, his knees already giving way beneath him so that the guards had to hold him upright to keep him from hanging himself until their lord gave the order.

Royce was not mentally present at his own execution, but was reliving another he had witnessed and had nearly lost his life in trying to prevent. "Run, Jessica!" He mumbled again as he tried to loose himself from his captors. His cry froze Justin's steps as Royce shook his own dark head and sobbed, "You killed her but you'll pay, you bastards.

You may kill me but Justin will hunt you down and make you pay with your lives." With that Royce fainted. His tall frame sagged between the two guards and he would have broken his own neck with the tight rope had his arms not been firmy held.

Justin's swarthy features paled and he was immobilized by the thief's words. He stared at the limp figure, his mind reeling with the knowledge that only one person could know of what had transpired that day on the cliffs near Clairemont—Richard, the brother he had thought dead for over ten years.

Lord St. Claire's strange actions drew interested mumbles from his men as they watched their leader kneel beside the thief and take his unconscious form into his arms. They had been unable to hear Royce's words, but this new turn of events aroused their curiosity to a fever pitch until none paid any heed to the lone rider who entered the gate.

Anthony reined in his mount before the gibbet, his eyes going to Justin and the man in his arms before casting a curious glance in Jacob's direction. Jacob shrugged, admitting he knew nothing of the events taking place before his eyes. He was as puzzled by Lord St. Claire's actions as any of the other men.

Dismounting, Anthony took the oak steps two at a time, his gaze sweeping past the tall, redheaded man who stood frozen with a look of undisguised awe upon his weather-beaten features. Placing a hand on Justin's shoulder to draw his attention away from the scar-faced man, Anthony called his name. He had to shake his friend's shoulder with more force to gain his recognition. "Justin, what is amiss here?"

Dazed, Justin looked up at Anthony, all past grievances forgotten in this moment of joy. A wide smile spread his craggy cheeks as he said, "'Tis Richard, Anthony. I've found my brother."

Anthony looked from one dark head to the other, his confusion reflected by the frown that etched its way across his handsome face. True, both had raven hair, but that was all the resemblance Anthony could see. "Justin, is this the man who has been robbing the pack train?"

Not wanting to think of the events that had brought his brother to him, Justin shook his head. "'Tis Richard, Anthony. Help me get him into the castle and I will explain everything to you."

Anthony did as Justin bade. He removed the noose from about Royce's neck and helped Justin lift the limp form into his arms before turning to the hangman. "Take the other Scot back to the dungeon until all of this has been cleared up." With that he followed Justin back into the black granite walls of Raven's Keep.

Justin strode briskly to his own chamber as if Royce's huge weight affected him little. He placed him upon the bed and tenderly soothed back the blue-black curls that clung to his damp forehead before turning to Anthony. Rubbing his temples, Justin crossed to the wine decanter and poured himself a goblet. He downed the contents before speaking. Anthony remained silent, waiting for Justin's explanation of the strange turn of events he had briefly witnessed. His friend's gaze traveled back to the man on the bed as he cleared his throat of the constriction his emotions aroused. "I nearly hanged my own brother. Had I not heard his words, Richard would now be swinging from the gallows."

Bemused, Anthony poured himself a hearty goblet of wine, swirling the ruby liquid as he looked from Justin to the unconscious man. "How do you know he is Richard? It could be a ruse to stay his execution."

Justin shook his head and smiled. "Nay, Anthony, 'tis Richard. It is not a lie to save his neck; he did not even realize his own demise was near. He was delirious from the wound I inflicted upon him today."

Still not satisfied, Anthony said, "How can you be certain? Many know of your missing brother."

Refilling his goblet, Justin crossed to the bed and gazed down at the scarred face. "True, it would be hard to recognize him as a St. Claire now, Anthony. It has been ten years since he disappeared and we thought him dead. However, Richard would be the only one to know what happened to Jessica, and it was her name that came to his lips today."

Anthony downed the wine. It left a bitter taste in his

mouth, as did his need to know the truth. Anthony had watched his friend grieve over his wife and brother far too long to let his hopes be revived by a lie from a thief, possibly to be dashed once again. "Still, that does not prove anything, Justin. It would not be hard for anyone to find out about Jessica and Richard. Don't let a lie make you blind."

Justin's gaze flashed with irritation as he looked at Anthony. His mouth was held in a firm, stubborn line as he said, "Damn it, man! 'Tis Richard. I know it could be a trick, but something in his voice held the truth. This is my brother and when he awakes he will be able to tell me who killed Jessica. Can't you understand that after all this time I will know for sure who murdered my wife? As you well know, I have fallen easily for lies in the past, but this man spoke the truth, Anthony. 'Tis more than I can say for you and my dear departed wife."

Justin's words struck home. The blood drained from Anthony's face as he looked at his friend, then it suffused once more with color. He had hoped things would be different, but he knew that if he did not get away from Justin for a few minutes, their friendship would be irreparable. If he stayed he would tell Justin how foolish he had truly been in the past and was now acting again. Instead, he would give himself time to cool off before it was too late and he could not mend the friendship, as he had set out to do.

Anthony paused at the door, his gaze traveling from the unconscious man on the bed to the tall, raven-haired knight. Justin's last statement puzzled Anthony and he wondered what he had meant by saying his dear *departed* wife. However, the present moment was not the time for him to mention Jamelyn. The fuse that had been lit at Windsor would only ignite an explosion between them if he questioned Justin about his wife. Without another word to his friend, Anthony silently left the chamber and strode briskly to the great hall to order a cooling ale.

Anne's gasp from the doorway drew Justin's attention away from his patient. He smiled as she entered, her face pale, her wide blue eyes nervously dancing from the unconscious form to Justin's smiling face.

"Anne, 'tis Richard. At long last I have found my brother," he told her.

Anne slowly nodded as she choked back the scream of hysteria that was trying to cut off her breathing in its effort to escape. She had heard such a rumor from one of the guards who had been near when Justin had spoken to Anthony Godfrey, but she could not believe it. That was the reason she had come to see for herself. Terror crept up her spine as she gazed from one man to the other, seeing the slight resemblance between them. She said, "Justin, how can you be sure? The man is a thief and could be lying like all the other deceitful Scots you have met. I would not see you hurt by his lies."

Exasperated, Justin ran his long fingers through his blueblack curls as he wearily said, "Nay, it is the truth."

Stilling her feet, which wanted to flee with rapid steps, Anne tried to remain calm through this new dilemma placed in her path. She had succeeded so far, but now her future looked bleak as death if it was indeed Richard and he remembered who killed Jessica on that far-off day.

A faint sheen of perspiration beaded Anne's brow as she crept up on tiptoes and placed a kiss on Justin's cheek. "Then I am happy for you. So many things have happened today. All this excitement has fatigued me. I think I will retire now for the night and let you celebrate your reunion with your long lost brother when he awakens."

Justin dropped a light kiss on Anne's brow as he smiled down into her blue eyes. "Aye, you have gone through much today, as have we all. Rest well, Anne."

She nodded and cast one last worried look at the man on the bed before fleeing the chamber. How vulnerable she felt at that moment. Her ability to plan seemed to evaporate as she faced the fact that Justin would soon learn the truth.

Anne knew she had to be gone before the wounded man— if it was Richard—regained consciousness. When Justin learned it was her men who had killed his wife and maimed his brother, the agonies of hell would be more welcome than his vengeance. With steps made fleet as a stag's from the fear gnawing at her insides, Anne hurried down the corridor to the great hall in search of her sergeant at arms. She did not see the puzzled look that crossed Anthony's face as she entered the room. He could not hear her words as she quickly explained to her man that she must leave Raven's Keep as soon as night settled. She stressed to her sergeant that it would be best for them to travel alone, as it was imperative for her to reach England as soon as possible; her men would only slow their progress.

The only hope left to Anne was to reach Edward and ask his mercy and protection against the rage she knew Justin would feel when he learned of her duplicity.

Anthony walked slowly back up the stairs toward Justin's chamber. His smooth brow was etched with lines as it puckered into a frown. Something nagged at the back of his mind, just out of reach of memory; for the life of him, he could not put his finger on it. Pushing the notion from his mind, he opened the door and entered. The encroaching twilight had darkened Justin's chamber and Anthony stood silently at the door, watching his friend light the tapers at the bedside of his presumed brother. During the past hour Anthony's thoughts had kept returning to Justin's earlier words. They kept prodding at his mind until he could stand it no longer. He had to know what his friend had meant by his remark.

Anthony suspected he would rekindle Justin's anger by mentioning Jamelyn, but the tartan that still lay across his saddle made it necessary for him to voice his concern. Bracing himself for Justin's fury, Anthony said, "Justin, you spoke of Jamelyn before. What has happened to her?"

Wringing out the damp cloth, Justin placed it once more upon Royce's fevered brow before he said, "She fled with her lover. But the bitch will pay when I find her."

"What do you mean?" Anthony asked, his confusion deepening.

"Exactly what I said. I left her with Anne and her men

for protection, but her lover attacked the group and they escaped together after tying Anne and her men up."

Releasing a deep, perplexed sigh, Anthony shook his blond head. "I don't believe it."

Justin swung about to face Anthony, his face hardening with the fury Jamelyn's deceit aroused within him. "'Tis true. You have always protected Jamelyn, but I have little time to listen to your bleeding-heart vows of her goodness. I would not expect anything more from you since your earlier actions."

Justin turned his attention back to the man on the bed. He changed the cloth again, hoping desperately to reduce the fever. He had no time to argue over his wife's lies at the moment. He would deal with her when Richard had recovered from his wounds.

The pieces of the puzzle slowly began to fall into place as Anthony remembered the cloaked figure with Anne's men. Until that moment he had forgotten it because of his concern over Jamelyn when he had found her tartan. Now he understood what had hounded him since he had seen Anne in the great hall a short while before. She should not be at Raven's Keep. "Justin, it is not true. Jamelyn did not flee with her lover."

Disgusted that his friend kept wanting to pursue the subject, Justin turned on him, furious with himself for letting Anthony's words cause a small hope to bloom within his own heart. "I'll hear no more of it. I have Anne as a witness to her treachery and that is all I need."

A chair crashed loudly to the floor as Anthony kicked it out of his way, striding across the chamber to grab Justin's arm, swinging his friend to face him. His boyishly handsome face had hardened into a mask of anger as he said, "You're a fool to believe Anne, Justin. She would say anything to keep you from another woman. Can't you understand that?"

Jerking free of Anthony's grasp, Justin confronted him. "Just as you would say anything to protect Jamelyn. I have seen the looks you cast in her direction when you think no one is observing you, Anthony. You are in love with Jamelyn, though she is a scheming bitch. You have let her beauty blind you to all else, even our friendship."

Anthony's hands fell to his sides and his shoulders seemed to sag under Justin's verbal assault. He looked up into his friend's flinty gaze and knew Justin had known his feelings for Jamelyn possibly longer than he himself had known them. He had tried to keep them hidden but now knew he had been unsuccessful. A weary sigh escaped as he said, "True, I care for Jamelyn. She is a lovely and desirable woman, if you have forgotten, but I would not trespass upon your relationship with her. I regret my past actions and had hoped you and I could put our grievance away and start anew. But though you won't believe me, I have proof that Jamelyn did not flee as Anne would convince you."

Desperately, Justin tried to quell the elation that swept over him and gruffly spat, "What proof have you? Show me Anne lies."

Anthony's gaze lingered on Justin's handsome face. He saw the spark of hope that flared within his blue eyes and knew that for all of Justin's protests, he still cared for his wife. Anthony placed one hand on his friend's shoulder, his fingers trying to impress the truth of his words upon him. "Justin, I saw Anne's men today riding toward England and a woman was with them. Until a few moments ago I thought Anne had decided to leave Raven's Keep. I had hoped you and Jamelyn had reestablished the relationship you found so briefly together at Windsor."

"Did you see Jamelyn?" Justin asked firmly.

Anthony shook his head. "Nay, the lady was cloaked, but who else could it have been if Anne is still in residence here? I also found Jamelyn's tartan. Do you think she would carelessly leave it behind unless she had been forced to?" Anthony saw the flicker of doubt in Justin's expression. "Justin, the tartan means too much to her. She has worked too hard to gain that woolen badge of honor to discard it even for a lover."

"Damn!" Justin swore as the truth hit him like a battle-axe between the eyes. But before he could organize his thoughts on the matter, a moan came from the occupant of the large bed.

Royce blinked as he tried to focus his eyes. Gradually the shadowy images sharpened and he looked up at the tall, raven-haired man. Through dry lips that trembled slightly from the effort, his voice a hoarse whisper, Royce said, "Justin, is it truly you?"

Justin bent over the bed, feeling the cooling forehead of his younger brother. A smile invaded the grim line of his lips as he said, "Aye, 'tis truly me, Richard. How do you feel?"

Royce's hand covered his aching head and he closed his eye against the light of the tapers to prevent the nausea the brightness aroused. "To be honest, I feel like living hell. How did I get here and where is Thomas?"

Justin settled his large frame on the side of the bed. "Thomas McFarland is still in the dungeon. Had you not mumbled Jessica's name, I'm afraid you both would be well beyond man's reach at this hour."

Royce's eye flew wide at the mention of Jessica. He wet his dry lips as a great tear brimmed in his unmaimed sapphire eye. "I tried to save her, Justin, but the Chester men were too much for me."

Anthony saw Justin stiffen and placed a calming hand on his shoulder. He shook his head to silence his friend, counseling him to wait for his brother's words. Justin nodded his silent agreement, though he wanted to question Richard immediately. Instead, he held his peace, knowing it would be better to let his brother tell him.

Royce's scarred face screwed up in agony at the memories that flooded his brain. "I had forgotten it all until now, wiped it out of my mind. Jessica and I went to pick wildflowers for your chamber. We had packed a lunch and Prince kept running about, upsetting the wine she had brought. It was near the cliffs where the yellow daffodils grew that we met the Chester men.

"At first we did not think anything of it until one speared Prince with his lance. Jessica screamed and ran forward and that was when they grabbed her. I fought to reach her but they were too many against my meager strength."

A sob caught in Royce's throat. He seemed to shake from head to toe at the gruesome memory. "They slit her throat before they turned on me. The last I remember was the blade that took my eye and the blow that knocked me over the cliff's edge. And until this day it was blotted from my mind. Thomas McFarland found me, doctored my wounds, and treated me like a son."

Tears ran unchecked down the men's cheeks as Royce's words vividly evoked that terrible day for all who were present. His story confirmed Justin's belief that this was indeed his brother. No one could have made up such a story, and he bore the scars to prove it.

The chamber was silent as the three men shared one another's grief. Justin clasped his brother's hand firmly as Anthony stood at their side, knowing well the pain that both men had lived with for more than ten years.

At last Justin cleared his throat, his eyes glassy with tears as he looked from his brother to his friend. "Your pain and Jessica's, as well as all I have experienced, will be avenged, for the one behind it now lies sleeping peacefully down the corridor."

Exhausted, Royce could only say, "Anne."

A muscle twitched in Justin's cheek as his lips firmed into a hard, narrow line. He nodded. "Aye, Anne. She has caused much pain for us all in the past and now I find again today she has connived to rid me of Jamelyn."

At the mention of Justin's wife, Royce tried to raise himself on one elbow but failed in the attempt. "Jamelyn? Has something happened to Jamelyn?" Using the last of his strength, he tried to throw back the covers and get up, but Justin's hand stayed his movements. "Lie still. You will only aggravate your wound. I will see that nothing befalls Jamelyn. She will be returned safely to Raven's Keep." Justin sent a silent prayer to heaven that his words would prove true.

Royce's movements had drained him of what little strength he possesed. Though his mind cried out for him to go and find Jamelyn, his body would not obey. Clasping his brother's strong hand, he drifted into a troubled sleep.

Justin's features looked as if they were chiseled from granite as he turned to Anthony. Deep grooves etched his mouth and his eyes held a deadly glint. "It has been Anne all along. How could I have been such a fool not to have seen that side of her?"

Placing a comforting arm about his friend's shoulder, Anthony said, "We are all fools at some point, but now is not the time to reflect upon things of the past. Jessica is dead, but Jamelyn may still be alive, and that is what we must now hope and pray for."

Abruptly Justin stood and reached for his sword belt. Fastening it about his lean waist, he said, "Aye, you organize our men and have Anne's guard secured in the dungeon. I have business to attend with my Lady Anne of Chester, and then we will find Jamelyn."

Anthony opened the door, but Justin's words halted him. "Anthony, thank you."

The blond knight nodded and smiled grimly. "We will find her, Justin. I'll send Nora up to see to Richard."

Justin smiled as he saluted his friend and then strode down the corridor toward Anne's chamber. He did not knock, but kicked the portal open with the heel of his boot. He was prepared to face the woman who had taken all he had ever loved from him, and at that moment he was not certain that he would be able to refrain from crushing the evil life from her. His hands itched to encircle the slender ivory column of her throat and press until her eyes bulged wide with terror and her lips turned blue.

"Anne!" he raged as he stepped across the threshold, but only silence greeted him. "Anne!" he called again as he searched the adjoining dressing room. She was nowhere to be found.

With anger seething in hot currents through his blood, building with each step he took, Justin began to search for Anne of Chester. To his amazement, she was not within the castle walls. He questioned her men briefly, but to no avail. They knew nothing of their mistress.

Stealthily, Anne and her sergeant at arms made their way along the dark passageway that she had traveled when she had followed Jamelyn on her way to meet Royce. Intrigued by Jamelyn's secretive flight, Anne had paid little heed to the exact turns in the pathway. It was that mistake that now made her veer in the wrong direction. The candle she carried illuminated only a small circle about herself and her man and she did not realize that the path she chose would lead to the trap set by the first Lord of Raven's Keep more than a hundred years earlier when the secret tunnel had been constructed.

Only the people familiar with Raven's Keep knew of the swiftly flowing, silent danger that ran toward the sea beneath the castle. Unaware of her deadly error, Anne veered to the left. Soon it was too late for them to turn back; there was no solid earth beneath their feet. A high-pitched scream of terror escaped Anne of Chester, echoing eerily through the darkness as the light from the candle flickered and went out, like her own life and that of her sergeant at arms a moment later.

No sound of their deaths penetrated the upper quarters of the keep, as Justin gave up his search for his treacherous mistress, and hurriedly galloped from the castle to find the woman he loved.

Chapter 16

The sun was sinking low over the Chevoit Hills when Jamelyn felt her bonds finally begin to give way. It had taken all afternoon, constantly working at the hemp rope, moving it steadily back and forth, to receive any reward for her torturous efforts. Her wrists were raw and the rope that bound them was moist and slippery with her blood, but her deep, burning anger made her heedless of the stinging pain. All her thoughts were centered on one thing—escape.

Furtively, Jamelyn glanced at her guards. The two men now rode silently along, though it had not been so all through their journey. She was well aware of the fate that awaited her. The two men had made their intentions clear with their obscene comments and vulgar jests. It had taken all of Jamelyn's self-control to keep from whimpering and cringing when their hands touched her breast or ran along her slender thigh to linger on her rounded bottom. She had clenched her teeth and pointedly ignored their actions, determined they would not have the pleasure of seeing her cower.

Feeling the rope slip further, she bit her lip and could

taste the sweetness of her blood as she strained against the bond. It slipped again as cold sweat beaded her brow. Taking a deep breath, she gave a jerk and the hemp fell free of her wrists. Shielding her actions with the cloak, she stealthily gathered the loose reins of her mount and before the guards could stop her, kicked Red Devil violently in the side, the harsh treatment sending the roan into a rapid gallop away from Anne's guards.

Jamelyn could hear the men's curses and shouts as she leaned low over Red Devil's neck in her effort to gain as much speed as possible and sent a silent prayer heavenward for help. Her prayer went unanswered. The ruffians soon gained on Red Devil and grabbed the reins from her hands, jerking the animal to an abrupt halt.

Red Devil reared, throwing Jamelyn off balance. She would have fallen from his back had she not grabbed the pommel of her saddle. Her seat on the roan's back was precarious as Red Devil pranced nervously, spooked by the abuse to his mouth. Jamelyn gasped in surprise as her guard's rough hands clamped brutally about her waist and jerked her from the horse's back. A hard slap across the face dazed her senses and she staggered from the blow as the heavyset guard spat, "Bitch, you'll pay for that."

Her auburn hair cascaded into her face and about her shoulders as she shook her head to orient her thoughts. She looked up at the two men, her face flushed, her breathing rapid. She could see the lust that glinted in their eyes, but did not cringe. Gathering all of her courage, she faced them bravely. "You may kill me as you have been ordered, but will your mistress protect you when my husband learns of the deed? Justin St. Claire will see you dead for the act."

A snarl curled the lips of the taller man as he looked down at the tousled woman who dared to threaten them. "Bitch, he won't ever know." His voice was a low growl as he jerked Jamelyn roughly from the other man and leaned close, his fetid breath nearly making her gag. "I'll be the first to sample your charms and see if the Scots women have as much to offer as our English ladies do."

His thick lips lowered toward her before a sudden, star-

tled look widened his eyes and then a moan of pain escaped
him as her knee came up abruptly and caught him in the
groin. His hand fell away from her as he doubled over,
clasping his injured member.

Taking advantage of the moment of freedom, Jamelyn
sprang away and turned to run. Her escape was halted as
the other, heavyset man jumped forward, grasping her about
the waist. He swung her easily off her feet and avoided her
thrashing heels as she kicked at him. He chuckled as his
hand captured one swollen breast and squeezed it brutally.
"*I'll* have to be the first to take you, since you've put Henry
out of commission for the moment."

Jamelyn struggled, but his fingers bit with agonizing
pressure into her tender breast, stilling her movements.
Trembling with pain, she cursed her body for being so weak.

"That's better," the short, heavyset man said, his voice
growing husky as he began to roam over Jamelyn's body
with his free hand. He explored her breast and down her
rounding belly to the hidden valley below. Hiking up the
front of her gown, his fingers found bare flesh. In his hurry
to touch the object of his desire, he did not feel the narrow
strip of leather about her thigh that contained her dirk. His
breath grew ragged and short as his fingers began to probe
her woman's center. The heavyset man failed to take note
of Jamelyn's furtive movement, too absorbed with the lust
that ran through him at the touch of that moist, soft flesh.
His senses were dulled and his eyes glazed as his lips traveled along the nape of her neck.

Jamelyn leaned back, bracing her heels against the hard
earth as she reached for her dirk. Her captor chuckled,
thinking his touch had aroused her to passion. Her action
was so swift that he had no time to avoid the deadly point
that ripped along his arm and entered his chest, sinking
neatly between his ribs to bring his life to an abrupt end.
He gasped for air and his arm fell away from her as a stunned
expression played over his face, before he sank to the earth
at Jamelyn's feet.

She took no time to consider the warm blood still on her
hands as she swung to face the dead man's companion. The

last of the sun's rays glinted along the narrow steel of her dagger as she grabbed her skirt and pulled it up, wrapping it about her other arm to keep it from hindering her steps.

A look of surprise mingled with anger marked her opponent's face and she smiled, the gesture deadly as she bent forward, preparing herself for his attack. "Now you see we Scots are not like you English bastards."

The guard roared with rage as he dived at Jamelyn, rashly not considering the events of a few moments past. She nimbly avoided him, but her dagger sank into his stomach, its sharp edge slashing silently across the man's middle, leaving a gaping wound that would mark the end of his life within minutes. Stunned that so small a woman could wreak so much havoc on two burly men, he clasped his belly and sank to his knees, his eyes never leaving her face as his life drained away through his fingers.

Jamelyn stood rigid and looked at the two dead men. Her heart was still racing within her chest, and the sight of so much blood turned her stomach. Nausea rose in bitter bile to her throat and she doubled over and clasped her stomach as it ridded itself of the morning meal. The full impact of all that had transpired that day took its toll on her and she sank slowly to her knees, her empty stomach still heaving.

After several minutes, she wiped the sweat from her brow and staggered to her feet. It took all the strength left within her to make her way to Red Devil and climb into the saddle. She turned the horse in the direction of Raven's Keep as shadows danced before her eyes. With an effort she leaned over the horse's neck, trying desperately to remain alert. However, exhaustion and pain overcame her just as she found the road to the castle, and she slumped across the pommel of the saddle.

Justin was the first to sight Jamelyn's mount and spurred his destrier forward. Red Devil, nibbling grass at the side of the road, neighed at the scent of the other approaching horses. His rider lay unconscious at his feet. Justin saw the dark shape in the grass and dismounted even before his steed had come to a complete halt.

He knelt beside Jamelyn, touching the pulse in her throat to see if she still lived. Relief swept over him as he felt the tiny beat of her heart and he gently lifted her into his strong arms. As if she were rare porcelain, he carried her to his mount and without a word urged his horse back to Raven's Keep, a deep frown of worry etching his handsome brow.

Anthony followed close on Justin's heels as he made his way to Jamelyn's chamber and laid her carefully upon the large bed. The haggard expression on his friend's face wrenched Anthony's heart as he placed a comforting hand on Justin's shoulder. "She'll be all right. Jamelyn is strong and will not let something so small defeat her. Come away and let her women tend her."

Justin shook his head without taking his eyes away from her pale face. "Nay, I'll stay with her. 'Tis time I acted the husband instead of some uncaring monster. My actions have caused her too much pain as it is without leaving her to the servants."

Understanding Justin's feelings, Anthony left without a word, his own thoughts turned toward Jamelyn's well-being. Nora and Maille silently entered as he left the chamber, their eyes wide with worry as they looked down upon their mistress's pale form. With nervous glances cast in Justin's direction, they bathed the dirt from Jamelyn and removed her clothing to see if she was injured beyond the abrasions on her wrists. With much relief, the two girls found no wounds and as they finished their task, Nora smiled up at Justin reassuringly. "My lord, I think my lady will be fine. If no harm has come to the child, then she will recover."

Justin jerked alert at the girls' words. With startled eyes, he looked up at the servant and asked, "Child?"

Maille and Nora nodded in unison. "Aye," said the more vocal Nora as she brushed a stray auburn curl from Jamelyn's forehead. "She carries your babe."

Stunned speechless, Justin could only stare in bewilderment at the two women as they curtsied to him and quickly exited the chamber. Numbed, he turned to gaze down upon his wife's pale features and gently lifted her small hand in his. Tenderly he placed his lips against her fingers and closed his eyes as he thought, I'm to be a father.

Joy surged through him and his blue eyes glowed as he opened them once more. A look of pleased surprise crossed his chiseled features as he saw Jamelyn's emerald gaze resting speculatively upon him. Her voice was calm, without emotion, as she said, "I heard what Nora told you."

Justin nodded and smiled. "Aye, she told me of the babe."

Jamelyn pulled her hand free of his and pushed herself up on the pillows, her eyes never leaving his face. A grimace flickered across her wan features from the soreness caused by her fall and instinctively her hand went to her rounded abdomen. "How do you feel about it?"

Justin arched one dark brow over his keen eyes as he looked down at his wife. Her tone did little to assure him that he or his child was wanted in her life. Struggling for the right words, he said, "It is mine and I will accept it."

Justin's words cut more harshly through Jamelyn than the sharp edge of a dagger. They pierced her heart and Anne's mocking statement flashed into her turbulent thoughts: "He may despise you and the babe, but he could not bring himself to be rid of you because of it. He will feel obligated to let you remain his wife."

Taking a deep, steadying breath to keep her voice from revealing the pain she suffered, Jamelyn turned her face away from her husband and quietly said, "I wish to be alone now."

Confusion swept over Justin as he rose from the bed. He wanted to explain his feelings to her and the reasons for his actions in the past. But now was not the time; she needed rest after her ordeal with Anne's men. He would wait to discuss it with her when she had recovered completely. Bending, he placed a light kiss on her brow as he said softly, "Rest now. You must take care of yourself for the babe's sake." Then he left her chamber.

Jamelyn's fist balled at her side until her knuckles were white from the pressure. She stared up at the soot-blackened beams without seeing them and let her agony consume her. Finally, when the tears were spent and nothing was left except dry, hiccuping sniffles, she wiped her red-rimmed eyes and sat up.

She had fought for Raven's Keep and it had been lost to her. She had tried to win her husband's love and had failed in that endeavor also. She would not lose her child because of Justin's feelings of obligation. If she remained at Raven's Keep, he would undoubtedly have his heir taken from her.

Jamelyn knew that if that happened she would die, for her heart could stand no more pain. The child within her womb was her last hold upon life. It represented all the things that had been taken from her and she was determined that no one would take it away. Justin could have Raven's Keep, but he would not have her child. It was part of her body, its blood was her own, and no one—not even its sire—would ever keep it from her.

Jamelyn sat up and swung her slender, graceful legs off the bed. She must leave Raven's Keep before Justin had time to stop her. Aching from head to toe, she managed to dress herself. She glanced briefly about the room in which she had grown up, knowing this would be her last look. When she left the gates of Raven's Keep, she could never return and expect to keep her child as her own. Justin would never allow the woman he despised to rear his child.

Tears clogged her throat, but she stoically forced them away and whispered, "Farewell, Raven's Keep. I have fought to keep you, but now my babe means more to me than a great pile of cold granite." With that she flung her mantle about her shoulders and crept from the room.

Jamelyn could hear the voices of Justin's men coming from the great hall as she made her way to the armory. She could not venture out alone without a means to protect herself. That lesson she had learned well from harsh experience. Silently she crept along in the shadows and waited with her back pressed against the cold stone wall until the armory guard turned his back to her. Drawing from a reserve of strength she did not realize she possessed, she picked up a heavy wooden stool and brought it down on the guard's head.

Breathing heavily from the exertion, she glanced warily toward the dark corridor to make sure the man's groan of pain had gone unnoticed. Releasing a sigh of relief, she entered the armory. Taking a heavy sword and a sturdy lance, she quickly and stealthily made her way to the stables.

Jamelyn knew it would have been better if she had used the secret passageway, for she would have had less chance of being caught, but she could not reach her destination without a mount. Time was of the essence and Red Devil would carry her swiftly northward. There she would meet with the Scotsmen she had freed after Justin had captured Raven's Keep. Staying in the deepest shadows, she breathed a silent prayer of thanks as she entered the stables and found no grooms in attendance.

Saddling Red Devil, Jamelyn led the horse to the entrance and secured him near the gate so she could make a quick exit after lowering the heavy portal for her departure. With the agility and ease of one trained for battle, she silently made her way up the stone steps to the rampart. Her breath held and nerves taut, she raised the heavy sword and brought the flat side of the blade down on the guard's head. He stumbled forward and then sank to the stone walkway without alerting the men further along the wall.

Jamelyn had to use all of her strength to keep the huge wheel from flying from her hands as she released the rope that secured it in place. With her teeth tightly clenched and her weight braced against the stone wall, she eased the wheel clockwise and prayed the gate would not squeak on its great iron hinges as it opened downward. Her muscles trembled from the exertion and she took great gulps of air into her lungs to still the pounding of her heart as the gate touched the ground. Moving swiftly, she raced back down to the bailey and mounted Red Devil before anyone was the wiser. With a quick kick to her mount's side, she galloped through the lowered portal, toward the north and freedom.

Passing over the last hill before Raven's Keep became invisible to the eye, Jamelyn could hear the shouts that echoed from the keep. Soon Justin would have men searching for her and she must put as much distance between herself and her husband as possible.

With that thought in mind, she leaned low over the roan's sleek, muscular neck and gave him his head. His hooves flew over the ground, throwing clumps of sod in the air in his wake. Jamelyn breathed in the crisp, cool air and experienced a sense of freedom she had not known since the English had come to disrupt her life. A bubble of laughter escaped into the night air as she threw back her gilded head and looked up at the blue velvet sky. "I am Jamelyn of Cregan, Chieftain of the Clan Cregan, and carry the heir of my clan within me. My child will rule after me and will not suffer the yoke of his kin."

Her vow was swept away by the breeze, as was the joy of the moment. She slowed Red Devil to a gentler pace and rubbed the ache that nagged at the small of her back. It grew stronger with each passing minute. The babe kicked as if to deny her words and Jamelyn shook her auburn head as moisture glistened on her sooty lashes. "You are also half-English, little one," she whispered to the night. "But I cannot allow your father to take you from me."

The ache grew more pronounced and Jamelyn took deep breaths in her effort to quell it, but at last she realized she could go no further. Reining Red Devil to a halt, she dismounted with care and her gaze turned once more toward Raven's Keep before she sank slowly to the ground.

A new fear sprang to life in Jamelyn's mind as the pain increased. Placing her hand on her swollen belly, she paled as she realized something might be amiss with her pregnancy. Biting her lower lip, she rested her head on her bended knees and prayed that nothing would happen to her child.

The thunder of hooves roused her and she looked up to see Justin and his men approaching. "No!" she cried as she forced herself to her feet. Grabbing her sword, she turned to face the group of men that surrounded her. Her eyes scanned the group and came to rest upon Shawn McDougal.

Jamelyn's tone pleaded with the Scotsman to come to her aid as she said, "Will you let them take me back?"

A troubled frown marred Shawn's ruddy features as he looked from Justin to Jamelyn and nodded. "Aye, lass. It is for the best."

Bitterness boiled within her at Shawn's second betrayal and she hissed derisively, "I should have expected as much from you. Call yourself a Scotsman no more, Shawn McDougal, for at your hand you have given the heir of the clan to the English."

Jamelyn's accusation hit Shawn like a blow, but he loved the young woman too well and could not let her stubbornness ruin the rest of her life. "Lass, I am a Scotsman to the core but will not see you commit this folly. My lord has told me of your condition and I will see the heir of Cregan born within the granite walls of Raven's Keep, as all of his ancestors have been birthed."

Tears welled in Jamelyn's emerald eyes as she looked up at Shawn. "Be damned that great pile of stone, I will not go back and have my child taken from me. I will fight to the death before I let that happen."

Justin had remained silent as Jamelyn and Shawn spoke. He heard the pain and heartbreak in his wife's words and his heart gave a gentle twist within his chest as he slowly dismounted. He faced Jamelyn, the love he felt for that small, fierce warrior glowing brightly in the depths of his indigo eyes.

Jamelyn watched the tall knight as he came forward and prepared herself to do battle. Like the first day, she confronted her enemy, but in a far different manner. The handsome man before her could devastate her life totally without the use of his sword. She loved him with a fierce, abiding love, but her death was preferable to knowing he did not love her and would take her child away because of it. Raising her weapon, she determined she would not return to Raven's Keep. It was better to die under the sword than to slowly wither away from a broken heart and loneliness.

Trying to hide her emotions, Jamelyn eyed the tall knight

and spat, "I will never return with you. Fight me now, Justin, or your life will be forfeit to my sword."

He stopped before her and she raised her sword to strike, but his next move stayed her hand. Justin let his sword fall to the ground and knelt before her. Tenderly he took her free hand within his own strong one and looked solemnly up at her face. His eyes pleaded for understanding and Jamelyn had to swallow back the rush of tears that nearly blinded her.

Justin's next action was her undoing, as he leaned forward and laid his head against her swelling abdomen, his words soft as he said, "Slay me now, Jamelyn, or it shall be your last chance. I feel the stirring of my babe within your belly and will never let you go. I love you, you stubborn vixen. If you spill my blood upon this rocky ground, I will die loving you."

Jamelyn's sword fell from her nerveless fingers. It clattered to the ground to lie beside Justin's blade as her arms wrapped about his wide shoulders and she held him close. She gazed down at the raven head pressed to her body and a thrill of pleasure swept over her. Justin loved her. He had offered his life as proof of his love. With tender fingers, she brushed the damp tendrils of hair from his forehead and the look he bestowed upon her made her lips tremble with happiness. "I shall not slay the sire of my babe. Who would teach him to be a great warrior if you were to die?"

A pleased chuckle rumbled through Justin's wide chest as he rose and pulled Jamelyn into his arms. Looking out across the rugged Scottish countryside, he said, "I'm sure his mother could do as well, my love. As I remember it, you came close to defeating his father in battle and have very adeptly done so in love."

His fiery blue gaze caressed her glowing features. "Let us put our swords away, my love. I much prefer doing battle with you upon the soft down mattress of our chamber. It is much more satisfying and a lot less painful." As he pulled her tightly against his chest, his eyes smoldered with passion. His voice was husky as he said, "I love you, Jamelyn, as I have never loved another. Your spirit has enthralled me and is kindred to my own. The loves I have experienced in the past were gentle and boyish loves, but now I am a man and need a woman my equal. All I ask in return is that you love me a small bit. After all I have done, I cannot expect you to love me as fiercely as I love you. I only beg you to be kind and give me a small portion of your heart."

Jamelyn pressed her cheek against his chest as she wrapped her arms about his lean waist. She could hear the rapid beat of his heart and could feel the tension within his muscular frame. He was afraid of her rejection and her heart swelled with her love as she said, "You do not have to ask for a small bit of my heart, Justin. You have had all of it for a very long time. I think I began to love you when you kissed my hand after saving my life the day of the boar hunt. I never dreamed I would say this to an Englishman, Justin, but I love you."

Forgetting that they stood surrounded by their men, Jamelyn and Justin sealed their love with a kiss that told more than words could ever say.

About the Author

Cordia Byers was born in the small north Georgia community of Jasper and lives there still, with her husband, James, and their two children, Michelle and Michael. Cordia likes to think of her husband as being like one of the heroes in her novels. James swept her off her feet after their first meeting, and they were married three weeks later. After eighteen happy years together, Cordia is looking forward to at least another fifty.

From the age of six, Cordia's creative talents had been directed toward painting. It was not until late 1975, when the ending of a book displeased her, that she considered writing. That led to her first novel, HEATHER, which was followed by CALLISTA, NICOLE LA BELLE, and now SILK AND STEEL. Cordia is at work on her fifth book. Finding more satisfaction in the world of her romantic novels, she has given up painting and now devotes herself to writing, researching her material at the local library, and then doing the major part of her work from 11:30 P.M. to 3:00 A.M.

Cordia enjoys hearing from her readers. Her address is Route 1, Box 63E, Jasper, GA 30143.